EXEMPLARY STORIES

MIGUEL DE CERVANTES, who was born in 1547 and died in 1616, a few days after William Shakespeare, had only three more years to live when he published his *Exemplary Stories* in 1613. Literary success was late in coming to the author who has become known as the father of the modern novel, beginning with the publication of *Don Quixote, Part I*, in 1605. He served as a soldier in Philip II's forces in the Mediterranean area, and was held captive for five years in North Africa. After his ransom and return to Spain he was a minor government functionary, tax-collector, and aspiring dramatist. Writing and modifying the *Exemplary Stories* and other works for publication occupied the last decade of his life. These stories deserve to be better known. Like his acknowledged masterpiece, their strength and originality lie in the almost perverse pleasure Cervantes takes in subverting the literary conventions of his day. He pushed forward the frontiers of popular prose fiction in his experimentation with character, genre, and register.

LESLEY LIPSON was born in South Wales (in 1962). She was educated at Maesteg Comprehensive School and New Hall, Cambridge where she gained a PhD. She taught Golden Age Literature at Birkbeck College, University of London for several years and has written various articles and reviews on Cervantes and other Golden-Age topics.

OXFORD WORLD'S CLASSICS

*For almost 100 years Oxford World's Classics have brought
readers closer to the world's great literature. Now with over 700
titles—from the 4,000-year-old myths of Mesopotamia to the
twentieth century's greatest novels—the series makes available
lesser-known as well as celebrated writing.*

*The pocket-sized hardbacks of the early years contained
introductions by Virginia Woolf, T. S. Eliot, Graham Greene,
and other literary figures which enriched the experience of reading.
Today the series is recognized for its fine scholarship and
reliability in texts that span world literature, drama and poetry,
religion, philosophy and politics. Each edition includes perceptive
commentary and essential background information to meet the
changing needs of readers.*

OXFORD WORLD'S CLASSICS

MIGUEL DE CERVANTES

Exemplary Stories

Translated with an Introduction and Notes by
LESLEY LIPSON

Oxford   New York
OXFORD UNIVERSITY PRESS
1998

Oxford University Press, Great Clarendon Street, Oxford OX2 6DP

Oxford New York

Athens Auckland Bangkok Bogota Bombay Buenos Aires
Calcutta Cape Town Dar es Salaam Delhi Florence Hong Kong Istanbul
Karachi Kuala Lumpur Madras Madrid Melbourne Mexico City
Nairobi Paris Singapore Taipei Tokyo Toronto Warsaw

and associated companies in
Berlin Ibadan

Oxford is a trade mark of Oxford University Press

© Lesley Lipson 1998
Chronology © E. C. Riley 1992

First published as an Oxford World's Classics paperback 1998

British Library Cataloguing in Publication Data

Data available

Library of Congress Cataloging in Publication Data

Cervantes Saavedra, Miguel de, 1547–1616.
[Novelas ejemplares. English. Selections]
Exemplary stories / Miguel de Cervantes ; translated with an
introduction and notes by Lesley Lipson.
(Oxford world's classics)
Includes bibliographical references.
Contents: The little gipsy girl—Rinconete and Cortadillo—The
glass graduate—The power of blood—The jealous old man from
Extremadura—The illustrious kitchen maid—The deceitful
marriage—The dialogue of the dogs.
I. Lipson, Lesley. II. Title. III. Series: Oxford world's
classics (Oxford University Press)
PQ6329.A6L56   1998   863'.3—dc21   97-42329

ISBN 0-19-283243-3 (pbk. : alk. paper)

1 3 5 7 9 10 8 6 4 2

Typeset by Best-set Typesetter Ltd., Hong Kong
Printed in Great Britain by
Caledonian International Book Manufacturing Ltd.
Glasgow

For Andrew, Joel, and Zachary

CONTENTS

ACKNOWLEDGEMENTS

I am indebted to my various readers, who made many helpful comments and suggestions with a rare tact and sensitivity. Special thanks to my husband Andrew both for his wordsmithing and for being more realistic about deadlines than I was. I am also grateful to Vince Milner for advice on matters Catholic. Last but not least, I must thank my young son Joel, for allowing me to spend quite so much of his first two years in the company of another man.

INTRODUCTION

Life and Works

None of the extant portraits of Miguel de Cervantes can be authenticated, and even the verbal description he offers of himself in the Prologue to his *Exemplary Stories* borders on self-parody. As an author he likes to hide behind his narrators and the man himself remains elusive, disappearing from his biographers' sight for months, even years at a time. Born at Alcalá de Henares, near Madrid, in September 1547, he was the third child of an impecunious surgeon with pretensions to nobility who restlessly wandered from one city to another in an unsuccessful attempt to improve his lot. Cervantes himself was also to become a wanderer, dogged by poverty, an unhappy marriage, and a failure to achieve his professional ambitions until the very last years of his life.

Due to the itinerant life-style of the family little is known of his formal education until he turns up in Madrid as a rather mature pupil of the Erasmist[1] Juan López de Hoyos in 1568. In that same year he produced four poems, elegies on the death of Elizabeth of Valois, third wife of Philip II. These were to be his first publications, appearing in print in 1569. A voracious reader (he refers to picking up scraps of paper in the streets of Toledo to satisfy his thirst for words in *Don Quixote*, I, 9), it is generally believed that the undisciplined nature of his education is the main factor contributing to his originality.

In 1569 he seems to have left Madrid rather suddenly, and documents discovered in the nineteenth century reveal that he was charged with wounding a man in a duel. He went to Italy, where he was briefly employed as chamberlain to a Cardinal Acquaviva. He then enlisted with the Spanish army and served with Don John of Austria's fleet when it won its decisive victory over the Turks at the Battle of Lepanto in 1571. It was here that he lost his left hand as the result of a wound. Returning to Spain upon completion of his service in 1575, his ship was captured by Algerian pirates and he

---

[1] A scholar in the tradition of the Dutch Humanist Desiderius Erasmus (1466–1536).

spent the next five years in captivity in Algiers until he was ransomed by Trinitarian monks, an experience he draws on both in his prose fiction and some of his plays.

Cervantes did not find it easy to become reintegrated into civilian life after a decade of soldiering and captivity abroad. It is probably no coincidence that many of the characters in his *Exemplary Stories* find themselves marginalized or isolated, some of them through temperament, others through some twist of fate. It is on these margins of conventional society, in a semi-literary and half-real land-scape, that Cervantes locates many of his fictional worlds. His first full-length publication in 1585, however, was a relatively orthodox contribution to the vogue genre of the time, a pastoral romance en-titled *La Galatea*. Since the genre relies heavily on the lyric poetry which is interwoven with the prose narrative and Cervantes was not a particularly accomplished poet, this work was not an overwhelm-ing success. It did go into a second edition five years later, however, and Cervantes himself speaks of writing a sequel on four separate occasions.

His early drama seems to have met with only moderate success, his first plays being staged in 1582 and 1583. When he published his *Eight Plays and Eight Interludes* in 1615, he acknowledged that these particular works had never been performed. By this time the Spanish theatre had been transformed by its most prolific exponent, Lope de Vega, who published his blueprint for the dramatic form in his *New Art of Writing Plays* in 1609. We must assume, then, that Cervantes's theatrical successes were among the works that have been lost. The full-length plays or *comedias* that have survived only serve to illus-trate that Cervantes's talent lay in the more flexible form of prose narrative, and he probably only managed to publish his drama on the back of his prose successes. His interludes, on the other hand, reveal a gift for comic dialogue and a penchant for social satire which figure prominently in the *Exemplary Stories*.

In 1584—the same year he is believed to have fathered an illegiti-mate daughter, Isabel, by a certain Ana Franca de Rojas—he married Catalina de Salazar, a young woman half his age. The most notable fact about the marriage is that Cervantes spent little time in the marital home. As early as 1587 he began wandering the dry and dusty byways of Andalusia on a mule as a minor government func-tionary, first as a requisitioning commissary for the Armada as it prepared to sail for the Protestant England of Elizabeth I, and then as a tax-collector. In spite of successive major setbacks, such as not being paid for months on end and spending at least two periods in prison (in 1592 and 1597) for faulty accounting, he continued to work in Andalusia until about 1600. It was in prison in Seville that he gained first-hand experience of criminal life and inspiration for such stories as *Rinconete and Cortadillo*. Although he presents taking passage to the New World as the last resort of the desperate in *The Jealous Old Man from Extremadura*, Cervantes himself wrote a petition to the Council of the Indies in 1590 requesting a government post of some sort. This again met with failure and he continued to traverse southern Spain as a tax-collector.

After a short period in Valladolid he returned to Madrid in 1605. The bulk of his work was published in the final ten years of his life although much of it was written earlier and has proved difficult to date with any confidence or accuracy. *Don Quixote, Part I*, was published in 1605; the *Exemplary Stories* in 1613; *The Journey to Parnassus*, his long, allegorical poem, in 1614; and *The Eight Plays and Eight Interludes* in 1615, along with *Don Quixote, Part II*. He remained in Madrid until his death on 22 April 1616, four days after completing the dedication to his final work, an epic romance entitled *The Travails of Persiles and Sigismunda*, which was published posthumously the following year.

Literary success came late and probably not where Cervantes might have hoped or predicted. He could never have foreseen that his reputation as the author of the first modern European novel would rest almost exclusively on a work which was originally conceived as a simple burlesque, his parody of chivalric literature, *Don Quixote*. He seems to have felt a greater affection for his first publication, *La Galatea*; although he never produced the promised sequel he did write some wonderful short parodies of the genre, the best of which figures in *The Dialogue of the Dogs*, the last story in the present collection. This shifting approach to the pastoral genre reflects his ambiguous attitude to this and other literary conventions of his time, respectfully adhering to them in one work and then comically subverting them in another. He probably took greater pride in his final work, *The Travails of Persiles and Sigismunda*, at least half of which is devoid of the irony and realism of his most enduring works. In it he seems to be at pains to prove that he is perfectly conversant with the prevailing literary canon of his day, although he often chose to flout the rules elsewhere. It goes without saying that the qualities of his work for which he is most celebrated in the twentieth century are not those which Cervantes himself would have held in highest esteem. Prose fiction, especially comic prose, simply did not enjoy the same status as poetry or drama. In essence, then, Cervantes became the father of the novel after failing as a poet and a dramatist.

While it is conjectured that the early sections of *Persiles and Sigismunda* pre-date this late period of creativity, because the style and ideology of the first half of the book differ so greatly from the second, we know for a fact that some of the *Exemplary Stories* were written ten years before their publication in the exemplary collection because they are present in what has become known as the Porras manuscript, dating from about 1604. The prebendary of Seville Cathedral, Francisco Porras de la Cámara, compiled this anthology of stories for the entertainment of the Archbishop, Fernando Niño de Guevara, and it contains earlier versions of *The Jealous Old Man from Extremadura* and *Rinconete and Cortadillo*. The fact that the former in particular was amended for inclusion in the *Exemplary Stories* a decade later has earned Cervantes the title of hypocrite in some quarters. The manuscript also contains one other tale, entitled *The Imposter Aunt*, which has been generally, though by no means universally, attributed to the same author. He also produced a considerable amount of verse which he intercalated in his prose works.

When the *Exemplary Stories* were first published in 1613 by Juan de la Cuesta they were an immediate success, going into four editions in ten months and twenty-three in all in the course of the century. The original collection comprised twelve stories: *The Little Gipsy Girl*, *The Generous Suitor*, *Rinconete and Cortadillo*, *The English Spanish Girl*, *The Glass Graduate*, *The Power of Blood*, *The Jealous Old Man from Extremadura*, *The Illustrious Kitchen Maid*, *The Two Damsels*, *The Lady Cornelia*, *The Deceitful Marriage*, and *The Dialogue of the Dogs*.[2] They inspired imitations in Spain, where writers such as Castillo Solórzano, Salas Barbadillo, and María

---

[2] The present volume contains eight of the twelve titles, omitting *The Generous Suitor*, *The English Spanish Girl*, *The Two Damsels*, and *The Lady Cornelia*. See the Note on the Text and Translation for further details.

de Zayas made their own contributions to the genre, while free adaptations and translations were also produced for an enthusiastic readership in England. In fact they remained more popular than *Don Quixote* until the eighteenth century, when the comic masterpiece began to be reassessed and has eclipsed them ever since.

After *Don Quixote*, however, the *Exemplary Stories* have generated most critical interest and admiration, and studies have tended to identify two contrasting types: the 'idealist' stories or romances, with their love interest, aristocratic protagonists, and more formal narrative style; and the 'realist' tales, in the seventeenth-century sense of comic realism, with plebeian characters, more-colloquial dialogues, and humour with an unmistakeable satirical edge. In fact, Cervantes's prose fiction as a whole has generally been categorized in the same way. While some critics have tried to establish a correlation between the early and idealist works and prefer to see the 'realist' ones as a product of his creative maturity, Cervantes's short prose fiction does not lend itself to such convenient classification. It is probably more realistic to concede that Cervantes did not wholly abandon one approach for another, but shifted between them as it suited his purpose. It should come as no surprise to learn that the critical reception of the stories and reading tastes have changed over the centuries. While there was a marked preference for the 'romantic' stories in the seventeenth century, in the late twentieth century the predilection is for all the others.

The comic and ironic realism that developed as a reaction to the enormous vogue of heroic chivalric literature in the sixteenth century found expression in one particularly influential form—the picaresque novel. The immediate forerunner of this genre was the brief but brilliant anti-clerical satire *Lazarillo de Tormes*, which was published anonymously in 1554. However, it is the monolithic *Guzmán de Alfarache*, published in two volumes by Mateo Alemán in 1599 and 1604, and therefore contemporaneous with *Don Quixote*, that has come to be recognized as the archetype of the genre. Instead of chronicling the worthy exploits of an aristocratic hero, it charts the descent into vice of a low-born figure who provides the reader with a satirical, pseudo-autobiographical account of the society through which he passes, interspersed with long moralizing passages. Cervantes's precise attitude to the picaresque genre is another area of critical contention, since he exploits some of its conventions without fully embracing its vision of society and its mores.

No single work in the present collection could be labelled purely 'idealist' or 'realist', even within the terms of reference of Cervantes's own culture. It is a trademark of much of Cervantes's prose fiction to deflate and challenge literary conventions with comic or satirical everyday detail, and consequently his approach might more appropriately be labelled 'experimental', and the results 'hybrid'. Much of his language is ambiguous and his approach to much of his material is fundamentally ironic. A basic literary precept of the day was the need to inspire *admiratio* or a sense of wonderment in the reader, and Cervantes achieves this by displacing recognizable character types into unexpected contexts and frequently dismantling generic conventions to create new combinations with which to surprise and challenge the reader. Thus he transposes a noble gentleman to a gipsy camp in one story, puts the words of satirical *pícaros* in the mouths of talking dogs in another, and presents one of his eponymous heroines as the 'illustrious' kitchen maid. In this way he creates an essential tension between the 'ideal' and the 'real', the 'literary' and the 'everyday', the plausible and the unlikely. In his *Journey to Parnassus* he speaks of producing 'fantasy with perfect naturalness'; in his *Exemplary Stories* he is more concerned to surprise his readers and stretch their imaginations by persuading them to suspend their disbelief than to recreate a realistic picture of his society.

Another important aspect of Cervantes's prose fiction is the often ambiguous relationship between narrator and reader. Recent criticism has focused on the reader's responsibility to read between the lines. The problem of interpreting the *Exemplary Stories* and understanding exactly what Cervantes meant by 'exemplary' is compounded by what the author himself says in his Prologue to the collection. The prologues to his prose works after *La Galatea* are characteristically coloured by irony and ambiguity, but the Prologue to his *Exemplary Stories* is probably the most provocative and challenging. He may open in a typically self-deprecating mode, explaining why there is no portrait of the artist gracing the frontispiece, and end with the hope that God will protect him from unfavourable comments, but the Prologue thus circumscribed is a confident one. He makes two sweeping claims, one with regard to the originality of the stories and the other to their exemplary quality; he also makes several other statements which are either tongue-in-cheek or a forthright challenge to look beyond the literal word. He tells you what you can expect to find in the collection, that is, harmless entertainment; in fact, he challenges you to find anything to the contrary (and promises to cut off his remaining hand if indeed such material is discovered). Yet a brief resumé of the violence of a few of the plots would suffice to undermine this claim. As if anticipating our problem with the term 'exemplary', he playfully announces that if he did not wish to labour the point he would explain precisely what sort of 'wholesome fruit' is to be gathered from each individual story as well as the collection as a whole. Could a master of irony be more provocative? The responsibility lies with the reader to extract the moral lesson; the author himself refuses to be prescriptive.

His emphasis on the exemplary nature of his stories poses more questions than it answers. He is primarily attempting to distinguish his work from the dubious morality of some of his Italian models and acquire for the *novela* in Spain a respectability that it did not yet possess. He probably chose the title of the collection precisely for its contentious and provocative nature. The very concept of 'exemplary' short stories must have appeared a contradiction in terms to contemporary readers familiar with Boccaccio's *Decameron* (translated into Spanish in the early sixteenth century and placed on the Index of prohibited books in 1589) and his frequently licentious treatment of his subject-matter. Cervantes would probably not have thanked the contemporary playwright, Tirso de Molina, for calling him 'the Spanish Boccaccio'. Matteo Bandello (whose *Tragic and Exemplary Stories* were published in Spanish in 1589) had already perceived the need to clean up the new genre when he gave his own collection an exemplary focus. Some of Cervantes's plots may involve rape or violence, but they do not exploit lewdness for its own sake. Having thus provided some sort of defence of his fiction, Cervantes then proceeds to challenge the objection of the contemporary moral lobby that imaginative prose fiction, such as the romance, was harmful to its readers, in as much as it endangered both their minds and their souls by its power to persuade. The spirit of the Counter Reformation demanded that reading be an enlightening and morally uplifting experience and that it provide its readers with examples of conduct worthy of emulation in real life. With the same end in view, though employing different means, *Guzmán de Alfarache* focused on vice in order to present its readers with examples not to follow, and reinforced this message at every possible opportunity. Cervantes's response to this demand for didacticism in literature was to say that 'we cannot spend all our time in church' and to make a case for purely recreational reading. It is enough that his work does not inspire lewd or improper thoughts; he does not want to tell his readers what they should think—he prefers to suggest.

Some of the stories do indeed conclude with a brief moral statement tagged on to the end, ostensibly in keeping with the tradition of the short moral tales of the Middle Ages, such as the *exempla* of Don Juan Manuel in the fourteenth century. Modern readers of Cervantes tend to find these glib and simplistic rather than enlightening. He seems merely to be paying lip service to a convention. Some stories reach their conclusion but do not necessarily achieve closure; that is, the ending does not appear completely compatible with the dramatic situation or vision of society presented in the preceding story. The suggestion that some characters will live happily ever after, for example, is not invariably convincing. The final lines of *Rinconete and Cortadillo* promise a sequel which will chronicle Rinconete's exploits in terms of the life of a saint rather than the petty criminal he is. Moreover, the final emphasis is placed on the exemplary and admonitory lessons contained, not in the preceding story, but in the sequel which we have not yet had the opportunity to read and which was probably never written. Cervantes is playfully manipulating a convention.

The short story was by no means a new narrative form. Independent or self-contained short stories or episodes which are linked together in some way to form a larger narrative structure stretch back to antiquity and were commonplace in medieval literature. In the sixteenth century chivalric, pastoral, and picaresque narratives were all basically modelled on the same pattern and Cervantes exploits it extensively in his own works. When he claims that he was the first to *novelar* or write short stories in Spanish, Cervantes is referring to a newer form of short prose fiction which is independent of this larger framework. His claim is in essence a valid one in spite of the obvious debt he owes the aforementioned collections of Italian *novelle*, for he is drawing a fundamental distinction. Although his own short stories might share elements of plot and ideology with these Italian models, his stories are original rather than adaptations or translations.

Cervantes is tantalizing the reader and inviting him to search for subtexts and counter-texts when he comments that, although he may speak with a stammer, the truth will be understood even if he has to resort to signs. Many of his characters, too, are searching for signs, proof, evidence, and the solution to riddles. Cervantes further compounds the problem of interpretation when he claims at the end of the Prologue that, since he is bold enough to dedicate the collection to the Count of Lemos,[3] then each story must contain 'a mystery which elevates it . . . Enough said'. We must beware, however, like Berganza during his time as a sheepdog in *The Dialogue of the Dogs*, of running up hill and down dale in pursuit of an imaginary wolf. The combined power of Cervantes's statements and insinuations has prompted some elaborate theorizing over the years. One contemporary critic, however, was quite satisfied to class all the stories alike when he dismissed them as 'prose plays' and condemned them as 'more satirical than exemplary'. This perceptive critic was Alonso Fernández de Avellaneda, the pseudonym of the still-unidentified author of the spurious sequel to *Don Quixote*, which was published in 1614. It was the publication of this work that spurred Cervantes to complete his own *Don Quixote, Part II*, which he published the following year. Intended to be highly uncomplimentary, Avellaneda's remarks nevertheless afford valuable insight into Cervantes's achievement in the *Exemplary Stories*. In the first place, they draw attention to Cervantes's indebtedness to the theatre. Indeed, his elaboration of colloquial speech and the revelation of character through dialogue are considered to be among his major contributions to the early modern novel. The very visual and 'choreographed' nature of much of the action may also be influenced by the drama of the period.

As for Avellaneda's reference to the stories' satirical quality, this is the most helpful signpost he could have erected for us. Since we undoubtedly live in a more cynical age, it is inevitable that we should find it satisfying to discover a certain critical nuance in Cervantes's words and perspective. Avellaneda's comment reveals that he too, in

[3] Pedro Fernández Ruiz de Castro y Osorio, nephew and son-in-law of the powerful Duke of Lerma and a generous patron of the arts.

his own age, sensed that these unusual and varied stories, in which Cervantes was exploring new narrative territory, were underpinned by a degree of critical intent, with regard not only to narrative forms but also to society and its norms.

The Little Gipsy Girl

Critical studies of *The Little Gipsy Girl* tend to fall into two categories: the first concentrates almost exclusively on the ideal or romance elements of the tale, such as love overcoming all obstacles and leading to an ideal union, complicated plot twists, disguised or mistaken identity, and the creation of suspense; the second adopts a more sceptical, even cynical attitude, perceiving that these elements of romance are organized ironically. Preciosa is certainly cynical in her attitude to language, which she distrusts. In fact the whole story tests and judges aspects of language as varied as exaggerated, poetic declarations of love and the confession of a prisoner who believes he is awaiting a death sentence. It is a romance which accepts nothing at face value.

A young nobleman, Juan Cárcamo, falls in love with a gipsy girl, Preciosa, and to prove his love for her he agrees to become a gipsy for two years. The story reaches a crisis when a soldier insults him, believing him to be a common, thieving gipsy. True to his noble origins, Juan kills the soldier in an act of revenge for his offended honour. While he is imprisoned, awaiting execution, it is revealed that Preciosa is really the daughter of the Chief Magistrate of Murcia, who was kidnapped as a baby. Her father can therefore use his authority and power to bring this crisis to a happy conclusion.

No one can deny that this plot contains the elements of romance: a young man submits to a trial to prove his love for a lady and must overcome his jealousy and the presence of a romantic rival; at the end we discover that the heroine of the tale is not who she thought she was. There is a return to origins and a restoration of the *status quo* after a typical delay in the denouement for the sake of creating suspense. The young man, however, undergoes a change of identity, not at the behest of some princess, but of a gipsy girl. The incongruity of a gipsy as the heroine of romantic fiction at that time cannot be exaggerated. Moreover, she is presented in the idealized terms of a heroine of romance or the object of desire in amorous poetry, with her golden hair and emerald eyes, so that even in physical terms she is strikingly different from her fellows. Cervantes places this heroine in the sordid, ambiguous context of anti-romance, where she dismisses the rhetoric of love with its exaggerated poetic metaphors and shows herself to be made of more practical stuff than her sentimental suitor. She seems to be challenging literary representations of love and proposing a real, achievable experience rather than a set of clichés. Preciosa has been viewed by some critics as the embodiment of all that is admirable in poetry, but she is just as often the voice of common sense and occasionally that of sexual innuendo. Like Cervantes's collection as a whole, the heroine of his opening story speaks in many voices and ambiguous tones.

The gipsies had begun to enter Spain in the fifteenth century and were marginalized and persecuted thereafter, yet in this story Cervantes integrates them into a romantic fiction and presents us with the idea of a virtuous gipsy. The invective of the opening lines, the categorical statement that the gipsies are nothing but a race of thieves, is immediately contradicted by the character and nature of Preciosa. The two worlds—the external spaces of the gipsy camps and the interiors of urbane society—are ironically juxtaposed. The story starts off by condemning and stereotyping the gipsies, but ends up questioning the standards of more conventional society.

Consider, for instance, Juan and the fact that he kills the soldier who insults him. A gipsy who had committed such an atrocity would have merited the death penalty, but when the Chief Magistrate discovers Juan's noble identity a matter of murder is commuted to a matter of honour. Juan could not have reacted in any other way and remained true to himself, and the dead man's uncle must be satisfied with material compensation for his loss. The incest and the violence of gipsy society leave much to be desired, but conventional society is equally flawed. This criticism is, of course, implicit. The only explicit reference that Preciosa makes to corruption is in her advice to an assistant magistrate in Madrid to accept bribes in order to live more comfortably.

Preciosa herself is presented as articulate and outspoken in her views on such subjects as courtship, fidelity, and virginity. She enthrals her audience when she sings, recites poetry, or engages them in lively dialogue. As soon as she is restored to her parents and her rightful place in society, however, she immediately becomes the almost silent, submissive daughter. Instead of having a voice of her own, her words are conveyed by the narrator. The shift from wilful independence to unquestioning obedience introduces a jarring note into the story. In a sense, Preciosa has abandoned the ambiguous world of the burgeoning novel and returned to that of romance.

This opening story sets the tone for the rest of the collection. Its heroine defies conventional definitions and the story itself appears to add up to more than just the sum of its parts.

Rinconete and Cortadillo

The satirical intentions of *Rinconete and Cortadillo* are more apparent. It is a colourful satire centring on an underworld crime syndicate in Seville, headed by a grotesque fool, which models itself on a religious brotherhood. It is the first of three stories in the present collection which bear affinities with the picaresque genre. The *pícaro* or anti-hero of the genre is one of life's underprivileged, who has been obliged to leave the paternal home and live off his wits. He becomes the peripatetic servant of many masters, learning worldliness and vice from the social stereotypes he encounters, and he narrates his pseudo-autobiography with a satirical voice. Although Cervantes's story is not a satire on the church in the manner of *Lazarillo de Tormes*, it nevertheless draws comic attention to the doctrinal and spiritual ignorance of the common man and the emptiness of religious observance. It is perhaps the funniest of the stories, yet there may well be a more serious comment beneath the mirth: that the ignorance of such people is itself criminal.

Two young delinquents meet up at a roadside inn. The comic note is established in the way their scruffy appearance is at odds with the airs and graces they put on for one another. Language cannot conceal the obvious. They provide each other with a potted life-story and it transpires that one is a card-sharper and the other a pickpocket, but that is the extent of the picaresque autobiography in this tale. They decide to join forces and their joint picaresque thieving brings them to the attention of the criminal fraternity of Seville, when they are duly summoned to register with the head of the underworld, Monipodio. From then on they act as observers of the sublime follies of this guild of thieves. In a sense, then, the picaresque detail is merely a means to an end, and the story Cervantes seems to be writing at the beginning is not the story he completes. It is not so much about Rinconete and Cortadillo as about what they witness. This story differs from others in the collection, because while most of the other characters are searching for some truth or revelation, in this story the truth is irrelevant. There is scant plot and little action, no crisis or climax, except for a few moments of comic panic when the police are spotted outside, and nothing is resolved. The characters are discovered in their moral ignorance and they continue to act in ignorance.

The actions, words, and both external and internal spaces of the story are circumscribed by religious references. Rinconete's father is a pardoner, 'an agent of the Holy Crusade'; the boys arrive in Seville to indulge their life of crime at a time of public prayer and a merchant is targeted for a stabbing before the hour of evening prayer. They admire the magnificence of the Cathedral and then Cortadillo irreverently returns to commit a theft on the Cathedral steps. Monipodio's mangled references to religious practices and the fact that a room in his house is dominated by the alms-box, the holy water, and the tawdry statue of the Virgin Mary reflect the extent to which religious observance has been subverted.

Unlike more authentic *pícaros*, Rinconete and Cortadillo are not drawn into this world they observe, but remain ironically detached from it, rather like Cervantes himself in his stance towards the genre as a whole. Rinconete's summation of events at the end of the story coincides with our own. We laugh and are appalled at the same time at the way these people are preparing places for themselves in hell, even if their earthly allies can keep them out of jail. The ironic detachment and good humour with which these criminals are depicted contrasts greatly with Mateo Alemán's more sombre and preachy treatment of crime and morality in *Guzmán de Alfarache*.

The Glass Graduate

If ignorance and folly support the satire in the previous story, in *The Glass Graduate* the focus is knowledge and madness. In linguistic terms it is the least ambiguous story in the collection, due to the aphoristic nature of the language, yet it is the most puzzling in terms of its interpretation. It begins with picaresque references to the River Tormes, birthplace of Lazarillo, and a poor young lad who has left

home in the hope of making something of his life. With the help
of wealthy patrons he embarks on a brilliant academic career, then
interrupts it to travel extensively in Italy, occasionally in the company of a Spanish regiment. This part of the story amounts to
little more than a travelogue. When he returns to Salamanca to
resume his studies, he is poisoned by a love potion which deludes
him into thinking that he is made of glass. Afraid of physical contact
with normal society, he stands aloof and alienated and his only
contact with other people is to stand at a distance and utter satirical
remarks.

He delivers the kind of wounding, personal satire that is deplored
by the protagonists of *The Dialogue of the Dogs* until he is cured by
a cleric. Restored to sanity he wishes to resume his legal career, but
no one wants to hear the truth stated so baldly by a sane man.
He once again abandons his career, goes to Flanders, and dies
honourably on the battlefield.

Parallels have been drawn between this strange and disjointed
piece of fiction and Cervantes's own experiences as soldier and artist.
Comparisons have also been drawn between Tomás Rodaja and the
Renaissance figure of the melancholy scholar, who often suffered
similar delusions, while another critic has seen in his alienation
an echo of the Cynics of Ancient Greece. In his deluded isolation
Tomás also brings the insanity of Don Quixote to mind, since both
suffer from book-induced madness and both embody the debate
between Arms and Letters. While Don Quixote quotes chivalric
precedent to justify his mad actions, the Graduate quotes Latin to
make his satirical point and flaunt his humanistic erudition. In fact,
it is almost as if his education separates him from his fellows. His
knowledge of the world derives from books rather than from personal experience. Although he remains an enigma, Tomás Rodaja
does reflect Cervantes's interest in deviant, unconventional characters who find themselves at odds with normal society.

The satire speaks for itself: it is sometimes funny and often malicious, but due to the large proportion of quotations it is for the main
part unoriginal. As for Tomás, his character does not evolve and
Cervantes has made no attempt to give him a voice of his own,
making him somewhat unique among the 'exemplary' characters.
Even before his induced madness, his motives are shaped by received
ideas. His knowledge is received, bookish wisdom and his cynicism

is similarly second-hand. Is Cervantes implying that the conventional satirist has nothing new to contribute to literary discourse?

The Power of Blood

While *The Glass Graduate* presents us with several distinct parts that refuse to fit together coherently, *The Power of Blood* is the most tautly constructed of all the stories. It is a balanced and symmetrical work exploiting contrasts of character, social privilege, sin and atonement, and light and dark, among others. Leocadia, the daughter of a poor but noble family, is kidnapped and raped by a young nobleman, Rodolfo, who then abandons her in the street and proceeds to forget that the incident ever took place, while she is left to bear a child and live in seclusion. When the son is injured seven years later the opportunity arises for Leocadia to inform the child's grandparents of what happened. Rodolfo's mother then arranges for Leocadia and Rodolfo to meet again, they fall in love, are married, and, we are informed, live happily ever after.

The contrasts are established early on: Leocadia's family are going up the hill that Rodolfo and his companions are descending; the former are depicted as sheep, the latter wolves. There are various parallel scenes: the injured child is taken and laid on the bed where his mother was raped; when Rodolfo sees Leocadia for the second time he is once again struck by her beauty, although his admiration this time round is deepened by awe; Leocadia twice falls unconscious in Rodolfo's arms. The crisis and its resolution are dominated by the image of the cross, itself a symbol of sin and redemption, from its first appearance in a dimly lit room to its re-emergence in the brilliant light of the final scene.

It is possible, however, to read the story differently if you look beyond these formal structures. While the 'power' of 'blood' is generally understood to refer to the blood the child Luis spills on the ground when he is injured, thus setting off a series of events which reunite his parents, it also refers to blood as inherited privilege and the power granted to one class over another. Luis is trampled by the fury of the horse while his mother is trampled by the lust of her assailant. In a story where external signs are all-important, there is one at the centre of the narrative which is highly ambiguous. Luis showed every sign of being the son of a 'noble' father. What is true nobility? Moreover, the fairy-tale ending regards the numerous and 'illustrious' descendants of Rodolfo and Leocadia as a sign of their happiness. Yet this illustrious descent originates in rape. The ending could also be read as the triumph of power and privilege. Otherwise condemned to a life of isolation, what other choice could Leocadia have made in the circumstances? While money is often being counted, dowries set, and fortunes flaunted in the other stories, in this tale economic power is implicit rather than explicit. The literal message of the tale may be exemplary in the way that sin is redeemed by the cross, but the underlying implication is that privilege, money, and power are the undisputed masters.

The Jealous Old Man from Extremadura

This is not the only portrait of a fateful May–December marriage in the Cervantine opus. In fact, it is one of three, and if any story brings the issue of exemplarity to the fore and makes it contentious it is this one.

A dissolute gentleman, Felipe Carrizales, squanders his wealth on wine and women, and finding himself destitute takes passage to the Indies where he makes his fortune. Returning to Spain twenty years later he decides to marry, and takes a child-bride whom he proceeds to lock up in a house which resembles both convent and harem. In spite of his determined efforts the edifice is brought crashing to the ground by the embodiment of his worst fear: the intrusion of a virile, young, would-be seducer.

In the earlier Porras edition the intruder, Loaysa, succeeds in seducing the young wife; Carrizales discovers them together, recognizes his role in his own downfall, and forgives his wife. In the 'exemplary' version Leonora resists her seducer's advances and remains faithful to her husband, in deed if not in thought. We have to accept the implausibility of Leonora both resisting Loaysa and then falling asleep in his arms. This crucial plot change has brought accusations of hypocrisy raining down on Cervantes's head, although just as much ink has been spilled in trying to justify the modifications.

The main characters and situations are drawn from farce; indeed, the theme is treated in conventionally bawdy fashion in Cervantes's comic interlude entitled *The Jealous Old Man*, in which the seducer shows the young wife what she has been missing behind a locked door while the husband and audience listen in. Although there are moments of pure farce in the 'exemplary' story, Cervantes invests the main character with a psychological complexity previously unknown in such a stereotype. His child-bride, too, invokes sympathy in her stunted emotional, sexual, and linguistic development. The potentially farcical material is injected with the suspense of honour drama,[4] especially when Carrizales considers exacting a bloody revenge on the apparent adulterers. The fact that Carrizales revises his intentions and decides to forgive is the crucial, exemplary moment in the story.

Although the jealous old man is the anti-hero of the story, he is not physically present in many of the scenes. He merely conditions the environment and imposes a kind of censorship on the women he has imprisoned within it. There is no direct speech in this story until a third of the way into the narrative. Healthy communication among the women is stifled as much as their sexuality is repressed, but their fear as well as their sensuality find almost surreal expression in the silently choreographed mime of their sarabandes and other dances.

Some of the most outstanding drama of the period is infused with male paranoia concerning their honour, and marital honour in particular. Husbands feel threatened by the fragile reputations and moral constitutions of their wives. In this story Leonora is therefore domesticated in keeping with the moral thinking of the time on the condition of women. She has contact with no man other than her husband, she is not encouraged to think of the world outside her home, is rarely allowed outside its walls, and freely admits that she has no will of her own. Carrizales's precautions are based on the presumption that she must not be exposed to the world's temptations because in her weakness she will inevitably succumb, but when temptation eventually enters her own world she stubbornly resists. Both old husband and young wife challenge the stereotype.

---

[4] The term may sound unusual to readers more familiar with English revenge drama. A preoccupation with honour permeates much of the literature of the period. The honour play was a popular sub-genre of the drama of the early seventeenth century, and even the lowly *pícaro* was concerned about his honour.

The Illustrious Kitchen Maid

While in *The Jealous Old Man from Extremadura* Cervantes subtly
blends elements of farce and tragedy, the texture of *The Illustrious
Kitchen Maid* is more blatantly heterogeneous, and the contrast contained in the title should alert us to Cervantes's treatment of his
material. The story opens in romance mode with the reference to distinguished gentlemen and the illustrious city of Burgos. The son of
one of these gentlemen immediately breaks with convention and
enthusiastically embraces the life of the *pícaro*. He then returns to
the world of romance only to persuade a friend to join him in his
sordid picaresque adventures. On their way to Zahara in southern
Spain the friend falls in love with a kitchen maid, reintroducing an
element of romance, although a subversive one, because gentlemen,
even in picaresque clothing, do not fall in love with kitchen maids.
So within the space of a few paragraphs the story has changed direction, and register, several times.

The incongruities are numerous and the language does not stabi-
lize until the boys' fathers turn up at the inn where they are working
and Carriazo's father narrates his own tale. It is an ignominious tale
of rape and greed, yet contained within the refined and measured
tones of high romance the violence is muted and abstracted. The
boys are duly restored to their proper milieu, as is the kitchen maid,
who, like Preciosa earlier in the collection, turns out to be the dis-
placed daughter of privileged stock. The anagnorisis or final recog-
nition scene of romance is comically foreshadowed by Carriazo's
father not being able to recognize his son because he has covered his
bloodied face with a handkerchief.

The story is full of abrupt juxtapositions; violent clashes are part
of the style as well as the action. Even the story of the kitchen maid's
true origins is a romance which is literally cut in two, told by several
different voices and interrupted by more violent picaresque episodes.
Convention, however, appears to triumph; the *status quo* is restored,
or so it seems until the closing lines. Privilege is perpetuated in a
series of multiple marriages, the conventional happy ending one
expects after the vicissitudes of romance, yet the colloquial and
'satirical' voice of his picaresque past returns to haunt the now-
respectable Carriazo. Anti-romance has the last word.

The Deceitful Marriage

The Deceitful Marriage can be read in its own right as a witty and amusing, though unremarkable tale of a trickster tricked. The moral of the story is clearer here than anywhere: if you yourself are a cheat, you cannot complain if you too are cheated; and appearances are deceptive. This confidence trickster, however, has another tale to tell: this self-confessed liar becomes the narrator of an incredible story which he wants his reader to believe. Campuzano, another soldier and aspiring artist who is down on his luck, tells his friend Peralta that while he was undergoing treatment for syphilis, and therefore feverish and possibly hallucinating, he overheard two dogs talking and faithfully transcribed their conversation. It is the ensuing dialogue of the dogs Berganza and Scipio, probably Western literature's first literal shaggy dog story, that has received most critical attention.

The Dialogue of the Dogs

Imaginative prose fiction was viewed with great suspicion in certain quarters, as we have seen. Cervantes's own *Don Quixote* explores and parodies the idea that literature not grounded in empirical reality is dangerous stuff. In *The Deceitful Marriage* and *The Dialogue of the Dogs* Cervantes is most overtly concerned with a reader's suspension of disbelief. He playfully places a quasi-picaresque autobiography, the most 'realist' fiction of its time in its baring of society's vices, in a totally fantastic framework of rational, talking dogs. He then defies us, like Peralta, not to get caught up in it. Like so many other stories, it is modelled on a variety of sources: the Lucianic dialogue, Aesop's fables, and of course, the picaresque pseudo-autobiography, a satirical form in its own right which Cervantes takes the opportunity to satirize further.

Time and time again the dogs return to the subject of gossiping, backbiting, or making critical judgements about people. They fear being labelled as cynical, preachy, and satirical. Scipio even quotes Juvenal as saying that it is difficult not to write satire, and the dogs' ultimate failure to restrain their satirical vision is a central irony in the story. Cervantes places the conventional picaresque autobiography within the framework of a dialogue in order to comment on what he sees as the shortcomings of the genre, namely, the narrowness of a single viewpoint and the protracted, shapeless preachiness of *Guzmán de Alfarache*.

It is a picaresque narrative with its own in-built critique—a story about the creative process and how to cast a critical eye over the expanding text; Scipio is forever interrupting Berganza's story to question where it is leading or to comment on its digressiveness or its tendency to moralize. It is also about the process of reading and the power of the imagination. The witch at the centre of the story claims that during their sabbath orgies it is impossible to ascertain whether the experience is real or fantasy. The analogy is clear. If the fantasy is powerful enough we can find ourselves believing that dogs are capable of rational speech and worry about the satirical nature of their words.

As for the issue of exemplarity, this too is clear. Unlike his *pícaro* predecessors, Berganza is not contaminated by his environment; he merely abandons vice and runs off to find another master. True virtue is immutable, Scipio announces at the end, however many layers of artifice or deceit may be superimposed on it. When critics fail to defend the case for moral exemplarity in the collection as a whole, they often speak of aesthetic exemplarity instead. *The Dialogue of the Dogs* is certainly an impressive and complex structure of writers, speakers, readers, and listeners, who to different degrees ponder the truth of oral, hand-written and published words. The true ending of the story, however, is not the end of the dogs' dialogue but Peralta's admission that the story is aesthetically satisfying even though it is implausible. Cervantes is overtly challenging a literary principle of his age which asserted that fiction could not convince without reflecting empirical reality. Furthermore, he openly defies another rule, that implausible events be relegated to a sphere outside of everyday reality, when he brings the supernatural to the streets of Valladolid.

Paradoxically, readers of the collection are more likely to identify with these two dogs than with any other 'exemplary' character; they are trying to fit the puzzling pieces of their experiences together to form a coherent whole, interpreting signs and searching for meaning. In the Prologue Cervantes challenges us to make sense of his stories just as the dogs are trying to make sense of their lives. As they grapple with the problem of satire in a picaresque context, their words seem to reinforce the satirical messages we have been reading between the lines in all the stories.

While encouraging us to come to our own moral conclusions, Cervantes is also anxious that we accept the coincidental, improbable, and downright impossible dimensions of his plots. He attempts to achieve this by situating the more bizarre details in a relatively familiar context. While the writers of chivalric romances placed their fantasies in distant lands, Cervantes locates his Don Quixote in La Mancha. Similarly, in the *Exemplary Stories* the reader does not need to go far to encounter the extraordinary: the talking dogs do their philosophizing in a ward full of sweating syphilitics; and his near-perfect literary heroines are given a flesh-and-blood reality when Cervantes subjects Preciosa to a fairly intimate physical examination by her mother and inflicts Costanza with bad toothache. He domesticates fantasy by firmly anchoring it in the houses, churches, hospitals, streets, and highways of seventeenth-century Spain, and in so doing charts new novelistic territory by placing the extraordinary within the context of the ordinary.

NOTE ON THE TEXT AND TRANSLATION

This translation has been written with reference to the *editio princeps*
of 1613 and that of Harry Sieber (Madrid: Ediciones Cátedra, 1992).
I have omitted four stories—*The Generous Suitor*, *The English
Spanish Girl*, *The Two Damsels*, and *The Lady Cornelia*. Since they
reflect the more traditional format of love and adventure, they are
stylistically and conceptually less adventurous than the rest. This also
makes them less representative of Cervantes as innovator.

I have retained most Spanish proper names and place-names
and only translated card games when there is an obvious English
equivalent. Similarly, I retain the old Spanish currency in the fre-
quent references to money. The only change I have made to the
shape of the narrative is to break up many of Cervantes's long and
complicated sentences.

SELECT BIBLIOGRAPHY

Biographies

Byron, William, *Cervantes: A Biography* (New York: Doubleday & Company, 1978).

Canavaggio, Jean, *Cervantes*, trans. J. R. Jones (London: Norton, 1990).

McKendrick, Melveena, *Cervantes* (Boston: Little, Brown & Co., 1980).

Russell, P. E., *Cervantes* (Oxford: Oxford University Press, 1985).

General Studies

Close, Anthony J., 'Characterization and Dialogue in Cervantes's *Comedias en prosa*', *Modern Language Review*, 76 (1981), 338–56.

Dunn, Peter, 'Shaping Experience: Narrative Strategies in Cervantes', *Modern Language Notes*, 109 (1994), 186–203.

El Saffar, Ruth, *Novel to Romance: A Study of Cervantes's 'Novelas ejemplares'* (Baltimore: Johns Hopkins University Press, 1974).

Forcione, Alban, K., *Cervantes and the Humanist Vision; A Study of Four Exemplary Novels* (Princeton: Princeton University Press, 1982).

——*Cervantes and the Mystery of Lawlessness* (Princeton: Princeton University Press, 1984).

Gerli, E. Michael, *Refiguring Authority: Reading, Writing and Rewriting in Cervantes* (Lexington: University of Kentucky Press, 1995).

Hart, Thomas R., *Cervantes's Exemplary Fictions: A Study of the Novelas ejemplares* (Lexington: University of Kentucky Press, 1994).

Ife, Barry W., *Reading and Fiction in Golden-Age Spain* (Cambridge: Cambridge University Press, 1985).

Nerlich, Michael and Nicholas Spadaccini (eds.), *Cervantes's Exemplary Novels and the Adventure of Writing*, Hispanic Issues, 6 (Minneapolis, 1989).

Riley, Edward C., *Cervantes's Theory of the Novel*, 3rd edn. (Oxford: Clarendon Press, 1968).

——'Cervantes: A Question of Genre', in F. W. Hodcroft *et al.* (eds.), *Medieval and Renaissance Studies on Spain and Portugal in Honour of P. E. Russell* (Oxford: Society for the Study of Medieval Languages and Literature, 1981).

Studies on Individual Stories

Calcraft, R. P., 'Structure, Symbol and Meaning in Cervantes's *La fuerza de la sangre*', *Bulletin of Hispanic Studies*, 58 (1981), 197–204.

Casa, Frank P., 'The Structural Unity of *El licenciado vidriera*', *Bulletin of Hispanic Studies*, 41 (1964), 242–6.

Clamurro, William H., 'Identity, Discourse and Social Order in *La ilustre fregona*', *Cervantes*, 7 (1987), 39–56.

Dunn, Peter N., 'Cervantes De/Re-Constructs the Picaresque', *Cervantes*, 2 (1982), 109–31.

El Saffar, Ruth, *'El casamiento engañoso' and 'El coloquio de los perros'*, *Critical Guides to Spanish Texts*, 17, ed. J. E. Varey and A. D. Deyermond (London: Grant & Cutler in association with Tamesis Books Ltd., 1976).

Lambert, A. F., 'The Two Versions of Cervantes's *El celoso extremeño*: Ideology and Criticism', *Bulletin of Hispanic Studies*, 57 (1980), 219–31.

Lipson, Lesley, '"La palabra hecha nada": Mendacious Discourse in Cervantes's *La gitanilla*', *Cervantes*, 9 (1989), 35–53.

Pierce, Frank, '*La gitanilla*: A Tale of High Romance', *Bulletin of Hispanic Studies*, 54 (1977).

CHRONOLOGY OF CERVANTES
AND HIS TIMES

1585   Publication of *La Galatea*, Part One.

1587–8 Commissary for requisitioning provisions for the Armada; working in Andalusia; defeat of the Armada.

1590   Applies unsuccessfully for a government posting in America.

1592   Imprisoned briefly in Castro del Río, charged with irregularities in his accounts; contracts with impresario Rodrigo de Osorio to supply six plays.

1594   Tax collecting in Granada.

1596   Travelling in Andalusia and Castile on tax business; sack of Cadiz by English fleet;

1597   September, gaoled in Seville because of a confusion over the administration of public finances.

1598   Released by April; death of Philip II; accession of Philip III.

1599   Mateo Alemán, *Guzmán de Alfarache*, Part One; plague in Spain.

1600   Probably returns to Castile from Seville; birth of Calderon.

1601   The court moves to Valladolid; Duke of Lerma in power.

1603   Shakespeare, *Hamlet*, first quarto; death of Elizabeth I; accession of James I.

1604   Cervantes joins his wife and sisters in Valladolid. Porras de la Cámara prepares MS for the entertainment of the Archbishop of Seville.

1605   January, publication of *Don Quixote*, Part One; June, one Gaspar de Ezpeleta killed in a duel outside Cervantes's house—Cervantes and his household arrested and charged with immoral and disorderly conduct, but are quickly released.

1606   Isabel recognized by Cervantes and takes the name of Saavedra; The court returns to Madrid.

1607   Cervantes and his family move to Madrid.

1609   He joins a fashionable religious brotherhood, the Slaves of the Most Holy Sacrament, with literary affiliations; Lope de Vega, *Arte Nuero de Hacer Comedias* (*New Art of Writing Plays*); expulsion of the Moriscos from Spain begins.

1610   He fails to be chosen for the entourage of the Count of Lemos on his appointment as Viceroy of Naples.

1612   Participates in meetings of literary academies and salons in Madrid.

1613   Moves to Alcalá de Henares; Becomes a tertiary of the Franciscan Order; Publication of the *Novelas ejemplares* (*Exemplary Stories*).

1614   The long poem *Viaje del Parnaso* (*Journey to Parnassus*) published; Alonso Fernández de Avellaneda publishes sequel to *Don Quixote*.

EXEMPLARY STORIES

PROLOGUE

I would prefer, if it were possible, dearest reader, not to have to write this prologue, for the one I put in my *Don Quixote* was not such a success that I am eager to follow it up with another. The fault lies with a friend of mine, one of the many I have acquired during the course of my life, thanks more to my temperament than my wit. This friend could easily, in keeping with established practice, have engraved and printed my likeness on the first page of this book, since the famous don Juan de Jauregui* had given him my portrait. That way my ambition would have been satisfied, together with the curiosity of those people who want to acquaint themselves with the face and figure of the man who dares to display such inventiveness in the market-place and expose it to public scrutiny. Beneath the portrait he could have written:

'The man you see before you, with aquiline features, chestnut-coloured hair, smooth, unwrinkled brow, bright eyes, and curved though well-proportioned nose, silver beard that not twenty years ago was golden, large moustache, small mouth, teeth neither large nor small—since he boasts only six of them, and those he has are in poor condition and even worse positions, for not one of them cuts against another—of medium build, neither tall nor short, a healthy colour in his cheeks, fair rather than dark complexion, slightly stooping, and not very light on his feet. This, then, is a description of the author of *La Galatea* and *Don Quixote of la Mancha* and the man who wrote *Journey to Parnassus*, which was modelled on the one by César Caporal Perusino,* and other works which have gone astray, perhaps without their owner's name upon them. He is commonly known as Miguel de Cervantes Saavedra. He was for many years a soldier and a prisoner for five and a half after that, during which time he learned to cultivate patience in adversity. He lost his left hand in the naval battle of Lepanto to a blunderbuss shot, and although the injury is ugly he considers it beautiful because he incurred it at the most noble and memorable event that past centuries have seen or future generations can ever hope to witness, fighting beneath the victorious banners of the son of that thunderbolt of war, Charles V of happy memory.'

And if this friend, of whom I complain, could not remember anything else to say about me save what I have already said on my own account, I could compose two dozen testimonials myself and secretly share their contents with him, thus spreading my fame and confirming my ingenuity. For it is absurd to imagine that such eulogies convey the absolute truth, for praise and condemnation have no fixed or constant value.

In short, since that opportunity was lost and I have been left blank and faceless, I shall have to rely on my gift of the gab. Although I may speak with a stammer, the truths I have to say will be clear enough, for even when they are conveyed by means of signs, they are usually understood. And so I say again, amiable reader, that you will in no way be able to make a fricassee of these stories I offer you, for they possess no feet, nor head, nor entrails, nor anything of the kind. What I mean is that the amorous compliments that you will find in some of them are so proper and so tempered by reason and Christian discourse, that they could not inspire undesirable thoughts in any reader, whether careful or otherwise.

I have called them 'exemplary', and on close examination you will see that there is not one from which you cannot extract some profitable example; and were it not for the fact that I do not wish to labour the point, I might show you the delicious and wholesome fruit to be gathered from each individual story as well as from the collection as a whole.

It has been my intention to set up a billiard table in the public square of our nation, where anyone may come and amuse himself without injuring anyone else; in other words, without causing harm to either body or soul. For proper and agreeable exercise is more beneficial than harmful.

Indeed, for we cannot spend all our time in church; the oratories cannot always be occupied; we cannot be always attending to business, however important it may be. There is a time and place for recreation, when the weary spirit may rest.

For this reason poplar groves are planted, fountains created, slopes levelled, and gardens neatly laid out. One thing I shall dare to say to you and it is this: if it somehow transpired that reading these stories provoked an improper thought or desire in one of my readers, I would sooner cut off the hand with which I wrote them, than see them published. I am no longer of an age to trifle with the life to come, for at fifty-five, I may have nine years left and beat my readers to it.

So it was to this that I applied my imagination; this is where my natural inclination leads me, especially since it is my opinion and it is true, that I am the first to write short stories in Castilian. For the many examples that are already in print in Spanish are all translated from foreign languages, while these are my very own, neither imitated nor stolen. They were conceived in my imagination, brought into the world by my pen, and are now growing up in the arms of the printing press. After them, if life does not desert me, I shall offer you *The Travails of Persiles and Sigismunda*, a book which dares to compete with Heliodorus,* unless it takes a drubbing for its boldness. Firstly, however, you will soon see the further adventures of *Don Quixote* and the witty remarks of Sancho Panza, and then *Weeks in the Garden*.*

This is a great deal for a man of my weak constitution to promise: yet who can put a rein on desire? I only wish you to consider this; that since I have been bold enough to dedicate these stories to the great Count of Lemos, they must contain some hidden mystery which elevates them.

Enough said, except to desire that God keep you and give me patience to bear the starchy and sarcastic comments that are bound to be forthcoming. Vale.*

THE LITTLE GIPSY GIRL

It seems that all gipsies, both male and female, are born into this world to be thieves. They are born of thieves, raised among thieves, study to be thieves, and eventually turn into thoroughgoing, dyed-in-the-wool thieves themselves. In such people the desire to steal and the act of stealing are inseparable instincts which remain with them until they die.

One member of this society was an old gipsy woman who could be regarded as a past mistress in the subtle art of thieving.* This old woman raised a young girl as her granddaughter, calling her Preciosa, and taught her all the gipsy customs, the tricks of her fraudulent trade, and her methods of stealing. This same Preciosa grew into the most extraordinary dancer in the whole of gipsydom, and the most beautiful and intelligent woman to be found anywhere, not just among gipsies but among all women everywhere who were cele-brated for their beauty and intelligence. Neither the sun nor the wind, nor any inclement weather——to which gipsies are more exposed than other people——could dull the lustre of her complexion or roughen the softness of her hands. What is even more remarkable is the fact that the tough upbringing she had received only served to reveal that she had been born of better stock than a line of gipsies, for she was exceedingly polite and well-spoken. And yet, in spite of this, she was somewhat brazen, but not to the extent that it gave way to any impropriety. On the contrary, although she was quick-witted, she was so virtuous that in her presence no female gipsy, whether young or old, dared to sing lascivious songs or use indecent language. In short, her grandmother recognized the treasure she possessed in such a granddaughter and so the wily old bird decided to teach her nestling how to fly and live by her claws.

Preciosa had a rich repertoire of carols, folksongs, serenades, sara-bandes,* and other songs and dances, especially ballads, which she sang with a special grace. To her crafty grandmother it was more than obvious that such arts and charms, combined with her grand-daughter's youth and considerable beauty, were bound to be power-ful attractions and enticements with which to accrue her fortune. She therefore used every means at her disposal to get hold of such verses

and there was always some poet to keep her supplied. For there are
poets who have an arrangement with gipsies and sell them their com-
positions, just as there are poets who compose for blind beggars,
inventing false miracles for them and taking a share of the profits. It
takes all sorts to make a world, and the bane of hunger sometimes
forces talented people into uncharted territory.

Preciosa was brought up in various parts of Castile and when she
was fifteen years old her putative grandmother took her back to
Madrid and her former camp in the fields of Santa Bárbara, the usual
haunt of gipsies. She did so with the intention of plying her trade
at Court, where everything is bought and sold. Preciosa went into
Madrid for the first time on the Day of St Anne,* patron saint and
advocate of the city, and performed a dance comprising a group of
eight, four elderly women and four girls, accompanied by a very
talented male dancer who led them. Although all the women were
looking neat and well groomed, Preciosa was so immaculately turned
out that she gradually captivated every eye that gazed upon her.
Amid the sound of the tambourine and the castanets and the motion
of the dance, there rose a murmur of praise for the beauty and grace
of the little gipsy girl and youths rushed to take a look at her and
men to gaze more intently. When they heard her sing—for it was
a dance accompanied by singing—they were in ecstasy. That was
the moment when the little gipsy girl's fame was established, and
the judges presiding over the celebrations unanimously decided
to award her the first prize for the best dance. When they came to
perform it in the Church of Holy Mary and all the other women had
finished dancing, Preciosa took up her position in front of a statue
of St Anne. She picked up her tambourine and as she played it and
danced in wide and exquisitely delicate circles, she sang the following ballad:

> Most precious, most lovely tree,
> Quite barren of fruit for years,
> Thus burdened with mourning
> And the grief of many tears.
>
> Reducing the pure desires
> Of consort and companion
> To fragile, uncertain hopes,
> And hollow expectation.

And from those years of waiting
Was engendered that disgust
Which cast out from the temple
That poor gentleman most just.*

Holy and infertile earth,
Which was at last to nurture,
The richness and the bounty
Which sustains all of nature.

The mint and source of all wealth,
Where God elected to make
The mould which then shaped the form
He as flesh and blood would take.

Mother of such a daughter,
In whom our God surely would
Display his grandiose power,
By mankind scarce understood.

For both you and she are, Anne,
The true sanctuary pure,
Where we in our misfortune
Seek and find our holy cure.

And after your own fashion
You, I do not doubt, hold sway,
Over your mighty grandson,
In your just and gentle way.

As lowly occupiers
Of heaven's great citadel,
A thousand of your own kin
Would most gladly with you dwell.

What daughter and what grandson
And son-in-law you possess;
You've right and proper reason
To sing loud of your success.

But you, so meek and lowly,
Were the live illustration
Who gave your holy daughter
Her humble education.

Now forever at her side,
And she close at God's right hand,
You enjoy the majesty
I but dimly understand.

The sweetness of Preciosa's singing filled all those who listened with
wonder. Some exclaimed, 'God bless you, young lady!' while others
said, 'What a pity the girl's a gipsy. If the truth be told, she deserves
to be the daughter of some great lord.' There were others who made
cruder comments: 'Let the youngster grow up and she'll soon be up
to her tricks! She's already weaving a fine net to ensnare men's hearts.'
Another spectator, who was more sympathetic yet more down-to-
earth and plain-speaking, commented on the lightness of her steps:
'Go for it, lass, go for it! Come sweetheart, and make the dust fly!'
And she replied, without halting her dance, 'I'll make the dust fly!'

The evening's entertainment and the feast day of St Anne drew
to a close, leaving Preciosa rather tired but so celebrated for her
beauty, wit, intelligence, and prowess as a dancer that wherever
people gathered together to talk in that city she was the subject
of their conversations. Fifteen days later she returned to Madrid
with three other young girls, tambourines, and a new dance. All four
were well-versed in lively but decorous ballads and other songs,
for Preciosa would not allow her companions to sing bawdy verses,
nor did she sing such songs herself, and many appreciated this fact
and greatly respected her for it. The old gipsy woman, her self-
appointed Argus,* never wandered far from her side, fearing that she
might be snatched away or abducted. She addressed her as granddaughter and was, in turn, regarded by the girl as her grandmother.

They began to dance in the shade of Toledo Street and her band
of followers gathered round in a large circle. As they danced the old
gipsy asked the bystanders for money, and ochavos and cuartos*
rained down upon them like stones thrown at a target, for beauty also
has the power to awaken dormant charity. When she had finished
dancing Preciosa said, 'If you give me four cuartos I'll sing you a solo
ballad, a very fine one indeed, which tells of how our sovereign lady,
Queen Margaret,* attended her first Mass after giving birth at the
Church of St Lawrence in Valladolid. As I say, it's a splendid song,
written by a poet of high rank, like the captain of a battalion.'

She had scarcely finished speaking when each and every one of the onlookers who stood around her exclaimed, 'Sing it. Preciosa, for here are my four cuartos.'

As the cuartos showered down upon her like hailstones the old gipsy had her work cut out collecting them all. When this abundant harvest had been gathered in, Preciosa shook her tambourine and in a gay and lively manner she sang the following ballad:

> The sovereign queen of Europe
> Went to Mass, after giving birth;
> In name and reputation
> A gem of great beauty and worth.
>
> Every eye is fixed upon her
> And all souls to her surrender,
> As they watch and gaze in wonder
> At such devotion, such splendour.
>
> She has, to show mere mortals
> She is of heaven on earth born,
> On one side the Austrian sun,*
> On the other tender dawn.
>
> In her wake there follows a star,
> Which shone forth its untimely glow
> In the black darkness of that day,
> That filled heaven and earth with woe.*
>
> If in the firmament are stars
> Which in bright chariots light the sky,
> In other chariots living stars
> Her private heaven beautify.*
>
> Here Saturn, old and ailing,
> Combs his beard and youth restores;
> Though he's slow his step is agile,
> For pleasure remedies gout's sores.
>
> The prolix God steps forth in words
> Of flattery and affection;
> Cupid in diverse shape and form
> Of pearl and ruby ostentation.
>
> There goes furious, warring Mars,
> His bravado just skin-shallow
> In more than one dashing hero
> Who's afraid of his own shadow.

There too goes mighty Jupiter,*
Right next to the house of the Sun,
For nought is denied the privilege
Which through prudent acts has been won.

The moon shines forth from every cheek
Of every heavenly mortal;
Chaste Venus in the loveliness
That forms this body celestial.

A myriad Ganymedes* small
Weave in and out, rotate and veer
Along the studded, starry belt
Of this ornate and wondrous sphere.

And so that all may fill with awe,
There's nought falls short of liberal;
In order to cause wonderment
No thing is less than prodigal.

Milan in its rich materials
Attracts numerous, curious eyes,
And with the gems of the Indies
And the scents of Arabia vies.

While evil-minded malcontents
Breed biting envy in their breast,
Pure loyalty, fair constancy,
In every Spanish soul doth rest.

Universal celebration,
Fleeing from all woeful cares,
Runs dishevelled and half crazy
Through all the streets and squares.

Then silence, open-mouthed with awe,
Finds its tongue to sound its praise;
Boys repeat the thousand blessings
In which all men their voices raise.

One voice shouts out, 'O, fertile vine,
Send forth your shoots and upward climb,
Your elm felicitous entwine;
May it shade you an eternal time,

'For the sake of your own glory,
For the good and honour of Spain,

For the support of Holy Church,
For the end of Mahomet's bane.'

Another tongue exclaims and cries:
'White dove, to you long life is owed,
Who in your offspring offers us
Eagles with two heads bestowed,*

'To banish savage birds of prey
From their dominion of the sky;
To defend frighted honesty
If safe beneath their wings she'll lie.'

A wiser, more distinctive voice,
More astute and by far graver,
Says, with a smile upon its lips,
Eyes sparkling with good cheer:

'Rare Austrian Mother of Pearl,
This gem for its value renowned,
What conspiring it can frustrate,
What treacherous intrigue confound,

'What hopeful illusions inspire,
What unworthy intentions thwart,
What fear in opponents augment,
What ill-conceived scheming abort.'

They reached the church of the Phoenix,*
Who burned in Rome a great martyr,
Whose sanctity remained alive
In glorious fame ever after.

To the sacred image of life,
To the reigning queen of heaven,
To her, who through her modesty,
Now treads upon stars all-sovereign,

Reverent and kneeling before her,
Who's mother and virgin both,
Both daughter and consort of God,
Margarita duly speaks forth:

'I return what you have bestowed,
Oh, ever-generous regent,
For where your favour is absent,
Suffering is always abundant.

'My first fruits I give unto you,
Wonderful, beautiful Virgin;
Pray accept them, such as they are,
For your care and melioration.

'I commend his father to you,
Who, a human Atlas, inclines,
'Neath the weight of so many realms,
And so many faraway climes.

'I know that the heart of the king
In the hands of God rests secure,
And that you in majesty may
All you desire from God procure.'

When she had finished thus praying,
Great hymns and fine voices resound
In another prayer to proclaim
God's glory on earth does abound.

And when Mass had come to a close,
With due pomp and ceremony,
This heaven and marvellous sphere
Took its place in God's harmony.

Preciosa had scarcely finished her ballad when the illustrious and worthy audience which had gathered to listen to her united in one voice to declare, 'Sing another song, dear Preciosa, for there'll be no shortage of cuartos.'

More than two hundred people were watching the gipsies' dance and listening to their song, during the course of which one of the town magistrates happened to pass by. On seeing so many people assembled together he asked what was going on, and was told that they were listening to the beautiful gipsy girl who was singing. The magistrate moved closer to satisfy his curiosity and stood listening for a while although, to preserve his dignity, he did not wait to hear the ballad through to the end. Since the young gipsy girl had made a particularly good impression on him he ordered one of his pages to tell the old gipsy woman to bring the girls to his house at nightfall, because he wanted his wife, doña Clara, to hear them. The page did as he was instructed and the old woman said that she would come.

They finished their song and dance and moved on to another place, whereupon a very well-dressed page approached Preciosa and, handing her a folded piece of paper, said, 'Preciosa, sing the ballad on this sheet of paper because it's a very good one, and I'll give you others from time to time, which will earn you the reputation of being the best ballad singer in the world.'

'I'll learn it very willingly,' replied Preciosa, 'and sir, make sure that you don't fail to give me the ballads you mentioned, as long as they are decent; and if you want me to pay you for them, let's agree on batches of a dozen, a dozen sung and a dozen paid for. For if you think I'm going to pay you in advance, then you're thinking the impossible.'

'If señorita Preciosa pays for the paper alone,' said the page, 'then I'll be content; and what's more, if the ballad turns out to be anything but good and decent, then I won't charge you.'

'But you must leave it to me to choose them,' replied Preciosa.

They proceeded along the street, and from a window grille some gentlemen called out to the gipsy girls. Preciosa went up to the grille, which stood close to the ground, and looked in on a very elegantly furnished and airy room, where many gentlemen were taking their leisure, some of them walking up and down the length of the room while others sat playing various games. 'Good thirs, would you care to give me thome of your winningth?' lisped Preciosa in keeping with gipsy tradition, for this is deliberate artifice on their part and not a natural characteristic. When they heard Preciosa's voice and saw her face, the players abandoned their gaming and the walkers their pacing and to a man they hurried to the window to see her—for they had heard about her—and said, 'Let the gipsy girls come in, let them come in, for we'll share our winnings with them.'

'It'll cost you dear if you get too near,' replied Preciosa.

'No, I give you my word as a gentleman,' replied one of them, 'You can come inside, child, safe in the knowledge that no one will so much as touch the tip of your shoe. No indeed, I swear by the insignia I bear on my chest.' He raised his hand to touch a cross of Calatrava.*

'If you want to go inside, Preciosa,' said one of the three gipsy girls accompanying her, 'feel free to go ahead; because I've no intention of entering a place where there are so many men.'

'Look, Cristina,' replied Preciosa, 'what you've got to beware of is a solitary, unaccompanied man when you're also alone, and not many gathered together; because the fact that there are lots of them dispels the fear and threat of being insulted. Take heed, Cristina, and be sure of one thing; that a woman who's determined to be virtuous can remain so in the midst of an entire army. It's true that it's sensible not to invite opportunity; but I'm speaking of private rather than public occasions.'

'Then let's go in, Preciosa,' said Cristina, 'for you're wiser than a sage.' The old gipsy woman urged them on and they went in. No sooner had Preciosa entered the room when the gentleman bearing the knightly insignia saw the paper which she was carrying in her bodice and went up to her and removed it, prompting Preciosa to exclaim,

'Please don't take that, sir, for it's a ballad which I've just been given and I haven't had time to read it yet.'

'And can you read, child?', asked one of the gentlemen present.

'And write,' replied the old woman, 'for I've brought my grand-daughter up as if she were the daughter of a scholar.'

The gentleman opened up the paper and saw that there was a gold escudo inside, and said, 'Well now, Preciosa, this letter bears its fran-chise on the inside; take this escudo which comes with the ballad.'

'So,' said Preciosa, 'the poet's decided I'm poor. It's certainly more of a miracle for a poet to give me an escudo than for me to accept it; and if all his ballads are to come with an escudo enclosed, then I hope he'll copy out the whole of the *Great Ballad Anthology** and send them to me one by one. I'll feel them and if they come with hard currency, then I'll receive them ever so softly.'

Everyone who was listening to the little gipsy girl was astounded not only by the wisdom but also by the wit of her words.

'Read it, sir,' she said, 'read it aloud; let's see whether this poet's as gifted as he's generous.'

The gentleman recited the following poem:

> Little gipsy girl, 'tis with just cause
> Your fair face should win you such applause;
> Yet your heart, this cold insentient stone,
> Earns you the title of Precious One.
>
> You will, I am quite sure, verify,
> As the truth of the case will testify,
> That such beauty and hardness of heart
> Can seldom or never be apart.

If, as your renown spreads far and wide,
You grow likewise and apace in pride,
I regard not with envy but scorn
That wretched age in which you were born.

A basilisk springs up within you,
Slaying all who come into view;
Your imperiousness, albeit sweet,
Is a tyranny we'll ne'er defeat.

Among wand'ring folk, so ill-perceived,
How was beauty so awesome conceived?
From Manzanares' humble verge
How did perfect creation emerge?

Bearing such fruit 'twill be as famous
As the revered, gold-bearing Tagus,*
And in rank and fame subordinate
Even mighty Ganges in full spate.

The ill fate of men you ceaseless spell,
When to us our fortunes you foretell,
For your rare beauty and benevolence
Will forever be at variance.

They place themselves in mortal peril,
Fully apprised that your look can kill;
Your lack of malice will exculpate
You, though your gaze render death their fate.

They say all women of your nation
Are witches, skilled in conjuration;
Although the sorceries you incant
Have genuine power to enchant.

And so to carry off the plunder
Of those whose lives you cast asunder,
While their gaze affixed upon you lies,
There's deadly charm in your lovely eyes.

You use such potent gifts to your gain,
When we dance in your thrall remain;
You look and our very lives supplant,
You sing and with the first note enchant.

You charm in a thousand diff'rent ways,
With a word, in silence, song, or gaze;
Whether you draw near or take flight,
The fire in our breasts you set alight.

Such absolute power to you imparts
Sovereign rule o'er indifferent hearts;
As my own heart bears witness true,
Content to resign its will to you.

Jewel of love, priceless precious stone,
This I humbly write for you alone;
I gladly live and would die for you,
Grant the grace to a poor suitor due.

'The last line contains the word "poor",' said Preciosa at that point. 'A very bad sign. Lovers should never say that they're poor because at the beginning, it seems to me, poverty's the arch-enemy of love.'

'Who taught you all these things, child?' asked one of the gentlemen.

'Who d'you think taught me? asked Preciosa in reply. 'Don't I have a soul in my body? Haven't I reached the ripe old age of fifteen? I'm neither lame, nor crippled, nor mentally deficient. The wits of gipsy girls obey different laws from those of most other people. They're always in advance of their years; there's no such thing as a stupid gipsy, or a slow-witted gipsy girl; since their survival depends on them being quick, astute, and deceitful, they're constantly sharpening their wits, and like rolling stones they gather no moss. Do you see these companions of mine, who say nothing and look a bit foolish? Well, stick a finger in their mouths and have a feel of their wisdom teeth, and you'll know what I mean. There's no girl of twelve who doesn't know as much as a woman of twenty-five, because they've got the devil and experience as their tutors and teachers and in one hour these give them a year's worth of lessons.'

With these words the little gipsy girl held her audience spellbound and those who were gambling gave her a portion of their winnings, and even those who were not gave her something. The old gipsy woman collected thirty reales in her pouch, and feeling richer and merrier than an Easter Sunday she gathered her lambs together and went off to the magistrate's house, promising to return with her flock another day to entertain such generous gentlemen.

Doña Clara, the magistrate's wife, had already been informed that the gipsy girls were coming to her house, and was looking forward to seeing them as much as the gentle rains of May, as she awaited Preciosa's arrival in the company of her maids and duennas and those of another señora who lived nearby. The gipsy girls had only to step inside for Preciosa to shine out among them, like the blazing flame of a torch among other lesser lights. Consequently they all converged upon her; some embraced her; others just stood gazing at her; some blessed her, while yet others praised her. Doña Clara said, 'This can really and truly be called golden hair! These are genuine emerald eyes!'

Her good neighbour examined her very closely and made a detailed inspection of every limb and joint. When she came to praise a small dimple in Preciosa's chin, she exclaimed, 'Oh, what a dimple! Any man who looks upon her will fall into the abyss.'

An attendant of doña Clara's, an old man with a long beard who was standing nearby, overheard this comment and remarked, 'Do you call that a dimple, my lady? Well, if I know anything about dimples, that is no dimple, but a tomb where desires are buried alive. Good heavens, the little gipsy girl is so pretty that were she made of silver or sugar paste she could not be lovelier. Can you tell fortunes, child?'

'In three or four ways,' replied Preciosa.

'That too?' said doña Clara. 'On the life of my husband, you must tell me my fortune, golden, silver, heavenly child, precious as pearls and carbuncles, I can think of no other words to praise you.'

'Show her, show the girl the palm of your hand and give her a coin to cross it with,' said the old woman, 'and you'll see what manner of things she has to tell you; for she knows more than a doctor of medicine.'

The magistrate's wife thrust her hand into her pocket and found that it was quite empty. She asked her maids for a cuarto, but no one had one, her good neighbour included. When Preciosa saw this, she said, 'All signs of the cross, because they are crosses, are valid; but the ones made with silver or gold are best. You should know that crossing a palm with a copper coin reduces the value of the fortune told or, at least, the fortune I tell. That's why I prefer to cross the first palm with a gold escudo, or a real, or at the very least with a cuarto, for I'm like those church vergers who rejoice when the offering's a generous one.'

'Upon my word, you have wit,' remarked the neighbour. Turning to the squire, she said:

'Señor Contreras, do you happen to have a cuarto? Let me have it and when my husband the doctor comes home I will return it to you.'

'I do indeed,' replied Contreras, 'but twenty-two maravedís of it are already vouched against last night's supper. If you can give me the twenty-two maravedís, then I can run and retrieve my cuarto.'

'We haven't a single cuarto between us,' said doña Clara, 'and you're asking for twenty-two maravedís? Away with you Contreras, you always were impertinent.'

Recognizing how short of money the household was, one of the young maids spoke to Preciosa, 'Child, would it be appropriate to cross a palm with a silver thimble?'

'Indeed it would,' replied Preciosa, 'you can make the best crosses in the world with silver thimbles, as long as there are lots of them.'

'I have one,' replied the young maid, 'and if this is good enough, take it, on condition that you tell me my fortune too.'

'So many fortunes for the price of one thimble?' exclaimed the old woman. 'Granddaughter, make haste for it's getting dark.' Preciosa took the thimble and the magistrate's wife's hand, and said:

> Lovely lady, lovely lady,
> With your delicate silver hands,
> Your own spouse loves you more dearly
> Than Moorish kings their Spanish lands.
>
> You are as gentle as a dove,
> But you can be as ferocious
> As a lioness from Oran,
> Or a wild Hyrcanian tigress.
>
> Yet like a shot and on the spot
> Your anger's quick to curb and calm,
> And you're as sweet as almond paste
> Or e'en a gentle, docile lamb.
>
> You quarrel much, eat too little,
> And eye the world with jealous glower;
> The Magistrate, a frisky lad,
> Likes to wield his staff of power.
>
> As a maiden you were courted
> By a very handsome sire.

All intermediaries be cursed,
They frustrate our best desire.

If you'd become by chance a nun,
Today you would run the convent,
Because four hundred clear lines
Mark you as abbess incumbent.

Though I don't want to tell you this,
It's so trivial I'll not tarry,
You'll be a widow at least once
And then once or twice remarry.

Don't cry, I beg you, my lady,
For we gipsies, 'tis my belief,
Don't always speak the Gospel truth,
Don't cry, my lady, cease your grief.

If you should die before your spouse,
The good and noble Magistrate,
Then we'll never see you widowed,
Or name your husband as 'the late'.

You will very soon inherit
A vast, immensely rich estate,
And your son will be a Canon,
But of which church I can't relate.

In Toledo he'll not travail.
You'll have a daughter fair and pale,
To be a prelate she'd not fail,
Were she to take the holy veil.

If in the coming four short weeks
You're not grieving o'er his loss,
You'll see your spouse Chief Magistrate
Of Salamanca or Burgos.

You have a beauty spot, I see,
Of such delightful sweetness made,
'Tis like a dazzling southern sun,
Illuminating vales of shade.

It's a sight many a blind man
Would give a fortune to behold;
It's good to see you smile and laugh,
When jokes and pleasantries are told.

Take heed, beware of falling down
And landing on your back prostrate;
'Tis a posture fraught with danger
For all ladies of your estate.

There remains much more to tell you,
If until Friday you can wait;
Then I'll tell all, for there's good news
And tales of bad luck to relate.

Preciosa finished her fortune-telling, whereupon everyone else present passionately wanted to have their own fortunes told too and they begged her to oblige. She, however, deferred until the following Friday, when they promised to have silver reales to cross her palm.

At that moment the magistrate returned home to hear marvellous reports about the little gipsy girl. He had them dance a little, which convinced him that the praises Preciosa had received were truthful and justified. He put his hand in his pocket to indicate that he wished to give her something, but after searching, shaking, and scratching every inch of it, he pulled out his empty hand and said, 'Good heavens, I seem not to have any money on me at all. Doña Clara, you give Preciosa a real and I shall give it back to you later.'

'That's a fine suggestion, indeed, sir. The very real we're looking for! We haven't a single cuarto between us and you're asking us to produce a real?'

'Then give her one of your lace collars, or some small token, for she can come and see us another day and we shall reward her more generously then.'

To which doña Clara replied, 'Then in order to make her come again, I won't give her anything now.'

'On the contrary,' said Preciosa, 'if you give me nothing, I'll never set foot in this place again. And yet, I will return, to oblige such distinguished company: but I'll take it for granted that you won't give me anything and so save myself the bother of expecting something. Bribes, my good magistrate, bribes are the answer to your money problems. Don't try changing the way things are, or you'll die of starvation. Listen, my lady, I've heard it said somewhere or other (and although I'm still young I know it's a cynical remark) that you've got to milk public posts for all they're worth in order to pay for the penalties accrued at the end of your term* and in order to buy your way into new posts.'

'That is what the unscrupulous say and do,' replied the magistrate, 'but a judge who serves his term well will not have penalties to pay, and the fact he has carried out his duty properly will guarantee him further posts.'

'Your Excellency speaks in a very saintly fashion;' replied Preciosa, 'carry on in this vein and we'll be cutting pieces off your clothing to preserve them as holy relics.'

'You know a great deal, Preciosa,' replied the magistrate. 'Be quiet now and I shall arrange for the king and queen to see you, for you are truly a specimen fit for a king.'

'They'll want me to be their jester,' replied Preciosa, 'and I won't know how to go about it, and it'll be a complete and utter disaster. If they wanted to know me for my good sense, then that might tempt me; but in some palaces jesters fare better than sensible people. I'm happy to be a poor gipsy, and let my fate lead me wherever heaven desires.'

'Now then child,' said the old gipsy woman, 'don't say any more, for you've already said enough, and you know more than I've ever taught you. Don't get too subtle, or you'll end up out of your depth; speak of something more appropriate to your age, and don't get haughty, for pride always comes before a fall.'

'These gipsies are as wily as the devil himself!' said the Magistrate at that point.

The gipsies took their leave, and as they were departing the maid who had given her the thimble said, 'Preciosa, tell me my fortune or give me back my thimble, for I've nothing to do my sewing with.'

'Young lady,' replied Preciosa, 'assume that I've already done so and get yourself another thimble, and don't sew a stitch until Friday when I'll come back and pronounce more fates and feats than you'll read in a tale of chivalry.'

They left and joined up with the crowd of peasant girls who made their way out of Madrid as night fell to return to their respective villages. Many went home in this company and the gipsies always went with them, for there is safety in numbers (and the old woman lived in constant fear that Preciosa would be stolen from her).

It so happened that one morning when they were going into Madrid again to ply their trade and were walking through a small valley about five hundred yards outside the city, they saw a dashing young man dressed in expensive travelling clothes. The sword and dagger he carried were, as they say, a blaze of gold; he also wore a hat with an expensive-looking band and decorated with multi-coloured feathers.

The sight of him stopped the gipsy girls in their tracks and they looked at him long and hard, surprised to see such a handsome young man in such a place at such an hour, alone and on foot. He went up to them and, addressing the oldest gipsy, he said, 'Friend, I beg you and Preciosa to do me the honour of listening to a few words in private, which will be to your advantage.'

'As long as we don't go out of our way or take too long, so be it,' replied the old woman.

She called to Preciosa and the three of them moved away from the others. When they were some twenty paces distant the young man said, 'I come to you in submission, captivated by Preciosa's intelligence and beauty. After striving desperately not to reach such extremes, in the end I realized that I was more captivated than ever and even less capable of avoiding the inevitable. I, my dear ladies (for I shall always address you in this manner, if heaven favours my aspirations), am a nobleman, as this insignia manifestly shows'—and opening his cloak, he revealed one of the most distinguished in Spain. 'I am the son of So-and-So'—his name is not disclosed here out of respect—'and I am under his guardianship and protection. I am an only child and can expect to inherit a considerable estate. My father is here at Court seeking an appointment, for which he has been recommended and which he is almost certain to obtain. Although I am of the rank and nobility I have indicated to you and which must by now be manifestly obvious to yourselves, even so I could wish I were a great nobleman in order to elevate to my rank the humble status of Preciosa, by making her my equal and my wife. I do not woo her in order to deceive her, for the sincerity of the love I feel for her can never condone any form of deceit. I wish only to serve her in the manner which best pleases her. With regard to her desires, my soul is wax wherein she may leave whatever impression she chooses; her wish is my command and her desires will be preserved and treasured, not merely imprinted in wax but sculpted in marble, the hardness of which resists the ravages of time. If you believe in the truth of what I say, then my hope will never allow itself to falter, but if you do not believe me, then I will forever live in fear of your doubts. My name is'—and he told them what it was—'my father's name I have already told you. The house in which he lives is in such-and-such a street and you can recognize it by this and that detail. You may make enquiries of his neighbours and even of those who are not, since my father's rank and name, as well as my own, are not so obscure that they are not known in the courtyards of the palace, and even throughout Madrid. I have here one hundred gold escudos which I wish to give you as surety and as a sign of what I intend to give you in the future, for he who pledges his soul will not withhold his worldly wealth.'

While the gentleman delivered this speech Preciosa studied him intently, and it was obvious that both his words and his appearance were making a favourable impression on her. Turning to the old woman she said, 'Forgive me, grandmother, for taking the liberty of replying to this gentleman who's so very much in love.'

'Answer as you wish,' replied the old woman, 'for I know that you've got sense enough to deal with anything.'

Preciosa replied, 'Although, my dear gentleman, I am a gipsy of humble birth, I cherish deep within me a tendency to dream, which makes me aspire to greater things. Promises do not persuade me, gifts do not break my resolve, gestures of submission do not incite my favour, and fine declarations of love do not frighten me. Although I am only fifteen (or I shall be, according to my grandmother, on St Michael's Day), I am mature in thought and I understand more than might be expected from someone so young, through natural intelligence rather than experience. By means of the one or the other I know that amorous passion in those who have recently fallen in love is like a crazy impulse which renders the will senseless, with the result that, crashing through all obstacles, it hurls itself recklessly after the object of desire and where it intended to attain the glory it beholds, it plunges instead into the hell of its sorrows. If the will attains its desire, then desire itself diminishes with the possession of the object desired, and should the eyes of understanding perchance to open at that moment, it would rightly see that it should detest what it previously adored. This fear inspires in me such caution that I give credence to no word and I distrust many actions. I possess a single jewel, which I esteem more highly than life itself, my integrity and my virginity, which I am not about to sell in exchange for promises and gifts, for in the end it will be something that can be bought and sold and will therefore be considered to be of very little value. Trickery and deception will not steal it from me either. I would rather take it with me to the grave, and perhaps even to heaven, than expose it to the danger of being attacked or damaged by delusions and wild dreams. Virginity is a flower which, if possible, should not allow itself to be offended, even by the imagination. Once a rose is cut from a bush, how quickly and easily it withers. One man touches it, another enjoys its perfume, another strips it of its leaves until finally it falls apart in rough hands. And if, sir, you have merely come in pursuit of this prize, then you will not carry it off unless it's bound with the ties and bonds of marriage. For if virginity is to be surrendered, it will be surrendered to this holy yoke alone. For it would no longer be a case of losing it but of trading it in exchange for the rich profits to come. If you wish to be my husband, I will be your wife; but first many conditions have to be stipulated and many enquiries made.

'First of all, I must know whether you are who you claim to be, and when this truth is confirmed, you must leave your parents' house and exchange it for our camps. You will dress as a gipsy and train for two years in our schools, and during this period I will satisfy myself as to your character and you may do the same with regard to mine. At the end of this same period, if you are happy with me and I with you, then I will become your wife; but until then I shall treat you as if I were your sister and humble servant. And you should bear in mind that during the course of this novitiate you may recover the vision which you seem for the moment to have lost or at least impaired, and you may realize that it would be more sensible to flee what you are currently pursuing with such determination. And when you have recovered your lost liberty, sincere repentance pardons all errors. If you wish to enlist as a soldier in our army under these conditions, the decision rests in your hands, for if you fail in any one of them, you will never touch a finger of mine.'

The young man was stunned by Preciosa's words and he stared at the ground for a while, deep in thought, indicating that he was pondering how best to reply. When Preciosa saw this she spoke again, 'This is not such a trivial matter that it can or ought to be resolved in the few moments at our disposal; return to the city, sir, and take time to decide what action you consider most appropriate. You can talk to me in the same place on any feast day you care to choose, on my way into or out of Madrid.'

The gentleman replied, 'When heaven decreed that I should love you, my dear Preciosa, I resolved to do for you whatever you cared to ask of me, although it never occurred to me that you would ask what you are indeed asking. However, since it is your pleasure that my own should adapt and conform to yours, then you may consider me a gipsy already, and subject me to all the tests and trials that you will. For you will always find me to be exactly the person I have described to you. Decide when you want me to change my costume, for I should like it to be very soon. I will deceive my parents with the excuse of going to Flanders,* and this will get me enough money to cover several days' expenses. It may take me as long as a week to arrange for my departure. I shall find some way of deceiving anyone who goes with me, so as to be able to carry out my plan. What I ask of you (if I may be so bold as to make a request of you) is this: except for today, when you can make enquiries about my rank and parentage, please do not go into Madrid any more. For I could not bear one of the all-too-frequent opportunities that may arise there to snatch away from me the good fortune which is costing me so dearly.'

'I will have none of that, young sir,' replied Preciosa. 'Let me make it perfectly clear that as far as I am concerned liberty must always be uninhibited and not stifled and bedevilled by the burden of jealousy; at the same time, you must also understand that the liberty I enjoy is not so excessive that it is not obvious from a mile off that my virtue is equal to my free and easy manner. And so the first obligation I want to impose on you is that you have confidence in me. And bear in mind that lovers who start off feeling jealous are either stupid or conceited.'

'You've got the devil himself inside you, girl,' the old woman interrupted at that point. 'Do you realize that you're saying things that wouldn't enter the head of a student at Salamanca?* You know about love and jealousy and confidence. How can this be? You're driving me crazy and I'm listening to you as if you were someone possessed and speaking Latin without knowing any.'

'Be quiet, grandmother,' replied Preciosa, 'believe me when I say that all you've heard me say so far is trivial and said in jest, compared with the profounder truths that remain unspoken in my breast.'

All that Preciosa said and the intelligence she displayed served only to add fuel to the flames that blazed in the heart of the enamoured gentleman. They finally agreed to meet in the same place a week later, when he would come and report on the progress of his affairs, and they, in turn, would have had time to enquire into the truth of what he had told them. The young man pulled out a brocade purse which he said contained one hundred gold escudos, which he presented to the old woman. Preciosa wanted her on no account to accept them, but the old woman thought differently and said,

'Be quiet, child, for the best sign this gentleman's given of being totally conquered is the fact that he's offered up his weapons as a token of his surrender; and in any case, giving, whatever the circumstances, has always been an indication of a generous heart. And remember that proverb which goes "God helps those who help themselves". And what's more, I wouldn't want to be responsible for the gipsies losing the reputation they've had for centuries of being greedy and grasping. You want me to refuse one hundred escudos, Preciosa, and gold ones at that . . . , which could easily be sewn into the seam of a skirt costing less than two reales, and once they're in there, we'd feel we had grazing rights in Extremadura. Should any of our sons, grandsons, and relatives through some mischance fall into the hands of the law, what better way to gain the ear of the judge and notary than with these coins, if they get into their pockets? Three times for three different crimes I almost found myself mounted on the ass ready for a whipping; the first time a silver jar set me free; the second time a string of pearls; and the third time forty reales which I swapped for cuartos, making twenty reales' profit from the exchange. Look, child, our business is a dangerous one, full of stumbling-blocks and awkward situations, and there's no defence comes so readily to our aid and protection as the invincible coat of arms of our great Philip. There's no getting past his *plus ultra*.* At the sight of a double-headed doubloon the miserable faces of the prosecutor and his agents of torture break into a smile. They're harpies to us poor gipsy women; they take more pride in fleecing and skinning us than they would a highwayman. No matter how bedraggled and down-on-our-luck we look, they never assume we're poor. They say we're like the jerkins of Belmonte's henchmen,* ragged and greasy but laden with doubloons.'

'Grandmother, I beg of you, say no more; for you're well on your way to citing so many laws in favour of keeping the money, that you'll get through every code of law the emperors ever dictated. Keep the money, and much good may it do you, and God grant that you hide it in some tomb where it'll never see the light of day again, or need to. We'll have to give something to our companions, because they've been waiting a long time and they must be annoyed by now.'

'They're more likely to see Turks,' replied the old woman, 'than get their hands on any of this money. Let this good gentleman see whether he's got any coins left—silver ones or cuartos—which he can share among them, for it won't take much to please them.'

'Yes I have,' replied the young man. And from his pocket he took out three reales which he shared among the three gipsy girls, who felt more pleased and gratified than an actor-manager who, in spite of the competition, finds his name inscribed on street corners.*

In a word, they agreed, as has been said, to meet there again a week later and that he would be known as Andrés Caballero when he became a gipsy, for there were other gipsies among them of that name. Andrés, as he shall be known from now on, was not bold enough to kiss Preciosa. Instead, he surrendered his soul to her with his eyes and left it with her, so to speak, when he took his leave of them all and returned to Madrid, and they, in very high spirits, did the same. Preciosa, who was quite taken with Andrés's gallant manner, was eager to discover whether he was who he claimed to be, although her curiosity was inspired more by goodwill than by love. She went into the city, and had only made her way through a few streets when she met the page-poet who had given her the verses and the gold escudo, and when he saw her he came up to her and said:

'It's a pleasure to see you, Preciosa. Have you read the verses I gave you the other day?' To which Preciosa replied:

'Before I answer that question, you must tell me something truthfully, and swear by what you hold most dear.'

'That is a request', replied the page, 'which I could not refuse, even if telling the truth were to cost me my life.'

'Then the truth I wish you to tell me', said Preciosa, 'is whether you are by any chance a poet.'

'If I were,' replied the page, 'it would be by some happy chance indeed. But you must know, Preciosa, that very few people deserve to be called poets, and that is the reason why I am not a poet but a lover of poetry. And to satisfy my needs, I am not going to seek out or ask for other people's verses: the ones I gave you are mine, as are those which I am giving you now, but that does not make me a poet, God forbid.'

'Is it so bad to be a poet?' asked Preciosa.

'It is not so bad,' replied the page, 'but I do not approve of people calling themselves poets without justification. Poetry has to be handled like a very precious jewel, the owner of which does not wear it every day, and does not show it to all and sundry at every opportunity, but rather when it is appropriate and proper to do so. Poetry is a very beautiful young girl, chaste, virtuous, sensible, sharp, retiring, who keeps herself within the limits of the highest good sense. She is fond of solitude, streams entertain her, meadows console her, trees calm her spirit, flowers cheer her, and finally, she delights and teaches whoever comes into contact with her.*

'Even so,' replied Preciosa, 'I've heard that she's very poor and might even be considered a beggar.'

'Quite the contrary,' replied the page, 'there is no poet who is not rich, for they are all contented with their lot, a philosophy attained by few. But, Preciosa, what prompted you to ask this question?'

'What prompted me was this,' replied Preciosa, 'that since I assumed that all poets were poor, I was amazed by that gold escudo which you gave me wrapped up in your verses; but now that I know that you are not a poet, but a lover of poetry, you may be rich, although I doubt it. I say that because your inclination to write verses must surely exhaust whatever worldly wealth you possess. For rumour has it there's no poet who can hold on to his money or earn money he doesn't have.'

'Well, I am not one of those.' replied the page, 'I write verses, I am neither rich nor poor; and without regretting it or charging it to a business account, as the Genoese* do with their guests, I am well able to give an escudo or two to whomever I choose. Precious pearl, please accept this second piece of paper and this second escudo which comes with it, without worrying whether I am a poet or not; I only want you to think and believe that he who gives you this would like to possess the wealth of Midas in order to surrender it to you.' With these words he handed her a piece of paper, and when Preciosa felt it she realized that there was an escudo inside and said:

'This piece of paper will live for many years, because it contains two souls, the one belonging to the escudo, and the other to the verses, for they always come full of "hearts and souls". But I want you, good page, to understand that I don't want to be burdened by so many souls, and unless you remove one of them, then there's no hope of my accepting the other. I like you for your poetry, not your generosity, and when this is understood we'll enjoy a long and lasting friendship. For you may need an escudo, however strong you may be, before you lack inspiration for a ballad.'

'If that is how you want it,' replied the page, 'and you insist on my being poor, do not reject the soul I convey to you on this sheet of paper, and give me back the escudo, for if you touch it with your hand, I shall venerate it as a holy relic for the rest of my life.'

Preciosa removed the escudo from inside the sheet of paper and kept the sheet, although she did not want to read it in the street. The page bade her farewell and went off in a very happy mood, believing that Preciosa had been won over, since she had spoken to him in such a friendly manner.

Since Preciosa's principal aim was to find the house of Andrés's father she did not want to stop and dance anywhere, and soon found the street she was looking for, a street she knew well. About half-way along she looked up and saw a balcony with gilded bars by which she was to identify the building. Inside she saw a gentleman of about fifty, who wore the insignia of a red cross emblazoned across his chest and who cut a grave and imposing figure. As soon as he saw the little gipsy girl he said, 'Come up, girls, and we'll give you alms.'

When he said this three other gentlemen came out onto the balcony, one of whom was the enamoured Andrés. When he saw Preciosa he turned pale and almost fainted, so great was his shock at seeing her there. All the gipsy girls went upstairs but the old woman remained below in order to ascertain from the servants whether Andrés's claims were true.

As the girls entered the room the old gentleman was saying to the others, 'This is, without doubt, the beautiful little gipsy girl who they say is in Madrid these days.'

'It is she,' replied Andrés, 'and she is, without doubt, the most beautiful creature ever beheld.'

'So they say,' said Preciosa, who had heard all that had been said as she came in, 'but they must be grossly exaggerating the facts. I can well believe that I'm pretty, but I'm nowhere near as beautiful as some people claim.'

'On the life of my son, don Juanico,' exclaimed the old man, 'you are even more beautiful than people say, my lovely gipsy.'

'And which one is your son, don Juanico?'* asked Preciosa.

'The young man standing beside you,' replied the gentleman.

'I honestly thought', said Preciosa, 'that you were swearing on the life of some two-year-old child. What a fine don Juanico, indeed. I'll wager he's old enough to be married and, judging by some lines on his forehead, he will be before three years are out, and very happily, unless his taste or inclination changes between then and now.'

'Upon my word,' said one of those present, 'can the little gipsy girl read fortunes in the lines on our faces?'

At this point all three girls accompanying Preciosa removed to a corner of the room where, signalling to each other to keep their voices down, they huddled together so as not to be overheard. Cristina said, 'Girls, this is the gentleman who gave us three reales this morning.'

'So it is,' replied the other two, 'but let's not say anything about it to him, in fact let's not say anything at all, unless he mentions it first. For all we know, he may not want to draw attention to himself.'

While the three of them were conferring in this way Preciosa replied to the question about reading fortunes, 'What I see with my eyes I can confirm with my finger. I know, for instance, even though he has no lines on his forehead, that don Juanico has a tendency to fall in love, that he's impetuous and impulsive, and that he's very fond of promising things which seem impossible. I pray to God that he doesn't tell fibs, for that would be worst of all. He's soon to make a long journey, but the best-laid plans may go awry, man proposes and God disposes, and so on; he may think he knows where he's going and end up somewhere else.'

To which don Juan replied, 'Indeed, little gipsy girl, you have guessed right about many aspects of my character, but as for my being a liar, there you are very wide of the mark, because I pride myself on telling the truth in all circumstances. As for the journey, you have again guessed right for, God willing, I shall indeed be setting out for Flanders within the next four or five days. Although you threaten that I am to change direction, I would not want anything to go wrong along the way to deflect me from my purpose.'

'Say no more, young sir,' replied Preciosa, 'put your trust in God and everything will turn out well. Please understand that I know nothing about what I'm saying, and it's not surprising, since I talk so much and in such broad terms, that I should hit the mark from time to time. I should like to be equally successful in persuading you not to go away, but to calm down and stay with your parents instead, and support them in their old age, for I don't approve of this toing and froing between here and Flanders, especially in young men of your own tender years. Wait until you've grown up a little and are able to shoulder the hardships of war, especially since there are hostilities enough to contend with at home; your heart is besieged by its own sentimental battles. Calm down a while, restless youth, and think carefully before you marry, and give us some alms in God's name and your own, for I'm convinced of your good birth. If in addition to this you're also truthful, then I'll triumphantly boast that I'm correct in what I've said.'

'I have already told you, young lady,' replied don Juan, who was about to become Andrés Caballero, 'that you are correct in everything except your fear that I am not to be trusted. You are most certainly wrong about that. The word I give in the country I keep in the city and anywhere else, without prompting, for a man who prides himself on being a gentleman does not indulge in falsehood. My father will give you alms for God's sake and mine; for the fact is I gave all I had to some ladies this morning. If these same ladies are as agreeable as they are beautiful, especially one of them, then I am the most fortunate man I know.'

When Cristina heard him say this she turned to the other gipsies and said in the same low voice as before, 'Hey, girls, I bet my life that he's talking about the three pieces of eight he gave us this morning.'

'That can't be right,' replied one of the others, 'because he said they were ladies and we aren't. And if he's as truthful as he claims, then he wouldn't lie about that.'

'A lie's of little consequence,' replied Cristina, 'if it's said without injury to anyone and without undue advantage or profit to the person who lies. All the same, though, it doesn't look as if they're going to give us anything, and they're not asking us to dance.'

The old gipsy appeared from downstairs at that moment and said, 'Granddaughter, cease now, for it's late and there's much to do and talk about.'

'What news do you bring, grandmother?' asked Preciosa, 'Is it a boy or a girl?'

'A boy, and a fine one at that,' replied the old woman. 'Come, Preciosa, for I've got truly wonderful things to tell you.'

'God forbid that he die so soon after his birth!' said Preciosa.

'Everything's under control,' replied the old woman, 'especially since the birth was without complication and the child's a treasure.'

'Has some lady given birth?' asked Andrés's father.

'Yes, sir,' replied the old gipsy, 'but the birth was kept so secret that only Preciosa and I know about it, and one other person, though we can't say who that is.'

'Nor do we wish to know, either,' said one of those present, 'but I pity the woman who deposits her secret on your lips for safekeeping and entrusts her honour to your protection.'

'We're not all bad,' said Preciosa. 'There may be some gipsy here who prides herself on keeping a secret and embracing the truth as fervently as the most punctilious man in this room. It's not as if we're thieves or begging favours.'

'Don't be angry, Preciosa,' said Andrés's father, 'I don't think anyone could assume anything bad about you at least; for your fine face seals your reputation and vouches for your good works. I beg you, Preciosa, dance a while with your companions; for I have a doubloon with two heads, though neither is a match for yours, in spite of their royalty.'

As soon as the old woman heard this, she said, 'Right then girls, hitch up your skirts and give these gentlemen a treat.'

Preciosa took the tambourine and they turned about, alternately linking and unlinking their arms, with such graceful and fluid movements that the eyes of all who watched were transfixed by their dancing feet, especially Andrés's which followed Preciosa's feet as if he could see the glory of paradise there. A sudden reversal of fortune, however, plunged him into hellish torment; for in the vigour of the dance Preciosa dropped the piece of paper which the page had given her, and as soon as it fell the man who had expressed such a low opinion of the gipsies picked it up, opened it immediately, and said, 'Well, now, we have a little sonnet here! Stop the dance and listen, for if the first line is anything to go by, I declare it's far from bad.'

Preciosa was dismayed because she did not know what the sonnet contained, and begged them not to read it and to give it back to her, but her insistence merely increased Andrés's desire to hear it. Finally the gentleman read it aloud and it went like this:

When Preciosa plays the tambourine each day,
And weightless air carries forth delightful sound,
With her hands she scatters pearls upon the ground,
And from chaste lips fragrant flowers fall away.

Souls are enthralled and all tears gently halted,
By such mesmeric, heavenly harmony,
Sound and motion merge in perfect euphony,
And her fame in highest heav'n is exalted.

From her finest strand of hair a thousand minds
Hang captivated, while gathered at her feet
Love's arrows lie in sweet resign prostrated.

Each lovely sun both illuminates and blinds,
And through them her sov'reign power is made complete,
Uncharted grace deep within adumbrated.

'Good heavens,' exclaimed the reader of the sonnet, 'the poet who wrote that has talent.'

'He's not a poet, sir, but a very gallant page and a man of honour,' said Preciosa.

Heed what you have said, Preciosa, and beware what you say now, for these words are not so much praise of the poet as lances which pierce Andrés's heart as he listens to you. Do you need proof, child? Then turn round and you will see that he has fainted into a chair and broken out in a mortal sweat. Do not think, young lady, that Andrés's love for you is so superficial that the least thoughtlessness on your part will not wound and hurt him. Go to him and whisper a few words in his ear which will go straight to his heart and bring him round from his faint. Or, go ahead and bring him a sonnet which sings your praises every day, and see the effect they have on him!

All this occurred as described: when Andrés heard the sonnet he was assailed by a thousand jealous thoughts. He did not faint, but turned so pale that when his father saw him, he said, 'What's wrong, Juan? You look as if you're going to faint, you've grown so pale.'

'Wait,' Preciosa intervened, 'let me say a few words in his ear and watch how it stops him fainting.' Going over to him she said through scarcely parted lips, 'That's a fine gipsy spirit you're showing there. Andrés, how will you ever endure the water torture if you can't cope with the paper test?'

After making half-a-dozen crosses over his heart, she moved away and then Andrés breathed a little and gave everyone to understand that Preciosa's words had helped him. They finally gave Preciosa the doubloon with the two faces, and she generously told her companions that she would change it and share it with them. Andrés's father asked her to write down the words which she had said to don Juan, for he wanted to know what they were for future reference. She said that she would gladly divulge them and added they should realize that, although they might seem nonsensical, they were particularly effective in protecting against nausea and giddiness, and these were the words:

> O little head, o little head,
> Steady on there, pray don't fall,
> On your reserves of patience call,
> On this support rely instead.
>
> And then you must—
> 'Tis good and just—
> Confide your trust.
>
> Let not your mind
> To perverse thinking be inclined.
>
> You'll surely see
> Marvel, wonder, prodigy.
>
> With God's succour
> And a giant St Christopher.

'If you recite just half of these words and make six signs of the cross over the heart of someone who feels giddy,' said Preciosa, 'they'll be as right as rain.'

When the old gipsy heard the incantation and the bluff, she was amazed, and Andrés even more so, because he knew that it was all the invention of her quick wit. They kept the sonnet, because Preciosa did not like to ask for it back and in so doing cause Andrés further anguish. For she already knew without being taught what it was to prompt alarm and fits of jealousy in devoted admirers.

The gipsies took their leave, and as they were going out Preciosa said to Juan, 'Now listen sir, any day this week's propitious for going away and none's bad. Hasten your departure as much as possible, for there's a free, unfettered, and very pleasant life awaiting you, if you're willing to adapt to it.'

'A soldier's life is not so free, in my opinion,' replied don Juan, 'that it does not entail more submission than liberty; but, all the same, I shall see what happens.'

'You'll see more than you think,' replied Preciosa. 'God go with you and bring you back safely, as your noble mien deserves.' These last words made Andrés happy, and the gipsies went off feeling even more contented. They changed the doubloon and shared it out equally amongst themselves, although the old woman (who kept watch over them) took a share and a half of their joint takings because of her seniority and also because she was the compass which guided them through the hurly-burly of the dances, the witty repartee, and the deception.

The day finally arrived which brought Andrés Caballero, early in the morning, to the place where he had made his first appearance, riding on a hired mule and with no servants in attendance. There he found Preciosa and her grandmother who, on recognizing him, welcomed him warmly. He asked them to guide him to their camp, before the sun came up and made him more easily recognizable if anyone decided to search for him. The two gipsies who, as if forewarned of his arrival, had ventured out alone, turned back and soon all three of them had arrived at their huts.

Andrés went into one of them, which was the biggest in the camp, and soon ten or twelve gipsies, all of them handsome, strapping young men, approached to take a look at him, for the old woman had already told them about the new companion who was to join their ranks. She told them without having to swear them to secrecy because, as has already been said, they keep secrets with an unrivalled shrewdness and conscientiousness. Then the mule caught their eye, and one of them said, 'We can sell this in Toledo on Thursday.'

'Please do not do that,' said Andrés, 'for there is no hired mule that cannot be recognized by each and every muleteer who travels around Spain.'

'I assure you, señor Andrés,' said one of the gipsies, 'that even if the mule bore more signs than those announcing the Day of Judgement, we could disguise it so well that its own mother wouldn't recognize it, nor the owner who reared it.'

'All the same,' said Andrés, 'on this occasion my opinion must win the day. This mule must be put to death and buried where not even its bones will ever be discovered.'

'What a sinful shame!' said another gipsy. 'You want to take the life of an innocent? Don't say such a thing, good Andrés, but do something for me. Look at the mule very carefully, so that all its identifying marks are fixed in your memory, then let me take it away. If you can recognize it two hours from now you can brand me like a fugitive black slave.'

'I will never allow the mule to live,' said Andrés, 'however much you may guarantee its transformation. I shall fear being discovered until it is buried in the ground. And if you want to do it for the profit you would make from its sale, I have not come to this brotherhood so empty-handed that I cannot pay the price of four mules as my admission fee.'

'Well, if that's how Andrés Caballero wants it,' said another gipsy, 'then the blameless creature must die, although God knows it grieves my heart, not only because it's a young animal, for it hasn't got all its teeth yet (which is rare in hired mules) but also because it must be a good walker since it hasn't got any scabs on its flanks or injuries from spurs.'

Its death was postponed until that night, and during the remainder of the day the ceremonies marking Andrés's initiation as a gipsy were performed. They comprised the following: the gipsies cleared out one of the best huts in the camp and decorated it with branches and sedge; they seated Andrés on the stump of a cork oak and placed a hammer and some pincers in his hands; then, to the sound of two guitars strummed by two gipsies, they made him leap into the air twice; then they bared one of his arms and gave it two gentle twists with a garrotte of new silk ribbon. Preciosa witnessed all of this, as did many other gipsy women, both young and old, some of whom regarded him with awe and others with love. In fact, Andrés cut such a dashing figure that even the gipsy men eventually gained a healthy respect for him.

Then, when the aforementioned ceremonies had been carried out, an old gipsy took Preciosa by the hand and, standing in front of Andrés, he said, 'This girl, who is the flower and cream of all the gipsy beauties we know to be living in Spain, we hand over to you to be your wife or mistress; for in this matter you may do as you please, for the free and easy life we lead is not subject to finickiness and ceremony. Take a good look at her, and see whether she pleases you or whether there is something in her which is not to your liking, and if you see such a thing, choose from among the young girls present the one you find most appealing; for we will give you whoever you choose. But you must understand that once you have chosen her, you must not leave her for another, nor pester or get involved with married women or unmarried girls. We stalwartly uphold the laws of friendship: no man covets another man's property; our life is free of the bitter plague of jealousy. Although there is much incest among us, there is no adultery; and when we find our own wives guilty of it, or some misdemeanour in a mistress, we do not seek justice from the law. We ourselves are the judges and executioners of our wives and mistresses; we kill them and bury them in the mountains and deserts as readily as if they were wild animals: no relation will avenge them, no father will seek retribution for their deaths. With such a terrifying prospect to deter them they endeavour to be chaste and we, as I have said, have peace of mind.

'We have few possessions which are not common to all, except for our wives and mistresses, and we want each one to belong to the partner fate allotted her. Among our kind, old age is as good a reason for divorce as death. Any man who so desires may desert an ageing wife, if he is young, and choose another to suit the appetites of his years. With these and other laws and statutes we protect ourselves and lead a merry life; we are lords of the pastures, of the ploughed fields, of the woods and hills, of the springs and rivers. The woodlands provide us with free wood, the trees with fruit, the vines with grapes, the gardens with vegetables, the springs with water, the rivers with fish, and the preserves with game. The rocks give us shade, the mountain passes give us fresh air, and the caves give us shelter. For us the inclemencies of the weather are gentle breezes, snow refreshes us while rain bathes us, thunder is music while lightning flashes across the sky like a torch. For us the hard ground is a soft feather mattress, the tanned skin of our bodies an impenetrable armour which protects us. Our fleetness of foot is not impeded by fetters, nor delayed by ravines, nor stopped in its tracks by solid walls; ropes cannot squeeze the spirit out of us, racks cannot weaken it, gags cannot stifle it, and stocks cannot crush it. Between "yes" and "no" we make no distinction when it suits our purpose; we take more pride in being martyrs than confessors. For our benefit beasts of burden are reared in the country and purses are cut in the cities. No eagle or any other bird pounces more swiftly on its prey than we pounce on opportunities to make a profit. Finally, we have many skills which promise success at the end of the day: for in jail we tell tales, on the rack we keep quiet, we work by day and we steal by night or, more precisely, we warn people not to be careless about where they leave their property.

'The fear of losing our honour does not worry us, nor does the urge to enhance it keep us awake at night; we do not support any factions, we do not get up early to present petitions or to appear in the company of important men or to beg favours. We cherish these huts and camps of ours as if they were sumptuous palaces with gilded roofs; we have our own Flemish scenes and landscapes in the lofty crags and snow-covered peaks, in the wide meadows and dense woodlands which surround us every step of the way. We are amateur astrologers, for since we nearly always sleep under the open sky we always know what hour of the day or night it is; we observe how Aurora banishes the stars from the sky and, with her companion the dawn, fills the air with joy, cools the water, and moistens the earth. Then, after the dawn, we see the sun "gilding the mountain tops" and "furrowing the hills", as some poet or other once said. We do not fear being frozen by its absence when its rays reach us only from a distance, nor being burned when they beat down upon us directly overhead. We face sun and ice, sterility and abundance with equanimity. In short, we are a people who live by our hard work and ready tongues, without having anything to do with the old saying: "Church, sea, or royal palace." We have as much as we want, for we content ourselves with what we have. I have told you all this, generous youth, so that you are not ignorant of the kind of life you have come to, or the customs you are to adopt, which I have outlined for you. In time you will learn countless other things no less worthy of your attention than those you have heard.'

At the end of this speech the eloquent old gipsy fell silent and the novice said that he was delighted to have learned of such laudable statutes, and that he intended to make his profession in that order, founded as it was on such sensible and wise principles. His only regret was that he had not discovered such a merry way of life earlier, and from that moment on he renounced his profession as a gentleman and the vanity of his illustrious lineage. He was submitting everything to the yoke, or rather, to the laws by which they lived, since they were so graciously rewarding his desire to serve them by giving him the divine Preciosa, for whom he would relinquish crowns and empires, which he would only ever desire in order to present them to her.

In reply to this Preciosa said, 'Since these legislators have found that according to their laws I am yours, and have placed me at your disposal, I have decided that according to the law of my own will I do not want to be yours except under the conditions which we agreed before you came here. You must live in our company for two years before you enjoy mine, so that you do not have any cause to regret your impulsiveness, nor I to be misled by my haste. Conditions break laws; you know the conditions I have imposed on you: if you want to keep them, perhaps I will be yours one day and you will be mine, and if not, the mule is not dead yet, your clothes are as you left them, and your money is untouched. You have still been away from home for less than a day; use what is left of it to give yourself time to reflect on what course of action is most appropriate. These men may well give you possession of my body, but they cannot give you my soul, which is free, which was born free, and which will continue to be free for as long as I wish. If you stay I will think highly of you; if you go back I will think no worse of you. For it seems to me that love's impulses go unchecked until they meet with reason or disillusionment. I wouldn't want you to treat me like the hunter who, when he catches up with the hare he is pursuing, seizes it and then releases it to go after the one which eludes him. Some eyes are deceived when at first sight they think that tinsel looks like gold, but they very soon come to recognize the distinction between what is real and what is false. This beauty which you claim I possess, which you esteem more highly than the sun and consider more precious than gold, how do I know whether, when you see it close up, you will think it a mere shadow, or whether when you touch it, you will realize that it is a base metal instead of gold? I am giving you a period of two years to reflect and consider what it will be wise to choose or proper to reject. For once the prize has been purchased, nothing but death can part us from it; it is sensible to spend time examining and re-examining it, looking at its respective vices and virtues. For I am not governed by the barbaric and appalling liberty which these kinsmen of mine have adopted, of abandoning or punishing their women whenever they feel like it. Since I do not intend to do anything requiring punishment, I do not want a partner who might cast me aside on a whim.'

'You are right, Preciosa,' exclaimed Andrés at that point, 'and so, if you want me to calm your fears and alleviate your suspicions by swearing that I will not deviate an inch from the orders you impose on me, just say what oath you want me to take, or what other assurance I can give you, and you will find me ready to do anything.'

'The oaths and promises a prisoner makes in order to win his freedom are rarely kept once his freedom is won,' said Preciosa, 'and the same goes, I think, for the promises of a lover who, to attain his desire, will promise the wings of Mercury and the thunderbolts of Jupiter, as a certain poet, who also swore by the Stygian lake,* once promised me. I do not want oaths, señor Andrés, nor promises; I want only to commit everything to the trial of this novitiate, and I shall be responsible for looking after myself, if you should attempt to offend me.'

'So be it,' replied Andrés. 'I ask only one thing of these gentlemen, my companions, and it is that they do not compel me to steal anything for the first month at least, for I do not think I will make a very good thief unless I first take many lessons.'

'Say no more, lad,' said the old gipsy, 'for we'll train you so thoroughly that you'll end up a true master of the art; and when you know how, you'll like it so much that your fingers will be itching to get on with it. It's great fun to leave empty-handed in the morning and return loaded to the camp under cover of darkness.'

'Covered with whiplashes is a better description of some I have seen,' said Andrés.

'You can't make an omelette, as they say . . .' replied the old man. 'Everything in this life's subject to its own dangers, and in his actions a thief risks such consequences as lashes, the galleys, or the gallows. But just because one ship ends up in a storm or sinks doesn't mean that no other ship should set sail. It'd be a fine thing if, because war devours men and horses, there were no more soldiers. Especially since any man among us who has been lashed by the law wears an insignia on his back that looks far more impressive than the finest one he could wear across his chest. The main thing is not to finish up dancing at the end of a rope while we're still in the first flower of youth or for our very first crimes. As for a tickle on our backs, or a bit of paddling in the galleys, we couldn't give a fig. Andrés, my son, stay in the nest under our wings for the time being, and in due course we'll teach you to fly where you won't come back without prey. And mind what I've said: after each theft you'll be biting your nails till the next one.'

'Well, to make up for what I might have stolen during this period of grace,' said Andrés, 'I want to share out two hundred gold escudos among everyone in the camp.'

He had scarcely finished speaking when a whole crowd of gipsies rushed towards him and, picking him up and hoisting him on to their shoulders, they chanted, 'Hurray, hurray for the great Andrés!' and 'Long live Preciosa, his cherished prize!' The gipsy women did the same with Preciosa, provoking envy on the part of Cristina and some other girls who were present at the scene. For envy inhabits barbarian camps and shepherds' huts as well as the palaces of princes, and it is annoying to see your neighbour, who seems no more deserving than yourself, exalted in such a way.

This gesture accomplished, they ate a large feast. The promised money was shared out fairly and equally, they sang Andrés's praises once more, and applauded Preciosa's beauty to the skies. At nightfall they slaughtered the mule and buried it so deeply that Andrés had no fear of its discovery leading to his own. With it they also buried its trappings, the saddle, bridle, and girths, in the manner of Indians who are buried with their most treasured possessions. Andrés was astonished by everything he had seen and heard, and determined to go ahead with his plan without participating in any way in their customs, or at least to avoid them by every means available to him. He hoped to buy his way out of the obligation to obey them in the unjust things they might order him to do.

The following day Andrés asked them to shift camp and distance themselves from Madrid, because he was afraid of being recognized if he remained there. They replied that they had already decided to make for the woodlands near Toledo and from there to go raiding the whole of the surrounding area. They therefore broke camp and gave Andrés a donkey to ride on, which he refused since he preferred to go on foot and act as Preciosa's lackey. Preciosa herself, riding on another beast, was delighted to see the power she wielded over her gallant squire, and he was no less pleased to find himself so close to the lady he had made mistress of his free will.

Potent is the force we idly and carelessly attribute to the sweet god of bitterness! How truly you enslave us and with what disrespect you treat us! Andrés is a highly intelligent nobleman who has spent most of his upbringing in the capital being indulged by his wealthy parents. Yet in the space of a single day he has effected such a transformation that he has deceived his servants and friends, frustrated the hopes his parents had of him, and abandoned the road to Flanders, where he was to demonstrate his courage and enhance the honour of the family line. He abandoned all these things to serve and prostrate himself at the feet of a girl who, when all is said and done, and in spite of her extreme beauty, was merely a gipsy. It is a prerogative of beauty to ride roughshod over the freest will and drag it by the hair to lie at its feet.

Four days later they arrived at a village two leagues distant from Toledo, where they set up camp after first giving the local alderman a few items of silver as a guarantee that they would steal nothing from the village or anywhere else within his jurisdiction. When they had done this all the old gipsy women, some of the girls, and the men dispersed to all the surrounding villages within four or five leagues from their encampment. Andrés went with them to receive his first lesson in thieving, and although they taught him many things during that expedition he learned nothing. On the contrary, and as was to be expected from someone of his genteel breeding, every theft that his instructors committed wrenched at his soul, and on occasion he even reimbursed the victims of his comrades' thieving out of his own pocket, so moved was he by their tears. The other gipsies despaired of him, explaining that his actions contravened their statutes and regulations, which forbade any charitable sentiment to disturb their consciences. If it were to do so, they would have to cease to be thieves, a prospect which they did not find at all appealing.

Seeing, therefore, that this was the case, Andrés announced that he wanted to steal on his own rather than in someone else's company. He was quick enough to run away from danger and he did not lack the courage to face it when it presented itself. In this way, the reward or the punishment for what he stole would be his and his alone. The other gipsies tried to dissuade him from this plan, explaining that situations might arise where company was essential, to attack as well as defend oneself, and one man by himself could not capture much booty. However much they tried to persuade him Andrés was determined to be a solitary and independent thief, since it was his intention to get away from the rest of the gang and use his own money to buy something which he would then pretend to have stolen. In so doing he would burden his conscience as little as possible. Employing this strategy, then, in less than a month he had brought more profit to the company than four of its most accomplished thieves. It was a source of great satisfaction to Preciosa to see that her tender suitor was such a fine and gifted thief. All the same, she was afraid that something might one day go wrong, and not for all the treasure in Venice did she want to see him disgraced; for the many services and gifts that he offered her obliged her to be well disposed towards him.

They remained in the region of Toledo for little more than a month, where they reaped a rich harvest during September, and from where they moved on into the prosperous and warm territory of Extremadura. Andrés shared in many modest, sensible, and sentimental conversations with Preciosa and she gradually began to fall in love with the good sense, and genteel manners of her admirer. If it is possible for such profound love to increase, then his love for her was also increasing, such was the modesty, good sense, and beauty of Preciosa. Wherever they went, he carried off more prizes for running and jumping than anyone else, he played bowls and *pelota** with expert skill, and he hurled the bar with great force and remarkable prowess. In short, his fame soon spread throughout Extremadura, and there was not a place on the map where the dashing gallantry, charms, and skills of Andrés Caballero were not discussed, while word of the young gipsy girl's beauty also spread far and wide. There was no town, village, or hamlet which did not invite them to enliven their religious festivals or other private celebrations. As a result the camp enjoyed a period of abundance, prosperity, and contentment, and the two lovers derived pleasure from merely looking at one another.

It so happened that in the middle of one night, while they were camped amongst oak trees some distance from the main highway, they heard their dogs barking more persistently than usual. Several gipsies, Andrés among them, went to see what they were barking at and found a man dressed in white trying to fend the dogs off while they held him firmly by one leg. The gipsies went over and released him from the dogs' grip, and one of them asked, 'What the devil brings you here, then, at such an hour of the night and so far off the beaten track? Have you come to steal by any chance? Because if you have, you've come to the right place.'

'I have not come to steal,' replied the man who had been bitten, 'and I do not know whether I am off the beaten track or not, although it is obvious that I have lost my way. But tell me, good sirs, is there an inn or some such place around here where I can lodge for the night and receive treatment for the wounds which your dogs have inflicted on me?'

'There's no inn or any other place that we can direct you to,' replied Andrés, 'but as for treating your wound and finding lodgings for the night, you'll find what you need in our camp. Come with us, for although we're gipsies, we're not without charity.'

'May God show you charity in return,' replied the man, 'and take me wherever you want, for the pain in my leg is very bad.' Andrés went up to him, accompanied by another compassionate gipsy—for even in a company of devils some are worse than others, and among many malevolent men there is usually one good one to be found—and they carried him between them.

It was a clear moonlit night, which enabled them to see that he was a handsome young man of fine stature. He was dressed from head to foot in white linen, and across his shoulders and fastened to his chest was a linen shirt or bag. They reached Andrés's hut or tent where they soon lit a fire and a lamp, and Preciosa's grandmother, who had already been informed of events, arrived soon afterwards to tend to the wounded man. She took some hairs from the dogs, fried them in oil, and then after washing the two bites on his left leg with wine, she placed the hair and oil over them, and on top of that some crushed green rosemary. She bandaged it up in clean cloths, made a sign of the cross over the wounds, and said, 'Sleep, friend, for with God's help you'll soon be well.'

While they were attending to the wounded man Preciosa stood by watching. She stared at him intently and he returned her gaze, with the result that Andrés saw how closely he watched her, but he attributed it to the fact that Preciosa's great beauty always attracted attention. Finally, when the young man had been treated, they left him alone on a bed of dry hay, not wanting for the moment to ask him where he was heading, or anything else for that matter.

As soon as they had left him, Preciosa called Andrés aside and said, 'Andrés, do you remember a piece of paper I dropped in your house while I was dancing with my friends, which I believe gave you a nasty turn?'

'Yes, I do,' replied Andrés, 'it was a sonnet in praise of you, and not a bad one at that.'

'Well, you should know, Andrés,' replied Preciosa, 'that the writer of that sonnet is the injured young man we have just left in the hut, and I know I am not mistaken because he spoke to me in Madrid two or three times and he even gave me a very good ballad. There, I think, he was a page, but no ordinary one, rather someone enjoying the patronage of some prince. Indeed, Andrés, he is sensible, clever, and extremely honourable, and I cannot imagine what brings him here dressed in such a way.'

'You cannot imagine, Preciosa?' cried Andrés. 'What else but the same power which has made me a gipsy has made him dress like a miller and come in search of you? Preciosa, Preciosa, how clear it becomes that you want to pride yourself on having more than one admirer. And if this is so, finish me off first and then slay this other one, don't sacrifice us together on the altar of your deceit, not to mention your beauty.'

'Heaven help me!' replied Preciosa, 'Andrés, how sensitive you are, and what a slender thread your hopes and my reputation are hanging on, if the cruel sword of jealousy has already pierced your soul! Tell me, Andrés, if there were some subterfuge or deception in this, would I not have enough sense to keep quiet and conceal the identity of this young man? Am I so foolish, by any chance, as to give you cause to doubt my goodness and integrity? Hush, Andrés, for goodness' sake, and tomorrow try to dispel your misgivings about where he is going and why he has come. Your suspicion might be ill-founded, although I am not mistaken in claiming he is who he is. And to satisfy yourself fully, since I have got to the stage of needing to satisfy you, by whatever means that young man came, and for whatever reason, get rid of him quickly, make him go away. Since everyone in our company obeys you, no one will give him refuge in his hut against your will. And if that does not work, I promise not to step outside my hut, or allow myself to be seen by him or anyone else you do not wish me to be seen by. Look, Andrés, it does not distress me to see you jealous, but it would distress me to see you act unwisely.'

'Unless you see me mad, Preciosa,' replied Andrés, 'no other state of mind would suffice to convince you of the cruelty and bitterness of jealous suspicions, or of how distressing they are. Yet, in spite of all this, I shall do as you command and I shall find out, if possible, what it is that this gentleman page or poet wants, where he is going, or what it is he is seeking. For it is just possible that by some thread which he carelessly lets slip I'll be able to unravel the whole skein which I fear has come to ensnare me.'

'Jealousy, as I understand it,' said Preciosa, 'never leaves the intelligence free to judge things as they are. Jealous people always look at things through magnifying glasses, which turn small things into big things, dwarves into giants, and suspicions into certainties. For the sake of your life and mine, Andrés, proceed in this matter, and everything else relating to our agreement, sanely and sensibly. For if you do, I know that you will concede that I deserve the highest merit for my virtue, modesty, and truthfulness.'

With this she took leave of Andrés who, with his soul in turmoil and beset by a thousand conflicting conjectures, had to wait until daylight to take the wounded man's confession. He could find no other explanation for the page's arrival except his attraction to Preciosa's beauty, for a thief thinks that everyone else is similarly inclined. On the other hand, the argument Preciosa had presented to him sounded so convincing that he was compelled to take heart and entrust his fate to her goodness.

Day came and he paid a visit to the injured man. He asked him his name and where he was going, and why he was travelling so late into the night and so far off the beaten track, although first and foremost he asked him how he was feeling and whether the bites had stopped hurting. The young man replied that he was feeling better and was not in any pain, and would be able to continue on his way. As for his name and where he was going, he revealed only that his name was Alonso Hurtado and that he had a matter of business to attend to at Nuestra Señora de la Peña de Francia.* He was travelling by night to get there quickly, but the previous night he had lost his way and had chanced upon the camp, where guard dogs had left him in the condition in which Andrés had found him.

To Andrés this statement did not ring true; on the contrary, it seemed full of inconsistencies and his suspicions began once again to torment his soul, so he said:

'Brother, if I were a judge and you had come under my jurisdiction for some crime, which would require me to put to you the questions which I have done, then the reply which you have given me would oblige me to press you further. I don't want to know who you are, what your name is, or where you are going. But be warned that if it's in your interest to lie during this journey of yours, then invent more plausible lies. You say that you're going to Peña de Francia, yet you left it back there to your right some thirty leagues from here. You are travelling by night to arrive quickly, yet you leave the main highway to make your way through woods and oak groves which scarcely have paths, let alone roads. Friend, get up, and learn to tell a better lie and good luck to you. But in exchange for this piece of good advice which I'm giving you, won't you reveal one truth? (I'm certain that you will, since you're such a poor liar.) Tell me: are you by any chance the person I've seen many times in Madrid, half page and half gentleman and reputed to be a great poet, the one who wrote a ballad and a sonnet for a young gipsy girl who was recently to be seen around Madrid and considered to be exceptionally beautiful? Tell me the truth and I give you my word as a gipsy gentleman to keep whatever secret you consider so important. Understand that to deny the truth, by denying that you are whom I claim you are, will get you nowhere, for the face I see before me now is the very one I saw in Madrid. It must be that your widely celebrated cleverness made me look at you many times as a rare and distinguished sort of man, so that your face remained fixed in my memory, and I have recognized you by it even in the clothes you are now wearing, which are different from the ones you wore then. Don't be alarmed; cheer up, and don't imagine that you've come to a den of thieves, but to a refuge which can guard and defend you from the rest of the world. Now listen, I have a theory, and if it's right then you're lucky to have bumped into me. This is my theory: you are infatuated with Preciosa, that beautiful young gipsy you wrote the verses for, and you've come to look for her, and I don't think less of you for that, in fact I think more highly of you. For although I'm a gipsy, experience has taught me how far the mighty power of love extends and the changes it imposes on those it draws under its influence and control. If this is the case, as I've no doubt it is, then the gipsy girl is here.'

'Yes, she is here,' said the injured young man, 'for I saw her last night.' This reply dealt Andrés a death-blow, for it seemed to be the final confirmation of his suspicions.

'I saw her last night,' the young man repeated, 'but I did not dare to tell her who I was, for it did not suit my purpose.'

'So,' said Andrés, 'you are the poet I spoke of.'

'I am,' replied the youth, 'for I cannot deny it, nor do I wish to. Just when I thought I was lost, I think I might have found refuge, if there is loyalty in the woods and a warm welcome in the wilderness.'

'There certainly is,' replied Andrés, 'and among us gipsies the greatest secrecy in the world. With this assurance you can, sir, open your heart to me, for in mine you will find precisely what is there, without a hint of duplicity. The gipsy girl's a relation of mine and has to submit to whatever I wish to do with her. If you want to marry her, then I and all her family will be delighted; if you want her as a mistress, we shan't let scruples get in the way, as long as you have money, for greed's forever present in our camps.'

'I have money,' replied the youth. 'In these shirt-sleeves which I have tied round myself I have more than four hundred gold escudos.'

Seeing him with so much money dealt Andrés another mortal blow, for it could only be for the purpose of conquering or purchasing his prize. In a faltering voice he said, 'That's a lot of money, now all you have to do is identify yourself and get down to business. For the girl, who's no fool, will see the advantage of being yours.'

'Ah, my friend,' said the youth at that point, 'I want you to know that the power that has made me change my dress is not love, as you say, or desiring Preciosa. Madrid has beauties of its own who can and do steal hearts and subjugate souls as well as, and even better than, the loveliest gipsies, although I concede that your relation's beauty exceeds that of any other gipsy I have ever seen. What brings me here on foot, wearing these clothes and bitten by dogs, is not love but misfortune.'

As the youth uttered these words Andrés gradually began to recover his spirits, since the explanation did not seem to be leading where he had expected. Eager to emerge from the confusion in which he found himself, he once again stressed to the youth that he could unburden himself with impunity, so the latter went on:

'I was in Madrid in the household of a titled nobleman, whom I served not so much as a master but as a relation. This nobleman had an only son and heir who, because we were related and of a similar age and character, treated me as an intimate and great friend. It happened that this young gentleman fell in love with a high-ranking young lady whom he would gladly have chosen to marry, if his will, like that of any good son, had not been subject to that of his parents, who wanted to marry him more advantageously. In spite of this, he kept his courtship of her secret from every eye and tongue which might have made his feelings public knowledge. My eyes alone were witness to his actions. Then one night, which ill fate must have chosen for the disaster I am about to recount, when we were walking along the young lady's street and past her door, we saw two handsome-looking men standing near it. My relation wanted to see who they were, and had scarcely moved in their direction when they deftly drew their swords and bucklers and came towards us. We did the same and attacked them with similar weapons. The fight did not last long, because our two opponents did not live long. Two sword thrusts guided by my relation's jealousy, together with the defense I offered him, put an end to them, a strange and rare outcome to such a confrontation. Triumphant, then, in a contest we had not sought, we returned home and, secretly gathering together as much money as we could, we took refuge in the monastery of St Jerome, where we waited for day, which would reveal what had happened and what deductions had been made about the killers.

'We learned that there was no evidence pointing to us, and the prudent monks advised us to return home and not cause or arouse suspicions by our absence. Just when we had decided to follow their advice they informed us that city law officers had placed the young lady and her parents under house arrest, and that among the servants from whom they had taken statements, one of the young lady's maids had told them how my relation used to walk up and down outside her lady's room day and night. With this clue they had gone to look for us and when, instead of us, they found the many signs of our flight, it was confirmed throughout the city that we had killed the noblemen, for such they were and of considerable rank. Finally, after we had spent a fortnight hiding in the monastery, on the advice of my relation the Count and that of the monks my companion left for Aragon disguised as one of the brothers and accompanied by another, with the intention of crossing to Italy and then making his way to Flanders, until we saw how the situation resolved itself. I decided that we should go our separate ways, rather than have us both suffer the same fate. Taking a different route, I set out on foot, dressed as a friar's servant and in the company of another brother of the order, who left me in Talavera. From there I have travelled alone and off the beaten track, until I arrived among these oaks last night, where you saw what happened to me. And if I asked about the way to Peña de Francia, it was to make some sort of answer to the question asked. To tell you the truth I don't know where Peña de Francia is, although I know it's the other side of Salamanca.'

'That's true,' replied Andrés, 'and you left it behind to the right of you some twenty leagues back,* that's how wide of the mark you were if that's where you were heading.'

'The place I was actually heading for,' replied the youth, 'was Seville, for I know a Genoese gentleman there, a great friend of my relation the Count, who regularly sends large shipments of silver to Genoa. It is my plan that he arrange for me to accompany the men who deliver it, as if I were one of them. By these means I will be able to get to Cartagena safely, and from there to Italy, because two galleys are shortly due to take the silver on board. This, my good friend, is my story. Consider whether I am justified in saying that it is the result of sheer bad luck rather than frustrated love. But if these good gipsies were willing to take me with them to Seville, if they are going that way, I would pay them very well for it, for I am convinced that I will travel more safely in their company, free of the fear I have experienced while travelling alone.'

'Be assured that they will take you,' replied Andrés, 'and even if you don't go with our company—because I don't yet know whether it's heading for Andalusia—you'll go with another which I believe we'll meet up with in a couple of days' time. If you give them some of the money you're carrying, you'll find that the unlikeliest things become possible.'

Andrés left him and went to report to the other gipsies what the young man had said and what he was trying to do, including the offer he had made to pay and reward them well. They were all of the opinion that he should remain in their company. Preciosa was alone in objecting to this, and her grandmother said that she could not go to Seville, nor anywhere near it, because of a trick she had played years earlier on a well-known capmaker there named Triguillos. She had persuaded him to stand naked and up to his neck inside a large pitcher of water with a crown of cypress on his head, and wait for the exact moment of midnight before getting out to dig up a great treasure which she had convinced him lay buried in a certain part of his house. She recounted how, when the good capmaker heard matins being rung, he was in such a hurry to get out of the pitcher at just the right moment that both he and the pitcher toppled to the ground. The impact of the fall and the pitcher fragments left him black and blue, the water spilled out, and he ended up swimming around in it, shouting out that he was drowning. His wife and neighbours came running up with lights and found him going through the motions of swimming, splashing and dragging his belly across the floor, flailing his arms and legs, and shouting 'Help me! I'm drowning!' He was so frightened that he genuinely believed that he was drowning. They took hold of him, pulled him out of danger, and when he recovered he told them of the old gipsy's ruse. 'Nevertheless, he dug a hole about two yards deep in the place indicated, although everyone around him kept telling him that it was a trick of mine. If a neighbour of his had not stopped him when he had reached the foundations of his own house, he would have brought both their houses down on top of him, if he had been allowed to dig as far as he wanted. This story spread throughout the city and even children pointed their fingers at him and recounted the tale of his credulity and my deception.'

This is the story the old woman told and this was her excuse for not going to Seville. The gipsies, who knew from Andrés Caballero that the youth had a lot of money with him, readily welcomed him into their company and promised to guard him and keep him hidden for as long as he wished. They then decided to veer left and go into La Mancha and the kingdom of Murcia. They called the youth and told him what they intended to do for him; he thanked them and gave them a hundred gold escudos to share amongst themselves. When they had received this gift they would have sat up and begged for him. Preciosa was the only one who was not happy that don Sancho—for this is what he said his name was—would be staying. The gipsies changed his name to Clemente and that is what they called him from then on. Andrés was also rather dismayed and disappointed that Clemente had stayed, for it seemed to him that he had abandoned his original plan rather too easily. However, Clemente, as if he could read his thoughts, said among other things that he was delighted to be going to the kingdom of Murcia, since it was close to Cartagena where, if any galleys came into port, as he was sure they must, he would easily be able to cross over to Italy. Finally, in order to keep him under closer observation, watch his every move, and guess what he was thinking, Andrés asked Clemente to be his close companion and Clemente interpreted this friendship as a great favour. They went everywhere together, spent a lot of money, showered the world with escudos, and ran, jumped, danced, and hurled the bar better than any of the gipsies. They were more than casually admired by the gipsy women and highly respected by the men.

So they left Extremadura and went into La Mancha and gradually made their way towards the kingdom of Murcia. In the hamlets and villages through which they passed they were challenged to games of *pelota*, fencing matches, and contests in running, jumping, hurling, and other feats of strength, skill, and speed. Andrés and Clemente were victorious in every competition, as Andrés alone had been in the past. In all this time, which was more than a month and a half, Clemente never had the opportunity to speak to Preciosa, nor did he seek one. Then one day, when she and Andrés were standing together, they called him over to join their conversation and Preciosa said:

'I recognized you from the very first moment you entered our camp and I was reminded of the verses you gave me in Madrid, but I didn't want to say anything then because I didn't know your reason for coming here. When I learned of your misfortune I felt truly sorry for you, but my heart was set at ease, because I had been alarmed to think that just as there were don Juans in the world who changed themselves into Andréses there might similarly be don Sanchos who also changed their names. I'm speaking to you so frankly because Andrés told me that he's explained to you who he is and why he's become a gipsy.' This was indeed true, because Andrés had related the whole story to him in order to be able to share his thoughts with him. 'And don't think that my knowing you was no advantage to you, because you have me and what I said about you to thank for your prompt welcome and admittance into our company, where I hope it may please God to grant you all the good fortune you desire. All I ask in return for this goodwill is that you don't criticize Andrés for what may seem like the indignity of his aim, nor point out to him the evils of remaining in this condition. For although I believe his will to be subject to my own, I would still be distressed to see him show the slightest sign of regret.'

To which Clemente replied, 'Do not think, peerless Preciosa, that don Juan revealed his identity to me lightly. It was I who first recognized him, his eyes which first disclosed his purpose; it was I who first revealed who I was and guessed the imprisoned state of his will. He in turn, duly taking me into his confidence, entrusted his secret to me and will bear witness that I applauded his decision and intention. Preciosa, I am not so stupid that I cannot appreciate how far the power of love extends, and your own all-surpassing beauty is sufficient excuse for even greater errors, if it is proper to define as errors actions which are inspired by such irresistible causes. I thank you, dear lady, for speaking in my favour, and I intend to reciprocate your goodwill by hoping that this affair has a happy ending, and that you will enjoy your Andrés and he his Preciosa with the blessing and approval of his parents. May we see from such a handsome union the fairest offspring benevolent nature can produce. This is what I shall desire, Preciosa, and this is what I shall always say to Andrés, and I shall say nothing to divert him from his excellent intentions.'

Clemente uttered these words with such feeling that Andrés was in some doubt as to whether they were spoken out of love or politeness. For the infernal disease of jealousy is so sensitive that it adheres to the tiniest particles of sunlight, and the lover is troubled and tormented when they touch the beloved object. Yet, in spite of this, his jealousy was never justified, and he trusted Preciosa's goodness more than his own good fortune, for people in love always consider themselves unfortunate until they attain what their hearts desire. Andrés and Clemente eventually became great friends and companions, their intimacy assured by the goodwill of Clemente and the modesty and prudence of Preciosa, who never gave Andrés cause to be jealous.

Clemente had an aptitude for poetry, as he had demonstrated in the poems he had given to Preciosa; Andrés also considered himself something of a poet, and they were both fond of music. So, to amuse themselves one night while they were camped in a valley four leagues from Murcia, they both sat down, Andrés beneath a cork oak and Clemente beneath an evergreen. With guitars in hand and inspired by the silence of the night, they sang the following song, Andrés leading and Clemente responding:

Look, Clemente, at the wondrous starry veil,
How this cold night in its own way
Vies with the radiance of the day.
As myriad lovely lights the heavens regale.
Hold this likeness in your sight,
If your divine wit can scale such lofty height,
Represent to me that face
Where sublime loveliness has its dwelling place.

Where sublime loveliness has its dwelling place,
Where Preciosa's purity
And beautiful chastity
Are refined to perfection in boundless grace,
There they in one form combine,
For there is no wit can praise her, lest divine,
Or lest it in full measure be
High, peerless, profound, extraordinary.

High, peerless, profound, extraordinary,
By means unprecedented,
To highest heav'n ascended,
Too sweet-toned for this orb sublunary,
Fair gipsy maid, may your celebrated name,
Raised upon the wings of fame,
Prompting wonderment and fear
Be duly lifted up to heav'n's highest sphere.

Be duly lifted up to heav'n's highest sphere,
'Tis our desire just and apt,
All the heav'ns will be enrapt,
When your name's sounds in their distant realm they hear,
Which down on earth below,
Wherever that name sweet-syllabled echo,
Music to our ears release,
Glory to our senses and to our souls peace.

Glory to our senses and to our souls peace,
Such the siren songs impart,
Captivating every heart,
'Til e'en the most avid watchmen vigil cease.
Preciosa the world disarms,
Radiant beauty quite the least of myriad charms;
My precious jewel sublime,
Sovereign wit, life's joys' reigning paradigm.

Sovereign wit, life's joys' reigning paradigm,
Of all gipsydom the flower,
Freshness of the morning hour,
Cool-breathing zephyr in blazing summertime.
Blind Cupid his arrow aims,
Transforming the iciest breast to ardent flames,
And she alone knows the way
Gently desire to satisfy, then to slay.

Both free man and slave showed every sign of continuing their
song when behind them they heard the voice of Preciosa who had
been listening to theirs. Hearing her silenced them and they listened
to her rapt and motionless. I do not know whether the following song,
which she sang with consummate grace, was improvised or whether
it had been composed for her at some time, but it was an apt response
to the men's song:

When I ponder the heart's affairs,
When I entertain thoughts of love,
I esteem virtue far above
Beauty's graces, whims and airs.

The very humblest plant of all,
If it grow straight at its own pace,
Nurtured by nature or by grace,
Will reach to heaven, strong and tall.

Though moulded from base copper ore,
Innate virtue refines my shine,
My every thought is good and fine,
Unburdened by riches galore.

It causes me no vexation
That no one esteem or love me,
I desire that my destiny
Be of my own fabrication.

I am bidden to do no ill
By the conscience that inspires me;
Let heaven dictate and decree
Henceforth whatsoever it will.

Yet it is beauty I should thank,
Were it a privilege heav'n sent,

To pluck me from humble descent
And raise me to far nobler rank.

If one soul is like another,
Then he who rudely ploughs the earth
Can boast a soul equal in worth
To that of any emperor.

My soul guards a wish deep within
That lifts me to a higher sphere,
For majesty and love sincere
Share not a common origin.

Preciosa ended her song and Andrés and Clemente stood up to greet her. The three of them engaged in pleasant conversation and in what she said Preciosa displayed her intelligence, virtue, and ready wit so clearly that Clemente was able to excuse Andrés's intention, which he had not until then been able to do, attributing his reckless decision to youthful waywardness rather than good sense.

That morning the gipsies moved on and camped in an area of Murcia, three leagues away from the city, where Andrés suffered a mishap which almost cost him his life. It happened like this: after handing over some cups and other items of silver to those in authority in that place, Preciosa, her grandmother, Cristina, and two other young girls and both Andrés and Clemente took lodgings at the inn of a rich widow. This widow had a daughter of about seventeen or eighteen who was more forward than she was beautiful and whose name was Juana Carducha. When this Juana had seen the gipsy men and women dancing, the devil took hold of her and she became so desperately infatuated with Andrés that she decided to tell him so and have him as her husband, if he so wished, even though it might grieve all her family. With this aim in mind she sought an opportunity to disclose her feelings, and she found one in the paddock where Andrés had gone to look at a couple of donkeys. She went up to him quickly, to avoid being seen, and said,

'Andrés'—for she already knew his name—'I'm a maiden and rich; my mother has no children besides me and this inn belongs to her. On top of that she's also got lots of vineyards and another couple of houses. I like the look of you; and if you want to marry me, it's up to you. Give me an answer quickly, and if you've any sense, stay here and we'll have a grand life.'

Andrés was astonished at Juana Carducha's boldness, and with the promptness she demanded he replied, 'Young lady, I'm engaged to be married, and we gipsies only marry gipsies. God bless you for the favour you wished to do me, of which I'm not worthy.'

Juana Carducha was mortified when she heard Andrés's cold reply, and would have retorted if she had not seen some gipsy girls entering the paddock. So she went off feeling embarrassed, wretched, and hell-bent on revenge. Being the sensible man he was, Andrés decided to put some distance between them and avoid the opportunity that the devil was offering him. For he could clearly read in Juana Carducha's eyes that she would give herself to him body and soul without the bonds of marriage, and he did not want to fight alone and on foot in that particular arena. He therefore appealed to all the other gipsies to leave that place that night. Ever obedient to his wishes, they began to prepare for departure and, having recovered their insurance that afternoon, they went on their way.

When Juana Carducha saw Andrés depart she realized that half her soul was departing with him, and since there was no time for her to satisfy her desires, she contrived to make Andrés stay behind by force, since she could not persuade him to stay of his own accord. So, with the cunning, subtlety, and secrecy engendered by her evil intent, she placed some costly coral necklaces, two silver lockets, and a few other trinkets amongst valuables which she knew to belong to Andrés. Then, almost as soon as they had left the inn, she started shouting and claiming that those gipsies had robbed her of her jewels, and in response to these cries the officers of the law and all the villagers came running. The gipsies halted their march and all swore that they had no stolen goods in their possession and that they would let them see all the bags and provisions of their camp. This greatly worried the old gipsy woman, who feared that such a search would bring to light Preciosa's jewels and Andrés's original clothes, which she had so carefully and cautiously guarded. However, the good Juana Carducha quickly resolved the problem by suggesting, when they were examining the second pack, that they should ask which one belonged to the gipsy who was such a good dancer, for she had seen him enter her room on two occasions and he might be the one who had the goods. Andrés realized that she was referring to him, and said with a laugh, 'Young lady, this is my luggage and this is my donkey; if you find in either one of them what you've lost,

I'll pay you back sevenfold, as well as submit to the punishment meted out to thieves.'

The law officers went to unload the donkey immediately and did not have to hunt far before they found the stolen property, which so horrified Andrés that he stood rooted to the spot and speechless, as if he had been turned to stone.

'Wasn't I right to suspect him?' said Juana Carducha at that point. 'Look how well he hides his thieving ways behind his handsome face!'

The mayor, who was present, began hurling insults at Andrés and the rest of the gipsies, calling them public thieves and highwaymen. In the face of all this Andrés remained silent, bewildered, and abstracted, not suspecting for a moment that Juana Carducha had betrayed him. At that moment a swaggering soldier, the mayor's nephew, went up to him and said,

'Just look at the state the rotten thieving little gipsy's in. I bet he'll kick up a fuss and deny the whole thing, although he was caught red-handed. You should be glad you aren't all thrown into the galleys. Don't you think he'd be better off there, serving his Majesty, rather than dancing from one place to another and stealing right, left, and centre? Upon my word as a soldier, I feel like knocking him to the floor.'

Without a further word of warning he lifted his hand and dealt Andrés such a vigorous blow that it shook him out of his abstraction and reminded him that he was not Andrés Caballero but don Juan and a gentleman. He rushed at the soldier, deftly unsheathed his sword, and furiously plunged it into his body, leaving him dead on the ground.

Suddenly the whole village was in uproar, the soldier's uncle the mayor was furious, Preciosa fainted, Andrés was distressed to see her faint, and everyone seized arms and ran after the murderer. The confusion increased, the shouting grew louder, and when Andrés went to attend Preciosa in her faint he neglected to defend himself. Fate ordained that Clemente did not witness this dreadful scene because he had already left the village with the baggage. So many of the villagers fell upon Andrés that they subdued him and shackled him with two heavy chains. The mayor would have gladly hanged him on the spot if it had been in his power to do so, but he had to send him to Murcia because he was under the jurisdiction of that city. They did not take him until the following day, and throughout the day he remained there he was subjected to an unceasing torrent of abuse and cursing from the enraged mayor, his men, and all the people of the village. The mayor arrested as many gipsies, both male and female, as he could, although most of the them had got away, Clemente among them, since he was afraid of being arrested and recognized.

Finally, carrying the indictment and with a large mob of gipsies in tow, the mayor and his officials marched into Murcia accompanied by many other armed individuals. With them went Preciosa and poor Andrés, who was bound in chains and wearing handcuffs and an iron collar. The whole of Murcia turned out to see the prisoners because they had already heard about the soldier's death. That day, however, Preciosa's beauty was so radiant that no one could look at her without blessing her and the news of her beauty reached the ears of the Chief Magistrate's wife. Eager to see her, the latter asked the Chief Magistrate, her husband, to give orders that the little gipsy girl should not be imprisoned, but that all the others should. They put Andrés in a narrow cell, the darkness of which, combined with the absence of Preciosa's light, had such a detrimental effect on him that he quite convinced himself that he would never leave that place except to go to his grave. They took Preciosa and her grandmother to where the Chief Magistrate's wife might see her, and when she finally laid eyes on her, she said, 'Her beauty is justly praised.'

Going up to her she embraced her tenderly, unable to take her eyes off her, and asked her grandmother how old she was.

'Fifteen,' replied the gipsy, 'and two months more or less.'

'My poor Costanza would be the same age. Alas, my friends, this child has brought back the memories of my misfortune!'

Preciosa then took the Chief Magistrate's wife's hands and kissed them many times, bathing them with her tears, and said:

'My dear lady, the gipsy who has been arrested is not guilty, because his action was provoked: they called him a thief and he is not a thief; he was struck across the face, and it is such a fine face that the goodness of his heart is expressed in it. In the name of God and because of who you are, please get his sentence postponed, and do not allow the Chief Magistrate to be hasty in dealing out the punishment with which the law threatens him. If my beauty has given you any pleasure, preserve it by preserving the prisoner, because the end of his life will mark the end of my own. He is to be my husband, and only just and virtuous impediments have prevented us from joining hands before now. If money were required to obtain the pardon of the injured party, the whole of our camp would be put up for public auction, and we would offer more than the sum of the fine. My dear lady, if you know what love is, and if you have had or indeed still have such feelings for your husband, take pity on me, for I love my husband tenderly and sincerely.'

The whole time she spoke she did not let go of the lady's hands, nor did she cease to look intently into her face, all the while shedding bitter and pitiful tears. The Chief Magistrate's wife held her hands just as tightly and looked at her with equal intensity and no fewer tears. They were still clutching each other's hands and staring at one another when the Chief Magistrate walked in. When he saw his wife and Preciosa weeping and clinging to each other so wretchedly, he was astounded, both by their weeping and by Preciosa's beauty. He asked them to explain this display of emotion, and in reply Preciosa released the lady's hands and threw herself at the Chief Magistrate's feet, saying:

'Sir, mercy, I beg you to show mercy! If my husband dies, I too am dead. He is not guilty, but if he is, punish me instead, and if that is not possible, at least delay the case until some possible means of remedy have been sought and found. For perhaps heaven will show grace and favour to someone who did not sin out of malice.'

With renewed amazement the Chief Magistrate listened to the reasoned pleas of the little gipsy girl, and had he not been reluctant to show a sign of weakness he would have wept with her. While this was happening the old gipsy woman was pondering many important and different matters, and after long and hard reflection said, 'My dear sir and madam, please wait a moment, and I'll turn this weeping into laughter, even if it costs me my life.'

So she briskly left the room, leaving everyone present confused by what she had said. While they waited for her to return Preciosa did not cease her tears nor her appeals that her husband's case be delayed, so that his father might be informed and come to intervene. The old gipsy woman returned carrying a small box under her arm, and asked the Chief Magistrate and his wife to go into another room with her, because she had important matters to discuss with them privately. Thinking that she wanted to give him information concerning some gipsy thefts, to make him favourable to the prisoner's case, the Chief Magistrate immediately withdrew with her and his wife to a side room, where the old woman, falling to her knees in front of them both, said, 'If the good news I wish to tell you doesn't merit the reward of pardon for a great sin I once committed, then here I am, ready to receive whatever punishment you wish to impose on me; but before I make my confession, I want you first to tell me whether you recognize these jewels.'

Bringing out the box which contained Preciosa's jewels she put it in the Chief Magistrate's hands, and when he opened it he saw some infant trinkets but he did not understand what they represented. His wife also looked at them, but she did not appreciate their significance either.

'These are the trinkets of some young child.'

'That's correct,' said the gipsy, 'and of which child in particular is written on this folded piece of paper.'

The Chief Magistrate quickly opened it up and read what was written: 'The child's name was doña Costanza de Azevedo y de Meneses, her mother was doña Guiomar de Meneses, and her father don Fernando de Azevedo, Knight of the Order of Calatrava. I stole her at eight o'clock on the morning of Ascension Day in the year fifteen hundred and ninety five. The child was wearing the trinkets which are kept in this box.'

The Chief Magistrate's wife had scarcely heard the words contained in the paper when she recognized the trinkets and raised them to her lips and, showering them with kisses, she fell to the floor in a faint. The Chief Magistrate rushed to her side before he had time to ask the gipsy about his daughter, but when his wife came round she said, 'Good woman, angel rather than gipsy, where is the owner, I mean the child to whom these trinkets belong?'

'Where, madam,' replied the gipsy, 'but here in this very house: they belong to that little gipsy girl who brought tears to your eyes, for she is, without shadow of a doubt, your daughter. I abducted her from your house in Madrid on the very day and at the very hour stated on that paper.'

When the lady heard this she shook off her shoes, and in her excitement rushed headlong out of the room to where she had left Preciosa, and found her surrounded by her duennas and maids and still in tears. She rushed up to her and, without a word of explanation, hurriedly unfastened her bodice and looked to see whether she had a small birthmark like a white mole below her left breast, and there it was, although it was by now much larger because it had grown over the years. Then, with the same urgency, she removed her shoe to reveal a snow-white foot of delicate ivory, and there too she found the sign she was looking for: the two smallest toes on the right foot were joined together by a small piece of skin, which they had not wanted to remove when she was a child for fear of hurting her. Her breast, her toes, the trinkets, the cited day of the abduction, the gipsy's confession, and the shock and joy her parents had experienced when they had seen her confirmed once and for all in the Chief Magistrate's wife's heart that Preciosa was their daughter. So, taking her in her arms, she led her back to where the Chief Magistrate and the old gipsy were waiting.

Preciosa was confused as she went with her, because she did not know why she had been examined in that way, and she was even more confused to find herself in the arms of the Chief Magistrate's wife who was covering her with kisses. Doña Guiomar finally delivered her precious charge to her husband, and transferring her from her own arms to his, she said, 'Sir, receive your daughter, Costanza, for I have no doubt it is she. Do not doubt it for a moment, for I have seen how her toes are joined together and the mark on her breast, and what is more, my soul has been telling me so since the first moment I laid eyes on her.'

'I do not doubt it,' replied the Chief Magistrate, holding Preciosa in his arms, 'for she has had the same effect on me as on you. And furthermore, how could so many details be consistent except by some miracle?'

All the domestic servants were mystified and asked each other what all the fuss was about, but no one's conjecture came anywhere near the truth. For who would have guessed that the little gipsy girl was the daughter of their master and mistress? The Chief Magistrate told his wife, his daughter, and the old gipsy woman that it should be kept secret until he himself made it known. He also told the old woman that he forgave her for the wrong she had done him in stealing his very soul, since the fact she had returned her deserved a greater reward, and his only regret was that, fully aware of Preciosa's rank, she had arranged for her to marry a gipsy, one who was into the bargain a thief and a murderer.

'Alas,' exclaimed Preciosa at his words, 'my dear sir, he is neither a gipsy nor a thief, although he has killed a man. But the man he killed tried to dishonour him, and he could do no less than act according to his true nature and kill him.'

'What do you mean by saying he is not a gipsy, my child?' asked doña Guiomar.

So the old gipsy woman briefly related the story of Andrés Caballero, how he was the son of don Francisco de Cárcamo, knight of the Order of Santiago, that his name was don Juan de Cárcamo, of the same Order, and that she still had the clothes he had exchanged for those of a gipsy. She also told them how Preciosa and Juan had agreed to wait for two years to test their feelings before deciding whether or not to marry. She stressed the virtue of both parties and the affable character of don Juan. They found this story as astounding as the recovery of their daughter, and the Chief Magistrate ordered the old woman to fetch don Juan's clothes. She did as she was instructed and returned with another gipsy who brought them with him.

While the old woman was absent, Preciosa's parents asked her a thousand questions, to which she replied with such good sense and grace that, even if they had not recognized her as their daughter, they would still have fallen in love with her. They asked her whether she had any feelings for don Juan and she replied that she felt only as much affection as made her grateful to a man who had been willing to humble himself enough to become a gipsy for her sake; but now that gratitude would extend no further than her parents considered appropriate.

'Hush now, Preciosa,' said her father, 'for I want you to keep the name Preciosa, in memory of how you were lost and found. I, as your father, shall undertake to arrange a marriage for you which is not unworthy of your rank.'

Preciosa sighed when she heard these words, and her mother, in her wisdom, realized that she was sighing because she loved don Juan and said to her husband, 'Sir, since don Juan is a man of rank and loves our daughter so much, it would not be such a bad idea to let her marry him.'

He replied, 'We have only just found her again and you want us to lose her so soon? Let us enjoy her for a while; because once we marry her off, she will not belong to us but to her husband.'

'You are right, sir,' she replied, 'but give the order for don Juan to be released, for he must be stuck in some dungeon.'

'Yes, he will be,' said Preciosa, 'for they will not have put a thief, killer, and above all a gipsy in any better quarters.'

'I wish to go and see him, since I have to take his confession,' replied the Chief Magistrate, 'and once again I charge you, madam, not to tell anyone this story until I wish it.'

He embraced Preciosa and then went to the prison, where he entered don Juan's cell and did not want anyone to accompany him. He found him with both feet in stocks, his hands in cuffs, and the iron collar still round his neck. The cell was dark but the Chief Magistrate had a skylight opened through which a feeble light was able to penetrate. When he saw Juan he said:

'So how is our prize catch? If only I had all the gipsies in Spain so neatly bound and chained, so that like Nero in Rome, I could finish off the lot of you in one go and in a single day. Let me tell you something, irascible thief, I am the Magistrate in this city and I have come to ask you face to face whether the little gipsy girl who travels with you is your wife.'

When Andrés heard this question he assumed that the Chief Magistrate must have fallen in love with Preciosa; for jealousy is a subtle beast and penetrates bodies without breaking, severing, or dividing them. In spite of his anxiety, he coolly replied, 'If she has said that I am her husband, then it is the absolute truth, and if she has said that I am not, she has also spoken truthfully, for it is not possible for Preciosa to lie.'

'Can she be so truthful?' asked the Chief Magistrate. 'That's quite an achievement for a gipsy. Well now, young man, she has said that she is your wife, but that you have never joined hands. She has learned that since you are guilty you are to die and asked me to marry her to you before you are executed, because she wants the honour of being the widow of such a great thief.'

'Then, please, sir, do as she requests. For if I marry her I will go contented to the next life, as long as I depart this life as her husband.'

'You must love her very much!' said the Chief Magistrate.

'So much so,' replied the prisoner, 'that it is beyond my powers of expression. Therefore, sir, let my case be decided; I killed the man who wanted to dishonour me; I love this gipsy girl; I will die content if I die in her good graces, and I know that God's will not fail me, for we have both kept our promise virtuously and conscientiously.'

'Then tonight I will send for you,' replied the Chief Magistrate, 'and in my house you shall marry Preciosa and tomorrow at noon you will hang. That way I will have satisfied the demands of justice and the desires of you both.' Andrés thanked the Chief Magistrate, who returned home and told his wife what had passed between himself and don Juan and other things he intended to do.

During his absence Preciosa described the whole course of her life to her mother, how she had always believed herself to be a gipsy and the granddaughter of that old woman, but how she had always had a higher opinion of herself than was to be expected of a gipsy. Her mother asked her to answer truthfully whether she loved don Juan de Cárcamo. With her eyes fixed bashfully on the ground she replied that, because she had thought she was a gipsy and was improving her lot by marrying a knight of an Order and of such high rank as don Juan, and because she had witnessed his good character and honourable behaviour, she admitted that she had occasionally looked upon him with affection. However, in short, as she had already stated, she had only the desires her parents wanted her to have.

Night fell, and when it was almost ten o'clock they led Juan out of prison, without his handcuffs and iron collar but bound head to foot in a heavy chain. He arrived in this manner, seen by no one save those who were escorting him, at the Chief Magistrate's house, where they led him silently and discreetly into a room and left him alone. Some time later a priest went in and told him to make his confession, because he was to die the following day. Andrés replied, 'I shall make my confession very willingly, but why am I not getting married first? And if I am to marry, it is certainly a very bleak marriage bed that awaits me.'

Doña Guiomar, who was aware of this exchange, told her husband that he was frightening don Juan too much and that he should be less harsh, or he might die from the shock. This seemed like good advice to the Chief Magistrate, so he went and called the priest who was confessing Andrés and told him that first they would marry that gipsy to Preciosa, and that he would make his confession afterwards. He advised Juan to commend himself wholeheartedly to God, for very often his mercies rain down when hope has almost withered and died.

Andrés was then led into a room occupied only by doña Guiomar, the Chief Magistrate, Preciosa, and two other domestic servants. When Preciosa saw don Juan bound and shackled by such a heavy chain, his face pale and showing signs of having wept, she swooned and leaned on the arm of her mother who was standing beside her and who, taking her in her arms, said, 'Don't lose heart, child, for everything you are witnessing will be for your benefit and pleasure.'

Preciosa, who did not understand what her mother's words meant, was inconsolable, the old gipsy was agitated, and the other on-lookers waited in silent suspense to see how the affair would end. The Chief Magistrate said, 'Curate, sir, this gipsy and this girl are the people you are to marry.'

'That I am unable to do unless certain prerequisite conditions are first fulfilled. Where have the banns been read? Where is the licence from my superior to authorize the nuptials?'*

'I have been negligent,' replied the Chief Magistrate, 'but I will arrange for your vicar to provide one.'

'Well, until I see it', the curate replied, 'these good people must excuse me.' And without further ado, and in order to avoid a scandal, he departed, leaving everyone in a state of confusion.

'The father has behaved very properly,' said the Chief Magistrate at that point, 'and this circumstance may be providential in allowing Andrés's punishment to be deferred. He is, after all, to be married to Preciosa, and if the banns have to be announced first, that will give us more time, which usually provides many a difficult situation with a happy outcome. Bearing all this in mind, I should like to ask Andrés something; if luck were to direct his affairs so that he could become Preciosa's husband without all these shocks and frights, would he consider himself more fortunate as Andrés Caballero or don Juan de Cárcamo?'

When Andrés heard himself being called by his proper name, he said, 'Since Preciosa has preferred not to be bound by silence and has revealed who I am, even if that same good fortune made me ruler of the world, I would only consider it fortune if it gave me Preciosa, in which case I should not dare to wish for any other blessing save that of heaven.'

'Then for the noble spirit you have shown, don Juan de Cárcamo, in the fullness of time I will see to it that Preciosa becomes your legitimate spouse, and now I give and betroth her to you as the richest jewel in my home, my life and my soul. Cherish her as much as you say you do, for I am giving you doña Costanza de Meneses, my only child, who, if she equals you in love, is not inferior to you in rank either.'

Andrés was astonished by the affection they were showing him, and so doña Guiomar briefly recounted how their daughter had been lost and found, with the irrefutable proof that the old woman had provided concerning her abduction, all of which left don Juan amazed and astounded, but also inexpressibly happy. He embraced them as his parents-in-law and addressed them as his lord and lady; he kissed Preciosa's hands and she, with tears in her eyes, wanted to kiss his.

In next to no time the secret was out. It left the house at the same time as the servants who had been present. When the mayor, the dead man's uncle, heard the news, he saw that all means of revenge had been removed, since the full weight of the law would not be brought to bear upon the Chief Magistrate's son-in-law. Juan put on the travelling clothes which the gipsy had brought; captivity and chains of iron were exchanged for liberty and chains of gold. The misery of the gipsies was transformed into joy when they were released on bail the following day. The dead man's uncle was promised two thousand gold ducados so that he would drop the charges and pardon don Juan. The latter did not forget his friend Clemente and ordered him to be looked for, but they failed to find him and knew nothing about him until they received reliable information four days later that he had boarded one of two galleys which were in the port of Cartagena, and had already sailed away.

The Chief Magistrate informed don Juan that he had heard it confirmed that his father, don Francisco de Cárcamo, had been appointed Chief Magistrate of that very city, adding that it would be sensible to await his arrival, so that the wedding could take place with his blessing and consent. Don Juan said that he would do only what the Chief Magistrate commanded; but first and foremost he wished to be officially betrothed to Preciosa. The Archbishop gave permission for the betrothal to take place after just one reading of the banns. The whole city celebrated the day of the betrothal with fireworks, a bullfight, and a jousting tournament, for the Chief Magistrate was a popular figure. The old gipsy woman remained in the house because she did not want to be separated from Preciosa.

News of the affair and forthcoming marriage of the little gipsy girl reached Madrid. Don Francisco de Cárcamo learned that his son was the gipsy and that Preciosa was the little gipsy girl he had seen, whose beauty was sufficient to excuse in his eyes the irresponsible behaviour of his son, whom he had given up as lost when he discovered that he had not gone to Flanders. He was even more inclined to excuse him when he saw how advantageous it was for him to marry the daughter of such a rich and high-ranking gentleman as don Fernando de Azevedo. He hastened his departure so that he might see his children without delay, and within twenty days he was in Murcia. When he arrived the celebrations recommenced, the wedding took place, and their life-stories had to be narrated once again. The poets of the city, of whom there are several very fine ones, undertook to record the strange tale and the peerless beauty of the little gipsy girl. The famous scholar Pozo* wrote so exquisitely that Preciosa's fame will last as long as time itself.

I forgot to mention that the infatuated innkeeper's daughter explained to the officers of the law that the accusation of theft against Andrés the gipsy was unfounded. She confessed her love and her guilt, and went unpunished because, in the joy that accompanied the return of the happy couple, vengeance was laid to rest and mercy restored.

RINCONETE AND CORTADILLO

One hot summer's day two lads chanced to meet at the Molinillo Inn, which is situated at the edge of the famous plain of Alcudia, on the road from Castile to Andalusia. About fourteen or fifteen years of age and neither of them more than seventeen, they were both good-looking lads but very shabbily dressed in ragged, threadbare clothing. Neither owned a cloak, their breeches were made of canvas, and their stockings of bare flesh. It is quite true that their footwear was more impressive, for the one sported rope sandals which were so well worn that they were worn out, while the other's shoes were all holes and no soles, with the result that they looked more like stocks than shoes. One wore a green hunting cap, the other a flattish, wide-brimmed hat without a band. One carried a shirt that was chamois-coloured with grime, buttoned and folded up in a bag slung across his shoulder and fastened at the front. The other travelled lightly and carried no bags, although there was a bundle stuffed inside his shirt front, which later turned out to be one of those Walloon collars,* stiff with grease and so frayed that it was nothing but threads. Wrapped up and protected inside was a pack of oval-shaped playing cards, the corners of which had been worn away through constant use and then trimmed and left in that shape so that they would last a little longer. Both lads were sunburnt, with long, neglected fingernails and grubby hands; one of them carried a cutlass and the other a horn-handled knife, such as are used by slaughterhouse workers.

Both went to have their siesta in a porch or shelter at the front of the inn. Sitting opposite one another, the one who appeared to be the elder of the two said to the younger one, 'From where do you hail, good sir, and whereabouts are you heading?'

'I do not know, sir,' replied the other, 'where I am from, nor where I am going either.'

'Well,' replied the elder, 'you haven't just appeared out of thin air, that's for certain, and no one settles down in a place like this, so you must be on your way somewhere else.'

'And so I am,' replied the younger lad, 'but I spoke the truth when I said what I did. For the place I have come from is not my home and I have only a father there who does not acknowledge me as his son and a stepmother who treats me like a stepson. The road I am taking leads God knows where and I will halt when I find someone who will provide me with the means to get by in this wretched life.'

'And do you have some trade?' asked the elder lad and the younger one replied,

'I only know how to run like a hare, leap like a buck and use a pair of scissors with great skill.'

'That is all very good, useful, and beneficial,' said the elder lad, 'because you will come across some sexton who will give you the All Saints Day collection if you cut him paper flowers for the monument on Holy Thursday.'

'That is not my style of cutting,' replied the younger one, 'for my father, by the mercy of heaven, is a tailor and stocking-maker by trade and he taught me how to cut gaiters which, as you well know, are knee-high leggings which cover the upper part of one's shoes and which, to give them their proper name, are normally known as spattees. I am so good at cutting them that I could pass a master craftsman's exam, except that my luck has been cut short and left me in the lurch.'

'All this and worse happens to the best of us,' replied the elder lad, 'and I have always heard it said that true talent is what usually goes to waste; but you are still young enough to improve your fortune. But unless I am mistaken or my eye is deceiving me, you have other hidden gifts, which you do not want to reveal.'

'Yes, I do,' replied the smaller boy, 'but they are not for public consumption, as you have rightly supposed.'

In reply the elder boy said, 'Well, I can tell you that I am one of the most discreet chaps you will find for miles around; and to make you unburden yourself and confide in me, I shall oblige you by opening my heart to you first. I imagine it is no coincidence that fate has brought us together here, and I believe that from this day until the end of our lives we are to be true friends. I, good sir, am from Fuenfrida, a place made famous and well known by the illustrious personages who are constantly travelling through it. My name is Pedro del Rincón, my father is a man of some standing because he is an agent of the Holy Crusade, in other words he is a seller of indulgences, or pardoner, as the vulgar mass is wont to call such men. Some days I accompanied him as he went about his business and was such a quick learner that in the sale of bulls I could not be outdone by any self-appointed champion of the art. However, since I was fonder of the money generated by the bulls than the bulls themselves, one day I embraced a sackful of coins and took myself and it off to Madrid. There the opportunities that usually present themselves left me scraping the bottom of the sack within a few days, and I threw it away more crumpled than a bridegroom's handkerchief. The man who had formerly been in charge of the money caught up with me. I was arrested and shown little clemency, although when these men recognized how young I was they contented themselves with tying me to a whipping post, swatting my back for a while, and exiling me from the capital for four years. I endured it all, shrugged my shoulders, suffered the lashes, and then left to fulfil the terms of my exile in such a hurry that I did not have time to find a mule to carry me.

'I grabbed what possessions I could and what seemed to be most essential, including these cards'—and at that point he took out the aforementioned cards which he was carrying round his neck—'With them I have earned my living in the various taverns and inns that lie between here and Madrid, playing pontoon. Although they look shabby and manhandled to you, they work wonders for the player who knows how to use them, for whichever way he cuts the pack, there will always be an ace at the bottom. And if you are familiar with this game, you will appreciate what an advantage it is to know that you will turn up an ace as the first card, which can count as one or eleven; and with this advantage, with everything staked on twenty-one, the money stays with the dealer. In addition to this, I picked up a few tips on how to play *quínolas* and *parar*, which is also known as *andaboba*,* from the chef of some ambassador or other. So if you could pass an exam in the cutting of gaiters, I could gain a master's degree in the art of card-sharping. With this skill I am certain of not dying of hunger, because even though I may only stop at a farm, there is always someone willing to spend a while playing cards. We shall shortly put this to the test, you and I. Let's prepare the trap and see whether one of these muleteers falls into it. What I mean is that we shall pretend to play pontoon, and if someone wants to make up a third he will be the first to part with his cash.'

'I will gladly play along,' said the other, 'and I am very grateful to you for the honour you have done me in telling me your life-story, thus obliging me not to withhold my own story from you. To tell my tale briefly, then, it goes like this: I was born in that pious place* between Salamanca and Medina del Campo. My father is a tailor and he taught me his trade, and to a man of my talents it was but a short step from cutting material to cutting purses. I was frustrated with the narrowness of village life and the coldness of my stepmother's attitude towards me. I left my village and went to Toledo to ply my trade, and there I accomplished great things, for there was no locket on a headdress, nor pocket so well-concealed that my fingers could not reach it or my scissors cut it, though they were guarded with the vigilance of an Argus.* During the four months I stayed in that city I was never caught in a tight spot, nor jumped on, nor chased by constables, nor squealed on by some sneak. It is true that about a week ago a double-crosser informed the Chief Magistrate of my skills and he, attracted by my fine qualities, wished to question me. Being a modest sort of chap, however, I wanted nothing to do with such important people and contrived not to meet him. So I left the city in such a hurry that I had no time to arrange transport, cash, or a lift in an empty coach or even some old cart.'

'Let's put all that behind us,' said Rincón, 'for now that we're acquainted there's no reason for these airs and graces; let's confess it openly, we haven't got two coins to rub together, let alone a pair of shoes.'

'So be it,' agreed Cortado, for that is what the younger of the two said his name was, 'and since our friendship is going to be eternal, as you, Mr Rincón have stated, let's inaugurate it with holy and laudable ceremonies.'

Diego Cortado got up and embraced Rincón and Rincón reciprocated warmly and enthusiastically. Then they both sat down to play pontoon with the aforementioned deck of cards, wiped clean of telltale marks but not of grease and malicious intentions. After dealing a few hands Cortado could turn up an ace as well as his teacher, Rincón. While they were playing, a muleteer came out on to the porch to get a breath of fresh air and he asked if he could make up a third. They very willingly cut him in and in less than half an hour they had won twelve reales and twenty-two maravedís from him, which was like dealing him a dozen spear wounds and twenty-two thousand sorrows. Thinking that such young lads would not be able to defend themselves, the muleteer tried to recover his money from them, but one of them drew his cutlass while the other grabbed his horn-handled knife and they put up such a fight that if his companions had not come out, he would surely have come off badly.

At that moment a group of travellers chanced to pass by on horseback, on their way to rest at the Alcalde Inn, which was half a league further along the route. When they saw the fight between the muleteer and the two boys, they broke it up and told the boys that if they happened to be going to Seville, then they could go with them.

'That where we're headed,' said Rincón, 'and your wish is our command.'

Without delaying for a moment longer, they leapt in front of the mules and went off with the travellers, leaving behind one aggrieved and annoyed muleteer and an innkeeper's wife who, impressed by the good breeding of the two rogues, had eavesdropped on their conversation without them knowing. When she told the muleteer that she had heard them say that the deck of cards they were using was stacked, he was beside himself with rage and wanted to go to the inn after them to recover his worldly goods, declaring that it was a huge insult and humiliation for two young boys to deceive a hulking great man like himself. His companions held him back and advised him not to go, if only to avoid publicizing his incompetence and folly. In short, although their arguments did not console him, they did persuade him to stay where he was.

Meanwhile, Cortado and Rincón ingratiated themselves so successfully with the travellers that they spent most of the journey hitching a ride on the mules' hindquarters; and although they had several opportunities to rifle through the saddlebags of their short-term masters, they did not do so, because they did not want to lose such a good chance of getting to Seville, where they both longed to be.

In spite of this resolution, as they were entering the city, at a time of public prayer, and halted at the customs gate for inspection and payment of import duty, Cortado could not resist cutting the saddlebag or travelling bag which a Frenchman in the company carried on the hindquarters of his mule. So, slashing with his knife he inflicted such a deep and gaping wound in it that its innermost contents were exposed. He carefully extracted two good shirts, a sundial, and a small notebook, items which did not give them much pleasure when they saw them. They reckoned that since the

Frenchman was carrying that bag on the back of his mule, he would not have filled it with items of such little worth as those objects they now had in their possession. They wanted to have another feel around but they refrained from doing so, imagining that the objects would already have been missed and that what remained would have been removed to a safer place.

They said goodbye to the people who had fed them on their journey before they stole from them, and the following day they sold the shirts in the second-hand shop outside the Arenal Gate and got twenty reales for them. Once this was accomplished they went off to see the city, and were impressed by the size and grandeur of its cathedral and the large crowd of people assembled at the river, because the fleet was being loaded up. The sight of the six galleys moored there made them both suck in their breath and fear the day when their crimes would surely send them to the galleys for life. They noticed that there were many young lads wandering round about with panniers; they inquired of one of them what exactly he was doing, whether it was hard work, and what the earnings were like.

The Asturian lad to whom they addressed the question replied that the work was undemanding and tax-free and some days he went home with five or six reales in his pocket, which enabled him to eat, drink, and be merry. He did not have to make promises to a master and was guaranteed a meal whenever he felt like it, because food was served at all hours of the day even in the smallest tavern in the city.

What the young Asturian had to say did not sound at all bad to the two friends, nor did the job itself displease them, since they got the impression that it would provide them with an ideal cover and smokescreen for their own activities, granting them access to all the houses. They decided there and then to buy the necessary tools of the trade, since they could practise it without first sitting an exam. They asked the Asturian what they needed to buy and he told them that they would each need a small, clean or brand-new bag and three palm-leaf panniers, two large and one small, in which to distribute the meat, fish, and fruit while the bread would go into the bag. He led them to the place where such items were sold, and using the money they had made from plundering the Frenchman they bought everything they needed. Within a couple of hours they were past masters in their new craft, judging by the way they manœuvred their baskets and balanced their bags. Their guide also advised them on what districts to make for: the meat market and San Salvador Square in the mornings, the fish market and Costanilla on fish days, the riverside every afternoon, and the fair every Thursday.

They committed the whole list of instructions to memory and early the following morning they took up position in San Salvador Square. They had scarcely got settled when they found themselves surrounded by other boys employed in the same line of business, who recognized that they were new to the square by their brand new panniers. They were asked a thousand questions, which they answered sensibly and politely. At that moment, a student and a soldier approached them, attracted by the clean condition of the baskets the two boys were carrying. The one who looked like a student summoned Cortado while the soldier beckoned to Rincón—'I greet you in the name of God,' they said in unison.

'Let business commence and prosper,' said Rincón, 'for you, sir, are the first man to employ me.'

The soldier replied, 'Then it will not a bad start, for I've got money to spend. I'm in love and today I have to prepare a feast for my lady love and some friends of hers.'

'Well, load me up as much as you like, for I'm willing and strong enough to carry off the whole square, and even if you need me to help you cook, I'll very willingly lend a hand.'

The soldier was pleased with the boy's good nature and told him that if he wanted a master to serve he would rescue him from such a demeaning activity. Rincón replied that since it was his first day on the job he did not want to leave it so soon, at least not until he had weighed up its pros and cons; but if he turned out not to be satisfied with it, he promised that he would rather serve him than a canon.

The soldier laughed, loaded him to capacity, and indicated in which house his lady lived so that he would know where it was in future and he would not need to go with him the next time he sent him on an errand. Rincón promised to carry out his duty faithfully and well. The soldier gave him three cuartos and in no time he was back in the square, anxious not to miss any opportunity, for the Asturian had also impressed upon them the importance of speed. He had also said that when they carried small fish, such as dace, sardines, or flounder, they should feel free to take a few and sample them against that day's expenses. However, they were to exercise good sense and judgement, so as not to damage their reputations, which was what mattered most in that line of business.

Although Rincón returned quickly, he found Cortado back in their spot before him. Cortado came up to Rincón and asked him how he had fared. Rincón opened his hand to show him the three cuartos, Cortado put his hand inside the breast of his shirt and withdrew a purse which smelled as if it had formerly been perfumed with amber and which was fairly bulging with money and said,

'This is what his reverence the student paid me, this and two cuartos; but you take it, Rincón, in case something happens.' When the object had discreetly changed hands, back came the student, seriously worried and in a cold sweat, and when he saw Cortado he asked whether by any chance he had seen a purse of such-and-such a description which he had lost with fifteen gold escudos, three reales, and so many maravedís in it. He asked him whether he had picked it up while he had been shopping with him. Looking the very picture of innocence, and without batting an eyelid, Cortado replied,

'All I can say about that purse is that it can't be lost, unless you were careless with it.'

'Of course, that's it! Sinner that I am,' replied the student. 'I must have been careless and I've had it stolen.'

'I'm inclined to agree,' said Cortado, 'but there's a solution for every problem, excepting death, of course, and yours, first and foremost, is forbearance; for God made us out of nothing and one day succeeds another and they give with one hand and take away with the other. It could happen that, in the course of time, the person who stole your purse will repent of his wrongdoing and return it to you perfumed with incense.'

'I'll settle for the purse without the incense,' replied the student.

Cortado went on, 'What's more, there are letters of excommunication from Pope Paul and there is diligence, which is the mother of good fortune; although, to tell you the truth, I wouldn't want to be the thief who took that purse, because if you're from some holy order or other, I'd think I'd committed some awful incest or sacrilege.'

'It certainly is a sacrilege!' said the aggrieved student, 'for although I'm not a priest, but a sexton in charge of some nuns, the money in the purse was the disposable part of a chaplain's stipend which a friend of mine who is priest asked me to collect, so it's sanctified and holy money.'

'He's made his bed, so he must lie in it,' said Rincón at that point. 'I don't envy him; there'll be a Judgement Day, when it'll all come out in the wash and then we'll see who we're up against and the insolent devil who dared to take, snatch, and rob the chaplain's salary. And what's the annual income? Pray tell me, Mr Sexton.'

'Yearly income? You must be joking! Am I going to stand round here talking yearly income?' spluttered the sexton, a touch overwrought. 'Tell me, brother, if you know anything about this business; if not, I'll bid you good day. I want the town crier to make an announcement.'

'That doesn't seem a bad idea,' said Cortado, 'but be sure to remember to describe the purse in detail and the exact amount of money inside; for if you're a coin or two out, it'll never turn up, and that's a promise.'

'There's no danger of that,' replied the sexton, 'for I know the details off by heart, better than the peal of church bells; I'll be accurate to the last maravedí.'

Then from his pocket he took a lace-trimmed handkerchief to wipe away the sweat which was streaming down his face like condensation in a still. As soon as Cortado saw it he marked it as his own, and when the sexton left he followed him and caught up with him at the cathedral steps, where he called him and took him to one side. Then he began to talk such utter drivel and spin such a yarn about the theft and recovery of his purse, raising his hopes and failing to finish a single sentence he began, that the poor sexton was quite mesmerized listening to him. Since he could not make head nor tail of what he was being told, he made Cortado repeat himself two or three times.

Cortado looked him steadily in the face and did not take his eyes off him. The sexton stared back at him, hanging on his every word. By holding his attention transfixed Cortado was able to conclude his business and very delicately remove the handkerchief from his pocket. Bidding him farewell, he told him that he would try to see him again that evening in that same spot, because it occurred to him that a lad in the same line of business and of the

same build as himself, who was a bit light-fingered, had taken his
purse and he felt compelled to find out, one way or the other, sooner
or later.

The sexton took some comfort from these words and said goodbye
to Cortado, who went and joined Rincón who had witnessed the
whole performance from a distance. Further down the street there
was another basket-carrier who had seen everything and how
Cortado passed the handkerchief to Rincón. Going up to them, he
said, 'Tell me, good sirs, are you from the wrong side of the fence,
or not?'

'We don't understand the expression, fine sir, ' replied Rincón.

'So you don't get my drift, my good gentlemen of Murcia?'*
replied the other.

'We're not from Murcia or Thebes either,' said Cortado. 'If you
want something else, say so; if not, go with God.'

'You really don't understand?' asked the lad. 'Then I'll explain and
spell it out for you. What I'm asking, sirs, is whether you are thieves.
But I don't know why I'm asking such a question, since I know that
you are. But tell me: why haven't you been to the customs house of
Mr Monipodio?'

'Do thieves in this area pay tax?' asked Rincón.

'If they don't,' replied the lad, 'then at least they register with Mr
Monipodio, who's like a father, teacher, and protector to them, so I
advise you to come with me to pay him your respects. If you don't,
don't you dare steal without getting the go-ahead from him or it'll
cost you dear.'

'I thought', said Cortado, 'that stealing was a free trade, with no
tax or duty to pay, and that if there is a price to be paid, then the
whole body pays it, with one's head and shoulders standing surety.
But since that's the way things are and each place has its own way of
doing things, let's observe the regulations here, for since it's the most
prestigious place in the world, then it must also have the best
customs. And so you may lead us to this gentleman you speak
of, because I'm already getting the impression, from what I've heard
said, that he's a very able and generous individual who's also good at
his job.'

'He's certainly able, skilled, and competent,' replied the lad. 'So
much so that in the four years he's held the post of father and leader
to us only four of us have been sent to the end of the world, about

thirty have been given the cat, and sixty-two sent on the voyage of a lifetime.'*

'We must confess, sir,' said Rincón, 'that all these terms are double Dutch to us.'

'Let's start walking, and I'll explain them as we go along,' replied the lad, 'and a few other things that you'll need to know like the back of your hand.'

So he started talking and spouting other expressions known as thieves' cant or jargon in the course of his speech, which was not a short one, for they had a long way to go. As they walked Rincón asked their guide, 'Are you, by any chance, a thief yourself?'

'I most certainly am,' he replied, 'in the service of God and decent people, although I'm not one of the more advanced students, for I'm still serving my year of probation.'

To this Cortado replied, 'It strikes me as rather unusual that there are thieves in the world in the service of God and decent people.'

The youth replied, 'Sir, I don't get mixed up in thologies; what I know is that every man can praise God whatever his trade, and more so with the order that Monipodio imposes on his adopted children.'

'Without doubt,' said Rincón, 'it must be a pious and holy order, since it makes thieves serve God.'

'It's so holy and pious,' replied the youth, 'that I don't know whether it can be surpassed anywhere in the profession. He's ordained that from the proceeds of our thieving we make some contribution, whether in the form of alms or otherwise, towards the oil for the lamp of a very sacred statue here in this city, and I assure you that we've seen great things come to pass as a result of this good deed. They recently gave a snaffler three dousings for pinching a pair of neddies, and although he was weak and sickly he endured the punishment without squealing, as if it were nothing. And those of us in the profession attribute this to his devout nature, because he wasn't strong enough to withstand even the initial attentions of the executioner. And because I know that you're bound to ask me the meaning of some of the words I've used, forewarned is forearmed, and I want to explain the meanings before you ask me. Understand that a *snaffler* is a horse-thief, a *dousing* is water torture, *neddies* are asses, begging your pardon, and the *initial attentions* are the first twists of the executioner's noose. We have other regulations: we recite our way through our rosaries once a week and many of us don't steal on Fridays or talk to any women called María on Saturdays.'

'I'm truly impressed,' commented Cortado, 'but tell me one thing, do you make any other form of restitution or perform any other penance than the ones you've mentioned?'

'On the matter of restitution,' replied the youth, 'there's nothing to say, because it's out of the question. Stolen property is divided up in any number of ways, with each agent and contractor taking his cut, and so the original thief cannot restore anything. Moreover, no one commands us to perform this deed, because we never go to confession, and if letters of excommunication are presented against us they never come to our attention, because we never go to church when they are read, except on jubilee days, when we are tempted by the rich pickings offered by the gathering of large crowds.'

'And by dint of this and nothing else,' asked Cortado, 'these people claim that they lead good and holy lives?'

'Well, what's bad about it?' retorted the youth. 'Wouldn't it be worse to be a heretic or a renegade, or to kill one's father and mother, or be a solomile?'

'I think you mean sodomite,' prompted Rincón.

'That's what I said,' retorted the youth.

'Everything, that's what's bad about it,' replied Cortado. 'But since our good fortune dictates that we enter this fraternity, get a move on, for I'm dying to meet Mr Monipodio, of whom such great things are said.'

'Your wish will very soon be granted,' said the youth, 'for you can see his house from here. Be so good as to remain at the door and I'll go inside to see if he's free, for this is the time of day when he usually grants an audience.'

'Please go ahead,' said Rincón.

Stepping ahead of them a little, the youth entered a run-down and ugly house and the two boys stood waiting at the door. He came back out and beckoned them inside. Their guide instructed them to wait in a small, brick-floored courtyard that was scrubbed so clean that it looked as if it was coloured with the finest red dye. On one side there was a three-legged bench and on the other an earthenware pitcher with a broken spout, and on top of it sat a small pot which was no less defective than the pitcher. In another part of the courtyard there was a rush mat and in the middle a flowerpot, which in Seville is called a *maceta*, planted with basil.

The boys took a good look at the artefacts of the house while they were waiting for Mr Monipodio to come down; and seeing that he was taking his time, Rincón ventured into one of the two small downstairs rooms that opened on to the courtyard. Inside he saw two fencing swords and two cork shields hanging on four pegs, a large chest without a lid or covering of any kind, and another three rush mats lying on the floor. To the facing wall was fastened a cheap and vulgar statue of Our Lady and beneath it hung a palm basket and, inserted into the wall, a large white basin, from which Rincón deduced that the basket served as an alms-box and the basin as a vessel for holy water, and he was right on both counts.

While Rincón was making these observations, two youths of no more than twenty years of age came in, dressed like students, and soon afterwards they were followed by two basket-carriers and a blind man who, without saying a word to one another, began pacing up and down the courtyard. It was not long before two elderly men came in, dressed in baize. They were wearing eyeglasses which lent them an air of *gravitas* and respectability, and they were both carrying a set of rosary beads that rattled noisily in their hands. Behind them came an old woman in voluminous skirts, and without saying a word she went into the room Rincón had examined and when she had taken some holy water she knelt with a great display of devotion before the statue. After some considerable time, having kissed the floor three times and raised her arms and eyes to heaven as many times again, she stood up, placed her offering in the basket, and went out to join the others in the courtyard. In summary, as many as fourteen people of varied dress and occupation had soon assembled in the courtyard. Among the last to arrive there were also two swaggering, tough-looking youths, with drooping moustaches, wide-brimmed hats, Walloon collars, coloured stockings, and thick gaiters. They both carried oversized swords, pistols instead of daggers, and their shields hung from their belts. When they came in they showed their surprise at seeing strangers and regarded Rincón and Cortado curiously out of the corner of their eye. They went up to them, and asked them whether they belonged to the fraternity. Rincón replied that they did and that they were very much at their service.

Then the long-awaited and momentous hour arrived: Monipodio, so highly esteemed by the whole of that virtuous company, was on his way down. He looked about forty-five or forty-six years old and was tall with a swarthy complexion, close-knit eyebrows, a bushy black beard, and deep-set eyes. His shirt was opened to reveal a veritable forest beneath, so thick was the hair on his chest. He wore a long, baize cloak which hung almost to his feet, which were shod in flat shoes, and his legs were draped in baggy linen breeches which flapped around his ankles. His hat was of the kind worn around the underworld, with its bell-shaped crown and broad brim; he wore a sword-belt slung across his shoulder and chest from which there hung a short, broad Perrillo sword.* His hands were stubby and hairy, with fat fingers and long, claw-like fingernails; his legs were not visible but his feet were noticeably broad and knobbly. In short, he embodied the coarsest, most grotesque ruffian in the world.

The lad who had been the boys' guide came down with him, and taking them both by the hand, he brought them before Monipodio, saying, 'These are the two worthy lads I told you about, Mr Monipodio, sir. 'xamine them an' you'll see they're good enough to join our congregation.'

'I shall be very happy to do so,' replied Monipodio.

I neglected to say that when Monipodio came down, all those who were waiting for him immediately bowed long and deeply, except for the two tough-looking individuals. They merely deigned to tug their forelocks, as they say, and resumed their pacing on one side of the courtyard while Monipodio strolled along the other, interrogating the newcomers about their occupation, place of origin, and parentage.

Rincón replied, 'Our occupation hardly needs to be spelt out, since we are standing before your good self, and I do not see the relevance of stating my origins, nor the identity of my parents, because you don't have to provide this much information even to enter a noble order.'

Monipodio replied, 'My son, you are right, and it is very sensible to conceal the details you mention, for if you have a run of bad luck, it is not desirable for there to be an entry in the register beneath the notary's signature: "So-and-So, son of So-and-So, inhabitant of such-and-such a place, hanged on such-and-such a day, or publicly flogged," or something along those lines which, at the very least, makes a bad impression on sensitive ears. So I repeat it's good policy to keep your origins secret, conceal the identity of your parents, and change your names; although amongst ourselves there is no need to hide anything and for now all I want to know are your real names.'

Rincón told him, and Cortado likewise.

'From now on, then,' replied Monipodio, 'I want, and it is my declared will, that you, Rincón, be called Rinconete and you, Cortado, Cortadillo, for these are names well befitting your age and our statutes. These require us to know the names of the parents of our brethren, for it is our custom to have certain Masses said for the souls of our deceased members and benefactors, taking the priest's stupendous out of what we pilfer, and these Masses, which are no sooner performed than paid for, are said to benefit the souls of our departed by way of salvage.* Our benefactors include: our defence counsel, the bailiff who tips us the wink, the hangman who takes pity on us, the fellow who, when one of us is tearing down the street pursued by a mob crying "Stop the thief, stop the thief!", stands in the way and confronts the posse with the words: "Leave the wretch alon:, he's been through enough already. Leave him be! Let his sins punish him!" Those charitable ladies who aid us by the sweat of their labours whether we are doing time inside or at sea, are also benefactors of ours, as are our mothers and fathers, who thrust us on the world, and the notary who, if he's in the right mood, either plays down the crime or softens the punishment. For all these people I've mentioned our brotherhood celebrates an adversary every year, with the greatest poop and solennity possible.'

'Well,' said Rinconete, for this name was now established, 'this work is indeed worthy of the highest and most profound intellect which we have heard that you, Mr Monipodio, possess. Our parents, however, are still alive, but if we outlive them, we shall notify this most fortunate and favoured of fraternities, so that a prayer of salvage or torment may be said for their souls, or so that the adversary day you mention be remembered, with all the customary pump and solitude, unless it is now better observed with poop and solennity, as you also remarked in your discourse.'

'It will indeed, cross my heart and hope to die,' replied Monipodio. Calling to the guide he said:

'Come here, Ganchuelo, are all the posts manned?'

'Yes,' said the guide, for his name was Ganchuelo, 'there are three sentries on the look-out and there's no danger of anyone catching us unawares.'

'So, getting down to business,' said Monipodio, 'I should like to know what you can do, my sons, so that I may assign you tasks and occupations appropriate to your inclinations and abilities.'

'I know a bit', replied Rinconete, 'about card-sharping; I know how to hide a card or two up my sleeve and I'm good at sighting marked cards; I'm a dab hand at dealing one, four, or eight cards; I never miss a scratch, pinprick, or rubbing. I can get a card into the gap as easy as saying ABC, and I'd dare to play a three-card monte better than three whole regiments and slip the sharpest player a better sweetener than a two-real loan.'

'This will do for starters,' said Monipodio, 'but all these tricks are old hat, and so commonplace, that every beginner is familiar with them, and they're only any use against some mug who let's himself get trounced before half the night is gone. But time will tell and then we'll see. Given half a dozen lessons on top of the rudiments you know, I truly believe that we'll make a first-rate player of you, perhaps even a master of the art.'

'Anything to oblige your good self and the honourable fraternity,' replied Rinconete.

'And what about you, Cortadillo, what can you do?' asked Monipodio.

'I can do the trick', replied Cortadillo, 'which they call "lucky-dipping", and I can pick a pocket with great skill and dexterity.'

'Anything else?' asked Monipodio.

'No, to my great shame,' replied Cortadillo.

'Not to worry, son,' said Monipodio, 'for you've come to a safe haven where you'll not founder and to a school where you'll not fail to become highly proficient in those skills most relevant to your needs. What's your nerve like, boys?'

'We've nerves of steel,' replied Rinconete, 'of course. We've courage to tackle any business relating to our craft and trade.'

'That's good,' replied Monipodio, 'but I should also like you to have the nerve to endure, if necessary, half a dozen dousings, without so much as parting your lips and uttering a word.'

'We know', said Cortadillo, 'what "dousings" are around here, and we've the nerve to face anything; because we're not so ignorant that we can't understand that we have to mind our P's and Q's or risk our necks. Heaven favours the man of courage, if that is the correct term, when he makes his control over his tongue a matter of life and death; as if it were more difficult to say "no" than "yes".'

'Stop, I've heard enough!' interrupted Monipodio. 'I declare that this argument alone convinces, obliges, persuades, and compels me to admit you forthwith as elders and dispense with your year of apprenticeship.'

'I am of the same opinion,' said one of the toughs, and all those present were unanimous in confirming it, for they had been listening to the whole conversation and they begged Monipodio to grant the boys permission to enjoy the privileges of the fraternity immediately, for their pleasant manner and agreeable conversation deserved no less.

He replied that in order to satisfy everyone he was granting them full rights as of that moment, stressing that the boys should consider it no small privilege, since it meant being exempt from paying half the first fruits of their thieving in tax; they wouldn't have to perform any menial duties that year, such as taking provisions to prison for a senior brother or to the brothel on behalf of the contributors; they could get sozzled and throw a party as, when, and where they wanted, without receiving permission from their leader; they would, of course, share the profits brought in by the senior brothers, being their equals, and other things which the boys deemed to be most singular favours and for which they thanked them profusely.

At that moment a young boy rushed in and breathlessly announced, 'The officer who deals with the vagrants is on his way to the house, but he doesn't have his bogey boys with him.'

'Nobody need be alarmed,' said Monipodio, 'for he's a friend and never comes to do us harm. Calm down, for I'll go out and speak to him.'

Everyone calmed down, for the news had rather startled them. Monipodio went to the door where he found the officer, with whom he remained a while in conversation, and then came back and asked: 'Whose turn was it to do San Salvador Square today?'

'Mine,' said the boys' former guide.

'Then how is it,' asked Monipodio, 'that I've seen no sign of an amber-scented purse which went missing this morning in that neck of the woods with fifteen gold escudos inside, plus two reales and I don't know how many cuartos.'

'It's true', replied the guide, 'that this purse went missing, but I didn't take it and I've no idea who did.'

'Don't try and be clever with me,' exclaimed Monipodio. 'The purse will have to turn up because the officer's asking for it, and he's a friend who does us a thousand favours every year.' The lad once again swore that he knew nothing about it. Monipodio began to get so angry that you could see the smoke coming out of his ears while he declared:

'No one should think lightly of breaking the smallest regulation of our order, or he'll pay for it with his life. The purse must show up, and if someone is keeping it under wraps to avoid paying duty, I'll give him what he's owed in full and I'll put up the rest from my own purse, because one way or another the officer must go away happy.'

The youth cursed his bad luck and swore again that he had not taken the purse, nor even laid eyes on it; but all he achieved was to fuel Monipodio's fury and throw the whole company into uproar when they saw that their statutes and ordinances were being violated.

When he saw all the commotion and agitation, Rinconete thought it would be wise to pacify and placate his leader, who could scarcely contain his rage. He conferred with his friend Cortadillo and, with their mutual approval, took out the sexton's purse and said, 'Let's put an end to the dispute, gentleman; this is the purse, with none of what the officer claims missing; for it fell into my companion Cortadillo's lap earlier today, along with a handkerchief which he took from the same owner as an added bonus.'

Then Cortadillo took out the handkerchief and held it up for everyone to see. When Monipodio saw it, he declared, 'Cortadillo the Good, for this is to be your title and reputation from now on, you may keep the handkerchief and I shall personally pay out compensation. The officer must take the purse away himself because it belongs to a sexton who's a relative of his, and it is only proper to comply with the saying that goes: "If someone gives you a whole chicken, the least you can do is give them a leg." This worthy officer turns a blind eye to more things in one day than we can or tend to give him in a hundred.'

They were unanimous in applauding the generosity of the two newcomers and in supporting the judgement and opinion of their leader, who went out to deliver the purse to the officer. Cortadillo's new nickname of 'the Good' was confirmed, as if he were don Alonso Pérez de Guzmán the Good, who threw a knife down from the walls of Tarifa, so that his only son's throat might be cut.*

When Monipodio came back in he was accompanied by two young women with their faces heavily made-up, their lips vibrant with colour, and their breasts thickly dusted with white powder. They wore short shawls and a brazen, shameless air; unmistakeable signs by which Rinconete and Cortadillo recognized that they were from the brothel, and in this they were not deceived. As soon as they came in they went with arms outstretched to the two toughs, one making a bee-line for Chiquiznaque and the other for Maniferro, for these were their names. Maniferro acquired his name from the iron hand he carried round in place of the original which had been cut off in the interests of justice. They embraced their ladies with great delight and asked them if they had brought them anything to wet their whistles.

'Would I let you down, my hero?' replied the one who was called Gananciosa. 'Your lad, Silbatillo, will be here soon with a laundry basket crammed full of what God has seen fit to provide.'

She was right, because at the very moment a young lad came in with a laundry basket covered with a sheet. Everyone cheered up when they saw Silbatillo, and Monipodio at once gave the order for one of the rush mats from the little room to be brought and laid out in the middle of the courtyard. Then he ordered everyone to sit around it, for they would get down to business while taking a bite to eat.

At this point the old woman who had prayed before the statue spoke up:

'Monipodio, my son, I'm not in the mood for revelry because I've had a giddy spell for the last couple of days which is driving me crazy. What's more, before midday I've got to perform my devotions and light my little candles at Our Lady of the Waters and the Holy Crucifix at St Augustine's, which neither hell nor high water could keep me away from. What I've come about is the fact that last night Renegado and Centopiés delivered a laundry basket, a bit bigger than this one here, to my house, full of whites, and as God is my judge, they still had soap suds on them, for the poor lads couldn't have had time to wipe them off, and they were sweating like pigs. It was pitiful to see them panting and with the sweat pouring down their faces, they looked like a pair of angels. They told me they were following a sheep farmer who had weighed a few livestock at the market, to see whether they could get their hands on a lovely fat bag of reales he had on him. They didn't empty the basket or count the contents, trusting in my good character; may God make all my wishes come true and keep us safe from the powers of law and order, for I swear I haven't laid a finger on the basket; it's as full as when it first turned up.'

'We believe you, mother,' replied Monipodio, 'leave the basket where it is and I'll come along as soon as it gets dark and take stock of the contents and give everyone their due, as is my custom.'

'Just as you say, my son,' replied the old woman, 'and since it's getting late, give me a quick swig, to settle this gippy old tummy of mine.'

'Down the hatch, mother,' interjected Escalanta at that point, for that was the name of Gananciosa's companion.

Removing the cover from the basket she revealed a leather wine-skin with about eight gallons of wine in it, and a cork cup that could easily hold a quart. Escalanta filled it up and gave it to the saintly old lady who, taking it in both hands and blowing some of the froth off the top, declared, 'That's a lot of wine, Escalanta, but God gives us the strength to do what we've got to do.' Lifting it to her lips, she knocked the whole lot back in one go, without pausing for breath and then commented, 'This little chap's from Guadalcanal, with just a trace of chalk in him. May God lift your spirits, daughter, for you've just lifted mine, except I fear it may do me some harm, since I drank it on an empty stomach.'

'It won't, mother,' replied Monipodio, 'because it's vintage.'

'By the Holy Virgin, I do hope so,' replied the old woman. Then she added, 'Listen, girls, could you lend me a cuarto to buy my little prayer candles. I was in such a hurry and so eager to bring the news of the basket that I left my bag at home.'

'I've got one, Pipota' (for that was the old woman's name), replied Gananciosa. 'Here, take these two cuartos and buy a candle for me with one of them, please, in the name of the good St Michael, and if you've enough for two, offer the other one to the good St Blas,* for they're my patron saints. I'd like to offer another to the lady Santa

Lucía, who I pray to about my eyes, but I don't have any more change on me; another time I'll have enough to do all three.'

'That'll be a wise move, my child, and mind you're not stingy; for it's very important to offer the candles yourself before you go and not wait for your heirs or executors to do it.'

'Mother Pipota speaks wise words,' said Escalanta. Putting her hand in her purse she gave her another cuarto and asked her to offer another two candles to the saints she considered to be most diligent and grateful. Then Pipota went off with these departing words:

'Have fun, my children, while time is still on your side; for old age will come and you'll regret the lost opportunities of your youth, as I regret mine. Commend me to God in your prayers, for I'm going to do the same for you and for myself, so that he'll deliver and preserve us from the assaults of justice in this dangerous business of ours.' And when she had said her piece, she was gone.

After her departure they all sat down around the rush mat and Gananciosa spread out the sheet by way of a tablecloth. The first items she took out of the basket were a large bunch of radishes and as many as two-dozen oranges and lemons, followed by a large pan filled with slices of fried cod. Next she removed half a Flanders cheese, a bowl of the finest-quality olives, a plate of shrimps, a large number of crabs in a thirst-making caper-and-pepper dressing, and three of the purest white loaves from Gandul. There were as many as fourteen people sitting down to the meal, each of whom pulled out his horn-handled knife, except for Rinconete who unsheathed his cutlass. It was the turn of the baize-clad old men and the guide to pour the wine using the cork cup. They had scarcely begun to get their teeth into the oranges when they were startled out of their skins by loud knocking at the door. Monipodio told them to keep calm and, going into the low room, he took down a shield and, putting his hand on his sword, went to the door and inquired, in a terrifying, booming voice, 'Who goes there?'

A voice from outside replied, 'It's me, no one of consequence, Mr Monipodio; it's me, Tagarete. I've been on duty since this morning and I've come to say that Juliana Cariharta's on her way here, all dishevelled and tearful. It looks like something dreadful's happened to her.'

At that moment the person he was talking about arrived, in tears. When Monipodio heard her he opened the door and ordered

Tagarete back to his post, with the caution that in future he should
report what he saw without quite so much banging; Tagarete said
that he would. Cariharta came in, a young woman bearing the same
stamp as the others and belonging to the same profession. Her hair
was in disarray and her face was all swollen and bruised, and as soon
as she stepped into the courtyard she fell to the floor in a faint.
Gananciosa and Escalanta rushed to her aid, and when they loosened
her bodice they found her black and blue all over, as if she had been
beaten. They splashed water on her face and she came round yelling,
'The justice of God and King fall on the head of that thieving face-
basher, that cowardly small-time crook and lousy rogue. After I've
rescued him from the scaffold more times than he's got hairs in his
beard! How unlucky can you get! To think I've wasted my youth and
squandered the best years of my life on that heartless, wicked, and
incorrigible villain!'

'Calm yourself,' intervened Monipodio, 'because I'm here and I'll
see that justice is done. Tell us your grievance, for you'll take longer
telling the tale than I will in arranging the revenge. Tell me if you've
had a bit of a tiff with your boyfriend, for if that's the case and you
want revenge, you have only to say the word.'

'What boyfriend?' retorted Juliana. 'I'll see myself befriended by
the devil rather than by that lion among the flock and lamb among
men. Do I have to eat at the same table as that man, let alone lie with
him? I'd rather see my flesh eaten by jackals, just look at the state
he's left me in.'

Lifting her skirt up to her knees, and even a little beyond, she
revealed them to be covered in weal marks.

'This', she went on, 'is what that ungrateful wretch Repolido has
done to me, although he owes more to me than to the mother who
bore him. And why do you think he did it? S'trewth, not that I've
ever given him cause to be so brutal. No, no indeed, he did it because
while he was gambling and losing, he sent Cabrillas, his lad, to ask
me for thirty reales and I only sent him twenty-four, and I pray to
heaven that the trouble and effort I put into earning them will cancel
out some of my sins. And in return for this favour and fine gesture,
convinced that I was cheating him out of some of the money he
believed me to have, this morning he took me out into the countryside, behind the King's Orchard, and there, among the olive trees,
he stripped me and not bothering to cover or withdraw the iron

buckle—I'll see him rot in irons as his punishment—he gave me such a beating with his belt that he left me for dead. These stripes you see before you are firm proof of the truth of my story.'

At this point she began yelling and screaming for justice again, and once again Monipodio and all the toughs present promised that she would get it. Gananciosa took her hand in hers to comfort her, and said that she would very willingly give up her most treasured possessions to have suffered as much at the hands of her own beloved.

'I want you to know, sister Cariharta,' she said, 'if you don't know already, that we punish those we love best; and when those black-guards give us what for, beat us and knock us about, it means that they adore us. If that's not so, tell me the truth, on your life: after Repolido had thrashed you and beaten you black and blue, didn't he show you some sign of affection?'

'Some sign?' bewailed the weeping Cariharta. 'A hundred thou-sand more like and he'd have given his right hand for me to go with him to his lodgings; and I even think that his eyes were brimming with tears after he had beaten me to a pulp.'

'No doubt about that,' said Gananciosa. 'And he'd cry like a baby to see what he's done to you; for such men, and in such circum-stances, are filled with remorse before they've finished committing their crime. You just wait and see, sister, whether he doesn't come looking for you before we go, asking you to forgive him for every-thing, with his tail between his legs and meek as a lamb.'

'I swear,' announced Monipodio, 'that cowardly thug is not to set foot in this place until he has done public penance for the crime he has committed. How dare he lay a finger on Cariharta's face, let alone the rest of her body!! For she can compete with Gananciosa here in purity of body and earning power, and I can't pay her a greater com-pliment than that.'

'Hush!' protested Juliana at that point, 'don't say anything bad about that wretch; for however bad he is I love him more than I can say, and the things my friend Gananciosa has said in his favour have helped me to recover my spirits and, to tell you the truth, I've a mind to go and look for him.'

'If you take my advice, you won't do that,' countered Gananciosa, 'because he'll come up with some tall story, give himself airs, and walk all over you. Relax, sister, for before long you'll see him here as contrite as you like, and if he doesn't come, we'll write him a letter in verse to annoy him.'

'Oh, yes,' exclaimed Cariharta, 'for I've got a thousand things to write to him.'

'I'll act as secretary, when necessary,' said Monipodio, 'for although I'm no poet, if a man rolls up his sleeves he'll produce a couple of thousand couplets in next to no time. And if they don't turn out all that well, I've got a barber friend who'll churn out the rhymes for us at any hour of the day. For the present, however, let's finish the meal we began, and everything will take its course afterwards.'

Juliana was happy to obey her leader, and so they all resumed their feasting and were soon scraping the bottom of the basket and draining the dregs in the wineskin. The old men drank like fish, the youths drank hard, and the ladies drank deep. The old men begged leave to depart and Monipodio immediately granted their request, charging them to report back anything they saw of use or advantage to the community. They replied that the matter was in capable hands, and they left.

Rinconete, who was by nature inquisitive, after first begging everyone's pardon and requesting permission to speak, asked Monipodio what contribution such venerable, dignified, and distinguished-looking people made to the fraternity. Monipodio replied that in the jargon and parlance of their community they were known as hornets, and it was their task to hover around the city during the day in search of houses that could be broken into at night. It was also part of their job to follow the men who carried money from the Board of Trade or the Mint to wherever it was being taken or deposited. Once they were in possession of these facts, they would test the thickness of the walls of the relevant house and mark the best place for burrowing—boring holes—in order to gain entry. In short, he said, they were among the most useful, if not the most useful, members of the fraternity, and they received a fifth of everything that was stolen as a result of their conscientiousness, just as the king was entitled to his share from the public coffers. In addition, they were very honest, upstanding men, who lived decent, respectable, God-fearing lives, and since they also feared for their consciences they attended Mass on a daily basis with extraordinary fervour.

'And some of these men are so obliging, especially the two who have just left, settling for much less than our list of tariffs entitles them to. Another pair are removal men, and since they are constantly moving house for their customers, they know their way in and out of every property in the city and which ones may be of use to us and which ones wouldn't.'

'A splendid arrangement,' said Rinconete, 'and I should like myself to be useful to such a first-rate fraternity.'

'Heaven always favours worthy desires,' said Monipodio.

While they were engaged in this conversation there was a knock at the door; Monipodio went out to see who it was and in answer to his question he heard this response: 'Open up, Mr Monipodio, it's me, Repolido.'

When Cariharta heard his voice she began raising her own, shouting loudly, 'Don't let him in, Mr Monipodio, don't let that sailor from Tarpeya, that tiger from Ocaña, in.'*

This did not prevent Monipodio from opening the door for Repolido; but when Cariharta saw that he was letting him in, she leapt to her feet and ran into the room where the shields were stored. Shutting herself in, she screamed from the other side of the door, 'Get that good-for-nothing out of my sight, keep that slaughterer of innocents and scourge of gentle doves away from me!'

Maniferro and Chiquiznaque restrained Repolido, who was bent on going into the room where Cariharta was hiding, but since they would not let him, he called to her from outside, 'That's enough, my angry love, for goodness' sake, calm down and you'll find yourself a married woman!'

'Me, married, you rotter?' was Cariharta's reply. 'He's singing a different tune now! You mean married to you, I suppose, when I'd rather be married to a pile of dead and rotting bones!'

'Come now, silly,' cajoled Repolido, 'let's stop this quarrelling and don't go getting ideas because I'm talking so gentle and I've come to you so meek; because, as God lives, if I blow my top, you'll fall harder the second time than you did the first! Don't get on your high horse with me. Let's all swallow our pride and not play into the devil's hands.'

'I'd play any game he likes,' retorted Cariharta, 'if he'd spirit you away some place where I never have to lay eyes on you again.'

'Haven't I warned you, wench?' said Repolido. 'Ye gods, I'm

running out of patience and I'm going to let rip and to hell with the consequences.'

This outburst prompted Monipodio to intervene: 'I'll not tolerate insolence in my presence; Cariharta will come out, not because she's being threatened but out of respect for me, and everything will end well. For squabbles among those who really love one another make the pleasure greater when peace is declared. Juliana! Child! My dear Cariharta! Come on out, for my sake, for I'll make Repolido get down on his knees and beg for mercy.'

'If he's prepared to do that,' commented Escalanta, 'we'll all be on his side and beg Juliana to come on out.'

'If this act of submission is about making me look silly in the eyes of my fellows,' pointed out Repolido, 'I won't submit to a whole army of rogues, but if it's about pleasing Cariharta, I won't stop at going down on my knees, I'll be her slave and knock a nail in my forehead.'

Chiquiznaque and Maniferro laughed when they heard Repolido say this, but he became so angry, thinking that they were making fun of him, that bursting with indignation he exclaimed, 'Whoever laughs or thinks of laughing at what Cariharta has said against me, or what I've said against her, or what either of us has said about the other, I swear that he's a liar and will be a liar every time he laughs or thinks of laughing, as I've already made clear.'

Chiquiznaque and Maniferro exchanged such ominous glances that Monipodio realized that something awful would happen if he didn't do something about it and so, positioning himself between them and Repolido, he said, 'Let this matter go no further, gentlemen; let the threats cease and die on your lips; and since the ones that have already been voiced have not touched our sword belts, then no one need take them personally.'

'We are quite confident', replied Chiquiznaque, 'that such warnings were not uttered for our benefit, nor will they ever be; because if we imagined that they were said with us in mind, then "the tambourine is in a hand that knows how to play it".'

'We've got another tambourine here, Mr Chiquiznaque,' retorted Repolido, 'and should it become necessary, we can also ring bells, and as I've already said, if anyone's amused, he's a liar, and if anyone's got other ideas, let him meet me outside and I'll show him what's what and who's boss.'

With these words, he made for the main door. Cariharta had been listening to him, and when she heard that he was leaving in a foul mood, she came out saying, 'Stop him, don't let him go or he'll be up to his old tricks. Can't you see the mood he's in and he's a Judas Mackerel* when it comes to courage. Come back, bravest of the brave and hero of my heart.'

When she got close enough she grabbed his cloak firmly and, with Monipodio also going to her aid, they held him back. Chiquiznaque and Maniferro did not know whether to be angry or not, and so waited quietly to see what Repolido would do. Seeing that Cariharta and Monipodio were begging him to stay, he turned round saying, 'Friends should never annoy their friends, nor make fun of them, especially when they see that their friends are annoyed.'

'There's no friend here', replied Maniferro, 'who wants to annoy or make fun of any other friend; and since we're all friends, let's shake hands like friends.'

Monipodio added, 'Spoken like true friends, and as such shake hands all round.'

They did so immediately and, removing one of her clogs, Escalanta began to beat a rhythm with it as if it were a drum. Gananciosa picked up a new palm-leaf broom which happened to be lying around and by strumming it she produced a sound which, though harsh and strident, harmonized with that of the clog. Monipodio broke a plate into two pieces and, holding them between his fingers and clicking them lightly like castanets, he added to the rhythm of the clog and the broom.

Rinconete and Cortadillo were astonished at this novel employment of the broom, because they had never seen anyone use it that way before. Maniferro recognized their astonishment and said, 'Does the broom surprise you? That's only natural, for nowhere in the world has anyone invented such spontaneous, light-hearted and cheap music. In fact, I heard a student say only the other day that not even Morphous,* who led Aridice from the Underworld, nor Marion,* who climbed on to the dolphin's back and escaped from the sea as if he were some gentleman on a hired mule, nor the other great musician* who founded a city with one hundred gates and an equal number of posterns, ever invented a better brand of music. It's so easy to pick up, so catchy to play, so free of frets, pegs, and strings and the need to be tuned. I swear they say it was invented by some fellow of this city who fancies himself as some musical Hector.'*

'I can well believe that,' replied Repolido, 'but let's listen to what our own musicians want to sing, for it looks as if Gananciosa has cleared her throat, a sure sign that she wants to sing.'

That was indeed the case, because Monipodio had asked her to sing a few of those *seguidillas** which were so popular. However, it was Escalanta who sang the first note, in a thin and trembling voice:

> My heart's been singed by a lad from Seville,
> With his thatch of red hair and fat Walloon frill.

Gananciosa took up the song:

> Mistaken is she who says she'll not fall
> For the man dressed in green, dark, handsome, and tall.

Then Monipodio, keeping time with his furiously clicking castanets, intoned:

> When two lovers fall out and then make their peace,
> A measure of wrath will their pleasure increase.

Cariharta did not want to enjoy herself in silence and so, taking another clog, she began to dance and join the other women in singing:

> Enough, angry love, put the whip down, I pray,
> For when you scourge me, it's your own flesh you flay.

'Sing in plain language,' protested Repolido at that point, 'and leave'istory well alone, for there's no need to go dredging that up. Let bygones be bygones, change the subject and that's that.'

Having just struck up their song, they were in no mood to stop when they heard an urgent knock at the door and Monipodio went to see who it was. The look-out told him that the Justice of the Peace had just turned into the end of the street and that ahead of him Tordillo and Cernícalo, two constables who were not open to their bribes, were coming this way. When those assembled inside heard this news, they flew into such a panic that Cariharta and Escalanta put their clogs on back to front, Gananciosa abandoned her broom and Monipodio his castanets, and the lively music was replaced by an anxious silence. Chiquiznaque fell silent, Repolido stood stock still and gaping, and Maniferro held his breath. Then, suddenly, scattering in all directions, they disappeared on to the terraces and rooftops to get away and gain access to other streets. No unexpected gunfire or sudden clap of thunder has ever startled a flock of doves caught unawares as much as the news of the impending approach of the Justice of the Peace filled all the worthy people in that assembled company with horror and panic. The two novices, Rinconete and Cortadillo, had no idea what to do with themselves, so they stayed where they were and waited to see how that sudden storm would end. It turned out to be no more than a storm in a teacup when the lookout came back to say that the Justice of the Peace had walked on past, without showing the slightest sign of suspecting anything at all.

While he was giving this information to Monipodio a young gentleman arrived in the doorway, dressed up to the nines, as the saying goes. Monipodio came back in with him and ordered Chiquiznaque, Maniferro, and Repolido to be summoned down, but no one else. Since Rinconete and Cortadillo had remained in the courtyard they could hear the whole of the conversation that took place between Monipodio and the gentleman who had just arrived. The latter asked Monipodio why the work he had commissioned him to do had been carried out so badly. Monipodio replied that he did not yet know how it had been done, but the agent to whom the commission had been entrusted was there and would give a very good account of himself. At that moment Chiquiznaque came down and Monipodio asked him if he had fulfilled the contract for the fourteen-stitch knifing commissioned to him.

'Which one's that?' asked Chiquiznaque. 'The one on the merchant at the crossroads?'

'That's the one,' replied the gentleman.

'Well, what happened there,' replied Chiquiznaque, 'is that I waited for him last night in his doorway and he came back before prayers. I went up close and took a good look at his face but could see that it was so small that it was totally impossible to fit a fourteen-stitch slash on it. When I realized that I couldn't fulfil the terms of the contract and follow my destructions . . .'

'You must mean *instructions*,' interrupted the gentleman, 'and not *destructions*.'

'That's what I meant,' replied Chiquiznaque. 'I was saying that when I realized that the proposed length of slash would not fit on to that small, narrow face, I knifed one of his lackeys instead, so that my journey would not be in vain and because I was sure of fitting it in because the target area was larger.'

'But I would have preferred you to give the master a sevenstitcher', replied the gentleman, 'than his servant the full four-teener. So, in effect, you've not carried out the commission properly; but it doesn't matter. I shan't miss the thirty ducados I left as a deposit. I bid you good morning.'

With these words, he removed his hat and turned round to leave; but Monipodio grabbed his tweed cloak and said, 'Hold on there a moment and keep your part of the bargain, good sir, for we've kept ours most honourably and efficiently. You owe us twenty ducados, and you'll not leave here unless you produce them, or some posses-sion of equal value.'

'So, this is what you call keeping your side of the bargain, is it?' protested the gentleman. 'Knifing the servant when you should have knifed the master?'

'This gentleman's really on the ball!' exclaimed Chiquiznaque. 'It looks like he's forgotten that proverb that goes: "Love me, love my dog."'

'How on earth can that proverb be relevant here?' asked the gentleman.

'Well, isn't it the same', Chiquiznaque expounded, 'as saying "Hate me, hate my dog"? It's like this, I'm the merchant and you hate me, my servant's my dog and by having a go at the dog you're getting at me. The debt is paid and the commission honoured appro-priately, so all that remains is for you to pay up right now and without haggling over prices.'

'I fully endorse that,' added Monipodio, 'and in all that you said, Chiquiznaque my friend, you took the words right out of my mouth. So, my fine fellow, don't go splitting hairs with your humble ser-vants and friends, just take my advice and pay up for work com-pleted. If you wish us to give the master another one, as big as his face can cope with, consider the wound as already receiving medical attention.'

'If that's so,' replied the dashing young fellow, 'then I will most willingly and gladly pay for both jobs in full.'

'You can be as certain of this as you can of being a Christian, that Chiquiznaque will give him a scar that suits his face so well, it'll look as if he were born with it.'

'With this assurance and promise, then,' replied the gentleman, 'take this chain to guarantee the twenty ducados already owing and the forty I'm offering for the knifing still to come. It's worth a thousand reales and it may well remain in your possession, because I suspect that another fourteen stitches will be needed before long.'

As he said this he removed a delicate chain from round his neck and gave it to Monipodio, who from its colour and weight realized that it was no cheap imitation. Monipodio received it with great pleasure and civility, for he was extremely well mannered. The commission was entrusted to Chiquiznaque, who set that very night as his deadline. The gentleman left well satisfied and Monipodio then summoned all those who had absented themselves in their alarm. They all came down and Monipodio positioned himself in the middle of them. He took out a notebook which he carried around in the hood of his cloak and gave it to Rinconete to read, for he was unable to read it himself. Rinconete opened it up and on the first page read the following heading:

'List of slashings to be carried out this week: Number one: on the merchant at the crossroads: price fifty escudos; thirty received in advance. Agent: Chiquiznaque.'

'I don't think there are any others, son,' said Monipodio. 'Move on and look for the heading: "List of beatings."'

Rinconete turned the page and saw 'List of beatings' written on the next one. Lower down the page it said: 'For the taverner in Alfalfa Square, twelve of the best, at an escudo a time. Eight escudos advanced. Deadline: six days. Agent: Maniferro.'

'You might as well cross that item off the list,' said Maniferro, 'because I'll see to that one tonight.'

'Are there any more, son?' enquired Monipodio.

'Yes, one more,' replied Rinconete, which reads like this: "For the hunchbacked tailor, nicknamed the Linnet, six of the best, at the request of the lady who left the necklace. Agent: Desmochado."'

'I'm surprised', remarked Monipodio, 'that item is still listed. Desmochado must certainly be out of action, because it's two days past the deadline and he's done nothing about this job.'

'I bumped into him yesterday,' said Maniferro, 'and he told me that since the hunchback was laid up sick, he hadn't carried out his duty.'

'I can well believe that,' said Monipodio, 'because I consider Desmochado such a good agent, that if it weren't for this just impediment, he'd already have carried out greater tasks. Anything else, laddie?'

'No, sir,' replied Rinconete.

'Then move on,' said Monipodio, 'and look where it says "List of common offences."'

Rinconete moved on through the book and found this heading on the following page: 'List of common offences, namely: hitting over the head with a bottle, daubing with juniper oil,* making people wear sanbenitos and horns,* tauntings and frighteners, disturbing the peace, mock stabbings, spreading slander, etc.'

'What does it say underneath?' asked Monipodio.

'It says,' replied Rinconete, '"daubing with juniper oil in the house of . . ."'

'Don't read out which house, for I know which one it is,' replied Monipodio, 'and I'm the driving force and agent in that particular piece of child's play and four escudos have already been advanced out of a total of eight.'

'That's correct,' said Rinconete, 'for it's all written down here and further down it says: "Sticking horns on people."'

'Don't read that address out either,' warned Monipodio. 'It's enough to commit the offence against them, without announcing it in public; which is a great burden on the old conscience. Speaking for myself, at least, I would rather stick on a hundred horns and as many sanbenitos, as long as I got paid for it, than mention it just once, even to the mother who brought me into the world.'

'The agent for this one', continued Rinconete, 'is Narigueta.'

'That's already been done and paid for,' said Monipodio. 'Look to see whether there's anything else, for unless I'm mistaken, there should be a twenty-escudo frightener in there somewhere. Half the fee's paid already and the agent is the whole community and we've got the whole of this month to do it in. Our orders will be carried out in full, without cutting any corners, and it will be one of the greatest events to take place in this city for a very long time. Give me the book, boy, for I know that there's nothing else and I also know that business is very slack at the moment. But things will get better and then we'll have more than enough to keep us busy. For the wind can't blow a leaf on a tree unless God wills it, and it's not our place to force anyone to take revenge, all the more because every man likes to be his own boss and doesn't want to pay someone else to do a job which he's perfectly capable of doing with his own two hands.'

'That's right,' agreed Repolido. 'But what do you order and

command us to do now, Mr Monipodio? For it's getting late and hotter by the minute.'

'What you must all do,' replied Monipodio, 'is go to your posts and not do any change-overs until Sunday, then we'll reconvene in this same place again for a share-out of whatever's come our way, without offending anyone. Rinconete the Good and Cortadillo are assigned the district from Torre de Oro, outside the city limits, as far as the gate of the Alcázar, where they can have a sit-down while working their card-tricks. For I've seen less talented players walk off every day with more than twenty reales in copper coinage, not to mention silver, with just one deck, and that was with four cards missing. Ganchoso will show them where this district is, and even if you wander as far as San Sebastián and San Telmo it doesn't really matter, although it's only fair that no one should encroach on anyone else's territory.'

They both kissed his hand to thank him for the favour he did them and promised to do the job efficiently and loyally and to be very vigilant and on their guard. Then, from the hood of his cloak Monipodio took out a folded piece of paper on which was written the list of the brethren, and he told Rinconete to sign his name on it. Since there was no inkwell to hand he gave it to Rinconete to take with him, so that he could write the following details at the first pharmacist's shop he came to: 'Rinconete and Cortadillo, brethren; probationary year: none; Rinconete, card-sharp; Cortadillo: thief, and the day, month and year, but omitting the names of parents and place of origin.' While Monipodio was reciting these instructions one of the elderly 'hornets' came in and said,

'I've come to tell you how this very minute I bumped into Lobillo, the one from Málaga, and he claims that he's so improved his game that he could wipe the floor with the devil himself even with a clean pack of cards. Because he's been knocked about a bit lately he won't come and report straightaway and pay his usual homage, but he'll be here on Sunday without fail.'

'I've always reckoned', said Monipodio, 'that this Lobillo fellow would be in a class of his own, because he's got the deftest and most nimble-fingered pair of hands for playing cards that you could wish for. To be good at your job, it's as essential to have good tools to work with as it is to have the brains to learn the basic rules.'

'I also bumped into the Jew,' said the old man, 'in one of the lodging houses on the Calle de Tintores. He was dressed up like a priest and had taken lodgings there because a little bird had told him that two fellows who'd come back rich from Peru are staying in the same place and he wanted to see whether he could get a game of cards out of them, even for low stakes, because great oaks from little acorns grow. He also says that he'll be sure to be at the meeting on Sunday and he'll give a full report of what he's been up to.'

'That Jew,' said Monipodio, 'is another great thief and really knows his stuff. I haven't seen him for days and that's bad form. I swear that if he doesn't mend his ways, I'll smash his head in, for the lying thief is no more ordained than a Turk and he knows less Latin than my mother. What else's new?'

'Nothing,' replied the old man, 'at least that I know of.'

'Very well then,' said Monipodio, 'take this pittance,' and he shared close on forty reales among them. 'I want you all back here on Sunday, for our earnings will be here in full.'

They all thanked him. Repolido and Cariharta hugged one another again, while Escalanta embraced Maniferro and Gananciosa turned her attention on Chiquiznaque. They all agreed, once the business of the house was done, to meet up at Pipota's. Monipodio said that he would also be going, to examine the contents of the laundry basket, and that afterwards he had to go and perform the juniper job and cross it off the list. He embraced Rinconete and Cortadillo and sent them on their way with his blessing, urging them not to lodge in one place or work the same area for very long, in the interests of everyone's health and wealth. Ganchoso went with them to introduce them to their patch, reminding them not to miss Sunday's meeting, for he was convinced that Monipodio was going to deliver a lecture on matters relating to their trade. Then he went off, leaving the two friends amazed at what they had witnessed.

In spite of his youth, Rinconete was a very bright and good-natured lad, and since he had accompanied his father in the papal bull trade, he was not unfamiliar with the correct use of language. He laughed aloud when he remembered the words he had heard spoken by Monipodio and the rest of his godly company and community. He laughed even louder when he recalled how instead of saying 'by way of suffrage' he had said 'by way of salvage', and instead of 'stipend' he had come out with 'stupendous', to describe what they were stealing, or how Cariharta said that Repolido was a sailor from Tarpeya and a tiger from Ocaña, instead of Hircania, along with a thousand other malapropisms like these and some that were even worse. He was especially amused to recall how she had said that heaven would accept the effort she had put into earning her twenty-four reales as a discount against her sins.

Above all, he was astonished at how certain and confident they were that they would go to heaven as long as they did not neglect their devotions, while their lives were dedicated to robbery, murder, and crimes against God. He also laughed at the old girl, Pipota, who had left the stolen basket of laundry under lock and key at home while she went to light candles before her precious statues and, by doing so, thought she would get to heaven clothed and shod. He was no less astonished by the obedience and respect that they all showed towards Monipodio, despite his being a vulgar and heartless barbarian.

Rinconete thought about what he had read in Monipodio's notebook and the activities in which they were engaged. In short, he was shocked by the laxity of law and order in that famous city, whose inhabitants made virtually no attempt to hide their wicked and monstrous ways. He resolved to advise his companion that they should not remain long in that God-forsaken environment which was so evil, dangerous, libertine, and corrupt. Yet, in spite of this resolution, led astray by his immaturity and lack of experience, he stayed on for several months longer. During this time things happened to him which demand a more lengthy exposition. So we must leave for another occasion the account of his life and miracles, together with those of his master Monipodio and the other members of that infamous academy, all of which will be of great consequence and serve as an example and warning to all who read them.

THE GLASS GRADUATE

While two gentlemen students were walking along the banks of the River Tormes they found, asleep beneath a tree, a boy of no more than eleven dressed in peasant clothing. They instructed a servant to wake him: he duly woke up and they asked him where he was from and what he was doing sleeping in that lonely place. To these questions the boy replied that he had forgotten where he was from and that he was going to Salamanca in search of a master whom he could serve in return for the opportunity to study there. They asked him if he could read and he replied that he could read and also write.

'In that case,' said one of the gentlemen, 'it is not lack of memory that has made you forget where you are from.'

'Be that as it may,' replied the boy, 'no one shall know where I am from or who my parents are until I am able to honour both the place and the people.'

'And how do you plan to honour them?' asked the other gentleman.

'Through my studies,' replied the boy, 'by becoming famous for my learning. For I've heard it said that even bishops are mortal men.'

This reply prompted the two gentlemen to receive him into their employ and to take him with them, which they did, thus giving him the opportunity to study in that university. The boy said his name was Tomás Rodaja, and from his manner of dress his masters inferred that he must be the son of some poor peasant. Within a few days they had dressed him in the black garb of the student and within a few weeks Tomás had shown signs of possessing a rare intellect. Yet all the while he served his masters so loyally, conscientiously, and diligently that without neglecting his studies for a moment he still managed to give the impression that he dedicated himself solely to their service. Since the faithful attendance of the servant inspires his master to treat him well, Tomás Rodaja was no longer the servant of his masters but their companion. In short, in the eight years he remained with them he became so famous in the university for his fine intellect and remarkable ability that he was esteemed and beloved by all kinds of people. His main subject of study was law, but the discipline in which he distinguished himself best was the humanities. He possessed such a formidable memory and it was so enlightened by his good judgement and breadth of mind that he was no less famous for the one than for the other.

The time eventually arrived for his masters to complete their studies and return home to one of the finest cities in Andalusia. They took Tomás with them and he stayed with them for a few days, but since he was tormented by his longing to return to his studies and to Salamanca—which casts a spell on all those who have enjoyed the pleasures of living there and compels them to go back—he asked his masters for permission to return. They, being obliging and liberal men, granted his request and provided him with the means to support himself for three years.

Expressing his gratitude in his departing words, he bade them farewell and left Málaga—for this was his masters' homeland. As he descended the hill from Zambra *en route* to Antequera he came upon a gentleman on horseback, who was dressed in colourful travelling clothes and accompanied by two servants who were also on horseback. Riding along with him he discovered that he was making the same journey. They decided to travel together and, conversing on a number of subjects, it was not long before Tomás revealed his rare intellect and the other gentleman his gallant and courteous manner. The latter explained that he was an infantry captain in His Majesty's army and that his ensign was recruiting men in the Salamanca region. He praised the military profession as a way of life; he vividly described to him the beauty of the city of Naples, the fun to be had in Palermo, the prosperity of Milan, the feasts of Lombardy, and the splendid food of the hostelries there. He charmingly and precisely imitated the way the soldiers said: 'Here, landlord; this way, you scoundrel; bring us *maccatella*, *polastri*,* and *macaroni*.' He praised to the skies the freedoms of the soldier and the free and easy ways of Italy. He said nothing, however, about the chill of sentry duty, the danger of attack, the horror of battle, the hunger of sieges, the devastation of land mines, and other hardships of this nature. For there are some who regard and accept them as additional burdens of the military life, while in actual fact they are the sum and substance of the soldier's lot. In short, the captain told him so much and did it so eloquently that the wisdom of our Tomás Rodaja began to falter and his will to lean towards that kind of life, where death is always close at hand.

The captain, whose name was don Diego de Valdivia, was delighted with Tomás's pleasant bearing, intelligence, and easygoing manner. He asked him to accompany him to Italy, if he felt so inclined, to satisfy his curiosity to see it. He added that he could offer him a seat at his table and, if it were necessary, his company's flag to serve under since his ensign was to quit the post soon. Tomás did not take much persuading before he accepted the invitation, reasoning with himself there and then that it would be a good idea to see Italy, Flanders, and other different lands and countries because long journeys make men wise. He also calculated that, being so young, he could afford to spend three or four years in this endeavour and that at the end of them he would still not be too old to resume his studies. As if everything were destined to accommodate his wishes, he told the captain that he would be happy to go with him to Italy, but on one condition: that he did not have to serve as ensign or enlist as a soldier, because he did not want to be committed to a flag. The captain told him that it would be of no consequence to enlist, and by doing so he would enjoy the allowances and pay allotted to the company, since he would give him leave whenever he requested it.

'That', said Tomás, 'would be to act against my conscience and your own: therefore I would prefer to be independent than under any obligation.'

'Such a scrupulous conscience', said don Diego, 'is more suited to a monk than a soldier. But be that as it may, we are now comrades.'

They arrived that evening at Antequera, and by spending many hours on the road it took them only a few days to reach the place where the newly formed company had halted. It had begun to make its way to Cartagena, quartering with four other companies in the villages they encountered along their route. It was there that Tomás observed the authority of the commissaries, the irritability of some of the captains, the solicitude of the billeting officers, the hard work and importance of the paymasters, the protests of the villages, the trading of billets, the irreverent behaviour of the new recruits, the quarrels among the hosts, the excessive baggage requests, and ultimately, the almost unavoidable necessity of doing all these things that Tomás observed but could not approve.

Shedding the uniform of the student, Tomás had put on a flamboyant costume and now cut quite a dash, as the saying goes. Of the many books he had with him he retained only the *Hours of Our Lady* and a *Garcilaso* without commentary,* which he carried in the pockets of his breeches. They reached Cartagena more quickly than they would have wished, for billet life is full of incident and variety and each new day brings some fresh novelty and pleasure.

There they boarded four galleys that were going to Naples and there too Tomás observed the peculiar way of life aboard those sea-going dwellings, where most of the time you are tormented by bugs, robbed by the galley-slaves, annoyed by the sailors, devoured by the rats, and exhausted by the motion of the waves. Tomás was terrified by the violent squalls and storms, especially in the Gulf of Lyons where they encountered two, one of which drove them towards Corsica while the other pushed them back to Toulon in France. Finally, deprived of sleep, soaked to the skin, and bleary-eyed, they reached the lovely and most beautiful city of Genoa. They disembarked in its sheltered harbour, and after visiting a church the captain and all his fellow soldiers entered an inn where they forgot the squalls of the past in the revelry of the present.

There they became acquainted with the smoothness of the Trebbiano, the full-bodied flavour of the Montefiascone, the strength of the Asperino, the generosity of the two Greek wines Candia and Soma, the grandeur of the Cinco Viñas, the sweetness and mellowness of the Vernaccia, the simplicity of the Centola, while the lowly Roman wines dared not appear in such illustrious company. After their host had listed all these different wines he then offered to display before them, without recourse to magic or any form of illusion, the genuine and authentic Madrigal, Coca, Alaejos, and Ciudad Real (in reality more imperial than merely royal), sanctum of the god of laughter. He also offered Esquivias, Alanís, Cazalla, Guadalcanal and Membrilla, not forgetting Ribadavia and Descargamaría.* In short, their host named and presented them with more wines than Bacchus himself could have stored in his own cellar.

Our good Tomás also marvelled at the blond hair of the Genoese ladies, the gallantry and elegant manners of the gentlemen, and the stunning beauty of the city where the houses look as if they have been mounted in the rocks, like diamonds in gold. The following day all the companies destined for Piedmont disembarked but Tomás did not wish to make that journey, preferring instead to go overland from there to Rome and Naples, which is what he did. He decided to return via the great city of Venice and Loreto to Milan and

Piedmont, where don Diego de Valdivia said he would find him if they had not been carried off to Flanders by then, as rumour suggested they might.

Tomás took his leave of the captain two days later and in another five he arrived in Florence after first visiting Luca, a small but very well-appointed town in which Spaniards are more favourably regarded and more warmly received than in other parts of Italy. He was delighted with Florence, not merely because of its pleasing situation, but because of its cleanness, its splendid buildings, its cool river, and peaceful streets. He remained there for four days and then he went to Rome, sovereign among cities and mistress of the whole world. He visited its shrines, worshipped its relics, and admired its grandeur. Just as one recognizes the size and ferocity of a lion by its claws, so Tomás measured Rome's greatness by its marble ruins, its damaged and intact statues, its fallen arches, the remains of its baths, its magnificent porticoes and amphitheatres, and its famous and holy river, which always fills its banks with water and blesses them with countless relics from the bodies of martyrs buried there. He also measured it by its bridges, which seem to be watching one another, and by its thoroughfares, the very names of which make them superior to all other streets in any other city anywhere in the world: the via Appia, Flaminia, Julia, and other equally prestigious sites. He was no less impressed by the topography of the hills within the city limits themselves: the Caelian, the Quirinal and the Vatican,* together with the other four whose names bear witness to the greatness and majesty of Rome. He also observed the authority of the College of Cardinals, the majesty of the Supreme Pontiff, and the crowds and variety of people and nationalities. He saw, observed, and made a careful note of everything. When he had made a tour of the seven churches, confessed to a penitentiary, kissed the foot of His Holiness, and provisioned himself with an ample stock of *agnus deis** and rosary beads, he decided to go to Naples. Since the weather was changeable at that time of year, and therefore unpleasant and unhealthy for anyone entering or leaving Rome overland, Tomás took a boat to Naples. There the sense of wonder that still lingered after seeing the sights of Rome was reinforced by the marvel of seeing Naples; a city which, in his opinion and that of everyone who has ever been there, was the finest in Europe and perhaps even the whole world.

From there he went to Sicily and saw Palermo and then Messina;

he admired the general situation and beauty of Palermo, the port at Messina, and the island as a whole he admired for the richness of its produce, for which it is rightly and appropriately called the grain-basket of Italy. He returned to Naples and Rome and from there he went on to Our Lady of Loreto,* at whose shrine he could see nothing of the inner or outer walls because they were covered with crutches, shrouds, chains, shackles, manacles, hair-pieces, wax busts, paintings, and altar-pieces, which testified to the infinite mercies which many had received from the hand of God as a result of the intercession of his divine Mother. For God wanted to enhance and give authority to that holy image through many miracles, as a reward for the devotion it inspired in those who adorned the walls of her house with these and other tokens. Tomás saw the very room and chamber where the most exalted and significant message* was delivered, witnessed but not comprehended by all the heavens, all the angels, and all those who dwelt in the eternal realms.

Embarking at Ancona he sailed to Venice, a city which would have no equal anywhere in the world if Columbus had never been born. Thanks be to heaven and the worthy Hernando Cortés who conquered the great city of Mexico so that the great city of Venice should, in some sense, have a rival. These two famous cities are alike in that their streets are water; the European city is a wonder of the ancient world while the American city is a marvel of the New. It seemed to Tomás that its riches were limitless: it was governed wisely, its position was impregnable, its prosperity was great, and its surroundings were delightful. In short, the whole city and its individual parts deserved the fame and reputation which they enjoyed throughout the world. The sumptuous architecture of its famous arsenal, where galleys and countless other vessels were built, only served to confirm the truth of its reputation.

The pleasures and distractions which our curious traveller discovered in Venice were almost as compelling as those of Calypso,* for they virtually made him forget his original plans. Once he had spent a month there, however, he returned via Ferrara, Parma, and Piacenza to Milan, the forge of Vulcan and envy of the Kingdom of France; in short, a city which, it is claimed, makes its promises and keeps them. It owes its magnificence to its grandiose proportions and those of its cathedral and the fact that it possesses in abundance everything necessary to sustain human life. From there he moved to

Asti, and arrived the day before the regiment was due to depart for Flanders.

He was very warmly received by his friend the captain and travelled in his company to Flanders and then to Antwerp, a city no less worthy of admiration than those he had visited in Italy. He saw Ghent and Brussels and observed that the whole country was preparing to take up arms to go on campaign the following summer.

Now that Tomás had satisfied the urge which had prompted him to see what he had seen, he decided to return to Spain and complete his studies at Salamanca. As soon as he made this decision he put it into action, to the very great regret of his companion, who urged him, when he was about to leave, to inform him of his health, safe arrival, and what he was doing. Tomás promised to do what he asked and travelled back to Spain through France without visiting Paris, since there was fighting there. In short, he reached Salamanca where he was warmly received by his friends, with whose support he continued his studies and eventually graduated in law.

It was at that time that a wily and artful lady happened to arrive in the city. All the birds in the neighbourhood immediately flocked to the bait and fell into her snare, and there was not a student in the place who did not pay her a visit. They told Tomás that this lady claimed to have been to Italy and Flanders, and so in order to find out whether he knew her, he paid her a visit. The consequence of this encounter was that she fell in love with Tomás but he, unaware of the effect he had had on her, would not have set foot in her house again if he had not been dragged there by others. To cut a long story short, she revealed her feelings to him and offered him her worldly wealth. However, since he was more attached to his books than to other forms of entertainment, he did not return the lady's affections in the slightest. When she saw herself scorned and, in her own eyes, despised, and realized that she could not conquer the resistance of Tomás's will by any common or ordinary means, she resolved to seek out other methods which she considered more effective and capable of satisfying her desires. So, on the advice of a Moorish woman she gave Tomás a so-called love potion in a Toledan quince, believing that it gave her the power to force his will to love her, as if there existed in the world some herb or spell or incantation capable of bending our free will. The people who administer such love-inducing drinks and aphrodisiac foods are known as poisoners, for they do no less than poison the people who eat and drink them, as experience has demonstrated on many different occasions.

Tomás ate the quince at such a fateful moment that he immediately began to shake from head to foot as if he were having a fit, and lost consciousness for many hours, at the end of which he regained his senses but seemed to have lost his wits. He stuttered and stammered that a quince he had eaten had killed him and he named the person who had given it to him. When the officers of the law were informed of the incident they went in search of the culprit. She, however, seeing how badly her plan had gone awry, had made herself scarce and was never seen again.

Tomás remained in bed for six months, during which time he lost so much weight that he was nothing but skin and bones, as the saying goes, and showed signs of having completely lost his senses. Although he received every available treatment, the sickness of his body was cured but not that of his mind. For although he was restored to physical health he was afflicted with the strangest form of madness ever witnessed. The unfortunate soul believed that he was made completely of glass, and under this delusion he would scream in the most alarming way whenever anyone approached him, begging and imploring them with eloquent words and arguments not to come any closer, because they would break him: for he really and truly was unlike other men, because he was made of glass from head to foot.

In order to shake him out of this delusion, many people ignored his shouts and pleas and, grabbing hold of him, they would put their arms round him and draw his attention to the fact that he was not in fact breaking. However, all they achieved by doing this was to make the poor wretch scream wildly and throw himself on the ground, where he would faint away and remain in that state for at least four hours. When he did recover it was only to renew his pleas and entreaties that they should not approach him again. He told them to speak to him from a distance and ask whatever questions they liked, for he would reply to each and every one of them with greater understanding, because he was a man of glass rather than flesh. For since glass was a fine and delicate substance his mind could function more quickly and efficiently in it than in a conventional body which was made of denser and earthier stuff.

Some members of the public wanted to test the truth of what he claimed and proceeded to ask him many difficult questions, to which he gave spontaneous and highly intelligent answers. This phenomenon amazed the most learned scholars in the university as well as the professors of medicine and philosophy, who were perplexed to see that in a single subject such a rare delusion as to believe you were made of glass could coexist with so fine an intellect that it was able to reply to any question correctly and intelligently.

Tomás asked them to give him some kind of covering to protect the fragile vessel of his body, so that he would not break by dressing in tight clothing. So they gave him a dun-coloured robe and a very loose shirt, which he put on very cautiously and belted with a cord made of cotton. He absolutely refused to wear shoes of any kind and instructed them to feed him by putting a basket on the end of a stick, in which they placed whatever fruit was in season at the time. He wanted neither meat nor fish; he drank only from the fountain or river and then only using his hands. When he walked through the streets he stayed in the middle of the road and kept an eye on the roofs, fearing that a tile might fall down and break him. In summer he slept in the country under the open sky and in winter he took refuge in some inn, burying himself neck deep in the hay loft, explaining that that was the most appropriate and safest bed a man of glass could wish for. Whenever there was thunder he would shake like a leaf and escape into the countryside, and would not return to the town until the storm had passed.

His friends kept him locked up for a long time, but when they realized that his unfortunate condition was not improving they decided to grant his request, which was to be allowed to move about freely. So they gave him his freedom and he went about the town, inspiring wonderment and pity in all who knew him.

Soon a group of young boys had gathered round him, but he was able to keep them at bay with his stick and he asked them to talk to him from a distance, for since he was a man of glass he was very fragile and delicate. The young boys, who are the most mischievous generation on earth, began to throw rags and even stones at him, in spite of his pleas and shouts, to see whether he was really made of glass as he claimed. He, however, screamed so desperately and became so distressed that some men were obliged to reprimand and punish the boys to stop them from throwing things at him.

Then one day, when they were annoying him a great deal, he

turned on them and said, 'What do you want of me, you tiresome boys? You keep buzzing round me like flies, you're as filthy as bed-bugs and brazen as fleas. Do you think I am Mount Testaccio,* for you to throw so many pots and tiles at me?'

Many people followed him to hear all his replies and rebukes, and the boys decided that it was more entertaining to listen to him than to throw things at him. On one occasion, while Tomás was passing through the cloth-market of Salamanca, a female draper said to him, 'My heart grieves for your misfortune, Mister Graduate, but what can I do, for I cannot weep?'

Choosing his words very carefully, he turned to her and said, 'Daughters of Jerusalem, weep for yourselves and for your children.'*

The draper's husband understood the malicious thrust of his words and said to him, 'Brother Graduate of Glass,' for this is what he called himself, 'you're more of a rogue than a madman.'

'I don't give a damn,' he replied, 'as long as nobody takes me for a fool.'

Another day, when he was passing in front of the brothel or house of ill-repute, he saw many of its residents standing in the doorway and commented that they were the baggage of Satan's army and lodging at the Inn of Hell.

One man asked him what advice or comfort he could offer a friend of his who was very sad because his wife had gone off with another man.

He replied, 'Tell him to give thanks to God for allowing his enemy to be removed from his house.'

'So, he shouldn't go and look for her?' asked the inquirer.

'By no means,' replied the Man of Glass, 'because finding her would be a lasting and reliable witness of his dishonour.'

'So, if that's the case,' replied the same inquirer, 'what shall I do to live in peace with my wife?'

The Man of Glass replied, 'Give her what she needs; let her give the orders to her domestic servants but never allow her to dictate to you.'

A boy said to him, 'Mister Glass Graduate, I want to get away from my father because he's always beating me.'

And the Glass Graduate replied, 'Take heed, child, that the beat-ings a father gives his son bring honour while those of a public executioner bring disgrace.'

Standing in a church doorway he saw a peasant of the sort who is always boasting of his Old Christian blood* go in, and behind him there followed another, who did not enjoy the same public esteem as the man in front of him. The Graduate called out loudly to the peasant, 'Domingo, wait, let Saturday go in before Sunday.'

With regard to schoolmasters he said that they were fortunate beings because they worked with angels, and they were very fortunate indeed if the angels did not have snotty noses. Someone else asked him what he thought of go–betweens. He replied that they did not live on the margins of society but next door.

News of his madness, his replies, and his sayings spread throughout Castile, and when they came to the attention of some prince or lord who was residing at Court he wanted to send for him and charged a nobleman friend of his who was in Salamanca with the task of sending him. When the said nobleman encountered Tomás one day, he said, 'The good Graduate should know that a grand personage at Court wishes to see him and has sent for him.'

To which the graduate replied, 'Your excellency must make my excuses to this lord, for I am not fit for palaces, because I have scruples and I do not know how to flatter.'

In spite of this reply the nobleman delivered him to the Court, and in order to transport him they employed the following strategy: they placed him in a wicker basket* packed with straw, of the kind used to convey glass, balancing the weight with stones and placing pieces of glass in the straw to give him the impression that they were carrying him like a glass vessel. They arrived in Valladolid* at night and unpacked him at the house of the nobleman who had sent for him, by whom he was very warmly received and who said, 'The Glass Graduate is very welcome. How was your journey? Are you well?'

To which he replied, 'No journey is bad if it comes to an end, except the journey to the scaffold. As for my health, I am neither one thing or the other, because my pulse and my brain are giving conflicting signals.'

Another day, when he had seen many falcons and hawks and other hunting birds on perches he declared that falconry was a worthy pastime for princes and great nobles; but they should be aware that in this exercise pleasure outweighed profit more than two thousand-fold. He opined that hare-hunting was very pleasurable, especially when the hounds were borrowed.

The nobleman was pleased with his madness and allowed him to go out and about in the city, guarded and protected by a man who ensured that the young boys did him no harm. In less than a week he had become a familiar figure to the young boys, and throughout the city, at every step, in every street, and on every street-corner, he replied to all the questions that were put to him. One such question came from a student who asked him whether he was a poet.

He replied, 'Up to the present time I have been neither so stupid nor so fortunate.'

'I don't understand what you mean by stupid and fortunate,' challenged the student.

The Man of Glass replied, 'I have been neither so stupid as to be a bad poet nor so fortunate as to deserve to be a good one.'

Another student asked him what he thought of poets. He replied that he held the art of poetry in high esteem, but the poets themselves he esteemed not at all. They asked him to explain why he said that. He replied that among the countless poets in existence, the good ones were so few and far between that they could scarcely be counted. Therefore, as there were no good poets, he had no regard for any of them; but he admired and revered the art of poetry because it embraced all other art forms. For poetry draws upon all other arts, at once refining them and being enhanced by them and presenting them to the world's view, thus enriching it with profit, pleasure, and wonder.

He continued, 'I know exactly how highly to esteem a good poet, because I am reminded of those lines of Ovid which say: "In former times poets were the delight of gods and kings, and the choirs of bygone ages were rewarded with rich prizes. Sacred was the majesty and venerable name of the bards of old and they often enjoyed great wealth."* I am even more mindful of the great worth of poets since Plato calls them the interpreters of the gods and Ovid says of them: "There is a god in us who stirs the fires in our hearts."* He also says: "But we poets are called soothsayers and favourites of the gods."* There is much to be said about good poets; as for the bad ones, the blabberers, what is there to say except that they are the most stupid and arrogant people in the world.'

He continued, 'What a spectacle it is to see one of those poets who has just one printing to his name when he wants to recite a sonnet to those of his circle, and the preliminaries he goes through when he says: "Pray lend an ear to a little sonnet which I composed last night for a certain occasion which, in my opinion, although it is of no consequence, possesses a certain charm." He then contorts his lips, raises his eyebrows, and rummages about in his pockets and from a dog-eared assortment of grubby papers, on which a thousand or more sonnets are scribbled, he extracts the one he wants to recite, and finally reads it out in unctuous, saccharine tones. And if by chance his audience, whether through ignorance or mischief, should fail to applaud it, he says: "Either you have not understood the sonnet or I have not read it properly. It would therefore be a good idea for me to read it again and for you to listen more carefully, for the sonnet really and truly deserves such attention." He recites it again in the same tone as before but with additional gestures and added pauses.'

'You should also see them letting fly at one another. How shall I describe the way the modern young pups bark at the dull old mastiffs of the past? I could say a thing or two about those who make snide remarks about a few excellent and worthy individuals from whom the true light of poetry shines forth and who, regarding poetry as a light relief and pleasant distraction from their many weighty labours, demonstrate the divine nature of their genius and the nobility of their ideas. They achieve this in spite of and notwithstanding the pedantic ignoramuses who pass judgement on what they do not know and despise what they cannot comprehend, and those who desire credit and esteem for the kind of stupidity that sits beneath canopies and the kind of ignorance that fawns around the seats of the mighty.'

On another occasion they asked him the reason why poets in general were poor. He replied that it was because they chose to be, since it was in their power to be rich, if they only knew how to take advantage of the opportunity that was constantly within their grasp. This was a reference to their ladies, for they were all exquisitely rich, possessing hair of gold, foreheads of burnished silver, eyes of emerald green, teeth of ivory, lips of coral, and throats of clear crystal, while the tears they shed were liquid pearls. Moreover, wherever they set foot, however hard and sterile the ground they trod upon, it would immediately flower with jasmines and roses; and their breath was pure amber, musk and civet, and all these things were signs and indications of their great wealth. He said this and other things about bad poets, but of the good ones he spoke highly and praised them to the skies.

One day he saw on the pavement in front of the Church of St Francis some badly painted images, and declared that good painters imitated nature while bad ones vomited it.

One day he approached a bookshop with very great caution in case he should get damaged, and said to the bookseller, 'I would be very happy with this business if it were not for a failing it has.'

The bookseller asked him to tell him what that might be. He replied, 'The fuss they make when they buy the copyright of a book and the trick they play on the author if he happens to be going to print at his own expense. For instead of one thousand five hundred books they print three thousand, and when the author thinks that his own works are being sold, the works of others are being despatched.'

It happened that six men who had been flogged passed through the square that same day, and when the town crier called out: 'The first, flogged for stealing', the Graduate shouted these words to the people who were standing in front of him, 'Stand aside brothers, unless you want the list to start with one of you.'

When the town crier said: 'The one at the back . . .', the Graduate added, 'He must be the one who gives his backside, I mean backing, to young boys.'

A boy said to him, 'Brother Glass, tomorrow they're going to whip a procuress.'

The Glass Graduate responded, 'If you had said they were going to whip a procurer, I would understand you to mean that they were going to whip a coachman.'

One of the men who carry sedan chairs was standing nearby, and said, 'Graduate, have you nothing to say about us?'

'No,' he replied, 'except that each and every one of you knows more sins than a confessor, but with this difference: the confessor learns his sins in order to keep them secret while you lot learn them to publicize them round the taverns.'

A mule boy heard this comment—because all sorts of people were listening to him all the time—and said, 'As for us, Mr Clever as Crystal, there is little or nothing to be said, because we're all decent people and essential to the State.'

The Glass Graduate retorted, 'A master's honour predicates that of his servant. So look at who you serve and you will see how honourable you are. You lot serve the lowest form of life to walk the earth. Once, when I was not made of glass, I rode a day's journey on a hired mule which was in such a state that I counted one hundred and twenty sores on it, all of them serious and harmful to humans. Every mule boy is a bit of a thief, rogue, and swindler. If their masters (for that is what they call the people who ride on their mules) are too gullible, they play more tricks on them than have been played in the whole city in recent years. If they are foreigners, they steal from them; if they are students, they curse them; if they are members of a religious order, they insult them with blaspheming; if they are soldiers, they tremble with fear.'

'These mule boys, together with sailors, carters, and mule-drivers, have a way of life which is unusual and peculiar to them. The carter spends most of his life in a space a yard and a half long, for there can be little more distance than that between the beasts's yoke and the front of the cart. He sings half the time and curses the other half. And another part of his life is spent shouting "Stay back", and if by chance he has to extract a wheel from the mud, he would sooner resort to two curses than three mules. Sailors are an ungodly, uncivilized mob, who know no other language than the one spoken on board. In fair weather they are diligent, in squalls they are lazy, and when there is a storm there are many who give orders and few who obey. Their god is their sea-chest and their mess, and their chief diversion is to watch the passengers being seasick. Mule-drivers are people who have severed relations with bedclothes and attached themselves to pack-saddles; they are so industrious and so quick that they would forfeit their souls rather than a day's work; their music is the beat of the mortar, their sauce is hunger, they celebrate matins by giving fodder to their animals and Mass by not going to church.'

When he uttered these words he was standing in the doorway of an apothecary's shop and, turning to the apothecary himself, he said, 'You'd have a healthy trade, sir, if you weren't so ruthless with your oil lamps.'

'In what way am I ruthless with my lamps?' asked the apothecary.

The Glass Graduate responded, 'I say this because when you need some oil you take it from the nearest lamp; and there is something else about this trade which is sufficient to ruin the reputation of the most skilled physician in the world.'

When he asked him what that was, the Graduate replied that he knew of an apothecary who, rather than admit that he did not have in stock what the physician prescribed, substituted for the items he did not have other substances which, in his opinion, had the same properties and quality, although this was not the case. Consequently, the wrongly made-up medicine had quite the opposite effect that the proper prescription would have had.

Someone else then asked him what he thought of physicians, and this is what he said: ' "Honour a physician with the honour due to him for the need which you may have of him: for the Lord has created him. For from the most High comes healing, and he shall receive honour from the king. The skill of the physician shall lift up his head: and in the sight of great men he shall be in admiration. The Lord has created medicines out of the earth; and he that is wise will not abhor them." '* 'This is what Ecclesiasticus has to say about medicine and good doctors, and quite the opposite can be said about the bad ones, because there are no people more harmful to the state than they are. A judge can manipulate or delay justice; a lawyer can uphold an unjust claim against us for his own profit; a merchant can eat into our estate; in short, everyone with whom we have to have dealings can injure us in some way. But as for taking our lives without fear of punishment, no one can do that. Only physicians can and do kill us without effort or fear of reprisal, and without baring any sword more lethal than a prescription. And there is no way of discovering their crimes because the consequences are buried immediately. I remember that when I was a man of flesh, rather than glass as I am now, a patient dismissed one of those second-rate physicians to consult another and four days later the first physician happened to pass by the apothecary's shop where the second had left his prescription. He asked the apothecary how his former patient was faring and whether the other physician had prescribed a purgative for him. The apothecary replied that he had a prescription for a purgative which the patient was to take the following day. The physician asked him to show it to him and when he saw that "To be taken shortly before meals" was written at the bottom he said, "I am happy with this prescription except for this business of being taken short, because it is too inconvenient." '

People followed him around to hear these and other things he said about the various professions, without doing him any harm, but without giving him any peace either. However, in spite of this he would not have been able to defend himself from the young boys if his guardian had not protected him.

Someone asked him what he would do not to envy anyone. He replied, 'Sleep: for as long as you are asleep, you will be the equal of the person you envy.'

Another asked him what means he would use to come by a commission which he had been trying to get for two years. He replied, 'Get on your horse and, keeping the person who has the commission in view, ride alongside him into the city and that way you will literally come by the commission.'

On one occasion a court judge happened to pass by in front of him on his way to a criminal case, accompanied by a large crowd and two constables. The Graduate asked who he was, and when he was told he said: 'I bet that judge has vipers in his bosom, pistols in his belt, and lightning in his fingertips to destroy everything that falls within his jurisdiction. I remember that I had a friend who passed sentence in a criminal case that was far in excess of the defendants' crimes. I asked him why he had passed such a cruel sentence and brought about such a manifest injustice. He replied that he intended to grant an appeal, thus leaving the way open for the gentlemen of the Council to show mercy by moderating that severe sentence and reducing it to its right and proper proportions. I replied that it would have been better to have passed an original sentence that would have saved them the trouble, and that way he would himself be considered a just and reliable judge.'

In the circle of people who, as we've been told, were forever crowding round to listen to him, there was an acquaintance of his dressed in the black garb of a lawyer, whom someone addressed as 'graduate'. Since the Glass Graduate knew that the man addressed as 'graduate' had not yet attained his degree, he said, 'Take care, friend, not to let the monks who ransom captives discover your title or they'll confiscate it as unclaimed property.'

The friend replied, 'Let us be civil with one another, Glass Graduate, for you are well aware that I am a man of lofty and profound learning.'

The Glass Graduate replied, 'I know you to be a Tantalus* in terms of your learning; it is so lofty it goes way over your head and so profound that it is quite beyond your reach.'

Standing near a tailor's shop one day, he saw that the tailor was twiddling his thumbs and said to him, 'Without doubt, master tailor, you are on your way to salvation.'

'What makes you say that?' asked the tailor.

'What makes me say that?' repeated the Glass Graduate. 'The fact that you have nothing to do and therefore you have no reason to lie.'

He added: 'Woe to the tailor who does not tell lies and who sews on festive days. It is a miracle of nature that among the great number who practise this trade you will scarcely find one who will make a suit without fault, since those who make them are largely a band of sinners.'

Of cobblers, he said that they never, by their own admission, made an ill-fitting shoe; for if the customer found his shoe too narrow or tight, he would be told that was how it was meant to fit, because fashionable people wore tight-fitting shoes, and after a couple of hours' wear they would be looser-fitting than sandals. If the customer found his shoes too wide, he would be told that was how they were meant to fit, out of respect for his gout.

A bright young lad, who worked as a clerk in a provincial notary's office, pressed the Graduate with questions and demands and brought him news of what was happening in the city, because he had something to say on every subject and had an answer for every question. On one occasion the young lad said to him, 'Glass Graduate, last night a money-lender who was condemned to hang died in his cell.'

He replied, 'He did well to make a hasty exit, before the executioner lent him a hand.'

On the pavement in front of the Church of St Francis there was a group of Genoese, and as he passed by one of them called to him, saying, 'Come here, Glass Graduate, sir, and tell us one of your priceless tales.'

He replied, 'No, I won't, because I don't want you transferring it to Genoa.'*

One day he came upon a shopkeeper who was parading one of her daughters in front of her, who was very ugly but decked out in baubles, finery, and pearls, and he said to the mother, 'You have done well to cover her with a layer of stones to make her fit for stepping out on to the street.'

With regard to pie-makers, he said that they had been playing the game of 'double your money' for years, without paying any penalty, by selling twopenny pies for fourpence, fourpenny pies for eight-pence, and eightpenny pies for twice that amount, simply because it seemed like a good idea. Against puppeteers* he inveighed at length, saying that they were vagrants who treated divine matters with an indecent lack of respect, because they reduced worship to mockery in the figures they paraded in their theatres. They also stuffed all or most of the Old Testament characters into a sack which they sat on while they ate and drank at inns and taverns. In conclusion, he said he was amazed that the authorities did not silence their theatres once and for all, or banish them from the realm.

On another occasion an actor dressed as a prince happened to pass by, and when the Glass Graduate saw him he commented, 'I remember seeing this fellow leave the theatre with his face covered in flour and wearing a sheepskin inside out, and yet when he's off-stage he's forever swearing by his noble blood.'

'He must be noble,' replied a member of the public, 'for there are many actors who are well born and of noble blood.'

'That may be so,' replied the Glass Graduate, 'but the last thing you need in a farce are persons of noble blood; dashing young men, yes, with charm and eloquent tongues. I can also say this to their credit, that they earn their daily bread by the sweat of their brows and unbearable hard work. For they are constantly memorizing their lines and live the life of nomads, moving from place to place and from one inn to another, going without sleep to satisfy others, because it is in the pleasure they give others that they derive their own profit. This can also be said in their favour, that in their line of business they deceive no one, for they are constantly exposing their mer-chandise to public scrutiny, so that everyone may see and judge it. The work-load of managers who are also players is incredible and the pressure they work under immense, for they have to make a large profit if they do not want to be so heavily in debt at the end of the year that they have to declare themselves bankrupt. Yet, in spite of these hardships, they are necessary to the state, like woodlands, boulevards, places of natural beauty, and all those things that provide honest recreation.'

He said that it was the opinion of a friend of his that the man who courted an actress paid court to a whole bevy of ladies in the one person, such as a queen, a nymph, a goddess, a chambermaid, and a shepherdess. It often happened that in the same person he also paid court to a page or a lackey, for these and other male roles were usually played by an actress.

Someone asked him who was the happiest man who ever lived. He replied, 'No one, because no one knows his father, no one lives a blameless life, no one is content with his lot, and no one ascends to heaven.'

Apropos of fencers, he said on one occasion that they were masters of a science or art which failed them when they needed it, and that they were inclined to be rather presumptuous in their efforts to break down into mathematical models (which are infallible) the movements and aggressive thoughts of their opponents. He was particularly hostile to men who dyed their beards, and on one occasion when two men were quarrelling in front of him, and one, who was Portuguese, said to the other, a Castilian, clutching his beard which was very thoroughly dyed, 'I swear, on my beard . . .', the Glass Graduate interjected, 'Don't say "swear", say "smear".'

To another, who was sporting a beard streaked with lots of different colours because it had been dyed badly, the Glass Graduate declared that his beard looked like a freckled dungheap. He advised another, whose beard was half white and half black, because it had been neglected and the white roots had grown through, not to try to challenge or quarrel with anyone because he was likely to be told that he was lying through half his beard.

One day he related how a bright and resourceful young woman, in order to comply with her parents' wishes, consented to marry a white-haired old man, who went on the eve of their wedding not to the River Jordan,* as the old wives' tale recommends, but to his flask of hair-dyeing tincture, with which he rejuvenated his beard so efficiently that when he went to bed it was as white as snow and when he got up it was as black as pitch. When the time came for them to join hands his appearance inspired the young girl, by dint of his tint, to tell her parents to give her the same husband they had shown her previously, because she did not want another. They told her that the man who stood before her was the very man they had shown her and given her as a husband. She replied that he was not, and had witnesses testify to the fact that the man her parents gave her was a venerable, white-haired man, and since the gentleman present did not have white hair, it was not he and she was being deceived. She would not budge from this resolve, the old man was humiliated, and the marriage did not take place.

He treated duennas with the same contempt as men who dyed their hair. At great length he criticized their ill-pronounced French vocabulary, their shroud-like coifs, their many affectations, their scruples, and their extraordinary meanness. He was irritated by their squeamishness, their empty-headedness, their manner of speaking which was more embroidered than their headdresses, and finally, their general uselessness and their sewing.

One person remarked, 'Why is it, Mister Graduate, that I have heard you speak ill of many professions, yet you have never criticized notaries when there is so much to be said?'

He replied, 'Although I am made of glass I am not so weak that I allow myself to be carried along by the current of public opinion, which is more often than not deceived. It seems to me that notaries are the grammar books of slanderers and the do-re-mi of singers. Just as you cannot advance to the other sciences except via the gateway of grammar, and just as the singer hums before he sings, so slanderers first show the evil potential of their tongues when they speak ill of notaries and constables and other agents of law and order. Yet without the work of the notary truth would be hidden, shamed, and ill-treated, as it says in Ecclesiasticus: "In the hand of God is the prosperity of man: and upon the person of the scribe shall he lay his honour."* The notary is a public figure and the work of the judge cannot be carried out effectively without his aid. Notaries have to be freemen and not slaves or the sons of slaves; they also have to be legitimate and not bastards or born of an inferior race. They pledge secrecy and loyalty and swear that they will not draw up documents in exchange for money. They also swear that neither friendship or enmity, profit or loss will prevent them from performing their duty with a good, Christian conscience. If the profession requires all these good qualities, why should we expect that from more than twenty thousand notaries working in Spain the devil should reap the richest harvest, as if they were shoots on his vine? I am unwilling to believe it, nor is it right for anyone to believe it; because the fact is that they are the most indispensable people in a well-ordered state and if they gross too much in fees, then they also commit gross injustices and between the two extremes there may be a middle way which will make them do their job more conscientiously.'

With regard to constables, he said it was not surprising that they should have one or two enemies, since it was their job either to arrest you or to remove your possessions from your home, or keep you under guard in their house and eat at your expense. He condemned the negligence and ignorance of attorneys and lawyers, comparing them with physicians who, irrespective of whether the patient is cured or not, claim their fee, and attorneys and lawyers do likewise, whether or not they are successful in the cases they are pleading.

Someone asked him which was the best land. He replied the sort that gave an early and generous harvest.

'That's not what I'm asking. What I want to know is which is the better place, Valladolid or Madrid?'

The Graduate replied, 'In Madrid, the outer limits and in Valladolid the central parts.'

'I don't understand,' repeated the man who had asked the question.

The Graduate said, 'In Madrid, the earth and sky, in Valladolid what lies between.'*

The Glass Graduate heard one man tell another that his wife had been taken ill the moment they had entered Valladolid, because the soil did not agree with her. The Graduate commented: 'She would have done better to eat it, if she happens to be jealous.'

Of musicians and foot messengers, he remarked that their prospects and fortunes were limited because the latter could only aspire to delivering their messages on horseback and the former to becoming musicians to the king.

Of ladies known as courtesans, he said that all or most of them were more courtly than sanitary.

One day while he was in a church he observed that at one and the same moment an old man was brought in for burial, a child for baptism, and a woman to be married, and he commented that churches were battlefields where the old ended their days, children conquer, and women triumph.

On one occasion a wasp stung him on the neck and he did not dare shake it off for fear of breaking, but he complained all the same. Someone asked him how he could feel the wasp if his body were made of glass. He replied that the wasp must be a scandalmonger, for the tongues and words of scandalmongers were sharp enough to pierce bodies of bronze, let alone glass.

When a very fat monk happened to pass by, a bystander remarked, 'Our brother has been feasting, I mean fasting, so long he can hardly move.'

Angered by this remark, the Glass Graduate retorted, 'Let no one forget the words of the Holy Spirit: "Touch not mine annointed." '*

His anger increased as he told them to give the matter some thought and they would realize that among the many saints that the Church had canonized and placed among the host of the blessed in recent years, there was no one called Captain So-and So, or Secretary Such-and-Such, nor the Count, Marquis, or Duke of Anywhere, but Brother Diego or Jacinto or Raimundo, all of them friars and brothers of religious orders. For the religious orders were the imperial gardens of heaven whose fruits were served at God's own table.

He said that the tongues of scandalmongers were like the feathers of eagles which abrade and damage the feathers of all other birds who come near them. He said extraordinary things about the keepers of gaming houses and gamblers: he said that gaming-house keepers were public confidence tricksters. Once they had received their tip from the winning player they then wanted him to lose and the deal to pass to the next person, so that his opponent would win and they would pick up their share. He warmly praised the patience of the gambler who would spend a whole night playing and losing and, although he had a fiendishly quick temper, would bite his lip and suffer the devil's torments rather than give his opponent cause to leave the table with his winnings. He also praised the scruples of a few honourable gaming-house keepers who would not even contemplate allowing games other than *polla* and *cientos** to be played in their establishments, and in this way, slowly but surely, without fear or hint of scandal, they amassed more commission at the end of the month than those who allowed their customers to play riskier games for higher stakes.

In short, he said so many things that, were it not for the cries of anguish he uttered when anyone touched or approached him, or his manner of dress, the frugality of his diet, the way he drank, his unwillingness to sleep anywhere but out of doors in summer and in hay-lofts in winter, as was stated earlier, no one would have thought he was anything but one of the sanest men on earth.

This illness lasted about two years, until a monk of the Jeromite order, who had a particular gift and skill in making the deaf hear and the mute speak, as well as curing madness, took it upon himself out of charity to cure the Glass Graduate. He cured him and restored him to health and his previous good sense, intelligence, and reason. As soon as he saw that he was healed, the monk dressed him as a lawyer and sent him back to Court where, showing as many signs of his sanity as he had formerly of his madness, he could practise his profession and thereby earn his reputation.

This he did and, calling himself Graduate Rueda rather than Rodaja,* he returned to Court. He was recognized by the children almost as soon as he got there, but when they saw him dressed so differently from the way he used to, they did not dare to shout after him or ask him questions, but followed him and said to one another, 'Isn't this the mad Glass Graduate? Yes, it's definitely him. He must be sane now, although he could be just as mad in his fine clothes as he was in his less conventional ones. Let's ask him something and put an end to our quandary.'

The Graduate heard every word but said nothing, and felt far more bewildered and embarrassed than when he was insane. The children communicated their discovery to the men, and before the Graduate reached the courtyard of the Royal Tribunals he was being followed by more than two hundred people of all descriptions. With this entourage, which was bigger than that of a professor, he reached the courtyard, whereupon the people already gathered inside merged with the crowd around him. When he saw himself surrounded by so many people he said in a loud voice:

'Gentlemen, I am the Glass Graduate, but I am no longer the man I was. I am now Graduate Rueda. Events and misfortunes which occur in the world at heaven's behest robbed me of my reason and the mercy of God has restored it to me. By the things I am told I said when I was mad you may judge what I shall say and do now that I am sane. I am a graduate in law from Salamanca, where I studied in poverty and where I achieved second place, from which you may infer that I earned my grade through merit rather than favour. I have come to this great sea of the capital to practise law and earn my living, but unless you leave me in peace, I will have come merely to row against the tide and die in the process. [In the original Spanish there is a pun on *abogar* (practise law) and *bogar* (to row).] For the love of God, if you must pursue me, don't persecute me or take away from me in my sanity the meagre living I earned when I was insane. Ask me in my own home the questions you used to ask me in the public squares and you will see that the man who gave good answers on the spur of the moment, as they say, will give better ones when he has the time to reflect.

They all listened and some went away. He returned to his inn with scarcely fewer people than when he went out. He went out the following day and the same thing happened; he delivered another speech but it had no effect on his audience. He was losing a great deal and earning nothing, and realizing that he would die of hunger he decided to leave the capital and return to Flanders, where he intended to avail himself of the strength of his arm since he could not avail himself of the powers of his intellect.

Acting upon this resolution, he said as he left the city, 'Oh Court, you nurture the ambitions of brazen suitors and shatter the hopes of virtuous and reserved men. You wine and dine unscrupulous rogues and let men of intelligence and principle starve to death.'

This said, he went off to Flanders. Accompanied by his good friend, Captain Valdivia, it was through feats of arms that he crowned the fame he had begun to acquire through learning. When he died he left behind him the reputation of having been a prudent and very valiant soldier.

THE POWER OF BLOOD

One warm summer night an elderly gentleman was returning from a day's recreation beside the river in Toledo with his wife, small boy, daughter of sixteen, and maid. The night was clear and the hour eleven o'clock; the road was deserted and their pace leisurely, for they had no wish to pay the price of weariness for the pleasures to be had in Toledo on the riverbank or along the river plain.

As the worthy gentleman and his honourable family made their way home, with the confidence inspired by the law and order of that city and the good character of its citizens, the furthest thing from their minds was that disaster might strike. However, since the majority of misfortunes which occur are unforeseen, contrary to all expectation a disaster befell them which interrupted their pleasure and gave them cause to weep for many years afterwards.

In that same city lived a nobleman of about twenty-two, whose wealth, noble blood, perverted inclinations, excessive liberty, and licentious companions incited him to behave with an audacity that belied his social position and earned him the reputation of a hell-raiser. This nobleman, then (whose name for the present, and with good reason, will remain undisclosed and whom we shall call Rodolfo), was descending the same hill that the old gentleman and his family were climbing, accompanied by four hotheaded and brazen young friends. The two squadrons, one of sheep and the other of wolves, met up with one another, and with shameless effrontery and their own faces covered, Rodolfo and his companions stared into the faces of the mother, the daughter, and the maid. This made the old man angry and he reproached and condemned them for their audacity. They responded by pulling faces and jeering, and without taking further liberties went on their way. However, the great beauty of the face which Rodolfo had seen, that of Leocadia (for this is how the gentleman's daughter will be known), began to impress itself so forcefully on his memory that it took possession of his will and awakened in him the desire to enjoy her regardless of any difficulties that might arise. He quickly shared this thought with his companions and they just as quickly resolved to go back and abduct her, to please Rodolfo. For rich people who happen to be generous always find someone to applaud their excesses and call their foul deeds fair. In this way, the formulation of the evil plan, the communication and approval of it, and the decision to abduct Leocadia and the act itself were virtually the actions of a single moment.

They put handkerchiefs over their faces, and with their swords drawn turned around and within a few paces had caught up with the people who were still thanking God for having saved them from the hands of those insolent youths. Rodolfo rushed at Leocadia and, snatching her up into his arms, he proceeded to run away with her. She did not have the strength to resist and the shock left her speechless and unable to protest, as well as blind because, fainting and senseless, she saw neither who was carrying her nor where she was being carried. Her father shouted, her mother screamed, her little brother cried, and the maid clawed at her face in anguish. The noises went unheard and the screams unheeded, the weeping moved no one to pity, and the maid scratched at her flesh in vain, for the solitude of the place, the hushed silence of the night, and the cruel disposition of the assailants suppressed every sound.

In short, one company went off in a merry mood while the other was abandoned to its sorrows. Rodolfo reached his house without hindrance, while Leocadia's parents reached theirs distressed, grieving, and desperate. Without Leocadia they were as if blind, for she was the light of their eyes; they were lonely, because Leocadia was their sweet and pleasant companion; they were confused, because they did not know whether it was advisable to inform the authorities of their misfortune since they were afraid of being the principal instrument in publicizing their dishonour.

As poor gentlefolk they were sadly in need of influential friends. Against whom could they lodge a complaint, except bad luck itself? The cunning and wily Rodolfo, on the other hand, had already smuggled Leocadia into his house and his room. Realizing as he carried her that she had fainted, he had covered her eyes with a handkerchief to prevent her from seeing the streets through which he carried her as well as the house and room in which she lay. It was in this room, and without being observed by anyone, since he had a separate apartment in his father's house (his father being still alive) and keys to this room and to the whole apartment—such independence is carelessness on the part of parents who want their children to live quietly and modestly—that Rodolfo was able to satisfy his lust before

Leocadia recovered from her faint. The lascivious impulses of youth rarely or never require proper or desirable circumstances to incite or arouse them more. Deprived of the light of understanding, he robbed Leocadia of her most precious possession in the darkness, and since the sins of sensuality generally aim no further than the moment of their satisfaction, Rodolfo immediately wished to be rid of her and it occurred to him to leave her in the street in her unconscious state.

He was about to put this plan into effect when he realized that she was coming round and uttering the following words:

'Where am I, unhappy wretch? What is this darkness, what shadows envelop me? Am I in the limbo of my innocence or the hell of my errors? Sweet Jesus, who is touching me? Why am I in bed and in pain? Are you listening to me, mother and mistress of my life? Can you hear me, my beloved father? Oh, I am accursed, for I realize that my parents cannot hear me and it is my enemies who touch me; I would consider myself fortunate if this darkness were to last forever and my eyes were never to see the light of day again, and if this place where I now find myself, wherever it may be, could serve as the tomb of my honour. For dishonour which remains secret is better than honour which is exposed to the judgement of the general public. Now I remember (and how I wish that I had not) that only a short time ago I was with my parents. Now I remember that I was attacked; now I fully appreciate that it is not right for people to see me. You who are with me, whoever you are'—and as she said these words she was gripping Rodolfo's hands—'if your soul will allow any form of plea to touch it, I beg you, now that you have triumphed over my reputation, to triumph over my life also. Take it now this very minute, for it is not proper that a woman without honour should have life. Consider that the degree of cruelty you exercised in offending me will be mitigated by the mercy you will show in killing me, and so you will be cruel and kind at the same time.'

Leocadia's words left Rodolfo confused and, being a youth of little experience, he did not know what to say or do. His silence astonished Leocadia as she sought with her hands to ascertain whether she was in the presence of a phantom or a ghost. However, since what she touched was of flesh and blood and she recalled the force that had been used against her when she was with her parents, the true nature of her misfortune began to dawn on her. With this realization dominating her thoughts, she resumed the speech which her many sobs and sighs had interrupted, with these words:

'Insolent youth, for your actions lead me to conclude that you are not very old, I will pardon the offence that you have committed against me solely on condition that you promise and swear to conceal it in perpetual silence and not mention it to a soul, just as you have concealed it in this darkness. I ask very little compensation for such a great injury; but in my opinion it is the greatest request I can ever make of you or you can ever grant me. Rest assured that I have never seen your face, nor do I wish to see it, because now that I remember the offence, I do not want to remember my offender nor retain in my memory an image of the perpetrator of my ruin. My complaints will be heard only by myself and heaven for I have no desire for the world to hear them, for the world does not judge things according to the facts but according to how they conform to its own criteria.

'I do not know how I am able to express these truths which are usually founded on the experience of many situations and on the passage of many years, while I am not yet seventeen. I deduce from this that suffering both ties and loosens the victim's tongue, sometimes exaggerating the ill to persuade people to believe, at other times saying nothing about it so that the wrong cannot be righted. Whatever the case may be, whether I remain silent or whether I speak, I believe that I must prompt you either to believe me or to aid me. For to refuse to believe me would be ignorance on your part and a refusal to aid me would make any hope of relief impossible. I shall not despair, because it will cost you little to grant what I ask, and this is my request. Do not for a moment expect or assume that the passage of time will temper the justifiable anger I feel toward you, nor desire to heap more injuries upon me. The less you enjoy me, now that you have already done so once, the less your evil desires will be aroused. Imagine that you offended me by chance, without giving reason any opportunity to intervene in the matter. I shall similarly persuade myself that I was never born into this world, or if I was, then it was only to be wretched. Leave me in the street or at least near the main church, because from there I shall be able to find my way home; but you must also swear not to follow me, or discover my address, or ask after my parents' name, or mine, or that of my relatives, for if they were as rich as they are noble I would not have brought such disgrace upon them. Give me some kind of answer, and if you are afraid that I might recognize you by your voice, I would have you know that with the exception of my father and confessor, I have never spoken to a man in my life, and I have heard few speak for long enough to be able to distinguish them by the sound of their voices.'

The reply which Rodolfo made to the wise words of the distressed Leocadia was none other than to embrace her, demonstrating that he wanted to confirm his desire and her dishonour once again. When Leocadia saw this she defended herself with a vigour surprising in one so young, using her feet, her hands, her teeth, and her tongue, saying:

'Be under no illusion, treacherous and heartless man, whoever you are, the spoils you have taken from me might as well have been taken from a tree trunk or a senseless pillar of stone, a conquest and triumph which can only win you notoriety and contempt. But the fresh conquest you are attempting you will achieve only over my dead body. You trampled on me and destroyed me while I was unconscious; but now that I have energy and determination you will have to kill me before you overpower me. For if, now that I am conscious, I were to yield without resistance to such a despicable desire, you might think that my faint was a pretence when you dared to destroy me.'

In short, Leocadia resisted so valiantly and so doggedly that Rodolfo's strength and desire waned; and since the outrage he had committed against Leocadia derived from nothing more than a lascivious impulse—which never engenders true and lasting love—in place of the fleeting impulse there remained, if not repentance exactly, at least less inclination to repeat the experience. Tired and no longer aroused, Rodolfo left Leocadia lying in his bed and in his house and, without saying a word, closed the door to his room and went to look for his companions to seek their advice as to what he should do.

Sensing that she was alone and locked in, Leocadia rose from the bed and explored the whole of the room, groping along the walls to see whether she could find a door to let herself out or a window to jump from. She found the door but it was firmly locked, and she came across a window which she was able to open and through which the moon shone so brightly that she was able to distinguish the colours in the tapestries decorating the room. She saw that the bed was inlaid with gold and so richly adorned that it looked more like the bed of a prince than of some private gentleman. She counted the number of chairs and desks, she noted the position of the door, but although she saw several picture-frames hanging on the walls, she could not make out the subjects they depicted. The window was large, ornate, and protected by a sturdy grille, and it looked out on to a garden which was also enclosed by high walls. All these obstacles thwarted her intention of jumping from the window into the street. Everything she saw and noted concerning the size and rich furnishings of that room convinced her that its owner must be a man of uncommon position and wealth. On a writing table next to the window she saw a small crucifix made of solid silver, which she picked up and placed in the sleeve of her dress, not out of devotion or any conscious intention to steal it, but prompted by a clever plan of her own. Once she had done this she closed the window again and returned to the bed to await the outcome of such ill beginnings.

It felt as if less than half an hour had passed when she heard the door to the room open and someone approach her who, without uttering a word, bound her eyes with a handkerchief and, taking her by the arm, led her out of the room; then she heard the door being closed again. The person who did these things was Rodolfo who, although he had gone in search of his companions, had preferred not to find them since it occurred to him that it was not in his interest to make them witnesses of what had passed between himself and the young lady. He decided instead to tell them that, regretting the foul deed and moved by her tears, he had let her go free along the road. With this resolve he hurried back to leave Leocadia at the main church as she had requested, before the new day prevented him from getting rid of her and obliged him to keep her in his room until the following night, during which time he wanted neither to resort to force again nor run the risk of being recognized. So he took her to the square known as Town Hall Square and there, speaking a mixture of Spanish and Portuguese in a disguised voice, he told her that she could safely return home, for no one would follow her, and before she had time to remove the handkerchief from her eyes he had retreated to a place where he could not be seen.

Finding herself all alone Leocadia removed the blindfold and recognized where she had been left. She looked around in all directions and saw no one; but suspecting that someone might be following her at a distance she halted with each step she took towards her house, which was not very far from there. In order to confound any spies who might be following her, she slipped into a house which she found open and from there shortly made her way to her own. There she found her parents in a state of shock and still dressed in the previous day's clothes, since it had not even occurred to them to get any rest.

When they saw her they ran to her with open arms and welcomed her with tears in their eyes. Distressed and agitated, Leocadia signalled that her parents should draw aside with her, which they did, and there she briefly recounted to them the whole disastrous episode in all its detail, and her lack of information concerning the identity of the man who had assaulted her and robbed her of her honour. She told them what she had seen in the theatre where the tragedy of her misfortune had been enacted: the window, the garden, the grille, the writing tables, the bed, the wall hangings, and finally she showed them the crucifix which she had brought away with her. At the sight of this they broke down in tears once more, they cried for mercy, they prayed for revenge, and they invoked miraculous punishments. She went on to say that although she had no wish to learn the identity of her assailant, if her parents desired to find out they could do so by means of that crucifix, by getting vergers to announce from every parish pulpit in the city that whoever had lost that crucifix would find it in the possession of a priest selected by them for this purpose. And so, when they discovered who owned the crucifix, they would also discover the house and identity of her enemy.

Her father replied: 'That would have been well said, daughter, if common mischief did not militate against your wise words, for it is obvious that this crucifix will this very day be missed from the room you speak of, and its owner will know for certain that the person he was with carried it off. Bringing it to his attention that some priest has it in his possession is more likely to identify the person who gave it to the priest than unmask the owner who lost it. The owner might arrange for someone else, whom he has briefed of the particulars, to come and claim it. If this happens we will be more confused than enlightened, although we could employ this very stratagem we suspect in others and deliver the crucifix to the priest via a third party. What you must do, daughter, is keep it and put your trust in it, for since it bore witness to your misfortune, it will also permit justice to be obtained on your behalf. Take comfort, daughter, from the fact that an ounce of public dishonour is more harmful than a hundredweight of private disgrace. And since you can live honoured before God in public do not grieve to be dishonoured in your own eyes in private; true dishonour resides in sin and true honour in virtue. A sinner offends against God in word, desire, and matters of honour, and since you have not offended against him in word, thought, or deed, consider yourself honourable, and I shall esteem you as such, without ever ceasing to regard you as your true and loving father should.'

With these prudent words Leocadia's father comforted her, and taking her in her arms again her mother also attempted to console her. She wailed and cried again and was obliged to keep her head down, as the saying goes, and live discreetly under the protection of her parents, dressing in a poor but respectable manner.

Rodolfo, in the meantime, who had returned home and noticed that the crucifix was missing, had no doubt who had taken it; but it was of no consequence to him. Since he was rich he attached little importance to it, nor did his parents ask him for it when he left for Italy three days later and placed in the charge of one of his mother's maids all that he was leaving behind in that room. Rodolfo had been intending for many days to go to Italy, and his father, who had been there, encouraged him to go. He told him that being considered a gentleman in one's own country alone was no recommendation, for it was also necessary to acquire the same regard abroad. For these and other reasons Rodolfo was ready to comply with the wishes of his father, who gave him generous letters of credit for Barcelona, Genoa, Rome, and Naples. Rodolfo departed soon afterwards with two of his companions, greedy to experience for himself what he had heard some soldiers say about the abundance of Italian and French hostelries and the freedoms which Spaniards enjoyed at the billets there. He liked the sound of 'Eco li buoni polastri, picioni, presuto et salcicie,'* and other such expressions which soldiers remember when they return from those parts and have to endure the austerity and discomforts of the inns and hostels of Spain. He ultimately went off with so scant a recollection of what had occurred between himself and Leocadia that it might never have happened.

She, meanwhile, lived as unobtrusively as possible in her parents' house, never allowing herself to be seen by anyone since she feared that her disgrace would be discernible in her face. Within a few months, however, she realized that she would be obliged to do out of necessity what until then she had done willingly. She saw that it was in her best interests to live in retirement and seclusion because she discovered that she was pregnant, a circumstance which brought back to her eyes the tears which had for a short period been forgotten, and her sighs and lamentations began once again to rend the air and her dear mother's prudence was powerless to comfort her. The time sped by and the moment of the birth arrived and was kept so secret that they did not even take a midwife into their confidence. With her mother performing this role, Leocadia gave birth to one of the most beautiful baby boys imaginable. With the same caution and secrecy that had surrounded his birth, he was taken to a village where he was looked after for four years. At the end of this period his grandfather conveyed him to his house where he was brought up as his nephew, if not in affluent circumstances, then at least in a very virtuous manner.

The child, whom they named Luis after his grandfather, had a beautiful face, a gentle disposition, and a keen intelligence. In all the things he was capable of doing at that tender age he showed signs of being the son of some noble father. His grace, beauty, and good sense so endeared him to his grandparents that they began to regard their daughter's misfortune as good fortune because it had given them such a grandson. When he went about the street he was showered with a thousand blessings: some blessed his beauty, others the mother who bore him; some blessed the father who sired him, while yet others blessed those who were bringing him up so well. Admired alike by those who knew him and those who did not, the child reached the age of seven and was already able to read Latin and Spanish* and write a good and elegant hand, for it was his grandparents' intention to make him virtuous and wise since they could not make him rich. Yet are not wisdom and virtue the very riches over which neither thieves nor so-called fortune have any jurisdiction?

It came about, then, that one day when the child went to deliver a message from his grandmother to a female relative of hers that he passed through a street where a horse-race was under way. He stopped to take a look, and in order to get a better view he crossed from one side to the other at a moment when he could not save himself from being knocked down by a horse whose rider could not restrain him in the fury of his gallop. It ran over him and left him for dead, sprawled out on the ground with blood pouring from his head. No sooner had this happened than an elderly gentleman who was watching the race jumped down from his horse with remarkable agility and approached the child. Taking him from a member of the public who was already holding him, he took him into his own arms and, without sparing a thought for his advanced age or his rank, which was of some distinction, he rushed to his house where he ordered his servants to leave him and go in search of a surgeon to attend to the child. Many gentlemen followed him, distressed at the suffering of such a beautiful child, because the news soon spread that the boy who had been knocked down was little Luis, the nephew of such and such a gentleman (naming his grandfather). This news spread from mouth to mouth until it reached the ears of his grandparents and his mother (who was pretending to be his cousin). Once the story had been confirmed they rushed out in search of their beloved child, frantic and beside themselves with worry. Since the gentleman who had taken him in was so well known and influential, many of the people they met could direct them to his house, and by the time they got there the child was already under the care of the surgeon.

Assuming them to be his parents, the gentleman and his wife, the owners of the house, asked them not to cry or raise their voices in anguish, because it would do the boy no good. When the renowned surgeon had attended to him with consummate care and skill, he announced that the wound was not as life-threatening as he had at first feared. Half-way through the treatment Luis came round and cheered up when he saw his aunt and uncle, who asked him through their tears how he was feeling. He replied that he was all right, except for the fact that his head and body hurt a lot. The surgeon ordered them not to talk to him, but to let him get some rest. They did as they were instructed, and his grandfather began to thank the master of the house for the great charity he had shown his nephew. The gentleman replied that there was no need to thank him, and he explained that when he saw the child knocked down and trampled, it was as if he had seen the face of a son of his, whom he loved dearly, and this prompted him to pick him up and bring him home, where he would remain until he was cured, with every necessary comfort it was within their power to provide. His wife, who was a noble woman, said the same and made even more earnest promises.

The grandparents were astonished at such Christian charity, but it was the boy's mother who was even more astonished. Now that her troubled spirit had been calmed by the surgeon's news she took a good look at the room in which her son lay and clearly recognized in its many distinguishing features that it was the very room in which her honour had ended and her wretchedness begun. Although it was no longer decorated with the tapestries it had formerly contained, she recognized the position of the furniture, she saw the window with the grille which looked out on to the garden, and because it was closed for the patient's sake, she asked whether that window had a view over a garden and was told that it did. What she recognized most clearly of all, however, was that the bed was the very one which she remembered as the tomb and resting place of her good name. What is more, the very writing table from which she had removed the crucifix was still in the same place.

In short, the truth of all her suspicions was confirmed by the steps which she had counted when she had been led blindfold from the room; that is, the steps which descended from there to the street and which she had had the intelligent foresight to count. When she left her son to go home that day she verified that there were the same number. Weighing up the facts she found her suppositions to be correct in every way. She recounted all the details to her mother and she, being the sensible person she was, inquired whether the gentleman with whom her grandson was staying had or used to have a son. She discovered that the young man we know as Rodolfo was his son, and that he was in Italy. Calculating the years she was told he had been away from Spain, she realized that they coincided with the seven years since her grandson's birth.

She informed her husband of all this, and together with their daughter they decided to wait and see what God would do with the injured child, who within a fortnight was out of danger and within a month was out of bed. During all this time he was visited by his mother and grandmother and pampered by the owners of the house as if he were their own son. Sometimes when doña Estefanía (for this was the name of the gentleman's wife) talked to Leocadia, she would say that the child so resembled a son of theirs who was in Italy that she could not look at him without getting the impression that she saw her own son before her. One day when she found herself alone with Estefanía, Leocadia used these remarks as an opening to tell her what she had resolved with her parents' assent to say to her, and her words were more or less as follows:

'Madam, the day my parents heard the news that their nephew had been injured, they truly believed that the heavens had closed against them and that the world had collapsed around them. It seemed that the light of their eyes had been extinguished and that the comfort of their old age had been taken away along with their nephew; for they love him with an affection over and above that which parents ordinarily feel for their children. But as the saying goes, "When God inflicts pain, he also provides the remedy", and the child found his in this house; and what I found prompted memories which I shall never be able to forget as long as I live. I, madam, am noble because my parents are noble, as all my ancestors have been noble, who with an average portion of wealth have happily preserved their honour wherever they have lived.'

Doña Estefanía listened to Leocadia's words in wonder and suspense, for she could not believe, although she saw it with her own eyes, that someone so young could be so wise, for she judged her to be little more than twenty years of age. Without opening her mouth or uttering a word of response she waited to hear whatever Leocadia had to tell her. In essence, she recounted Estefanía's son's transgression, her own dishonour, how she was abducted, blindfolded, and brought to this room, and the features that had confirmed her suspicions that it was the same room. To corroborate this she removed from her breast the crucifix which she had taken and which she addressed with these words: 'You, Lord, who witnessed how I was violated, be judge of the reparation that is owing to me. I took you from the writing table in order to remind you constantly of my grievance; not to ask for revenge, which I do not seek, but rather to beg of you some comfort to help me endure my wretchedness patiently. This child, madam, towards whom you have shown such charity, is your own true grandson. Heaven permitted him to be knocked down so that when he was brought to your house I might find in it, as I hope I shall find, if not the best remedy for my ill fortune, at least the means to be able to endure it.'

As she said this she fainted into the arms of Estefanía, still clutching the crucifix. Being a woman, after all, and moreover a noble woman, in whom compassion and mercy are usually as natural as cruelty in a man, Estefanía had scarcely seen Leocadia faint when she put her face next to hers and shed so many tears upon it that it was not necessary to sprinkle additional water on it to bring Leocadia round. They were still in this embrace when Estefanía's husband happened to come in leading little Luis by the hand, and when he saw Estefanía weeping and Leocadia in a faint he immediately demanded to know the reason. The child embraced his mother whom he believed to be his cousin and his grandmother whom he saw as his benefactress, and he also asked them why they were crying.

'We have momentous things to tell you, Sir,' Estefanía replied to her husband, 'the substance of which can be summed up by telling you to accept that this unconscious young woman is your daughter and this boy your grandson. This truth which I am now telling you was conveyed to me by this girl and it has been and is confirmed by the face of this boy, in which we have both recognized the face of our own son.'

'Unless you explain yourself, madam, I have no idea what you're talking about,' replied the gentleman.

At that moment Leocadia regained consciousness, and still clutching the crucifix, she dissolved into a sea of tears. All of this left the gentleman quite bewildered, but his wife dispelled the confusion by recounting to him all that Leocadia had told her. He was convinced by the divine grace of Heaven as if it had been confirmed by many reliable witnesses. He comforted and embraced Leocadia, kissed his grandson, and that very day dispatched a message to Naples advising their son to return immediately, because they had arranged a marriage for him with an exceedingly beautiful woman who was a perfect match for him. They would not allow Leocadia or her son to return to the home of her parents; the latter were overjoyed at their daughter's good fortune and offered up boundless thanks to God for it.

The message arrived in Naples, and within two days of receiving the letter Rodolfo, tempted by the prospect of enjoying such a beautiful woman as his father had described, took the opportunity of embarking with a fleet of four galleys which were about to depart for Spain; he was accompanied by his two friends, who had still not taken leave of him. With favourable conditions he arrived in Barcelona in twelve days, and hastening from there he arrived in Toledo in another seven and entered his father's house looking so handsome and dashing that he appeared the very epitome of elegance and gallantry.

His parents were overjoyed at their son's good health and safe arrival. For Leocadia, who was watching him from her hiding place, where she had been ordered as part of doña Estefanía's plan, the suspense was almost too much to bear. Rodolfo's companions wanted to go to their own homes immediately, but Estefanía would not allow it because they were essential to her scheme. Night was approaching when Rodolfo arrived, and while supper was being prepared Estefanía called her son's companions aside, convinced that they must be two of the three who, according to Leocadia, were with Rodolfo the night she was abducted. She earnestly begged them to tell her whether they remembered her son abducting a woman on a particular night so many years earlier, because ascertaining the truth affected the honour and peace of mind of all concerned. She was able to make this request of them so very insistently and assure them so persuasively that no harm whatever would come to them for acknowledging this abduction, that they felt it was safe to confess that it was true. They, Rodolfo, and another friend abducted a girl on the very summer night she had cited, and Rodolfo had gone off with her while they detained the other members of her family who were trying to defend her with their shouts of protest. The following day Rodolfo had told them that he had taken her to his house and this was all they could say in reply to the questions they were asked.

The confession of these two was enough to dispel any doubts Estefanía might have had about the matter, and she therefore decided to proceed with her good intention, which was as follows. Shortly before they sat down to supper Rodolfo's mother took him into a room where they could be alone, and placing a portrait in his hands she said, 'Rodolfo, my son, I want to give you an enjoyable supper by showing you your wife. This is her true likeness; but I want to warn you that what she lacks in beauty she makes up for in virtue: she is noble, intelligent, and reasonably wealthy, and since your father and I have chosen her for you, rest assured that she is the perfect partner for you.'

Rodolfo examined the portrait carefully and said, 'If the artists, who usually tend to be generous with the beauty of the faces they portray, have been equally generous with this one, I am convinced beyond any measure of doubt that the original must be ugliness itself. In truth, my dear lady and mother, it is just and right that children should obey their parents in whatever they are commanded to do; but it is also appropriate and more desirable that parents provide their children with the situation that will be most pleasing to them. And since the estate of matrimony is a knot that is untied only by death, it is sensible for both bonds to be equal and made of the same threads: virtue, nobility, intelligence, and the privileges of wealth may well please the mind of the man whose luck it is to have a wife with such qualities, but that her ugliness could ever be pleasing to her husband's eyes seems to me to be impossible. I know I am young, but I also appreciate that compatible with the holy sacrament of marriage is the right and proper pleasure which a husband and wife enjoy, and if this is lacking, the marriage is unstable and fails in its secondary purpose. For to think that an ugly face, which one has forever before one's eyes, in the drawing room, at the dining table, and in bed, can give pleasure—let me say again that I believe this to be virtually impossible. I implore you in your mercy, mother, to give me a companion who puts me in good humour rather than annoys me, so that together we may equally bear the yoke which Heaven imposes on us without straying from the straight and proper path.

'If this lady is noble, intelligent, and rich, as you say she is, she will not fail to find a husband who is of a different disposition from mine: some seek nobility, others intelligence, some money, and others beauty, and I count myself among the latter. As for nobility, I thank Heaven, my ancestors, and my parents for leaving it to me as my inheritance; as to intelligence, as long as a woman is not silly, foolish, or stupid, it is enough that she is neither witty to excess nor too stupid to be any use; as regards wealth, on this count also my parents' fortune means that I have no fear of becoming poor. I seek loveliness and I desire beauty, with no other dowry than chastity and good manners; and if my wife possesses these qualities, I will serve God gladly and give my parents a happy old age.'

Rodolfo's mother was highly delighted with his words, for they signalled to her that her plan was succeeding. She replied that she would try to arrange a marriage for him that was in accordance with his desire, and told him that he should not distress himself, for it would be easy to cancel the arrangements that had been made to marry him to that particular lady. Rodolfo thanked her, and since it was now time for supper, they approached the table. When Rodolfo, his father and mother, and his two companions had sat down, Estefanía exclaimed, as if she were just remembering something, 'How remiss of me! How well I am treating my guest! Go,' she said to a servant, 'and tell doña Leocadia not to be dictated to by her considerable modesty but to come and honour this table, for all those present are my children and her servants.'

This was all part of her ruse, and Leocadia had already been primed and instructed in all that she had to do. She was not long in making her entrance, and produced the most unexpected and stunning effect that enhanced natural beauty could ever do. Since it was winter she wore a long dress of black velvet studded with gold buttons and pearls, with a diamond waistband and necklace. Her hair, which was long and almost fair, served as decoration and headdress, and its arrangement of loops and curls, together with the shimmering of the diamonds inlaid among them, dazzled every eye that gazed upon them. Leocadia was a vision of grace and elegance. She led her son by the hand, and in front of her walked two maids who illuminated her way with two candles in silver candlesticks.

Everyone stood up to pay homage to her, as if she were some heavenly being who had miraculously appeared there. No one who stood gazing at her entranced was able, in that state of rapture, to say anything to her. Leocadia, with her graceful charm and gentle breeding, curtsied to everyone and, taking her by the hand, Estefanía seated her beside herself and opposite Rodolfo. The child was seated next to his grandfather.

Rodolfo, who now had a closer view of Leocadia's incomparable beauty, said to himself, 'If the bride chosen for me by my mother possessed only half this beauty, I would consider myself the happiest man on earth. Bless my soul! What is this vision I see? Am I by chance gazing upon some angel in human form?' As he said this Leocadia's beautiful image entered via his eyes and took possession of his soul. As for Leocadia, now that she could see so close to her the man she already loved more than the light of her eyes, she stole the occasional furtive glance at him as the meal progressed and began to relive in her imagination what had happened between Rodolfo and herself. The hope that his mother had inspired in her soul of becoming his wife began to ebb away, for she feared that his mother's promises could only be commensurate with her own wretched luck. She contemplated how close she was to being either happy or unhappy for the rest of her life. This reflection was so intense, and her thoughts were so turbulent and weighed so heavily on her heart, that all at once she grew feverish and pale. She felt herself growing faint, which obliged her to rest her head on doña Estefanía's arms who, seeing her in such a state, put her arms around her anxiously.

Everyone became alarmed and left the table to go to her aid. The one who displayed the greatest concern was Rodolfo, for he stumbled and fell over twice as he hastened to reach her. Neither unbuttoning her bodice nor throwing water in her face brought her round; rather, her arched chest and the absence of a pulse clearly indicated that she was dying. The maids and menservants of the house cried out and impetuously spread the word that she was dead. This bitter news reached the ears of Leocadia's parents, whom Estefanía had hidden away for a happier event. Together with the parish priest who was hiding with them, they disobeyed Estefanía's instructions and rushed into the room. The priest hastened to see whether she showed any signs of repenting of her sins so that he could absolve her of them, and where he expected to find one unconscious person he found two, for Rodolfo lay with his head on Leocadia's breast. His mother made way for him to reach Leocadia since she was destined to be his; but when Estefanía saw that he was also unconscious she herself was on the verge of losing her senses, and would have done so if she had not seen that Rodolfo was coming round. When he recovered fully he was embarrassed that they had witnessed his highly extravagant behaviour.

His mother, however, who could almost guess what her son was feeling, said, 'Do not be embarrassed, my son, by your lack of self-control, rather blush at your self-restraint when you know what I no longer wish to keep concealed from you, although I intended to save it for a happier moment. Understand, my dear son, that this unconscious woman I hold in my arms is your true wife; I say "true" because your father and I had chosen her for you, for the one in the portrait is a false substitute.'

When Rodolfo heard this, driven by his amorous and passionate desire, and since the title of husband swept away all the obstacles that the propriety and decorum of the place might have placed in his way, he threw himself on Leocadia, so that his face was close to hers, and lifted his lips to hers, as if waiting to welcome her departing spirit into his own. But when the tears of compassion of all those present were at their most copious, and the grief-stricken voices were growing louder, when Leocadia's mother was tearing at her dishevelled hair and her father at his beard, and the cries of her son were penetrating the heavens, Leocadia regained consciousness, and with her recovery the onlookers recovered the gaiety and contentment that had vanished from their hearts.

Leocadia found herself enveloped in Rodolfo's arms and tried with modest force to free herself from them, but he said, 'No, madam, such resistance is out of place. It is not right that you should struggle to leave the arms of the man who has you captive in his soul.' With these words Leocadia fully recovered her senses and doña Estefanía decided not to take her original plan any further and told the priest to marry her son to Leocadia immediately. This he did because there was no obstacle to prevent the wedding, for this incident occurred at a time when the willingness of both parties alone was enough for the marriage to take place, without the good and holy formalities and precautionary measures that are necessary today.*

Now that the marriage ceremony has been performed it can be left to another pen and another wit more delicate than my own to recount the general rejoicing of all those present: how Leocadia's parents embraced Rodolfo, how they thanked heaven and his parents; the astonishment of Rodolfo's companions who, on the very night of their arrival, unexpectedly witnessed such a beautiful wedding. Their sense of wonder increased when Estefanía announced in front of all those present that Leocadia was the young girl their son had abducted while in their company, a fact which left Rodolfo no less amazed than they. To establish the truth of the matter, he asked Leocadia to give him some sign to convince him fully of what he did not really doubt, for he assumed that his parents would have ascertained all the facts.

'When I regained my senses and came round after another faint I found myself, sir, in your arms without honour; but I consider the sacrifice worth making, since in coming round from my recent faint I once again found myself in the same arms as then, but this time with honour. And if this sign is not sufficient, let the sight of a crucifix suffice, for no one could have stolen it from you but me; if indeed you noticed its absence the following morning and it is the same one that the mistress of the house now has in her possession.'

'You are the mistress of my soul,* and you will continue to be so all the years that God ordains, my beloved,' replied Rodolfo.

When he embraced her again there were further blessings and congratulations.

Supper was served and the musicians who had been anticipating this moment made their entrance. Rodolfo saw himself in the mirror of his son's face, the four grandparents wept for joy, and there was not a corner of the house that was not visited by a spirit of rejoicing, contentment, and gaiety. And although the night flew by on weightless black wings, to Rodolfo it seemed that it dragged itself forward, not on wings, but on crutches; so urgent was his desire to be alone with his beloved wife.

The longed-for hour finally arrived, for there is no end which does not have its hour. They all retired to bed and the whole house fell as silent as the grave, but the truth of this story will not remain shrouded in silence, for the many children and illustrious descendants which this happy couple left in Toledo, and who are still alive today, will not permit it. They enjoyed each other, their children, and their grandchildren for many happy years, an enjoyment that was permitted by heaven and by the power of the blood which the brave, illustrious, and Christian grandfather of little Luis saw spilled on the ground.

THE JEALOUS OLD MAN
FROM EXTREMADURA

Not so long ago a noble-born gentleman set out from somewhere in
Extremadura* and, like a second prodigal son,* drifted through
various parts of Spain, Italy, and Flanders, frittering away both the
years and his fortune. After wandering extensively, with his parents
now dead and his inheritance squandered, he ended up in the great
city of Seville,* where he found ample opportunity to consume the
little he still possessed. Finding himself so short of funds and abandoned by most of his friends, he resorted to the same course of action
as many other desperate people in that city, namely, that of seeking
passage to the Indies. This was the refuge and shelter of the nation's
destitute, sanctuary of the bankrupt, safe-conduct of murderers,
asylum and hiding place of those players called sharpers by the
experts in the art, common attraction for loose women, the collective delusion of many, and the personal redemption of few.

Finally, when it was time for a fleet to depart for Tierrafirme,* he
came to some arrangement with the Admiral, equipped himself with
provisions and an esparto mat,* embarked at Cádiz, and bade farewell
to Spain. The fleet weighed anchor and in a spirit of general rejoicing hoisted its sails to the fair and gentle wind. Within a few hours
it had carried them out of sight of the land, confronting them instead
with the vast and panoramic expanses of the great father of all
waters, the Atlantic Ocean.

Our passenger was in pensive mood as he turned over in his
memory the many and varied dangers he had confronted during his
period of wandering, and the undisciplined behaviour that had
characterized the whole of his life. As a consequence of this self-
scrutiny he firmly resolved to alter his way of life, to be a better
steward of any property God might see fit to grant him, and to
proceed with more caution than previously in his dealings with
women. The fleet was enjoying calm conditions while this storm was
raging inside Carrizales (for this was the name of the man who gives
substance to our story). The wind began to rise again, propelling the
ships forward with such force that not a soul was left sitting in his
or her seat; and so Carrizales was obliged to abandon his thoughts

and devote himself exclusively to the preoccupations which the voyage imposed on him.

The conditions of the voyage were so favourable that without suffering any setback or reversal of fortune, they arrived at the port of Cartagena.* In order to dispense with any detail that bears no relevance to our purpose, I shall say only that Felipo was about forty-eight years old when he went to the Indies, and in the twenty years that he remained there, aided by his hard work and diligence, he managed to accumulate more than a hundred and fifty thousand solid gold pesos.

In his material comfort and prosperity, then, he was prompted by the natural desire that everyone experiences to return to his native land, and postponing the large profits that were pending he left Peru where he had accrued such wealth, transporting it all in gold and silver bars, which had been registered to avoid any difficulties.* Returning to Spain, he disembarked at Sanlúcar and arrived in Seville as replete in years as in riches. He retrieved his fortune without encountering any problems, and looked for his friends but found that they were all dead. He wanted to set off for his native region, although he had already received news that death had not spared him a single living relative. If on his way to the Indies, a poor and needy man, he was plagued by many thoughts that would not allow him a moment's peace in the midst of the ocean waves, he was no less troubled by them now in the peace and calm of dry land, although the cause of his anguish was different. If formerly he could not sleep because of his poverty, now he could derive no rest from his prosperity. For wealth is just as heavy a burden for someone unaccustomed to possessing it or ignorant of how to use it as is poverty for someone who knows no other condition. The possession of gold is a source of anxiety just as much as the want of it; but the anxieties of the poor are alleviated when they acquire some modest amount, while the anxieties of the rich are intensified as greater sums are amassed.

Carrizales considered his bars of gold, not out of miserliness—because in the several years he had been a soldier he had learned to be generous—but rather in an effort to decide what he should do with them. Preserving them in their present state was an unprofitable exercise, and keeping them at home would only tempt the greedy and invite the attention of thieves. Any desire to resume the restless life-style of a merchant had evaporated, and it seemed to him that, considering his age, he had more than enough money to live out the rest of his days, which he wanted to spend in his native region. He would invest his property there and pass his old age in peace and quiet, giving to God what he could, since he had already given to the world more than he ought. On the other hand, he considered the very great poverty of his homeland and its inhabitants, and how by going to live there he would make himself a target of all the importunities that the poor are wont to impose on the rich man in their midst, especially when there is no one else in the vicinity for them to turn to in their wretchedness. He wanted to have someone to bequeath his riches to when he died, and with this desire in mind he examined the state of his health and came to the conclusion that he could still bear the burden of matrimony. As soon as this thought occurred to him, it gave him such a fright that it weakened and broke his resolve, like a wind dispelling a mist, because he was by nature the most jealous man in the world,* even while he was still unmarried. For at the mere thought of the married state jealous thoughts began to disturb him, suspicions to torment him, and his imagination to alarm him so forcefully and so violently that he categorically gave up all intentions to marry.

Being resolved in this matter, and yet unresolved in what he was going to do with the rest of his life, it so happened that while passing through a particular street one day he looked up and saw a young girl standing at a window. She looked about thirteen or fourteen years of age, with such pleasing features and so beautiful that, powerless to offer any resistance, the venerable Carrizales surrendered the weakness of his old age to the youthfulness of Leonora, for this was the name of the beautiful young girl. So without losing any time, he began to reason and argue with himself at great length, saying:

'This girl is beautiful, and judging by the appearance of this house, she can't be very rich: her tender age calms my suspicions. I must marry her; I will lock her up and mould her according to my desires, and this way she will have precisely the temperament I will teach her to have. I am not so old as to have no hope of fathering children to succeed me. Whether she has a dowry or not is of no consequence, since heaven has given me enough to be generous towards others, and the rich should not seek profit in their marriages so much as pleasure. For pleasure prolongs life while conjugal displeasure cuts it short. Reason no more on the matter, then: the die is cast, and she is the one heaven wishes me to have.'

After repeating these words to himself, not once but a thousand times over the course of several days, he eventually spoke to Leonora's parents and ascertained that although they were poor they were noble; and informing them of his intention and of his status and fortune, he asked them for their daughter's hand in marriage. They requested time to make enquiries into his claims, and he would similarly have the opportunity to confirm their claim to nobility.* They took their leave of one another and conducted their various enquiries, each party finding the claims of the other to be truthful. Leonora finally became Carrizales's wife once he had given her a dowry of twenty thousand ducados,* so intense was the flame that seared the jealous old man's breast. He had scarcely uttered his marriage vows when he was overwhelmed by sudden and violent paroxysms of jealousy, and he began without reason to tremble and to suffer greater anguish than he had ever suffered before. The first outward indication that he gave of his jealous disposition was in not wanting any tailor to take his wife's measurements for the many dresses that he intended to have made for her. So he went in search of another woman of roughly the same build and proportions as Leonora herself, and he found a poor woman whose measurements he used to have a dress made. Trying it on his wife and finding that it fitted her well, he employed the same means to have the rest of her dresses made, which were so numerous and of such fine quality that the bride's parents considered themselves more than fortunate in having acquired such a good son-in-law, to their own and their daughter's mutual advantage. As for the child, she could only marvel at the sight of so many clothes, for the simple reason that in her whole life she had never worn more than a serge skirt and a taffeta dress.

The second indication that Felipo gave of his disposition was in not wanting to live with his wife until he had built a separate house for her, which he arranged in the following way. He purchased a house for twelve thousand ducados in a prestigious area of the city, with running water and a garden containing many orange trees. He blocked up all the windows which faced on to the street,* replaced them with skylights, and then proceeded to do the same with all the other windows in the house. In the main entrance, which in Seville is called a *casapuerta*, he installed a stable big enough for one mule and on top of it a hay loft and accommodation for the man employed to take care of it, an ageing black eunuch. He raised the walls enclosing the roof terraces in such a way that anyone entering the house had to look directly to heaven because there was nothing else to see, and he linked the main entrance to the patio by means of a turnstile.* He bought luxurious furnishings to decorate the house, which in its lavish tapestries, furniture, and canopies declared itself to be the property of a man of means. He also purchased four white slaves whose faces he branded and two other recently imported negro slaves.* He arranged for a caterer to deliver food, on condition that he neither slept in the house nor even set foot inside it except to hand whatever provisions he had brought through the turnstile. Once these arrangements had been made he leased out a portion of his estate in various affluent areas of the city, deposited another in the bank, and reserved a third portion for himself to cover everyday contingencies. He also had a master key made for the whole house, and locking up inside it everything that it was usual to buy in bulk and in season, he stocked up with provisions for the entire year. When he had everything thus organized and assembled, he went off to his parents-in-law's house and asked for his wife. They surrendered her to him with considerable sorrow, because they felt as if they were delivering her up to her grave.

Young and innocent Leonora still did not understand what had happened to her. Crying like her parents, she asked for their blessing and then, bidding them farewell, she arrived at her house surrounded by her slaves and maids and holding her husband's hand. As soon as they stepped inside Carrizales preached a sermon to them all, entrusting them with the care of Leonora and charging them never, by any manner of means, to allow anyone beyond the second door, not even the black eunuch. The individual he charged with the greatest responsibility for Leonora's care and comfort was a very prudent and serious-looking duenna, who would act as Leonora's governess. She would also supervise all the household business and give orders to the slaves and the other two young girls of Leonora's age, who had been acquired so that Leonora might be able to pass the time with girls of her own tender years. He promised that he would treat and indulge them in such a way that they would not resent their confinement, and he also promised that on holy days they would all, without exception, attend Mass; but so early in the morning that the light of day would scarcely catch a glimpse of them. The maids and slaves promised to do all that he required of them cheerfully, willingly, and enthusiastically. And as for the new bride, shrugging her shoulders she lowered her head and said that she had no other will than that of her husband and lord, to whom she was ever obedient.

When these precautions had been taken and the good Extremaduran had withdrawn into his house, he began to enjoy the fruits of marriage, at least as well as he could. To Leonora, who had no experience of any others, these were neither appetizing nor unappetizing. So she whiled away the hours with her duenna, companions, and slaves, and in order to pass the time more pleasurably they developed a sweet tooth and few days went by without them concocting a thousand delicacies sweetened with honey and sugar. They had more than ample provisions of what they needed to indulge this habit, and their master was more than happy to supply them with these things since it seemed to him that in keeping them entertained and occupied in this way, they had no opportunity to start thinking about their confinement.

Leonora treated her maids as equals, whiling away the time in the same pursuits, and in her simplicity even took to making dolls and other childish things, which reflected her artlessness and want of maturity. This was all a source of great satisfaction to the jealous husband, who believed that he had succeeded in choosing the best way of life imaginable, convinced as he was that neither diligence nor malice could ever find a way of disturbing his peace. His sole concern, therefore, was to bring his wife gifts and to remind her to ask for anything that entered her head, since her every desire would be fulfilled.

When, as was mentioned earlier, she attended Mass during the twilight hours, her parents also came to the church and spoke with their daughter in the presence of her husband. He gave them so many presents that, although they felt sorry for their daughter because of the confinement in which she lived, their pity was tempered by the many gifts that Carrizales, their generous son-in-law, gave them.

He would rise early in the morning and await the arrival of the caterer, whom he had informed the previous evening of what he needed to bring the following day by means of a list which had been left at the turnstile. On the arrival of the caterer Carrizales would go out of the house, usually on foot, leaving the two doors—the outer and the inner—locked behind him, and the negro enclosed between them. He would attend to his business affairs, which were few, quickly return home, and, locking himself inside, would spend his time indulging his wife and pampering her maids, who were all rather fond of him because of his unaffected and pleasant character, and especially, because he was so generous towards them all. They lived an entire novitiate year in this manner and took their vows in that way of life, fully intending to maintain such a life-style until the end of their days; and so they might have done if the Scheming Meddler in human affairs had not interfered, as you are about to hear.

He who considers himself more prudent and circumspect, let him now tell me what further measures the ageing Felipo might have taken, since he did not even allow any male animal to set foot in the house. The domestic mice were never chased by a tomcat, nor was the bark of a male dog ever heard inside it; they were all of the feminine gender. His days he spent thinking, and at night he went without sleep, as he patrolled and guarded his house like the Argus* of what he held dear. No man ever got beyond the door to the patio, for he conducted his business with his friends in the street. The figures represented in the wall hangings which decorated his halls and drawing-rooms were all women, flowers, and woodland scenes. The entire house was redolent of chastity, seclusion, and restraint: not one of the old wives' tales which the maids used to recount to one another around the fireside during the long winter evenings ever betrayed the slightest hint of bawdiness, due to his presence in their company. The silver hairs in the old man's white head looked like strands of pure gold to Leonora, because the first love that young ladies experience becomes imprinted on their souls like a seal impressing itself in wax. His excessive vigilance she interpreted as reasonable caution; she sincerely believed that her particular experience was that of all new brides. Her thoughts were never so undisciplined as to stray beyond the walls of her house, nor did she wilfully desire anything other than that which her husband wanted. Only on those days when she went to Mass did she see the streets, but at such an early hour that, except on her way back from the church, there was hardly enough light to see them at all. Never was a monastery so enclosed, nor nuns more cloistered, nor golden apples* so closely guarded; and yet he was quite powerless to prevent or avoid falling, or at least thinking that he had fallen, into the predicament he feared.

There exists in Seville a breed of idlers and loafers, commonly known as *gente de barrio* or men about town. These are the sons of the richer residents in each neighbourhood, affected, lazy, smooth-tongued individuals, concerning whose manner of dress and life-style, character, and peculiar rules of conduct much could be said but will, out of respect, remain undisclosed.

One of these young fellows, known in their parlance as a *virote*, a young bachelor (for the recently married are called *mantones*), turned his attention to the house of the circumspect Carrizales and, no-ticing that it was always shut up, was seized by the urge to know who lived inside. He went about his enquiries with such determin-ation and zeal that he managed to find out everything he wished to know.

He learned of the disposition of the old man, of the beauty of his wife, and of the means he employed to protect her, all of which aroused in him the desire to see whether it would be possible to infil-trate, either by force or by ingenuity, such a closely guarded fortress. And communicating this idea to one *mantón* and two *virote* friends of his, they agreed that it should be put into effect, for there is never a shortage of advisers and helpers in endeavours of this nature.

They stressed the difficulties involved in undertaking such a daunting task, and after discussing the matter on many occasions they came to the following agreement: Loaysa, for this was the name of the *virote*, would pretend to leave the city for a few days and dis-appear from his friends' sight, which he did. This achieved, he put on a fresh pair of linen leggings and a clean shirt, but on top of these he placed such torn and darned garments that there was not a pauper anywhere in the city who wore anything quite so shabby. He shaved what little beard he had, covered one eye with a patch, tightly ban-daged up one leg, and, leaning on two crutches, he made such a con-vincing invalid that the most authentic cripple was no match for him.

In this guise he stationed himself every night at his prayer post in the doorway to Carrizales's house, which was already locked up, with the negro, Luis, enclosed between the two doors. Once settled there, Loaysa would pick up his guitar, which was rather grimy and missing a few strings, and being something of a musician, he would begin to play a few lively and cheerful tunes, altering his voice so as not to be recognized. Then he would quickly progress into Moorish ballads, which he sang so pleasantly and with such gusto that every passer-by stopped to listen to him, and while he continued to sing he was constantly surrounded by children. Luis the negro, who was listening between the two doors, was mesmerized by the *virote*'s music and would have given his right arm to be able to open the door and listen to him more at his leisure; so strong is the desire amongst negroes to become musicians. And whenever Loaysa wanted his audience to leave him, he would stop singing, pick up his guitar, and, supporting himself on his crutches, move away.

He performed for the negro (for he was performing for him alone) four or five times, since he reckoned that to bring that edifice to the ground his best strategy must be to start with the negro. This assumption did not prove false. When he arrived at the door one night, as was his custom, and began to tune his guitar, he sensed that the negro was already alert and listening, and so he approached the crack at the edge of the door and said in a low voice:

'Would it be possible, Luis, to have a glass of water, because I'm feeling thirsty and can't sing?'

'No,' said the negro, 'because I don't have the key to this door and there's no hole through which I can pass it to you.'

'Who's got the key, then?' asked Loaysa.

'My master,' replied the negro, 'who's the most jealous man in the whole world. And if he knew that I were here now talking to someone, my life wouldn't be worth living. But who is it that's asking me for some water?'

'I', replied Loaysa, 'am a poor cripple, lame in one leg, and I earn my living by begging from our good citizens; and on top of that I also teach a few negroes and other poor people to play, and I've already got three negroes, slaves of three aldermen, whom I've taught well enough for them to be able to play at any dance and in any tavern, and they've paid me very handsomely for it.'

'I'd pay you far better,' said Luis, 'if I had some way of taking lessons; but it's impossible, because when my master goes out of a morning he locks the door to the street, and when he returns he does the same thing, leaving me cooped up between two doors.'

'Good lord, Luis,' said Loaysa, for by now he knew the negro's name,* 'if you could find some way of getting me inside at night from time to time to give you a lesson, in less than a fortnight I'd have you so skilful with the guitar that you could play without shame at any street corner; because let me tell you that I've a particular knack for teaching, and what's more, I've heard it said that you're very gifted, and from what I can intuit and judge from your voice, which is high-pitched, you must sing very well.

'I don't sing badly,' replied the negro, 'but what's the use, if the only song I know is the 'Star of Venus' and the one that starts off 'In a green meadow', and the one that goes:

> With trembling hand clasping
> The bars of a window . . .*

'All these are nothing,' said Loaysa, 'compared with what I could teach you, because I know all the ballads about the Moor Abindarráez and the ones about his lady Jarifa,* and all those that get sung about the history of the great Sufi Tumen Beyo,* and the sacred sarabands* which are so good that they even leave the Portuguese lost for words. And I use such simple methods to teach all this that even if you're in no hurry to learn, you'll scarcely have time to eat three or four pecks of salt before you're a decent player of all types of guitar.'

Having heard this the negro sighed and said, 'What's the use of all this if I don't know how to get you into the house?'

'I've got a suggestion,' said Loaysa. 'Try to get the keys from your master, and I'll give you a piece of wax for you to press the keys in hard enough for the wards to leave their impression; and because I've become quite fond of you, I'll get a locksmith friend of mine to make new keys. That way I'll be able to get inside at night and teach you better than I'd teach Prester John of the Indies,* because it seems a great shame to me that a voice such as yours should remain unheard because you lack the support of a guitar. For I want you to know, Luis, that the best voice in the world loses some of its essential quality when it's not accompanied by an instrument, whether it be a guitar or clavichord, organ or harp, but what's most suited to your voice is the guitar, being the easiest to handle and the least costly of instruments.'

'That's all very well and good,' replied the negro, 'but it's impossible, because the keys never come into my possession; my master doesn't let them out of his clutches during the day and at night they sleep beneath his pillow.'

'Then think of something else, Luis,' said Loaysa, 'if you really want to be an accomplished musician, because if you don't, then I'm wasting my time giving you advice.'

'What do you mean, if I really want to?' replied Luis, 'So much so that I'll stop at nothing, as long as it's humanly possible, in order to be a musician.'

'Well, if that's the case,' said the *virote*, 'I'll get something past these doors to you, if you'll make a space by removing some of the earth next to the hinge. As I say, I'll pass you some pincers and a hammer, so that at night you can use them to remove the nails from the lock very easily, and it'll be just as easy for us to put the plate back in place without anyone noticing that it's been removed. And once I'm inside, locked up with you in your loft, or wherever you sleep, I'll get the job done so quickly that you'll see even more than I've already said, which will enhance my reputation and improve your skill. And as to what we might eat, have no worries because I'll bring more than a week's provisions for both of us, for I've got pupils and friends who'll never see me suffer want.'

'As for food,' replied the negro, 'there'll be no need to worry on that score, what with the portion my master gives me and the left-overs which the slaves give me, there'll be more than enough food for two. Just let me have this hammer and pincers you speak of, and I'll make room next to this hinge for them to get through, and I'll hide and cover it with mud. Although it may take a few knocks to get the plate off, my master sleeps so far from this door that it'll take a miracle or really bad luck on our part for him to hear them.'

'Let's leave it in God's hands,' said Loaysa, 'for two days from now, Luis, you'll have everything you need to put our virtuous plan into effect; and beware of eating things that'll make your throat phlegmy, because they do no good at all and only a great deal of harm to the voice.'

'Nothing makes me quite so hoarse,' replied the negro, 'as wine; but I won't give it up for all the voices on earth.'

'Nor am I suggesting such a thing,' said Loaysa, 'and God forbid that I should. Drink, Luis my good fellow, drink, and much good may it do you, because wine drunk in moderation never did any harm at all.'

'I do drink in moderation' replied the negro, 'Here I've got a jug which holds four pints precisely and exactly; the slaves fill it up for me without my master knowing, and the caterer also brings me a little wineskin on the sly which holds exactly eight pints, which I use to top up the jug.'

'If only my own life were as good as yours sounds,' said Loaysa, 'for a dry throat can neither sing nor grunt.'

'God go with you,' said the negro, 'but be sure to come here and sing every night without fail until you bring what you need to get inside, because I'm itching to get my hands on the guitar.'

'You just try and stop me,' replied Loaysa, 'and I'll even bring you some new little tunes.'

'That's all I ask,' said Luis, 'and now you must sing me something, so that I can go off to bed in a good mood, and as far as payment is concerned, I wish you to know, sir, that I'll pay you better than any rich man.'

'I'm not concerned about that,' said Loaysa, 'you'll pay me for what I teach you, and for the moment, listen to this little tune, for when I'm inside you'll witness wondrous things.'

'The sooner the better,' replied Luis.

And when this long dialogue had come to an end, Loaysa sang a lively little ballad that left the negro feeling so happy and satisfied that he could scarcely wait for the moment when the door would be opened.

Loaysa had no sooner left the door than, with a lightness of step scarcely to be expected of someone carrying crutches, he went off to give his advisers an account of the good start he had made, which augured well for the equally happy ending he was anticipating. He found them and told them everything that he had arranged with the negro, and the following day they acquired tools efficient enough to break the toughest nails as if they were made of wood.

The *virote* did not neglect to go back and perform for the negro, any more than the negro neglected to prepare a hole big enough to accommodate what his teacher would give him, covering it up so well that, unless one were to search for it with a distrustful or suspicious eye, it was impossible to detect. On the second night Loaysa gave him the tools and Luis tested his strength and, almost without applying any, he found that the nails were broken, and holding the lock plate in his hand, he opened the door and drew his Orpheus and teacher inside. When he saw him with his two crutches, his clothes so ragged, and his leg so thoroughly bandaged, he stared at him in amazement. Loaysa was no longer wearing the patch over his eye, since it was unnecessary, and as he entered the house he embraced his good pupil, kissed his face, and placed in his hands a large wine-skin, a box of preserves, and other sweetmeats, of which he carried several well-stocked bags. Laying aside his crutches as if he had no disability whatsoever, he began to prance around, all of which left the negro more than a little surprised, and Loaysa said to him:

'Understand, brother Luis, that my lameness and disability are not the result of any illness but of the ingenuity I use to earn my living begging for the love of God. With the help of this craftiness and my music, I live the best life in the world, a world in which all those who are not ingenious or cunning will die of hunger; and you'll come to see this in the course of our friendship.'

'Time will tell,' replied the negro, 'but let's get on with the business of putting this plate back in place, so that no one'll notice that it's been removed.'

'That's a good idea.'

And taking nails from Loaysa's bag of provisions, they replaced the lock in exactly the same position as before, which greatly pleased the negro. Loaysa went up to the room which the negro occupied in the hay loft and made himself as comfortable as possible.

Luis then lit a wax taper and without more ado Loaysa took out his guitar and, playing it quietly and delicately, so entranced the negro's senses that listening to him sent him into transports of delight. After playing for a while he took out some more food and gave it to his pupil, who drank so sweetly and yet so heartily from the wineskin that it transported him even further than the music had done. Once this state had been achieved, he then insisted that Luis should have a lesson, and since more than a drop of wine had gone to the poor negro's head, he could not strike a single correct note. Yet, in spite of this, Loaysa had him believe that he already knew at least two songs; and the amazing thing is that the negro believed him and spent the whole night strumming the guitar, which was out of tune and missing a few of its strings.

They slept through what little of the night remained, and at about six o'clock in the morning Carrizales came downstairs and opened the inner door and also the one leading to the street and stood waiting for the caterer, who soon arrived, handed food through the turnstile, and went away again. He called out to the negro to come down and collect the barley for the mule and his own portion. Once he had taken them old Carrizales went out, leaving both doors locked behind him, without noticing what had been done to the street door, which more than cheered teacher and pupil.

The master of the house had scarcely stepped out when the negro snatched up the guitar and began to play in such a way that all the maidservants heard him and asked at the turnstile, 'What's this, Luis? Since when have you had a guitar or who gave it to you?'

'Who gave it to me? Only the best musician in the world, who's to teach me more than six thousand songs in less than six days.'

'And where is this musician?' asked the duenna.

'He's not far from here,' replied the negro, 'and if I weren't embarrassed and afraid of my master, perhaps I'd show him to you, for I swear that the sight of him would please you.'

'And where might he be that we should be able to see him,' retorted the duenna, 'if no other man except our master has ever entered this house?'

'Ah well,' said the negro, 'I don't want to tell you anything until you've seen what I know and what he's taught me in the short space of time I mentioned.'

'To be sure,' said the duenna, 'if this teacher of yours isn't some demon, I don't know who could make a musician of you so quickly.'

'You just wait,' said the negro. 'You'll see and hear for yourself soon enough.'

'That cannot be,' said another young woman, 'because we have no windows on to the street to be able to see or hear anyone.'

'The matter's taken care of,' said the negro, 'for there's a cure for every ill except death; especially if you're willing and able to keep quiet.'

'You just watch us keep quiet, brother Luis,' said one of the slaves. 'We'll be quieter than if we were dumb, because I assure you, my friend, that I'm dying to hear a decent voice, for since we got shut up in this place, we haven't even heard any birds sing.'

Loaysa was listening to all these exchanges with the greatest satisfaction, since it seemed that they were all contributing to the attainment of his pleasure and that good fortune had had a hand in guiding their words according to his wishes.

The maids went away with a promise from the negro that, when they least expected it, he would call them to hear a good voice; and fearing that his master might return and find him speaking to them, he left them and withdrew to the sanctuary of his quarters. He wanted to have a lesson but dared not play during the day, for fear that his master might hear him. The latter returned home shortly afterwards, and closing the doors behind him as was his custom, locked himself up in the house. When Luis was being given his food through the turnstile that day, he told the negress who was serving him that once their master had fallen asleep that night they were all to be sure to come down to the turnstile door to hear the promised voice. The truth is that before he said this he had petitioned his teacher with many requests to be so kind as to sing and play that night at the turnstile, so that he could keep his promise to the maids that they would hear an exceptional voice, assuring him that he would be extremely well treated by all of them. The teacher pretended to need some persuasion to do what he really desired to do above all else; but finally he said that he would do what his good pupil asked of him, for no other reason than to make him happy.

The negro embraced him and kissed him on the cheek to demonstrate how happy the promised favour had made him, and that day fed Loaysa as well as if he were eating in his own home, or perhaps even better, since it might have been the case that at home he would have gone wanting.

Night came, and at midnight, or just a little before, hissing could be heard at the turnstile and Luis immediately realized that the flock had arrived, and calling to his teacher, they came down from the loft with the guitar well strung and better tuned. Luis asked who and how many were gathered to listen. They replied that everyone was there except for their mistress, who was still sleeping with her husband, a fact which disappointed Loaysa. Nevertheless, he wanted to get his plan under way and satisfy his pupil and so, gently playing the guitar, he produced such wonderful sounds that they astonished the negro and amazed the flock of women who were listening to him.

How, then, shall I describe their sentiments when they heard him play 'How it grieves me'* and finish with the devilish tones of the saraband, recently introduced into Spain? There was not an old woman who did not join in the dance, nor a young one who did not work herself into a frenzy of motion, all the while treading noiselessly in a bizarre silence, and posting sentries and spies to warn them should the old man wake up. Loaysa also sang *seguidillas* which crowned his audience's pleasure, and they pestered the negro to reveal the identity of such a marvellous musician. The negro told them that he was a poor beggar, the most handsome and charming ever to emerge from amongst the wretched of Seville.

They begged him to find a way for them to see him, insisting that he should not leave the house for a fortnight and promising that they would treat him very well and provide him with whatever he might need. They asked Luis what means he had employed to get him inside the house, but to this question he made no reply. As to the other matter, he said that in order to be able to see him they should make a small hole in the turnstile and that afterwards they would fill it in with wax; and as for keeping him in the house, he would do his best to persuade him.

Loaysa also spoke to them, placing himself at their service in such persuasive terms that it was obvious to the women that they were no product of some poor beggar's wit. They asked him to come to the same place the following night; they would persuade their mistress to come down to listen to him, in spite of the fact that her husband was a light sleeper, a condition that did not arise from his advanced age so much as from his excessive jealousy. To this Loaysa replied that if they wished to hear him without fear of the old man suddenly bursting in upon them, then he would give them some powder to sprinkle in his wine, which would send him into a deeper and longer sleep than usual.

'Bless my soul,' said one of the young women, 'if that were true, what good fortune would have entered our doors without us noticing or deserving it. It wouldn't be a sleeping draught for him so much as an elixir of life for all of us and for my poor mistress, Leonora his wife, for he continually vexes her with his company and won't let her out of his sight for a moment. Oh, my good sir, bring this powder, and may God grant you all your heart desires. Go now and don't delay; bring it, good sir, for I offer to mix it with the wine myself and to be the cupbearer; and may it please God to make the old man sleep for three days and nights, which would mean as many days of glorious release for the rest of us.'

'Then I will bring it,' said Loaysa, 'and it's of such a nature that it does no more harm or mischief to the one who takes it than to provoke a very deep sleep.'

They all pleaded with him to bring it quickly and, agreeing to bore the hole in the turnstile the following night with a gimlet, and to bring their mistress to see and hear him, they separated. The negro, although it was almost dawn, wanted to have a lesson, which Loaysa gave him and convinced him that no other pupil of his had a better ear than he did; yet the poor negro neither knew, nor would he ever know, how to strike a single chord.

Loaysa's friends were faithful in coming at night to listen through the street door to see whether their friend had any information or request to communicate. When he heard the prearranged signal Loaysa knew that they were at the door and through the gap near the hinge he gave them an account of the favourable state of his endeavours, strongly urging them to look for some sleep-inducing substance to give to Carrizales, for he had heard talk of some powder which had this effect. They told him that they had a doctor friend who would give them the best concoction he could, if such a thing existed. Encouraging him to proceed with the enterprise, and promising to come back the following night with all due caution, they quickly departed.

Night came and the doves flocked together at the summons of the guitar. With them came the innocent Leonora, trembling and fearful that her husband might wake up. For although she had not wanted to come, overwhelmed as she was by this fear, her maids and especially the duenna said so much about the sweetness of the music and the gallant nature of the penniless musician (for without having seen him, she praised him more highly than Absalom* and Orpheus) that their poor mistress, convinced and persuaded by them, was obliged to do what she did not wish or would ever wish to do. The first thing they did was to bore the hole in the turnstile in order to see the musician, who was no longer dressed in his poor man's rags, but in full sailor-style breeches of fawn taffeta, a doublet of the same material with gold braid, a satin cap of the same colour, and a starched collar edged with long points and lace. For he had brought all this with him in his bags, anticipating that the occasion might arise when it would be appropriate to change his costume.

He was a graceful and fine-looking young man; and since they had for so long been accustomed to having only their old master to look at, it seemed to them that they were gazing upon an angel. They positioned themselves at the hole, one by one, to take a look, and to help them see him more clearly, the negro traced the contours of his body from his head to his toes with a lighted wax taper. And once they had all seen him, including the youngest black slave girls, Loaysa picked up his guitar and sang so beautifully that night that he left the whole of his audience, old and young alike, in a state of admiration and awe. They all pleaded with Luis to find the ways and means of getting his good teacher into the inner part of the house, so that they could hear and see him at closer quarters, rather than by peering through their little peep-hole as if it were a sextant. This would also remove the anxiety caused by being so far from their master, who might take them by surprise and catch them red-handed, which would not happen if they had him hidden inside.

Their mistress earnestly contradicted this proposal, insisting that they do no such thing nor allow him to come into the house, because it would sorely distress her, and anyway, they could see and hear him safely and without endangering their honour where they were.

'What honour?' asked the duenna, 'The king's got enough for everyone. Go lock yourself up with your Methuselah if you want to, but leave us alone to take our pleasure as best we can. And what's more, this gentleman seems so honourable, that he'll not require any more of us than we ourselves desire.'

'I, my good ladies,' said Loaysa at this point, 'did not come here with any other intention than to serve your honourable selves with my heart and soul, grieved by your extraordinary isolation and by the time you are wasting in this cloistered life-style. On the life of my father, I am a man of such a simple, gentle, and decent character, and so submissive, that I will do no more than is requested of me; and if any of you were to say "Teacher, sit here; teacher, move over there; lie down there, come over here," I would obey like the tamest and best-trained dog who jumps for the King of France.'*

'If that's the case,' said the naïve Leonora, 'how exactly will the good teacher get inside?'

'Well,' said Loaysa, 'your ladyships must do your utmost to get a wax impression of the key to this middle door; I'll arrange for a copy to be brought tomorrow night which we can use.'

'In getting a copy of that key,' said one young woman, 'we'll have copies of every key in the house, because it's the master key.'

'So much the better,' replied Loaysa.

'This is all very true,' said Leonora, 'but before he does anything else this gentleman is to swear that once he's inside he'll do nothing but sing and play when we say so, and that he'll remain shut up and quiet wherever we put him.'

'I do so swear,' said Loaysa.

'That oath is meaningless,' replied Leonora, 'for he must swear on the life of his father, and also on the cross and kiss it so that we can all be witnesses.'

'I swear on my father's life,' said Loaysa, 'and by the sign of the cross, which I kiss with my unclean mouth.'

And making the sign of the cross with two fingers, he kissed it three times. Then another young woman spoke up: 'Listen, sir, please don't forget about that powder, will you, because it's crucial to our plan.'

With these words that night's conversation came to an end and everyone was left feeling pleased with the arrangement. And at that hour, which was already the second after midnight, good luck, which was directing Loaysa's affairs ever more favourably, brought his friends to the street. They gave their customary signal, which was a few notes on a Jew's harp.* Loaysa spoke to them, explaining how far he had got in achieving his objective, and asked whether they had brought the powder or some other substance to make Carrizales sleep, as he had requested. He also told them of the business concerning the master key.

They told him that the powder or ointment would be brought the following night, and would be so effective that by simply applying it to the wrists and temples it would induce a very deep sleep from which the sleeper would not awaken for two days, unless the anointed areas were washed clean with vinegar. They also asked him to give them the wax key impression, for they would easily get another made. And so they departed and Loaysa and his pupil slept for what little of the night remained. Loaysa looked forward to the following night with great expectation and wondered whether they would keep their word concerning the key. And although time seems to drag and to tarry to those who are waiting, it eventually catches up with thought itself and the desired moment arrives, for time never slows down or stands still.

Night, then, arrived and with it the customary hour for assembling at the turnstile where all the household maids were gathered, young and old, black and white, since they were all keen to see the musician inside their seraglio. But Leonora did not come, and when Loaysa asked after her he was told that she was still in bed with her husband, who kept the door to their quarters locked, and after locking it placed the key beneath his pillow. They also informed him that their mistress had told them that once the old man was sleeping she would endeavour to get the key from him and press it in the wax, which was already softened for the purpose, and which they were shortly to go and retrieve through a cat-flap.

Loaysa was astonished by the old man's caution, but it did not cause his desire to falter. At that moment they heard the Jew's harp and Loaysa took up his position and found his friends outside, who gave him a small jar of ointment possessing the properties they had explained to him on the previous night. Loaysa took it and told them to wait a while, because he would give them the impression of the key. He went back to the turnstile and told the duenna, since she was the one who seemed most fervently to desire his entry into the house, to take it to Leonora, inform her of its properties, and stress that she should try to anoint her husband very gently so as not to rouse him, and she would witness a miracle. The duenna did as she was told, and as she approached the cat-flap she found Leonora already stretched out full-length on the floor with her face close to the hole. When she got there the duenna lay down in the same way, put her mouth to her mistress's ear, and in a low voice told her that she had the ointment and how she was to test its efficacy. Leonora took the ointment from her and explained to the duenna how it was quite impossible for her to get the key away from her husband, because it was not in its usual place under his pillow, but wedged between the two mattresses and virtually half under his body. But she was to tell the teacher that if the ointment worked as well as he said it would they could remove the key as often as they wished and so it would not be necessary to make a copy. She told her to go and tell him so, and then to come back and see whether the ointment was taking effect, because she intended to put some on her husband immediately. The duenna came down to communicate all this to the teacher Loaysa, and he sent away his friends who had been waiting for the key. Trembling and scarcely daring to exhale, Leonora set about tentatively anointing her jealous husband's wrists as well as his nostrils, and when she moved on to the latter she thought that she felt him shudder, and she became paralysed with fear, thinking that he had caught her in the act. However, she finished applying the ointment to all the places she had been told were necessary, which was tantamount to embalming him for the grave.

Before very long the sleep-inducing ointment was giving ample proof of its effectiveness, because the old man immediately began to snore so loudly that he could be heard in the street. This was music to his wife's ears and sweeter even than the music of the negro's teacher. Still unable to believe her eyes, she approached and shook him gently, and then with a little more force, and then more vigorously still, to see whether he awoke; she became so daring that she rolled him from one side to the other, without him waking up. As soon as she saw this, she went to the cat-flap in the door and in bolder tones than she had used earlier she called to the duenna who was waiting outside and said, 'Congratulate me, sister, Carrizales is dead to the world.'

'So what are you waiting for, mistress, why don't you get the key?' asked the duenna. 'Don't forget that the musician has been waiting for it for more than an hour.'

'Wait, sister, I'll get it right now,' replied Leonora. And returning to the bed, she slipped her hand between the mattresses and removed the key without the old man sensing the loss, then holding it in her hand she began to jump for joy, and without further delay she opened the door and gave it to the duenna, who took it with the greatest delight.

Leonora instructed her to let the musician in and bring him to the gallery, because she herself dared not wander from there because of what might happen; but above all she was to get him to re-confirm the oath he had sworn not to do more than they ordered him to do, and if he refused to re-confirm it, then they were not under any circumstances to let him in.

'As you wish,' said the duenna, 'and I assure you that he'll not enter unless he first swears and swears again and kisses the cross six times.'

'There's no need to set a limit,' said Leonora, 'let him kiss it as many times as he pleases, but make sure that he swears on the life of his parents and by everything that he holds dear, because this way we'll be safe and able to listen to him singing and playing to our hearts' content, for upon my word, he does perform exquisitely.

Away with you then, don't delay any longer, let's not waste the whole night talking.'

The good duenna picked up her skirts, and with an uncharacteristic fleetness of foot reached the turnstile where the whole household was assembled and waiting for her. When she showed them the key she was carrying, they were so delighted that they raised her aloft like a newly appointed professor,* chanting 'Long live the duenna'. They were even more delighted when she announced that it was no longer necessary to make a counterfeit key, because judging by the way the anointed man was currently sleeping, they could have access to the house key as often as they liked.

'Come on then, friend,' said one of the young women, 'open up that door and let the gentleman in, for he's been waiting a good while, and let's have our fill of music like we've never done before.'

'But there is something to be done before that,' replied the duenna, 'we must make him swear an oath, like last night.'

'He's so good,' said one of the slaves, 'that he won't be worried about oaths.'

At this point the duenna opened the door, and holding it ajar she called to Loaysa, who had been listening to the proceedings through the hole in the turnstile. When he reached the door he wanted to step inside straight away, but the duenna placed a restraining hand upon his chest and said:

'You must understand, my good sir, as God is my judge, that all of us within these doors are as virginal as the mothers who bore us, with the exception of my mistress; and although I must look about forty, whereas in reality I'm two and a half months short of thirty, I too, for my sins, am a virgin. And if I appear older, difficulties, trials, and hardships can quite indiscriminately add years to your appearance. In view of this fact, it would be unreasonable, in exchange for hearing at best a handful of songs, to risk all the virginity that is locked up in this house; because even this negress, Guiomar, is a virgin. And so, my very good sir, before entering our realm you must swear a very solemn oath to do no more than we specifically order you to. And if our demands seem excessive, consider that the risk we are taking is even greater. And if you come with good intentions, the oath you swear will cost you little effort, because a good payer is not afraid of giving guarantees.'

'Mistress Marialonso has spoken well and wisely,' said one of the young women, 'just as you would expect from a sensible person who knows just how things should be; and if the gentleman won't swear, then he's not to come in.'

This prompted the negress Guiomar to say in her ungrammatical Spanish:

'For me, even never he swear, him come in with the devil an' all, even when swear, if you here, he forget everything.'

Loaysa listened dispassionately while Mistress Marialonso had her say and replied with calm gravity and authority:

'Let me assure you, my good sisters and companions, that my intention never was, is, or ever shall be other than to give you all the pleasure and satisfaction it is within my power to provide. I will therefore have no objection to taking this oath you require of me; but I could have wished for more faith to be shown in my word, because the word of a person such as myself is equivalent to a binding obligation; and I want you to know that there's more to a person than meets the eye, and that beneath a ragged cloak there's often a good drinker. But in order to persuade you all of my virtuous intent, I intend to swear as a good Catholic and an honourable man. And so, I swear by the undefiled efficacy, where it is most sacredly and lengthily contained, and by the passes of the holy mountain of Lebanon, and by all that is encompassed in the preface to the true history of Charlemagne,* together with the death of the giant Fierabras,* neither to depart from nor overstep the limits of the oath as sworn, nor the commandments of the humblest and lowliest of these ladies, or face the penalty, should I do, or wish to do otherwise, that from the present moment henceforward and thencebackward until now, I declare it to be null, void, and invalid.'

The obliging Loaysa had reached this point in his oath when one of the servants, who had been listening intently to his words, declared in a loud voice, 'This is an oath to soften the hardest stone, if ever I heard one! On my head be it if I ask you to swear any further, for you could get into the Cave of Cabra* itself with what you've sworn already!'

And grabbing him by the breeches she pulled him inside and all the other women immediately gathered around him. Then she went off to communicate the news to her mistress, who was keeping watch over her sleeping husband. When the messenger told her that the musician was already on his way up, she was at once delighted and distressed and asked whether he had taken an oath. She replied that he had, and in the most original way she had ever come across in her life.

'If he's sworn an oath,' said Leonora, 'then we've got him. Oh, how sensible I was to insist on the oath.'

At that moment the whole crowd arrived at once, with the musician at its centre and the way lit by the negro and the negress Guiomar. And when Loaysa saw Leonora, he made as if to throw himself at her feet and kiss her hands. But she, without uttering a sound, gestured for him to get up, and then they all stood around as if they were dumb, not daring to speak, for fear of being overheard by their master. Correctly interpreting their silence, Loaysa told them that they should feel free to speak normally, because the ointment with which the old man had been anointed was so effective that, short of actually killing a man, it left him as good as dead.

'I can vouch for that,' said Leonora, 'for if it were not so he would have already woken up twenty times, his sleep is so disturbed by his many ailments; but since I rubbed the ointment in he's been snoring like an animal.'

'If that's the case,' said the duenna, 'let's go to the room across the way, where we can listen to the gentleman sing and enjoy ourselves a bit.'

'Let's go,' said Leonora, 'but let Guiomar stay here on guard, so that she can warn us should Carrizales wake up.' To which Guiomar replied:

'Me, black, stay; you, white, go: God pardon all!'

The negress stayed behind; the others went to the drawing room where there was an elegant dais, and placing the gentleman in the middle, they all sat down. The good Marialonso picked up a candle and began to examine the gallant teacher from head to foot, and one of them declared 'Oh, what a quiff he's got, so fine and curly!' Another 'Oh, how white his teeth are! Have you ever seen shelled pine-nuts so white and so fine?' Another 'Oh, look what big, wide eyes he's got! Upon my mother's soul, they are so green, they look like emeralds.'* One praised his mouth, another his feet, and all together they carried out a detailed study of the various parts of his anatomy. Only Leonora remained silent and gazed at him, as it gradually dawned on her that he cut a much more handsome figure

than her husband. Then the duenna took the guitar from the negro
and placed it in Loaysa's hands, asking him to play and sing a few
verses which were very much in vogue in Seville at that time, which
went like this:

> Mother, my dear mother,
> Though you try to enchain me . . .

Loaysa did as she requested. They all stood up and began to dance
as if possessed by the music. The duenna knew the verses, though
she sang them with more enthusiasm than natural talent, and they
went as follows:

> Mother, my dear mother,
> Though you try to enchain me,
> *Unless I guard myself,*
> *You will never restrain me.*
>
> They say it's in writing,
> Of its truth there's no doubt,
> That it's living without
> It, that makes love inviting.
> There's naught unrequiting
> In passion locked away;
> It's by far the better way
> To let me remain free.
> *Unless I guard myself, etc.*
>
> If of its own volition
> The will is not contained,
> It will never be restrained
> By status or contrition;
> And with this one ambition
> It will death itself defy,
> Its desires to satisfy.
> Why can't you see this plainly?
> *Unless I guard myself, etc.*
>
> When she's of a disposition
> To fall in love just so,
> Then to the light she'll go
> Like a moth to its perdition.
> Though guards set up position,
> And scrupulously try

> To keep a watchful eye,
> Like you, they strive but vainly.
> *Unless I guard myself, etc.*
>
> A maid of fairest feature
> Will metamorphose
> When deep in love's throes,
> A chimerical creature,
> Quite changed in her nature:
> Hands of wool, feet of flax,
> And in a heart soft as wax
> Love's flame burns insanely.
> *Unless I guard myself,*
> *You will never restrain me.*

The circle of young women, led by the good duenna, was reaching the end of its singing and dancing when Guiomar the look-out arrived on the scene, in severe distress and shaking from head to foot as if she were having a fit, and announced in a voice half hoarse and half attempting a whisper, 'Master wake, mistress; mistress, master wake, and get up and come.'

Anyone who has observed how a flock of pigeons which has been calmly feeding in a field on what other hands have sown will suddenly take fright and fly away at the violent crack of gunfire and, forgetting their meal, will flap and flounder through the air in confusion and surprise, will be able to imagine the terror and alarm that seized the band and circle of dancers on hearing the unexpected news that Guiomar had delivered. Each one sought her own particular excuse and all of them together their collective means of escape, as they scurried off in various directions to conceal themselves in the attics and corners of the house, leaving the musician alone. Abandoning his guitar and his song, and highly agitated, he had no idea what to do.

Leonora wrung her beautiful hands and the lady Marialonso slapped herself in the face, albeit not too roughly. In other words, it was a scene of confusion, shock, and terror. But the duenna, being the more astute and self-possessed of the two, instructed Loaysa to enter one of her rooms while she and her mistress remained in the drawing room, for they would easily find some excuse to give her master should he find them there.

Loaysa hid himself away immediately and the duenna listened carefully to see whether she could detect the approach of her master but, hearing no sound at all, her spirits revived. Gradually, step by tentative step, she approached the room where her master slept, and hearing that he was snoring as loudly as before, and reassured that he was sleeping, she picked up her skirts and hurried back to share the good news with her mistress, who was overjoyed to hear it.

The good duenna did not want to miss the opportunity which good fortune now offered her of enjoying, before any of the others, the charms which she imagined the musician to possess. So, telling Leonora to wait in the drawing room while she went to call him, she left her and went to where he was waiting, no less thoughtful than confused, for news of what the anointed old man was doing. He was cursing the failure of the ointment and complaining of the credulity of his friends, and also his own lack of foresight in not first testing it on someone else before using it on Carrizales.

At this point the duenna arrived and assured him that the old man was sleeping more soundly than ever. He heaved a sigh of relief and turned his attention to the many amorous words that Marialonso addressed to him, from which he was able to deduce her wicked purpose, and resolved to use her as bait to capture her mistress. And while the two of them were engaged in this conversation the other maids, who were hiding in various parts of the house, re-emerged from all directions to ascertain whether their master had indeed woken up. Finding that the whole house was as silent as the tomb, they reached the room where they had left their mistress and learned from her that their master was still sleeping. They asked after the musician and the duenna, and when she told them where they were they all went off, as silently as they had come, to eavesdrop on the two of them through the door.

Even Guiomar was one of those gathered there; the negro, however, was not. For as soon as he heard that his master had awoken, he grabbed the guitar and went to hide in his loft, where he now lay sweating out his fear under the blanket of his miserable bed. In spite of his fear he could not resist plucking at the guitar, so great was his fondness (the devil take him!) for music.

The young women overheard the old woman's amorous compliments and each one began to call her all kinds of bad names; no one referred to her as an old maid without adding an adjective or qualifier such as witch-like, hairy, fickle, and many other things besides, which out of respect will remain unrecorded. But what would have caused most amusement to anyone who heard them at the time were the expressions of the negress Guiomar who, being Portuguese and not very fluent in Spanish, cursed her in a peculiarly funny way. And the outcome of the conversation between the two of them was that he would submit to her demands only on the condition that she first of all deliver up her mistress to him to do with as he pleased.

It was no easy thing for the duenna to deliver what the musician requested; but in exchange for the fulfilment of her desire, which had by now taken possession of her soul and the very marrow of every bone in her body, she would have promised him the most impossible things imaginable. She left him and went to speak to her mistress; and when she saw all the servants crowding around her door, she told them to return to their quarters, saying that there would be opportunity to enjoy the musician the following night with less or no fear of interruption, because the commotion of this night had taken the edge off their pleasure.

They all understood perfectly well that the old woman wanted to be left alone; but they could not refuse to obey her because she was in authority over them all. The maids withdrew and she went to the drawing room to persuade Leonora to consent to the wishes of Loaysa, with a long speech that was so well structured that she gave the impression of having had it prepared for several days. She emphasized his courtesy, his valour, his elegance, and his many charms. She described how much more gratifying the embraces of a young lover would be compared with those of her old husband, assuring her that her pleasures would be secret and long-lasting. She added many other details of this nature which the devil put in her mouth, so full of colourful rhetoric, so convincing and effective, that they would be sufficient to soften the hardest marble let alone the tender and susceptible heart of the innocent and naïve Leonora. Oh, duennas, born and bred in this world to cause the destruction of a thousand virtuous and good intentions!* Oh, long and elaborate headdresses, chosen to impose authority in the halls and drawing rooms of the principal ladies of the land, how you contravene your obligations in the way you carry out your now inescapable duties! In short, the duenna was so eloquent, the duenna was so persuasive, that Leonora was forced to yield, Leonora was deceived, Leonora was ruined; and with her came crashing to the ground all the precautions of the prudent Carrizales, who was sleeping the slumber of the death of his honour.

Marialonso took her tearful mistress by the hand and virtually had to drag her to where Loaysa was waiting. Giving them her blessing with a false and demonic laugh, she closed the door behind her and left them shut up inside while she settled down in the drawing room to sleep, or rather, to await her own reward. But the wakefulness of recent nights got the better of her and she fell asleep on the dais.

It might have been an appropriate moment, if we did not know that he was asleep, to ask Carrizales what had been achieved by his painstaking precautions, his suspicions, his carefulness, his convictions, the high walls of his house, the exclusion from it, even in the form of a shadow, of anyone with a masculine name. What now of the narrow turnstile, the hefty walls, the darkened windows, the extraordinary confinement, the large dowry with which he had endowed Leonora, the gifts he continually gave her, his fair treatment of the maids and slaves, the fact that he never neglected for a moment to provide them with everything he imagined them to need or desire? However, it has already been stated that it would be pointless to ask him, because he was sleeping more soundly than necessity required. If he had heard the question and hazarded an answer, he could not have given a better response than to shrug his shoulders, arch his eyebrows, and say:

'All this was razed to its foundations by the cunning of an idle and ill-intentioned youth, the malice of a dishonest duenna, and the error of an impressionable girl, provoked and persuaded by the arguments of others. God deliver each and every one of us from such enemies, against whom no shield of prudence is sufficient to defend us, nor sword of caution sharp enough.'

However, in spite of everything, Leonora's courage was such that, precisely when she had greatest need of it, she was able to repulse the ignoble advances of her cunning seducer, which were inadequate to subdue her; he exhausted himself in vain, she was victorious in the struggle, and they both fell asleep. At that moment heaven ordained that, in spite of the ointment, Carrizales should wake up and, as was his custom, he explored the whole bed with his hand. When he found that his beloved wife was missing he leapt out of bed in terror and astonishment, with greater agility and determination than his advanced years would have led one to expect. When he discovered that his wife was not in the room and realized that it was open and that the key was missing from between the mattresses, he thought he would lose his mind. Regaining a little of his composure he went to the gallery and from there, placing one foot stealthily in front of the other so as not to be detected, he reached the drawing room where the duenna was sleeping. When he saw that she was alone and without Leonora, he proceeded to the duenna's room, and opening the door very quietly he saw what he would gladly have sacrificed his sight never to have seen. He saw Leonora lying in Loaysa's arms, and both of them sleeping as soundly as if it were they who were under the influence of the ointment rather than the jealous old man.

Carrizales's heart stopped beating as he gazed at this bitter spectacle; his voice stuck in his throat, his arms hung helpless at his side, and he stood as if turned into a cold marble statue. Although anger worked its natural effect on him by reviving his dying spirits, his grief was so overwhelming that it would not allow him to draw breath. Yet he would have exacted the revenge which that great misdeed demanded of him if he had had weapons to hand. He therefore decided to go back to his room to fetch a dagger, and then to return to remove the stains on his honour by shedding the blood of his two enemies, even the blood of the entire household. Having made this honourable and necessary resolution, he returned to his room as silently and cautiously as he had come, whereupon his grief and anguish weighed so heavily on his spirits that, too feeble to do anything else, he fell in a faint across his bed.

Daybreak arrived and caught the two new adulterers entwined in each other's arms. Marialonso awoke and wanted to go and claim what in her opinion was owing to her; but seeing that it was late, she decided to defer it until the following night. Leonora was alarmed to see the day already well advanced and cursed her carelessness and that of the wretched duenna, and the two of them approached her husband's room with frightened steps, praying fervently to themselves that they would find him still snoring away. When they saw that he was lying on the bed and making not a sound, they thought that since he was asleep the ointment was still working, and they hugged each other in great delight. Leonora approached her husband and, taking him by the arm, she rolled him from side to side to see whether he would wake up without them having to bathe him with vinegar, which they had been told would be necessary to bring him round. But with this movement Carrizales recovered from his faint and, letting out a very heavy sigh, he said in a feeble and pitiful voice, 'Oh, woe is me, what a sad end my fortune has brought me to!'

Leonora did not fully understand what her husband was saying, but seeing him awake and hearing him speak, and surprised that the effects of the ointment were not as long-lasting as indicated, she went up to him and, putting her face next to his and holding him close, she said, 'What's wrong, my lord, for you seem to be complaining of something?'

Hearing the voice of his sweet enemy the wretched old man opened his eyes and, as if in dazed astonishment, fixed their wild expression upon her and without blinking stared hard at her for some time, at the end of which he said, 'Be so good, my lady, as to send for your parents immediately on my behalf, because something is weighing on my heart which is sapping me of all my strength and I fear that before very long it will take my life, and I should like to see them before I die.'

Leonora readily believed the truth of her husband's words, thinking that the effects of the ointment and not what he had witnessed had reduced him to this state. She responded that she would do what he ordered, and instructed the negro to go without delay to fetch her parents. Then, hugging her husband, she showed him more affection than she had ever done, asking him what it was that troubled him in such tender and loving terms as if he were the thing she loved most dearly in the whole world. He continued to gaze at her in the same abstracted way, her every word and caress wounding him like a sword-thrust piercing his very soul.

The duenna had already informed the domestic staff and Loaysa of their master's illness, stressing that it had to be something serious because he had forgotten to order the street door to be shut when the negro went to summon their mistress's parents. They were equally surprised that he had been sent on such an embassy, because neither of them had set foot in the house since the marriage of their daughter.

In short, they all went about silent and puzzled, ignorant of the true source of their master's affliction, which caused him from time to time to sigh so heavily and so distressingly that with each sigh his soul seemed to tear itself from his body. Leonora cried to see him in that condition, and he laughed the laugh of the deranged when he contemplated the falsity of her tears.

At that moment Leonora's parents arrived, and finding the main door and the door to the patio open and the house as silent as the tomb and empty, their surprise and alarm were considerable. They went to their son-in-law's bedroom and found him, as has already been described, with his eyes riveted on his wife, whom he was holding by the hands, as the two of them wept profusely. She wept at the mere sight of her husband's tears; he wept to see how falsely she shed hers. As soon as her parents came in, Carrizales began to speak and said, 'Please be seated, all the rest of you may leave the room and only Mistress Marialonso should remain.' They did as they were instructed, and when the five of them were alone, without waiting for anyone else to speak, Carrizales wiped his eyes and said in a calm voice:

'I am quite sure, my good parents, that it will be unnecessary to call upon witnesses in order to convince you of a truth I wish to state to you. You will no doubt remember, for it is not possible that you could have forgotten, with what affection and how wholeheartedly one year, one month, five days, and nine hours ago precisely you gave your beloved daughter to me to be my lawfully wedded wife. You also know how generously I endowed her—the dowry was after all large enough for three women of similar status to marry and be considered rich. You will similarly remember the painstaking efforts I took to dress and adorn her with anything she happened to desire and I myself considered appropriate. You have seen no more and no less, my good people, how, prompted by my natural disposition and fearful of the misfortune from which I have no doubt I am to die, and schooled in the experience of my many years and by the different and strange things that happen in the world, I wanted to protect this jewel, which I chose and you gave me, as carefully as possible. I raised the outer walls of this house, I removed the view from the windows on to the street, I doubled the locks on the doors, I installed a turnstile, as if it were a convent; I condemned to perpetual exile everything possessing the mere shadow or name of male. I gave her maids and slaves to serve her; I refused nothing that either she or they cared to ask of me; I made her my equal; I shared my most intimate thoughts with her; I gave her all my worldly goods.

'All these measures were taken so that, if I planned correctly, I could be sure of peacefully enjoying what had cost me so much effort, and she would give me no reason to entertain a single jealous or anxious thought. However, since human endeavour cannot escape the punishment which the divine will wishes to visit upon those who do not exclusively place all their hopes and desires in it, it comes as no surprise that I should be frustrated in mine and that I should myself have been the source of the poison which is taking away my life. But since I am aware of the suspense in which I am keeping you all hanging on my every word, I want to conclude the long preamble to this speech by saying in one word what it is impossible to say in a thousand. Let me tell you, then, my good people, that from all that I have said and done it has transpired that this morning I found this young girl, born into the world to destroy my peace and put an end to my life'—and as he said this he pointed to his wife—'in the arms of a handsome youth, who is now shut up in the apartment of this foul duenna.'

Carrizales had scarcely pronounced these last words when Leonora's heart sank and she fell fainting at her husband's knees. The colour drained from Marialonso's face and a lump rose in the throats of Leonora's parents which prevented them from uttering a word. But going on regardless, Carrizales said:

'The revenge which I intend to take for this offence neither is nor should be of the kind that is ordinarily taken in such circumstances, for since my behaviour was extraordinary I want the nature of my revenge to be similarly unusual. I shall exact it on myself as the party bearing most guilt in the crime; I should have anticipated that this young girl of fifteen could not live at ease or in harmony with an old man of almost eighty.* I was the one who, like a silkworm, constructed around myself the house in which I would die. I do not blame you, ill-advised child'—and saying this he leaned forward and kissed Leonora's face as she lay unconscious—'I do not blame you, I repeat, because the arguments of cunning old women and the flattering words of enamoured young men easily conquer and triumph over the inexperienced minds of the young. But in order for all the world to see how willingly and faithfully I loved you, I want in this my dying moment to demonstrate it in a way that will be remembered as a model, if not of goodness, then at least of unprecedented sincerity. I therefore want a notary to be summoned immediately to rewrite my will. In it I will give instructions for Leonora's dowry to be doubled and I will request that when my days are over—and there are few remaining—she consent to marry—which she will be able to do without difficulty—that young man who was never offended by the white hairs of this tormented old man. Thus she will see that, if while I lived I never deviated for a moment from what I believed to be her pleasure, in death I shall do likewise, and I want her to be happy with the one she must love so dearly. I will give instructions for the rest of my wealth to be dedicated to other pious works, and to you, my good gentlefolk, I will leave enough for you to be able to live out the rest of your lives honourably. The notary must come soon, because my affliction is so great that it is rapidly cutting short my life.'

After he had said this he collapsed in a terrible faint and fell so close to Leonora that their faces touched: a strange and sad spectacle for the parents to behold as they looked at their beloved daughter and dear son-in-law. The wicked duenna did not want to wait around to face the recriminations she expected from her mistress's parents, and so she slipped out of the room and went to tell Loaysa what was happening, advising him to leave the house immediately, for she would be sure to inform him of developments via the negro, because there were no longer doors or keys to prevent it. Loaysa was astonished at this news and, following her advice, dressed up once more as a poor man and went to inform his friends of the strange and unexpected outcome of his amorous adventure.

While the two of them remained unconscious, Leonora's father sent for a notary friend of his, who arrived after both daughter and son-in-law had regained consciousness. Carrizales altered his will in the manner he had indicated without mentioning Leonora's indiscretion, except respectfully to request and plead with her to marry, in the case of his death, the man whom he had secretly named to her. When Leonora heard this she threw herself at her husband's feet and, with her heart pounding in her breast, said, 'Live many more years, my master and my whole world, for although you are not obliged to believe anything I say to you, I want you to know that I have not offended you except in thought.'

As she began to exonerate herself and explain the full truth of the matter, she became suddenly tongue-tied and once again fainted away. The grieving old man embraced her unconscious form; her parents also embraced her, and they all cried so bitterly that the notary who was writing the will was obliged, or rather compelled, to join them in their grief. In his will Carrizales provided for the basic needs of all the maids, he granted the slaves and the negro their liberty, and to the perfidious Marialonso he left nothing but the salary that was owing to her. But whatever it was, his distress was so severe that on the seventh day they carried him to his grave.

Leonora was left widowed, tearful, and rich; and when Loaysa expected her to fulfil the obligation which he knew her husband had had written into his will, he saw her a week later taking the veil in one of the most enclosed convents in the city. Despairing and almost ashamed, he went off to the Indies. Leonora's parents were very much saddened, although they derived consolation from what their son-in-law had left them and instructed in his will. The maids consoled themselves in the same way, as did the slaves with their liberty. Only the treacherous duenna was left poor and cheated in all her ill-conceived ambitions.

And as for me, I only desired to reach the end of this affair, example and illustration of what little faith can be placed in keys, turnstiles, and walls when the will remains free, and how much less faith should be placed in the immaturity of youth, especially when these duennas in their ample black habits and their long white head-dresses are whispering temptations in its ears. The only thing that leaves me perplexed is the reason why Leonora did not try harder to explain herself and convince her husband of how intact and inno-cent she had remained in that affair: but her confusion left her tongue-tied and the speed with which her husband died gave her no opportunity to absolve herself.

THE ILLUSTRIOUS KITCHEN MAID

Not very long ago in the illustrious and famous city of Burgos there lived two eminent and wealthy gentlemen, one of whom was called don Diego de Carriazo and the other don Juan de Avendaño. Don Diego had one son whom he named after himself and don Juan another whom he called don Tomás. In order to be economical with words, these two young gentlemen, who are to be the chief protagonists in this tale, will be known simply as Carriazo and Avendaño.

Carriazo was little more than thirteen years of age when he was inspired to try the picaresque way of life. Without being forced into such action by any ill treatment on the part of his parents, but by a mere whim and fancy of his own, he cut loose, as the slang of his generation would have it, from his parents' home and ventured out into the world. He was so content with the freedom of the road that even in the midst of the discomfort and hardship that came with it he did not miss the luxury of his father's house; travelling on foot did not tire him, the cold did not offend him, and the heat did not annoy him. As far as he was concerned each season of the year was like a mild and gentle spring; he slept as soundly upon unthreshed corn as he did upon a mattress; he bedded down in the hay lofts of inns with as much pleasure as if he were lying between fine linen sheets. All in all, he became such a successful *pícaro* that he could have taught the famous Alfarache himself a thing or two in the art of being a rogue.

In the three years it took him to reappear and return home he learned to play jackstones in Madrid, *rentoy* in the taverns of Toledo, and *presa y pinta** outside the city walls of Seville.* However, in spite of the fact that hardship and want are endemic to this way of life, Carriazo revealed a princeliness in all his dealings. His good breeding was clearly manifest in a thousand different ways because he was generous and open-handed towards his companions. He rarely paid homage to Bacchus, for although he drank wine he drank so little that he could never be counted amongst those poor devils who look as if they have painted their faces with vermilion and ochre whenever they drink too much of anything. In short, in Carriazo the world perceived a virtuous, clean, and well-bred *pícaro* of above-average intelligence. He ascended through all the grades of picaresque achievement until he graduated a master in the tunny fisheries of Zahara,* the *ne plus ultra* of picaresque activity.

Oh, kitchen skivvies, dirty, fat, and sleek, counterfeit beggars, false cripples, pickpockets of Zocodover* and the main square in Madrid, gaudy prayer merchants, basket carriers from Seville, lackeys of the underworld, and all the rest of that vast and motley bunch of people comprehensively known as *pícaros*! Curb that pride, don't give yourselves airs and don't call yourselves *pícaros* unless you have studied for two years in the academy of tunny fishing. That is where you will find hard work and idleness in their element. That is where you will find unmitigated squalor, plump fatness, urgent hunger, abundant satisfaction, undisguised vice, endless gambling, incessant brawling, sporadic deaths, vulgarities at every turn, the kind of dancing you find at weddings and the type of *seguidillas* you find in print, ballads with refrains and poems without. Here they sing, there they curse, on one side they quarrel, on the other they gamble, and everywhere they steal. That is where liberty reigns and work is conspicuous by its absence. That is where many noble fathers go or send someone else to look for their sons and that is where they find them; and the sons are so distraught at being removed from that way of life that you would think they were being carried off to their deaths.

However, the sweetness of the life-style I have sketched has a bitter edge to it: no one can sleep secure and free of the fear that at any moment they might be transported from Zahara to Barbary.* For this reason they retire at night to coastal towers and only by trusting in the eyes of watchmen and sentries are they able to close their own. For it has happened that sentries, watchmen, *pícaros*, foremen, boats and nets, together with all the rabble which congregates there have gone to bed in Spain and woken up in Tetuan.* However, this fear was not enough to prevent our Carriazo from turning up there three summers in succession to have a good time. During his final summer luck was so much on his side that he won almost seven hundred reales, with which he wanted to buy himself some new clothes and return to Burgos and the sight of his mother who had shed so many tears for him. He bade farewell to his friends, of whom he had many very good ones; he promised them that he would be with them again the following summer, for nothing but illness or death could prevent it. He left half of his soul there with them and gave his heart to those arid sands which in his eyes were fresher and greener than the Elysian fields.* Since he was accustomed to making journeys on foot he took this one in his stride, and wearing only sandals covered the distance between Zahara and Valladolid singing 'Three ducks, mother . . .'.* He stayed there for a fortnight in order to modify the colour of his complexion from its dark mulatto tone to a paler shade of brown, and to refashion his appearance by erasing the signs of the *pícaro* and reassuming the image of a gentleman.

He accomplished all this as well as the five hundred reales he took with him to Valladolid would allow, and even managed to keep back a hundred to hire a mule and a boy, in whose company he presented himself to his parents feeling happy and looking respectable. They received him with great delight and all their friends and relations came to congratulate them on the safe return of don Diego de Carriazo, their son. It should be noted that during his travels don Diego exchanged the name Carriazo for Urdiales, and this is what he was called by those who did not know his real name. Among those who came to see the new arrival were don Juan de Avendaño and his son don Tomás, with whom Carriazo struck up and maintained a very firm friendship since they were the same age and neighbours.

Carriazo spun his parents and everyone else present a thousand long and magnificent yarns concerning what had happened to him during the three years of his absence. He very carefully avoided the subject of the tunny fisheries, although they were constantly on his mind, especially when he saw the time approaching when he had told his friends he would return. He would not be distracted by the hunt in which his father engaged him nor enticed by the many respectable and enjoyable social gatherings which take place in that city. Compared with the grander amusements he was currently being offered he much preferred the pleasure he had experienced at the tunny fisheries.

Seeing him frequently melancholy and pensive, and trusting in their friendship, his friend Avendaño dared to ask him the reason for his downcast spirits and undertook to remedy them if he could, even if it meant shedding his own blood. Carriazo did not wish to conceal the truth from him because he did not want to compromise the great friendship they professed for one another. So he recounted, point for point, the life of the fishermen and explained how all his sad reflections sprang from the desire he cherished to return to such a way of life. He painted such an attractive picture that when Avendaño finished listening, he was more disposed to applaud than to condemn Carriazo's inclination.

In short, as a result of their conversation Avendaño was so swayed by Carriazo that he decided to go off with him and spend a summer enjoying the merry life that his friend had described to him. Carriazo was more than delighted with his resolve since it seemed that he had gained a witness to vouch for him and vindicate his ignoble intention.

They immediately devised a plan to collect together as much money as they could; and the best method they came up with was dependent on the fact that two months hence Avendaño was to go to Salamanca where, for his own pleasure, he had been studying Latin and Greek for three years. His father wanted him to continue and study the discipline of his choice, and the money he gave him would be available for their scheme.

Carriazo chose that moment to tell his father that he wished to go with Avendaño to study in Salamanca. His father fell in so readily with their proposal that after discussing the matter with Avendaño's father, it was arranged that they would set them up in a shared house in Salamanca and equip them with whatever else was required or deemed appropriate for the sons of two such fathers. When the time for their departure arrived, they were given money and put in the charge of a tutor who was more honest than intelligent. Their fathers handed them documents with instructions as to what they should do and how they should behave in order to progress in virtue and learning, which are the benefits which all students, especially the noble-born ones, must endeavour to derive from their long hours of toil and study. The boys looked suitably humble and obedient and their mothers cried; they received everyone's blessing and set off on their own mules, accompanied by two domestic servants as well as the tutor, who had grown a beard in order to lend more authority to his role.

When they reached the city of Valladolid they told the tutor that they wanted to stay there for two days in order to look around, for they had never been there before. He replied that anyone hastening to their studies as they were should not be detained even for an hour, let alone two days, by such trifling nonsense. It would weigh on his conscience if he allowed them to be detained even for a moment: they should leave at once, and if they did not, they would be sorry.

This was the limit of the efficiency of the good tutor or, if we prefer, steward. The young lads, who had already reaped an early harvest by stealing four hundred gold escudos from him, asked to be allowed to stay just one day, in which they wanted to go and see the Argales fountain, whose waters were being newly channelled to the city by means of a large and impressive aqueduct. In the end he granted them permission, albeit with a heavy heart because he wanted to avoid the expense of staying there overnight, preferring to stop at Valdeastillas, and cover the eighteen leagues that separate Valdeastillas from Salamanca in two days, rather than the twenty-two leagues from Valladolid. However, since devising a plan is one thing and bringing it to fruition is another, everything turned out contrary to his wishes.

The boys, accompanied by a servant and riding two very good domestic mules, went out to see the Argales fountain, famous for its antiquity and its waters and quite the equal of the Cano Dorado and the revered Priora, not to mention Leganitos and the sublime Castellana fountain, which easily outrivals Corpa and Pizarra de la Mancha.* They arrived at Argales, and when the servant thought that Avendaño was getting something to drink out of their saddle-bags he saw that in fact he took out a sealed letter, whereupon he instructed him to return to the city immediately and give it to their steward, and when he had done this he was to wait for them at the Campo Gate.

The servant obeyed, took the letter, and returned to the city while the boys turned their horses around and slept that night in Mojadas. Two days later they slept in Madrid and four days after that they sold their mules in a public market-place, having found one buyer who would advance six escudos in good faith and another who would even give them the full amount in gold. They put on peasant costumes, comprising short cloaks with tails, leather breeches or chaps, and coarse brown stockings. The following morning they found a draper who purchased their clothes from them, and by nightfall they were so altered that the mothers who had borne them would not have recognized them. Quickly rigged out, then, in the manner Carriazo knew and loved, they set out for Toledo on foot and without their swords for, although he had no use for them, the draper had bought these too.

Let us leave them to go on their way for a moment, since they are merry and content, and return to the story of what the steward did when he opened the letter that the servant delivered to him and found that it contained the following message:

'You will be so good, Master Pedro Alonso, Sir, as to bear with us and turn back to Burgos, where you will inform our parents that after lengthy consideration, and having come to the conclusion that the pursuit of arms is more appropriate for a gentleman than the pursuit of letters, we have decided to exchange Salamanca for Brussels and Spain for Flanders.* We have the four hundred escudos in our possession and we intend to sell the mules. Our honourable intention and the long road ahead of us are sufficient pardon for our error, although no one will judge it to be an error, unless he is a coward. Our departure is imminent, our return will be when God disposes; may He keep your good self as He is able and as we, your humble students, desire. We send these words from the Argales fountain, with our feet already in our stirrups to ride to Flanders. Carriazo and Avendaño.'

Pedro Alonso was astounded by what he read, and promptly turning to his saddlebags and finding them empty he was fully convinced of the truth of the letter. He immediately set out for Burgos on the mule remaining in his possession to deliver the news as speedily as possible to his masters, so that they with equal promptness might remedy the situation and devise some means of catching up with their sons. The author of this story, however, says nothing of these matters, because once he left Pedro Alonso on horseback he resumed the narrative of what happened to Avendaño and Carriazo as they entered Illescas. He tells us that on passing through the town gate they came across two mule drivers, who were Andalusian in appearance, dressed in wide linen breeches, slashed linen doublets, and buckskin jerkins, and carrying curved daggers and strapless swords. It appeared that one was coming from Seville and the other was heading that way. The one who was leaving was saying to the other, 'If my masters weren't so far ahead of me I'd stay a little longer to ask you a thousand things I'm eager to know; because I'm really amazed by what you've told me about the Count hanging Alonso Genís and Ribera without granting them an appeal.'

'What a to do', replied the one from Seville. 'The Count set a trap for them and caught them while they were within his jurisdiction, for they were soldiers and his treatment of them was unlawful, and the high court was unable to remove them from his custody. Let me tell you, friend, that this Count Puñonrostro* is the devil himself and he's turning the screw on us hard. Seville and the surrounding area for ten leagues in all directions are swept clean of villains. No thief hangs round in the vicinity. They all fear him like the plague, although rumour has it that he'll soon abandon his post as chief officer of justice; because he's not the sort to put up with the endless squabbling that goes on with the gentlemen of the high court.'

'Long may they live,' said the one who was on his way to Seville, 'because they're like fathers to the poor and a refuge for the unfortunate. How many poor wretches are dead and buried solely on account of the anger of an absolute judge or magistrate who was either under-informed or over-prejudiced. Many eyes see better than two. A single heart is sooner poisoned by injustice than are many together.'

'What a preacher you've become;' said the one from Seville, 'judging by the way you're prattling on, you're in no hurry to stop, but I can't hang around. Don't stay in your usual place tonight, but at the Sevillano Inn, because there you'll see the most beautiful kitchen maid. Marinilla at the Tejada tavern is odious by comparison. All I'll say for the time being is that the Chief Magistrate's son's supposed to be crazy about her. One of my masters who goes there swears that the next time he goes to Andalusia he's going to stay in Toledo for two months at that very inn just to be able to feast his eyes on her. As a token of my admiration I gave her a little pinch, and in return I got a slap in the face. She's as hard as marble, as unsociable as a peasant from Sayago, and as prickly as a nettle: but she's got the face and the features of an angel. In one cheek she bears the sun and in the other the moon; one's made of roses and the other of carnations, and in both there are lilies and jasmines too. All I'll say is that you must see her for yourself and you'll see that I've not said half of what I could say about her beauty. I'd gladly give her both those grey mules of mine as a dowry if they'd give her to me as a wife: but I know that they won't give her to me, for she's a jewel fit for an archpriest or a count. And so I repeat that if you go there you'll see what I mean. And farewell, for I'll be on my way.'

With this, the two mule-drivers parted company and the two

friends who had been listening to their conversation and chatter were left speechless, especially Avendaño. The simple account which the mule driver had given of the kitchen maid's beauty aroused in him an avid desire to see her. This same desire was awakened in Carriazo, but it did not weaken his resolve to get to his tunny fisheries, which he considered more desirable than taking in the sight of the Egyptian pyramids, or any of the seven wonders of the world, or even all of them together. They amused themselves on the road to Toledo by repeating the mule-drivers' words and by imitating and mimicking the mannerisms and gestures that had accompanied them. Then, with Carriazo who was already acquainted with that city acting as guide, they went down along Sangre de Cristo* and found themselves in front of the Sevillano Inn, but they dared not ask for lodgings there because they were not suitably dressed. Night had already fallen, and although Carriazo tried to prevail upon Avendaño to seek lodgings elsewhere, he could not get him to budge from the door of the Sevillano, where he waited in the hope that the widely acclaimed kitchen maid might appear. As the night advanced and the kitchen maid showed no signs of appearing, Carriazo grew desperate but Avendaño just sat quietly. In an effort to attain his objective, and under the pretext of enquiring after some gentlemen from Burgos who were on their way to Seville, Avendaño ventured as far as the inner courtyard of the inn. He had scarcely set foot inside when he saw a young girl emerge from a room which opened onto the courtyard: she looked to be about fifteen years of age, she was dressed in the costume of a peasant, and she was carrying a lighted candle in a candlestick.

Avendaño did not notice the young girl's costume and manner of dress, because his eyes were fixed on her face where he found himself gazing into the kind of eyes usually attributed to angels. Her beauty filled him with wonder and amazement and he was unable to make his planned enquiry of her, so overwhelming was his astonishment and rapture. Seeing him in front of her, the young girl said, 'What are you looking for, brother? Are you by any chance the servant of one of our guests?'

'I am no one's servant but yours,' replied Avendaño in considerable embarrassment and confusion.

Receiving such a reply, the young girl countered, 'Come now, brother, we who serve have no need of servants.' Calling to her master, she said, 'Sir, could you see what this young man wants?'

Her master emerged and asked him what he wanted. Avendaño replied that he was looking for some gentlemen from Burgos who were making their way to Seville, one of whom was his master, who had sent him on ahead via Alcalá de Henares where he was to do some important business. He had also instructed him to come to Toledo and wait for him at the Sevillano Inn where he would put up. He thought he would arrive that night or the following day, at the very latest. Avendaño told his lie so convincingly that the innkeeper accepted it as the truth, and said, 'Stay here at the inn, friend, for you may wait here until your master arrives.'

'I am much obliged, Sir,' replied Avendaño. 'Please have a room prepared for myself and a travelling companion who is waiting outside, for we have money with us to pay as well as the next man.'

'It will be my pleasure,' replied the innkeeper. Turning to the young girl, he said, 'Costanza, dear, tell Argüello to take these gentlemen to the corner room and to put clean sheets on their beds.'

'Yes, Sir,' replied Costanza (for this was the maid's name).

With a curtsey to her master she left them. Her absence had the same effect on Avendaño that the setting of the sun and the first shadows of the dark and gloomy night usually have on the traveller. In spite of this he went out to report to Carriazo what he had seen and arranged. Carriazo recognized the many signs that indicated to him that his friend had been infected with the plague of love, but he decided to say nothing for the moment, preferring to wait until he had seen for himself whether the subject which inspired such extraordinary praise and inflated rhetoric justified his lovesick state.

They finally entered the inn and Argüello, a woman of some forty-five years of age who was in charge of the beds and the preparation of the rooms, led them to one which was furnished for neither gentleman nor servant, but rather for someone whose condition in life fell between the two extremes.

They requested some supper, but Argüello replied that meals were not provided for anyone, although they cooked and prepared what the guests themselves purchased outside and brought to the inn. However, there were eating-houses nearby where they could eat whatever they liked with an easy conscience. The pair followed Argüello's advice and took themselves to an eating house, where Carriazo dined on what they served him while Avendaño was nourished by the fare he carried with him, namely, his thoughts and fantasies.

The fact that Avendaño ate next to nothing greatly surprised Carriazo. In order to acquaint himself fully with his friend's state of mind he addressed him in the following way when they returned to the inn: 'It would be a good idea to get up early tomorrow, so that we can be in Orgaz before it gets hot.'

'Count me out,' replied Avendaño, 'because before I take leave of this city I intend to see the so-called sights, such as the Sagrario, Giannello's engine, the views from St Augustine, the King's Garden and the great plain.'*

'That's fine by me,' replied Carriazo, 'that won't take more than a couple of days.'

'Let me make it clear that I intend to take things slowly, it's not as if we're off to Rome to be made bishops.'

'Pull the other one,' retorted Carriazo, 'I'd stake my life on it that you're keener to stay put in Toledo than to complete our unfinished journey.'

'That's very true,' replied Avendaño, 'in fact, it's as impossible for me to tear myself away from the vision of that maid's face as it is for someone to get to heaven without good works.'

'That's praise indeed,' said Carriazo, 'and your decision is worthy of such a generous heart as your own. How appropriate that a don Tomás de Avendaño, possessing all the qualities of a gentleman, comfortably rich, pleasingly youthful, and admirably sensible, should be besotted with a kitchen maid who serves at the Sevillano Inn.'

'It seems to me it's no more incongruous than the case of a don Diego de Carriazo, namesake of a father who's a knight of the Order of Alcántara,* who's about to come into his inheritance as eldest son, and is as graceful in spirit as in body. Although he's generously endowed with these attributes, whom do we find him in love with? I ask you! Queen Guinevere? No, nothing of the sort. He's in love with the tunny fisheries at Zahara which, as far as I can gather, are as disagreeable as the temptations of St Anthony.'*

'*Touché*, my friend,' replied Carriazo, 'you've given me a taste of my own medicine. Let's stop our quarrelling right now and be off to bed, for tomorrow's another day.'

'Look, Carriazo, you haven't seen Costanza yet; once you've seen her, I'll give you leave to insult and criticize me as much as you like.'

'I can already foresee how this business is going to end,' said Carriazo.

'How?' asked Avendaño.

'With me going off to my tunny fisheries and you staying with your kitchen maid.'

'I shan't be that fortunate,' replied Avendaño.

'Nor shall I be so stupid as to give up my good intention in order to comply with your wayward inclination,' replied Carriazo.

Such was the manner of their conversation as they arrived at the inn and they continued in a similar vein for half the night. When they had been sleeping for little more than half an hour, or so it seemed to them, they were woken by the sound of many flageolets* being played in the street. They sat up in bed and listened intently, and Carriazo said, 'I bet it's day already and there must be some celebration taking place at the convent of Our Lady of Song which is near here, and that's why they're playing those flageolets.'

'That's not the reason,' replied Avendaño, 'because we didn't fall asleep so long ago that it's morning already.'

They were still pondering these things when they heard a knock on their door and when they asked who was there someone outside replied, 'Young men, if you want to hear some good music, get up and look out through the window which gives on to the street, in that front room there, for it's unoccupied.'

The pair got up, but when they opened the door there was no one there and they had no idea who had given them the advice. When they heard the sound of a harp, however, they realized that there was indeed music to be heard and so, dressed as they were in their night-shirts, they went to the front room where three or four guests were already stationed at the window. They found a space for themselves and soon afterwards, to the accompaniment of a harp and a guitar, a marvellous voice sang the following sonnet, which fixed itself in Avendaño's memory:

> Rare and humble one, you rise
> In grace to an exalted height;
> Nature herself, awed at the sight,
> Offers a taste of paradise.
>
> Whether you speak or laugh or sing,
> Show meekness or incivility,
> (Sole effect of your gentility),
> Souls under your spell you bring.

> In order that the peerless beauty
> You possess, and the virtue sublime
> Of which you boast, gain more renown,
>
> Serve not; to be served is your duty,
> By those whose hands and temples shine
> Bright with sceptre and resplendent crown.

It was not necessary for anyone to explain to either of them that this music was being performed for Costanza's benefit, because the sonnet had left them in no doubt. It resounded so painfully in Avendaño's ears that he would have considered it a blessing to have been born deaf and to have remained so for the rest of his days, rather than hear those words. For from that very instant he began to suffer as violently as anyone whose heart has been pierced by the cruel arrow of jealousy. It only made matters worse that he did not know who should or could be the object of his jealousy. However, this uncertainty was soon removed from his mind by one of the guests at the window, who said, 'What a fool this Chief Magistrate's son must be to go around making music to a kitchen maid. It's true that she's one of the most beautiful girls I've ever seen, and I've seen many; but that's no excuse for wooing her so publicly.'

He was answered by another of the observers at the window: 'Well, as a matter of fact, I've heard it said on authority that he might as well not exist for all the attention she pays him. I'll wager that at this very moment she's fast asleep behind her mistress's bed, where she is rumoured to sleep, totally oblivious to singing and music-making.'

'Very true,' replied the other, 'for she's the most virtuous young girl that ever lived; and it's a miracle in the hustle and bustle of this establishment, with new people arriving every day, and she in and out of the rooms, that no one can accuse her of the slightest indiscretion.'

When Avendaño heard these words he began to take heart and rally his spirits to listen to the many other songs which the musician sang to the accompaniment of various instruments, all of which were addressed to Costanza who, as the guest had conjectured, was sleeping soundly.

As day approached the musicians went away, sounding their farewells on their flageolets. Avendaño and Carriazo returned to their room, where the one who was capable of sleep slept until morning.

They both got up with a desire to see Costanza, but while the desire of one was merely to satisfy his curiosity, the desire of the other was an amorous longing. Costanza, however, did her duty by both of them when she stepped out of her master's room looking so beautiful that they both felt that all the praises the mule-driver had lavished upon her fell short of the truth and were in no way exaggerated.

She was dressed in a chemise and bodice of a green material with a border of the same cloth. The bodice was low-cut but her chemise was high-necked and pleated at the throat with a collar of embroidered black silk and a necklace of jet black stars on an alabaster column, for her throat was no less white. She also wore a cord of St Francis around her waist and a large bunch of keys hung from a ribbon at her right side. She was not wearing clogs but double-soled red shoes. She wore her hair in plaits secured with ribbons of fine white yarn, and they were so long that they reached below her waist. Her hair was lighter than chestnut and almost fair but it was so lustrous, immaculate, and well groomed that nothing else, not even strands of pure gold, could compare with it. The gourd-shaped earrings which hung from her ears were of glass but looked like pearls. When she emerged from the room she made the sign of the cross and in a calm and devout manner genuflected deeply before an image of Our Lady which was hanging on one of the walls of the courtyard. Scarcely had she raised her eyes and seen the two who were watching her when she withdrew back into the room and called to Argüello to get up.

It remains to be said now what Carriazo thought of Costanza's beauty, for the effect it had on Avendaño the first time he saw her has already been described. I shall say only that Carriazo was just as impressed as his companion but he was much less infatuated; in fact, so much less so that he did not want to spend another night at the inn, but set off immediately for the tunny fisheries. At that moment Argüello appeared in the passageway, accompanied by two other hefty wenches who were also maids at the inn and reputed to be Galician. The employment of so many maids was justified by the large numbers who patronized the Sevillano Inn, which was one of the best and most highly frequented inns in Toledo. The guests' servants also came to the inn to request barley for their animals. The innkeeper went out to give them some, cursing his maids because it was their fault that he had lost a stable boy who had measured out the barley very diligently and accurately, apparently without a single grain going to waste. When he heard this Avendaño said, 'Don't worry yourself, Sir, give me the ledgers, for while I'm here I'll keep such a careful check on the distribution of the barley and straw that's required that you'll not miss the stable boy you say has left you.'

'I'm much obliged to you, indeed,' replied the innkeeper, 'I can't see to it myself, because I've got a lot of business to attend to outside the inn. Come on down, I'll give you the book, and bear in mind that these mule drivers are the devil in human form and they'll steal a ration of barley from under your very nose with no more scruples than if it were straw.'

Avendaño came down into the courtyard, examined the book, and then began to deal out rations of barley as if he were pouring water and to make such a careful record of it all that the innkeeper who was watching him was satisfied. In fact, he was so satisfied that he said, 'If only that master of yours might never arrive and you felt inclined to stay here, for I swear it would be worth your while. The lad who's gone off came here some eight months ago skinny and on his uppers and now he's got two very good suits of clothes and goes around looking as plump as a partridge. For I want you to know, son, that in this establishment there are many perks to be had on top of your basic wage.'

'If I were to stay,' replied Avendaño, 'I wouldn't be concerned about my earnings, for I'd be happy with anything so long as I could be in this city which, I'm told, is the finest in Spain.'

'It is, at least,' replied the innkeeper, 'one of the best and richest in the country; but there's something else we need to do now—and that's look for someone to fetch water from the river, for another lad also walked out on me. He used to fill the pitchers to overflowing and when he carried them on a spirited ass of mine he used to flood the place out. One of the reasons why the mule-drivers love to bring their masters to my inn is the plentiful supply of water that they always find here; they don't have to lead their animals to the river because they can drink from large troughs on the premises.'

Carriazo was listening to all this and when he could see that Avendaño was fixed up with a job in the establishment he did not want to be left out, especially when he thought how pleased

Avendaño would be if he humoured him. So he said to the inn-keeper, 'Bring me the ass, Sir, for I'll girth it and load it as well as my companion records his business in the ledger.'

'Yes,' said Avendaño, 'my companion Asturiano will be a wonderful water-carrier, I can vouch for him.'

When Argüello, who was listening to their conversation from the passageway, heard Avendaño say that he could vouch for his companion, she intervened, 'Tell me, good sir, who is going to vouch for *him*? For it seems to me that he's got greater need of someone to speak for him than he's got to speak for another.'

'Be quiet, Argüello,' said the innkeeper, 'don't interfere in matters which don't concern you. I'll vouch for them both, and you'd be wise not to go squabbling with the lads who work here, because it's your fault that they all leave me.'

'So these young men are staying at the inn, then?' said another serving wench. 'Well, I'll be blessed, but I wouldn't trust them with the wineskin if I were on the road with them.'

'That's enough of your cheek, madame Gallega,' replied the innkeeper. 'Get about your business and don't pester the lads, or I'll give you a good hiding.'

'Yes, indeed,' replied Gallega, 'and what treasures they are to have us hankering after them. I'm sure my master the innkeeper's never seen me so playful with the lads from the inn or from outside that I deserve the low opinion he's got of me. They're rogues, and they take off whenever they feel like it, without us giving them any cause whatsoever. A fine sort of people they are, to be sure, if they need incentives to make them leave their masters in the lurch when they least expect it.'

'You talk too much, sister Gallega' replied her master, 'hold your tongue and get on with your work.'

Carriazo had by now saddled the ass, and after leaping on to it he went off to the river, leaving Avendaño delighted with the gallant decision he had made. Let it be happily recorded that Avendaño was thus transformed into a stable boy calling himself Tomás Pedro, and Carriazo, taking the name Lope Asturiano, into a water carrier: metamorphoses impressive enough to eclipse the examples narrated by the big-nosed poet.* Argüello had scarcely digested the fact that they were both staying at the inn when she formed designs on Asturiano and marked him as her property. She resolved to pamper him so diligently that, even if he were of a shy and retiring nature, she would make him as pliant as a leather glove.

Gallega was entertaining the same thoughts with regard to Avendaño, and since she and Argüello were great friends, owing to their daily contact and conversation and the fact that they shared a room, they immediately confided their amorous intentions to one another and determined that very night to embark on their conquest of their two indifferent lovers. The first thing they realized, however, was that they would have to ask them not to be jealous of the way they saw them behave, for the girls would scarcely be able to indulge the lads on the inside if they didn't have generous admirers outside the inn. 'Be silent, brothers,' they would explain, as if the former were present and already their established young men or beaux. 'Say nothing and cover your eyes; leave the music to the musicians and let the dance be led by someone who knows the steps. There'll be no two canons in this town as pampered* as you two will be by your devoted servants.'

This and many other reassurances of this general nature and character were rehearsed by Gallega and Argüello. In the meantime our good friend Lope Asturiano was making his way to the river via Carmen Hill and thinking about his tunny fisheries and the sudden change in his status. Either for this reason or because fate ordained it, as he negotiated a narrow path on his way down the hill he collided with the ass of another water-carrier who was climbing up the hill with a full load. Since he was going down and his ass was spirited, willing, and under-worked, the collision knocked the tired and skinny beast which was coming up to the ground, and because the pitchers got broken the water also spilled out on to the earth. Incensed and enraged by his misfortune the old water-carrier attacked the new one, and before the latter could shake off his attacker and dismount, the former had dealt him a dozen good blows which Asturiano did not take kindly to.

He did eventually dismount and in such a foul mood that he fell upon his opponent and, throttling him with both hands, he pushed him to the ground. As he fell he hit his head so hard against a stone that his skull split in two and began to bleed so profusely that Asturiano thought that he had killed him.

Many other water-carriers who were in the vicinity and saw their companion in such a sorry state seized Lope and, holding him very firmly in their grip, shouted: 'Get the police! Get the police! This water-carrier's killed a man!'

No sooner had they uttered these cries and shouts than they set about beating and punching him. Others who went to the aid of the prostrate figure could see that his head was cracked open and that he was breathing his last. The news travelled up the hill from person to person as far as Carmen Square, where it reached the ears of the constable who, quick as a flash, appeared at the scene of the quarrel accompanied by two officers. By this time the injured man had already been laid across his ass while Lope's animal had been seized. Lope himself was hemmed in by more than twenty water-carriers, who pressed down upon him so hard and crushed his ribs so heavily that he was in greater danger of his life than his own victim, so thick and fast came the punches and blows which they rained upon him to avenge the other man's injuries.

The constable arrived, pushed his way through the crowd, and handed Asturiano over to his officers. Then, leading Lope's ass and the injured man who was still lying across his own animal, he took them to the jail with so many people and young boys thronging behind him that they could scarcely push their way through the streets.

The racket outside drew Tomás Pedro and his master to the door of the inn to find out what all the commotion was about. They caught sight of Lope being led by the two constables, his face and mouth streaming with blood. The innkeeper immediately scanned the scene for his ass and saw it in the charge of another officer who had joined the other two. He asked why they were being arrested and was told the full story.

The innkeeper was upset about his ass, fearing that he would probably lose it, or at the very least be obliged to pay a higher price to retrieve it than it was actually worth. Tomás Pedro followed his companion without being able to get close enough to say anything to him, so huge was the crowd that blocked his way and so closely was Lope guarded by the officers and the constable who were holding him. Tomás did not leave his friend until he saw him locked up in a cell and restrained by a pair of fetters. He also saw the injured man being taken to hospital, where he was present when his wounds were attended to. He saw that the injuries were serious, indeed very serious, and this opinion was confirmed by the surgeon.

The constable took the two asses home with him as well as five reales which the officers had taken from Lope. Tomás returned to the inn feeling very confused and miserable, and found that the man he already regarded as his master was feeling no less wretched than himself. He recounted his companion's circumstances, the injured man's critical condition, and the fate of his ass. That, however, was not all the bad news he had to relate. On top of this misfortune another had occurred which was no less distressing. A great friend of his master's had met him on the road and informed him that, in order to travel quickly and cut two leagues off his journey, his master had taken the Azeca ferry from Madrid and was that night sleeping in Orgaz. The friend had been given twelve escudos to pass on to Tomás with instructions to go on to Seville where his master would wait for him.

'But that's out of the question,' Tomás continued, 'for it wouldn't be right for me to leave my friend and comrade in jail and in such danger. My master will forgive me for the present moment: all the more so because he's such a good and honourable man that he'll condone any shortcoming in my service to him, as long as I don't neglect my companion. Good sir, do me the honour of taking this money and attending to this matter; and when this money runs out, I'll write to my master explaining what's happening and I know that he'll send me sufficient funds to get us out of any predicament.'

The innkeeper's eyes opened wide with interest, pleased to see that the loss of his ass showed signs of being partially compensated. He took the money and comforted Tomás, telling him that he knew many people of standing in Toledo who could pull strings with the magistrates, especially a nun who was related to the Chief Magistrate whom she could twist around her little finger. A washerwoman at this same nun's convent had a daughter who was a great friend of a sister of a monk, who was a great friend and intimate of this same nun's confessor, and the said washerwoman did the laundry at the inn . . .

'And if she asks her daughter, which she surely will do, to talk to the monk's sister, and she talks to her brother who'll then talk to her confessor, and the confessor in turn speaks to the nun, and the nun sees fit to give a note to the Magistrate (which will be easy to do), in which she earnestly pleads with him to look into Tomás's affair, we can without the shadow of a doubt anticipate a favourable outcome. All this is possible, of course, provided that the water-carrier doesn't die and that there's no shortage of oil to grease the palms of the various magistrates. For unless the wheels of justice are well oiled, they creak more than ox-carts.'

Tomás was amused by the offers of help which his master had made him and the endless twists and turns these offers had taken. Although he realized that he had spoken with more mischief than sincerity, he nevertheless thanked him for his good intentions and handed over the money, promising that much more would be forthcoming, so great was his confidence in his master, as he had already explained.

Learning that her new lover was in chains, Argüello went straight to the jail to take him some provisions, but was not allowed to see him and turned back bitter and disappointed. She did not, however, allow this to deter her from her good intentions. In short, within two weeks the injured man was out of danger and within three the surgeon declared him fully recovered. During this time Tomás had arranged for fifty escudos to be delivered to him from Seville, which he produced from his breast pocket and handed to the innkeeper with letters and a false seal attributed to his master. Since the authenticity of the correspondence was of little interest to the innkeeper, he took the money with great delight, especially as it came in gold escudos.

For the sum of six ducados the injured man withdrew from the dispute, while Asturiano was sentenced to pay a fine of ten ducados, the ass, and the costs. He was then released from jail but he did not wish to rejoin his companion, citing as his excuse the fact that while he had been in jail Argüello had visited him and made amorous advances, which he found such a tiresome nuisance that he would rather be hanged than respond to the desire of such an awful woman. Since he was determined to go ahead and stick to his plan, this is what he intended to do: buy an ass and exercise the office of a watercarrier for as long as they remained in Toledo. For with that cover he would not be sentenced or imprisoned as a vagrant, and if he collected just a single load of water he could entertain himself all day wandering around the city and watching foolish girls.

'You're more likely to see pretty rather than foolish girls in this city, which is famed for having the shrewdest women in Spain and their shrewdness is equal to their beauty. If you're unconvinced, just look at Costanza, who possesses more than enough loveliness to enhance the beautiful women not only in this city but all over the world.'

'Steady on there, Tomás,' retorted Lope, 'let's not be so hasty in our praise of our distinguished kitchen maid, unless you want me to think you a heretic as well as the madman you already are.'

'Did you call Costanza a kitchen maid, brother Lope?' replied Tomás. 'May God forgive you and reveal to you the error of your ways.'

'So she isn't a kitchen maid, then?' asked Asturiano.

'I've yet to see her wash her first dish.'

'It doesn't matter if you didn't see her wash her first dish, if you've seen her wash the second or the hundredth.'

'I tell you, brother,' replied Tomás, 'that she doesn't wash dishes. She occupies herself with nothing but her needlework and looking after the inn's silverware, of which there's a great deal.'

'So, why do they call her the illustrious kitchen maid throughout the city, if she doesn't wash dishes? But, of course, it must be because she polishes silver rather than washes dishes that they call her illustrious. But, all this aside, tell me Tomás, how hopeful are you?'

'Desperately unhopeful,' replied Tomás, 'because all the time you were in jail I was unable to say a word to her, and in response to the many speeches which the guests address to her she does nothing but lower her eyes and keep her lips tightly sealed. She's so chaste and modest that her modesty captivates her admirers as much as her beauty. What really exhausts my patience is the knowledge that the Chief Magistrate's son, who is a dashing and rather daring young man, is crazy about her and serenades her. Few nights go by without him making some musical offering, and he is so open in his admiration that his songs mention her by name, praise her, and celebrate her beauty. But she doesn't hear them, nor does she venture out of her mistress's room from dusk until the following dawn, a shield which nevertheless fails to protect my heart from being pierced by the bitter arrow of jealousy.'

'So what do you intend to do about this impasse you've reached in your conquest of this Portia, Minerva, and new Penelope,* who in the guise of a young damsel and kitchen maid has caused you to lose your heart, your nerve and your mind?'

'Make as much fun of me as you like, Lope my friend, for I know that I'm in love with the most beautiful face ever fashioned by nature and the most incomparable chastity to be found anywhere in the world today. Her name's Costanza, not Portia, Minerva, or Penelope. That she serves at an inn I can't deny, but what can I do when it seems that some invisible force of destiny impels me and choice clearly dictates that I should adore her? Look friend,' Tomás continued, 'I can't explain how love so elevates and ennobles the lowly condition of this kitchen maid that when she stands before me I don't see her poverty and although I'm well aware of it I don't recognize it. Although I try, I find it impossible to focus my mind on the lowliness of her status even for a fleeting moment, because this thought is immediately erased by the recollection of her beauty, her gracefulness, her composure, her virtue, and her modesty, which lead me to believe that locked and hidden beneath that rustic exterior there must be some treasure of great value and immense worth. Finally, whatever she may be, I love her dearly, and not with that vulgar love with which I've loved others, but with a love so pure that it seeks only to serve her and to win her love in return, so that she might repay with her virtuous desire the debt she owes my equally virtuous sentiments.'

At this point Asturiano uttered a loud cry and exclaimed:

'Oh, Platonic love! Oh, illustrious kitchen maid! Oh, what fortunate times we live in to see beauty captivating without malice, modesty kindling the passions without burning, grace giving pleasure without arousing, and the lowliness of a humble condition compelling it to be raised on what is known as the wheel of fortune. Oh, my poor tunny fish, who will not this year be visited by this your enamoured admirer! But next year I'll make such amends that the foremen of my beloved tunny fisheries will have no complaint to make of me.'

In reply to this Tomás said, 'I can see, Asturiano, how blatantly you're mocking me. What you could do is go off to your fishing with my blessing. I'll continue my own quest, and you'll find me here on your return. If you wish to take your share of the money, I'll give it to you at once. Go in peace, and let each of us follow the path mapped out for us by destiny.'

'I thought you more astute than that,' replied Lope, 'can't you tell that I'm only joking? But since I realize that you are speaking sincerely, I will sincerely serve you in all your heart desires. I beg only one favour, in return for the many I intend to do for you, and it's that you never put me in a position where Argüello might flirt with me and solicit my attentions, because I'd relinquish our friendship rather than expose myself to the danger of acquiring hers. As God lives, my friend, she talks more than a clerk of the court, and her breath smells of the dregs of bad wine a mile off; all her top teeth are false and I'm convinced that her hair's a wig; and in order to cover and make up for these defects, since she revealed her awful intention to me, she's taken to painting her face with white lead and applies it so thickly that her face looks like a hideous plaster mask.'

'That's all very true,' replied Tomás, 'even Gallega, who's making my life a misery, isn't as bad as that. What you could do is spend one last night at the inn and then tomorrow you can buy the ass you talk of and look for somewhere else to stay. That way, you'll avoid having to meet Argüello, while I'll still run the risk of encounters with Gallega and with the lethal rays which emanate from Costanza's eyes.'* The two friends agreed to this plan and went off to the inn, where Asturiano was greeted with a great show of affection from Argüello.

That night there was a dance at the door of the inn attended by many mule-drivers who were staying there and at neighbouring establishments. Asturiano played the guitar and in addition to the two Galicians and Argüello there were three other female dancers from another inn. Many other men came in disguise and were more eager to see Costanza than the dance, but she did not appear or come out to watch the dance, thus frustrating many expectations.

Lope played the guitar so well that he was said to make it sing. The young mule-drivers asked him to sing a ballad and Argüello pleaded with him even more energetically. He replied that he would if they would dance the way players sang and danced in plays, and to avoid making mistakes, they were to do exactly what he instructed them to do in his song, and nothing else.

There were several dancers among the mule-drivers as well as among the women. Lope cleared his throat and spat twice to give himself time to think about what he would say. Thanks to his quick, sharp, and ready wit he soon produced the following song in an impressive display of impromptu invention:

> Step forward, lovely Argüello,
> A maiden once, but not now,

> Take two more steps to the rear
> And then a courteous bow.
>
> Take your partner by the hand,
> The one they call Barrabas,
> Muleteer from the south,
> Holy father of the Compás.*
>
> Of the two Galicians girls
> Who in this tavern serve,
> Let the rounder-faced step forward
> Ready to dance with verve.
>
> Take hold of her, Torote,
> All four in time now stamp
> The shifting swings and steps,
> As the *contrapás* you tramp.

The men and women alike followed to the letter the instructions which Asturiano dictated to them in song; but when he reached the part where he told them to tramp a *contrapás*, the dancing mule-driver whose nickname was Barrabas retorted: 'Brother musician, keep your mind on your song and don't go calling anyone badly dressed, for there's no tramp here, and let each man dress as God provides him with the means.'

The innkeeper, who heard the mule-driver's ignorant outburst, explained, 'Brother mule-driver, he's referring to the steps of a foreign dance and not criticizing the way anyone's dressed.'

'If that's the case,' replied the mule-driver, 'then there's no call for this complicated stuff; let's hear the old familiar *sarabandas*, *chaconas*, and *folías*,* and let them dance any way they please, for there are people here who know how to have a good time.'

Without replying to this Asturiano continued with his song:

> Come hither, all you nymphs
> With your captive devotees,
> For the dance of the *chacona*
> Is vaster than the seas.
>
> Let the castanets resound,
> Bend down and rub your hands
> In the copious manure
> Or in the countless sands.

You've all danced so superbly,
I can correct you nought;
Pray a prayer and give the devil
Two fresh figs,* as you ought.

Spit at the old whoreson,
Then we'll all have a good time;
For he and the *chacona*
Are great partners in crime.

You're fairer than a hospital
Sublime Argüello, so divine,
I'll change my tune, please be my muse
And promise to be mine.

Dancing with such vigour
Will keep you fit and trim,
Shaking sloth and stiffness
From every lazy limb.

Let laughter fill the hearts
Of those who dance and play,
Those who heed the merry song,
Or watch the dancers sway.

Their feet just keep on moving,
They seem to lose control,
And their pleasure is redoubled
When each shoe parts with its sole.

The elderly and ageing
Find a lightness in their tread,
While the fresh and lively youths
Sing out lustily instead.

How very many times she's tried,
This most esteemed señora,
With the energetic saraband,
Pésame and *perra mora*,*

To infiltrate the walls, wherein
Devoted sisters dwell,
To discompose pure chastity
In its cold and holy cell.

How often she's been cursed
By the admirers she's wooed,
For she gives them lewd ideas,
And fools are always in the mood.

This dark maiden from the New World
Acquired her ill repute,
By inspiring more blaspheming
Than drink in a dispute.

And those who pay her tribute
Are too many to take stock;
The host of pages, maids, and men
Who to her banner flock.

She claims, and swears and stresses,
Her confidence quite fearless:
'Forget the *zambapalo*;
Among dances I am peerless'.

While Lope sang the drivers of mules and the washers of dishes, numbering twelve in total, danced with wild abandon. As he prepared to move on by singing songs of more weight, substance, and consequence than what he had just been singing, one of the many disguised spectators of the dance shouted, without removing his mask: 'Shut up, you inebriate. Hold your tongue, you sot. Be silent, you old wineskin, you old man's poet and bogus musician!'

After this others stepped forward and hurled so many insults and angry gestures in his direction that Lope felt it wise to keep quiet. The mule-drivers, however, were so incensed that had it not been for the innkeeper who calmed them down with soothing arguments, blood might have been spilled. Even with this intervention they would not have stopped shaking their fists at him if officers of the law had not arrived at that very moment and sent them all packing.

They had scarcely withdrawn when everyone in the neighbourhood who was still awake at that hour heard the voice of a man who, sitting on a rock in front of the Sevillano Inn, began singing with such marvellous and sweet harmony that they were filled with wonder and felt compelled to listen to the end. The most attentive listener of all was Tomás Pedro, since he was the most deeply affected, not only by the sound of the music but also by the purport of the words. He did not hear mere songs, but letters of excommunication which tormented his very soul, for the musician sang the following ballad:

> Where are you, for we see you not,
> Beauteous sphere* inviolate,
> Fair ornament of humankind,
> Divinity incarnate?
>
> Empyrean heaven, where perfect love
> Has its true and fixed abode;
> First cause, in whose relentless wake
> Our impending fates unfold.
>
> Crystal reaches of the heavens,
> Where in waters clear and undefiled,
> The ardent flames of love are chilled
> And then redoubled and refined.
>
> In this new and wondrous firmament
> Two stars emit their ray,
> And robbing light from no third star,
> They transform night into bright day.
>
> Joy so stark in contrast
> With the father* who so cruelly
> Gives his children burial,
> In the chamber of his belly.
>
> Humble, you shun the lofty heights
> Where praises raise the mighty Jove,
> Yet you have the power to sway him,
> Whom your gentleness alone can move.
>
> Invisible and subtle net,
> How securely you ensnare
> The warrior adulterer,*
> Triumphant in warfare.
>
> Fourth heaven and second sun,*
> You leave the other in the shade.
> What fortune and felicity
> As your brilliance you parade.
>
> Grave ambassador,* who speaks
> With a wisdom to inspire,
> In perfect silence you persuade,
> Achieving more than you desire.

If truth be told, you have no more
Than second heaven's fairness,
And of the first you are no more
Than the moonshine's likeness.

You are this sphere,* Costanza,
Condemned by cruel fate
To a place that ill befits you,
And obscures your true estate.

Determine your own fortunes,
Making certain to redress
Your stern manners with social graces,
Your haughty airs with tenderness.

And so you will see, señora,
That your fortunes are applauded
By those well proud of their descent,
And for their beauty lauded.

You'll achieve all this the sooner,
If you will accept in me
The richest and the purest will
That love in any soul will see.

Just as he concluded these last lines, two half-bricks came flying through the air. If instead of landing at his feet they had struck him square in the middle of his head, they would easily have knocked all the music and poetry out of his skull. The poor youth took fright and began to run up the hill so quickly that not even a greyhound could have caught up with him. Such is the unhappy lot of musicians, bats, and owls who forever run the risk of being showered with such violent insults. All those who had been listening to the pelted singer's voice were impressed by it, but it was most highly thought of by Tomás Pedro, who admired both the voice and the ballad. He would, however, have preferred someone other than Costanza to have been the inspiration for so much music, although not a single note ever reached her ears. Barrabas, the mule-driver, who had also been listening to the music, was of the opposite opinion: for when he saw the musician take flight, he said:

'Off you go, minstrel of Judas, I hope fleas eat your eyes out. Who the devil taught you to sing all that stuff about spheres and heavens to a kitchen maid and call her Sundays and Moondays and talk about wheels of fortune? The devil take you and anyone else impressed by your song. You should have said she's as stiff as a poker, as proud as a peacock, as white as milk, as chaste as a novice monk, as cantankerous and wild as a hired mule, and harder than a piece of plaster; and if you were to tell her this, she would understand you and take pleasure in what you say; but as for calling her ambassador, net, first cause, highness, and lowness, such talk is more suited to a child in a catechism class than a kitchen maid. It has to be said that there are poets in the world who write songs that no one on earth can figure out. Look at me, for example, I can't make head nor tail of the songs this musician has sung, although I'm Barrabas, so imagine what Costanza will make of it! But she's wiser; she's tucked up in bed making fun of Prester John of the Indies.* This musician, at least, isn't one of the Chief Magistrate's son's cronies; for there are lots of them and every now and then you can understand what they're on about; but as for this one, he's really put my back up.' All those who listened to Barrabas were highly entertained by his comments and considered that his opinions and criticisms hit the nail right on the head.

With that, they all went home to bed. Lope had scarcely had time to settle down when he heard someone knocking very softly on his door. When he asked who it was, he received this whispered reply: 'It's Argüello and Gallega: open up, for we're freezing to death.'

'That's very odd,' replied Lope, 'since it's the middle of summer.'

'Stop trying to be funny, Lope,' retorted Gallega, 'get up and open the door, for we're done up like two duchesses.'

'Duchesses at this hour of night?' replied Lope. 'I don't believe it; I'm more inclined to believe that you're either witches or shameless hussies. Go away at once, and if you don't, on the life of . . . I swear that if I have to get up, with the buckle of my belt I'll make your backsides as red as poppies.'

Finding themselves addressed in a manner that was so hostile and contrary to what they had expected, they were afraid of Asturiano's fury and, with their hopes frustrated and their plans come to nought, they returned to their beds dejected and defeated. However, venting her anger through the keyhole before leaving the door, Argüello announced, 'Honey's too sweet for the ass's mouth, anyway.' Then, as if she had pronounced an opinion of great substance and exacted just revenge, she returned, as has already been stated, to her melancholy bed.

When Lope heard them turn away he said to Tomás Pedro, who was also awake, 'Listen, Tomás, put me in an arena with two giants or in a situation where I'm obliged to crush, on your behalf, the jaws of half a dozen or a dozen lions, and I'll get on with it; but preserve me from the peril of a hand-to-hand encounter with Argüello. That I'll never consent to, even if the alternative's to be shot through with arrows. Look what Danish maids* fate's offered us tonight! Well, tomorrow's another day.'

'Friend, I've already told you', replied Tomás, 'that you can do what you like, either by going on your pilgrimage, or by buying the ass and becoming a water-carrier, as you've decided.'

'I'm still resolved to become a water-carrier,' replied Lope. 'Let's sleep for what little of the night is left before daybreak, for my head feels bigger than a barrel and I'm in no mood to talk to you now.'

They fell asleep, day broke, they got up, Tomás went to feed the animals, and Lope went to the nearby livestock market to buy himself an acceptable ass. It so happened that Tomás, prompted by his thoughts and the leisure afforded him by the solitude of the siestas, had in the course of several days composed a few amorous verses. He had written them down in the same book in which he kept the barley accounts, intending to copy them down somewhere else and rip out or erase the relevant pages. However, before he had done this, one day while he was out and had left the ledger on top of the supply of barley, his master picked it up. Opening it to examine the state of the accounts, he came across the verses which, once read, disturbed and alarmed him. He took them to his wife, and before he read them to her he called Costanza. Speaking with much gravity, interspersed with the occasional threat, they asked her to tell them whether Tomás Pedro, the stable lad, had ever addressed any compliment or uttered anything untoward in her direction, or whether he had given her any indication of his affection for her. Costanza swore that his first word to her, on that or any other subject, was still to be uttered, and that he had never, even with his eyes, given her the slightest hint of any improper thought. Her master and mistress believed her, accustomed as they were to hearing her answer truthfully, whatever the question. They told her to leave the room and the innkeeper said to his wife, 'I don't know what to make of this. You should know, wife, that

Tomás has written a few poems in this barley ledger which make me suspect that he's in love with Costanza.'

'Let me see the poems,' replied his wife, 'and I'll tell you what it's all about.'

'I'm sure you will,' replied her husband, 'for since you're a poet, you'll hit on their meaning straight away.'

'I'm not a poet,' retorted his wife, 'but you yourself know that I've got a good head on my shoulders and I know how to recite the four prayers* in Latin.'

'You'd do better to recite them in Spanish, for your uncle the priest's already told you that you made lots of mistakes when you recited in Latin and weren't really praying anything.'

'That arrow came from his niece's quiver, for she's jealous of the way I take my Book of Hours in my hand and make short work of it.'

'Think what you like,' said the innkeeper. 'Listen carefully, for these are the verses:

> On whom does love smile?
> He who's silent a while.
> What subdues its cruelty?
> Undaunted fealty.
> What secures love's elation?
> Determination.
> And so I might well expect
> To be happily triumphant,
> If my soul in this respect
> Be silent, firm, and constant.
>
> To what is love's health owed?
> To a favour bestowed.
> What mitigates its fury?
> Verbal injury.
> And when treated with disdain?
> Desire begins to wane.
> That my love will be enduring
> I may well conjecture,
> For the source of my suffering
> Will neither favour nor injure.
>
> What hope is there for him with none?
> Utter oblivion.

What kind of death makes the pain cease?
Semi-decease.
So to die would be wise?
Rather agonize.
For it is said to be the norm
And a truth to apprehend,
That after a raging storm,
Calm will usually descend.

Shall I reveal my passion's plight?
When the time is right.
And if it is always wrong?
You'll not wait long.
Death will sooner come to claim me.
May your hope and faithfulness
Prosper to such a degree,
That when Costanza knows your firmness,
She'll turn your sorrow into glee.

'Are there any more?' asked the innkeeper's wife.

'No,' replied her husband, 'but what do you make of these verses?'

'The first thing we need to do is make sure that Tomás actually wrote them.'

'There's no doubt on that score,' replied her husband, 'for the barley account and the verses are written in one and the same hand and no one can argue otherwise.'

'Look, husband,' said the innkeeper's wife, 'at the way I see it. Although the verses actually name Costanza, from which we can gather that they were written for her, that's no reason to accept it as absolute fact, as if we'd seen him write them down with our own eyes. What's more, there are other Costanzas in the world besides ours; and even if it's all addressed to her, he doesn't say anything to dishonour her, nor does he make any serious demands of her. Let's be on the alert and warn the girl, for if he's really in love with her there's no doubting that he'll write more verses and try to give them to her.'

'Wouldn't it be better,' asked her husband, 'to rid ourselves of the problem once and for all by throwing him out of the inn?'

'That,' replied his wife, 'is entirely up to you; but the fact is, as you yourself admit, that the lad does his job so well that it'd be a real shame to dismiss him for such a trivial reason.'

'I'll go along with that,' said her husband, 'let's keep our eyes open, as you say, and time will advise us what to do.'

They agreed and the innkeeper put the book back where he had found it. Tomás returned to the inn anxiously looking for his book, and when he found it, rather than go through the same nerve-racking experience again, he copied out the verses and tore up the original sheets. He also decided to risk disclosing his feelings to Costanza at the very first opportunity. However, since her every action was dictated by her chaste and modest character she gave no one a chance to look at her, let alone engage her in conversation. Since there were as a rule so many people and so many eyes in the inn, the problem of speaking to her was compounded and the poor lovesick lad despaired of the situation.

That very day, however, Costanza appeared with a kerchief around her face and when asked why she wore it she explained that she had bad toothache. Tomás, whose passion for her sharpened his wits, devised there and then the best plan of attack and said, 'Mistress Costanza, I'll give you a written prayer which, if you recite it twice, will get rid of the pain as if the tooth had been removed.'

'That's welcome news,' replied Costanza, 'I shall recite it, because I can read.'

'There's one condition,' said Tomás, 'that you must show it to no one, because I value it highly, and it would be a pity if it were scoffed at simply because so many people knew it.'

'I give you my word, Tomás,' promised Costanza, 'that I won't give it to anyone. Let me have it right now, because the pain is getting me down.'

'I'll write it down from memory,' replied Tomás, 'and then you may have it.'

These were the first words that Tomás addressed to Costanza and Costanza to Tomás in all the time that he had been at the inn, which was already more than twenty-four days. Tomás withdrew, wrote out the prayer, and managed to pass it to Costanza without anyone noticing. She, with much pleasure and even more devotion, went into a room by herself and when she opened the piece of paper she saw that it contained the following:

'Lady of my soul: I am a gentleman of Burgos; if I outlive my father I shall, as his first born, inherit an estate of some six thousand ducados a year. When I heard reports of your beauty, which have spread many leagues in all directions, I left my home, I altered my manner of dress, and in the clothes you now see me wear I came to serve your master. If you wish to be mine, in the manner and by the means most befitting your virtuous nature, tell me what proofs you require of me to convince you of this truth. Once you are convinced of it, if it is your wish, I will be your husband and I will consider myself the most fortunate man on earth. I only beg you not to dismiss such devoted and pure intentions as mine outright. If your master learns of them and gives them no credit, he will condemn me to exile from your presence, which would be the same as condemning me to death. Allow me, lady, to see you until you believe me, for he who has committed no other crime than that of adoring you does not deserve such a rigorous punishment. You may give your answer with your eyes, unheeded by all those who constantly have their eyes fixed upon you. For your eyes are such that in anger they slay and in their mercy they restore to life.'

Knowing that Costanza had gone off to read his piece of paper, Tomás waited with his heart pounding, one moment fearing his death sentence, the next moment hopeful of a reprieve. At that moment Costanza emerged looking very beautiful in spite of the fact that her face was partly hidden by her kerchief. If it were possible for her beauty to be enhanced by some sudden emotional upheaval, then the shock of having read in Tomás's paper something so far removed from what she expected to find there might be considered to have added to her loveliness. She appeared carrying the torn and shredded paper in her hands and said to Tomás, who could scarcely stand up:

'Brother Tomás, this prayer of yours reads more like a spell or a trick than a holy prayer, so I shall have no faith in it or use it, and for that reason I've ripped it up, to prevent someone more gullible than myself from seeing it. Learn some other, easier prayers, because this one will never get you results.' Saying this, she went in to her mistress, leaving Tomás in a state of some trepidation, although he was somewhat relieved to see that the secret of his desire was safely locked in Costanza's breast. He comforted himself that, since she had not informed her master, at least he was not in danger of being thrown out of the inn. He felt that in the first step he had taken towards the achievement of his ambition he had to contend with numerous difficulties, and in weighty and perilous enterprises the first moves are always the most fraught with danger.

While this was going on at the inn, Asturiano was in the process of buying an ass at the market. He looked at many but none of them satisfied him, although a gipsy was very eager to foist a particular beast on him, whose nimbleness owed more to the quicksilver which had been poured into its ears than to any natural lightness of hoof. What pleased him in its step was counteracted by what disappointed him about its body, which was very small and not the size or proportion that Lope required, since he was looking for an animal strong enough to bear his weight as well, whether the pitchers were empty or full. At this point a young man approached him and whispered in his ear:

'Good sir, if you're looking for an animal which is suitable for the office of water-carrier, I've got an ass in a meadow near here, and you'll not find a bigger or better one in the city. I advise you not to buy an animal from a gipsy, for although they may look healthy and in good condition, they've all been touched up and are riddled with hidden defects. If you want to buy one that's right for you, come with me and say nothing.'

Asturiano took him at his word and told him to lead him to the ass which he had praised so highly. The two of them went off, keeping themselves to themselves, as the saying goes, as far as the King's Garden where, in the shade of a waterwheel, they encountered a large number of water-carriers whose asses were grazing in a nearby field. The vendor showed Lope his ass, which was such an impressive-looking beast that it immediately caught Lope's eye, and all those present praised its strength, step, and stamina. They struck a deal without any further guarantees or information, and with the water-carriers acting as agents and go-betweens he paid sixteen ducados for the ass which came equipped with all the accessories of the trade.

Lope paid cash in the form of gold escudos. They congratulated him on his purchase and on his entry into the trade and assured him that he had bought a very lucky ass. Without it going lame or collapsing on him, its previous owner had, in addition to feeding himself and the ass honourably, earned himself two suits as well as the sixteen ducados with which he now planned to return to his native province, where a marriage had been arranged for him with a distant relative.

Apart from those who had acted as intermediaries in the sale of the ass there were another four water-carriers present who were playing *primera** stretched out on the ground, which served as their table while their cloaks served as a table-cloth. Asturiano began to watch them and saw that they played not like water-carriers but like archdeacons, for each of them had a stake of more than a hundred reales in copper and silver. One deal forced all the players to stake what they had left, and if one player had not given a share to his partner, he would have cleared the table. Eventually, two of the players in that deal ran out of money and left the game. When he saw this the vendor of the ass offered to join in if they could find a fourth player, for he was not in favour of three-hand games. Asturiano, who was very accommodating and would never let the soup go to waste, as the Italian saying goes, said he would make up the fourth hand. So they sat down, the game proceeded smoothly, and since he was gambling with money rather than time Lope soon lost the six escudos he had on him. When he realized that he had no money left he told them that he would stake the ass, if they were amenable. They accepted his offer and staked a quarter of the ass, explaining that they wanted to place their bets a quarter at a time. Lope was very unlucky, and in four successive stakes he lost the four quarters of the ass to the very man who had sold it to him. Just as the latter was getting up to take possession of it, Asturiano pointed out that he had only gambled the four quarters of the ass but not its tail, and if they would give it to him, he would take it and be on his way. The request for the tail made them all laugh and there were a few lawyers among them who were of the opinion that such a claim was invalid. They explained that when a ram or any other animal is sold, the tail is neither added nor subtracted, because it must necessarily be attached to the hindquarters. Lope retorted that Barbary rams are usually considered to have five quarters, the fifth being the tail, and when the said rams are cut up, the tail is as much a quarter as any of the others. As for the tail being included with a ram or any other animal sold as livestock, he was prepared to concede the point, but his own animal was not sold but wagered, and it was never his intention to gamble the tail, and would they please return it to him now, together with everything attached and belonging to it, namely, the whole of the brain and the backbone, where it began and from where it descended, as far as the very tips of its hairs.

'Let's imagine,' said one, 'that what you say is true and they give you what you're asking, then you'll have to sit down with the remains of the ass.'

'Precisely,' replied Lope. 'Bring me my tail, and if you don't, I swear that you'll not take the ass from me, not even if all the water-carriers in the world were to come after it. Don't go thinking that because there are so many of you you can pull a fast one on me, because I'm the kind of man who can go up to another and sink several inches of dagger into his belly without him knowing who did it, or where and how it happened. What's more, I don't want payment of the tail in instalments either, I want it whole and cut from the ass as I've requested.'

To the winner and the others it seemed unwise to settle the matter by force, perceiving that Asturiano was so determined that he would never let them get away with it. Accustomed as he was to the ways and manners of the tunny fisheries, where flamboyant and spirited gestures, extravagant oaths, and ostentatious posturing were the order of the day, he flung aside his hat, seized a dagger which he was carrying under his cloak, and assumed such a menacing stance that he instilled fear and respect in every member of that water-carrying company. Eventually one of them, who seemed to have more wits and common sense than the others, persuaded them to wager the tail against a quarter of the ass in a game of *quínola* or *dos y pasante*.* They agreed and Lope won the *quínola*; this annoyed the other man, who wagered another quarter, and three games later he was once again without his ass. He wanted to carry on and gamble the money but Lope refused, until the others insisted so much that he had no choice but to play. He won back the other man's honeymoon funds and completely wiped him out. The poor man was so grief-stricken that he threw himself on the ground and began beating his head against it. Lope, in accordance with his noble origins and his gener-ous and sympathetic character, lifted him to his feet and gave back all the money he had won from him, including the sixteen ducados he had paid for the ass, and he even shared some of his own money among the onlookers. Such unprecedented generosity left everyone speechless with amazement; and if this had happened in the time and reign of Tamburlaine,* they would have proclaimed him king of the water-carriers.

Lope returned to the city surrounded by a vast entourage, and there he told Tomás what had happened and Tomás, in his turn, related the good progress he had made. There was not a tavern, ale-house, or gathering of *pícaros* which had not heard the tale of how the ass had been wagered, won back by means of its tail, and the spirit and generosity of Asturiano. The vulgar herd, however, which is for the most part devilish, damned, and defaming, did not bother to recollect the generosity, spirit, and laudable qualities of the great Lope, they only remembered the tail. He had been selling water in the city for scarcely two days when he found himself pointed out by lots of people who remarked: 'That's the water-carrier who demanded his tail.'

The young lads pricked up their ears, discovered the full story, and subsequently Lope could not turn a corner without the whole street resounding with their shouts; on one side: 'Give us the tail, Asturiano!' and on the other: 'Asturiano, give us the tail!' Finding himself persecuted by so many sharp tongues and taunting voices Lope took refuge in silence, thinking that by refusing to respond he would stifle such impertinence. He was, however, quite mistaken, for the longer he held his tongue the more the young lads hounded him. So he adopted another strategy, and swapping forbearance for anger he jumped from his ass and chased the boys with a stick. This was tantamount to setting a powder-keg alight or cutting off the Hydra's head;* for each one that he chopped off, that is, for each lad that he thrashed, there immediately sprang up in its place, not seven but seven hundred others, who asked him for the tail with even greater vehemence and determination. He eventually saw fit to retreat to the inn, where he had taken accommodation far away from that of his friend, for the sole purpose of avoiding Argüello. He intended to remain there until the influence of his unlucky star had receded and the young boys' mischievous request for the tail had been forgotten.

He did not set foot outside the inn for six days, except at night when he went to see Tomás and enquire how he was faring. The latter told him that since he had given the paper to Costanza he had not been able to say a single word to her, and he thought her behaviour was even more reserved than usual, because on the one occasion when he was able to approach her, she saw him in time and, before he could get any closer, said, 'Tomás, I'm not in any pain, so I've no need of your words or your prayers: be satisfied that I don't denounce you to the Inquisition. Don't waste your breath.'

However, she said this without displaying any anger in her eyes or any other excess of emotion which might indicate severity. Lope recounted how the boys were pestering him by asking him for the tail because he himself had asked for the ass's tail, thereby recovering his notorious debt. Tomás advised him not to leave the inn, at least not on the ass, and if he did go out then he should use the quiet back-streets, and if these precautions were insufficient then he would have to give up the job, which would be the best way to put a stop to such an impudent demand. Lope asked him if Gallega had made any further advances. Tomás said that she had not, although she continued to bribe him with gifts and presents which she stole from the guests in the kitchen. With this Lope returned to his rooms, determined not to venture out again for another six days, at least not on the ass.

It must have been about eleven o'clock that night when a large number of officers of the law suddenly and unexpectedly entered the inn, followed by the Chief Magistrate. The innkeeper was alarmed, as were the guests. For just as sightings of comets invariably arouse fears of bad luck and misfortune, so too officers of the law, when they descend suddenly and in force upon an establishment, unnerve and intimidate even the clearest consciences. The Chief Magistrate withdrew to a room and summoned the innkeeper, who came in trepidation to see what he wanted. When he saw him the Chief Magistrate asked him very gravely, 'Are you the innkeeper?'

'Yes, sir,' he replied. 'At your service.'

The Chief Magistrate ordered everyone in the room to depart and leave him alone with the innkeeper. When the customers had gone and they were alone, the Chief Magistrate asked the innkeeper, 'Innkeeper, what servants do you have at this inn of yours?'

'Sir,' he replied, 'I have two Galician girls, a housekeeper, and a young lad who sees to the barley and hay.'

'No others?' asked the Chief Magistrate.

'No, sir,' said the innkeeper.

'So, tell me, innkeeper,' said the Chief Magistrate, 'where is the girl who is said to serve at this establishment, who is so beautiful that throughout the city she is known as the "illustrious kitchen maid"? It has even come to my attention that my son, don Periquito, is infatuated with her and not a night goes by without him serenading her.'

'Sir,' replied the innkeeper, 'it's true that this kitchen maid they speak of is here at this inn, and although she's not my servant, neither is she not my servant.'

'I do not understand what you mean, innkeeper, by this kitchen maid being and yet not being your servant.'

'I've only stated things as they are' continued the innkeeper, 'and if your Honour will allow me, I'll tell you the tale which I've never told another living soul.'

'Before you tell me any more, I wish to see the kitchen maid; have her come here,' said the Chief Magistrate.

The innkeeper put his head around the door and shouted, 'Wife, tell Costanza to come here.'

When the innkeeper's wife heard that the Chief Magistrate was summoning Costanza, she became anxious, began wringing her hands, and said, 'Oh, dear me! The Chief Magistrate wants to see Costanza and he wants to see her alone! Something awful must have happened; for this girl's beauty casts a spell on men.'

Hearing this, Costanza comforted her: 'Mistress, don't worry. I'll go and see what the Chief Magistrate wants and if something bad's happened, be assured that I'm not to blame.'

With this, and without waiting to be summoned again, she picked up a lighted candle in a silver candlestick, and with more modesty than fear she went to face the Chief Magistrate.

When he saw her he ordered the innkeeper to close the door, and when he had done so the Chief Magistrate stood up. He took the candlestick which Costanza was carrying and, lifting the light to her face, he examined her intently from head to foot. Since Costanza was nervous the colour in her face was heightened, and she looked so beautiful and innocent that the Chief Magistrate felt that he was gazing upon an angel that had descended to earth. When he had gazed at her for some time, he said, 'Innkeeper, this is not a jewel to be kept in the humble setting of an inn; seeing what I see I can say that my son, Periquito, is wise to have employed his thoughts on such a worthy object. May I say, young lady, that people can and indeed should call you not just "illustrious" but "most illustrious". Such adjectives, however, should not be applied to a kitchen maid but a duchess.'

'She's not a kitchen maid, sir' said the innkeeper, 'for within the establishment she's occupied solely in carrying the keys to the silverware of which, by the grace of God, I possess a few pieces, which I use to serve our more honoured guests.'

'Even so,' said the Chief Magistrate, 'let me say, innkeeper, that it is neither proper nor appropriate for this young lady to live in an inn. Is she a relative of yours, by any chance?'

'She's neither my relative nor my servant; if it please your Honour to know who she is, when she's dismissed your Honour shall hear things which will both please and astound you.'

'It would please me greatly to hear these things' said the Chief Magistrate. 'Costanza should leave us now, in the knowledge that she may rely on me as she would her own father: for her great modesty and beauty oblige all who see her to offer themselves in her service.'

Costanza uttered not a word in reply, but with great dignity she made a deep curtsey to the Chief Magistrate and left the room, to find her mistress waiting for her and anxious to know what the Chief Magistrate had wanted of her. Costanza told her what had taken place and how her master remained with him to tell him something or other that he did not want her to hear. This did not calm the innkeeper's wife's nerves, and she remained in an attitude of prayer until the Chief Magistrate left and she could see that her husband was still a free man. He, while he had remained with the Chief Magistrate, had recounted the following tale:

'Sir, by my calculations, fifteen years, one month, and four days ago a lady arrived at this inn dressed in the costume of a pilgrim. She was being carried in a litter and was accompanied by four servants on horseback, two female companions, and a young lady, who were travelling in a coach. She also brought two mules covered in rich caparisons and laden with a sumptuous bed and kitchen utensils. In other words, her possessions were those of a person of distinguished rank and the pilgrim herself appeared to be a noblewoman. Although she looked to be about forty years of age or thereabouts, this did not detract from her considerable beauty. On her arrival she was ill, pale, and so exhausted that she ordered her bed to be made immediately in this very room. They asked me to name the most reputable doctor in this city and I replied that Doctor Fuentes was their man. They went to fetch him immediately and he came without delay. She revealed her illness to him in private and as a consequence the doctor ordered her bed to be moved to some other part of the inn where she would not be disturbed by any noise. She was moved forthwith to a more private room upstairs, which had all the comforts the doctor requested. None of the male servants entered their mistress's room and she was served only by the two companions and the young girl.

'My wife and I asked the servants who the lady was, what her name was, where she came from, and where she was going, whether she was married, widowed, or a spinster, and the reason why she was dressed as a pilgrim. To all these questions which we asked many times they all made the same reply, which was to say that the pilgrim was a rich and high-ranking lady from Old Castile, that she was a widow, that she had no children to inherit her estate, that because she had been ill for some months with the dropsy she had pledged to make a pilgrimage to Our Lady of Guadalupe, and it was with that undertaking that she was dressed in that manner. As for revealing her name, they were under strict instructions to call her the lady pilgrim and nothing else. That was all we were able to learn at first. However, when her illness had detained the lady pilgrim at the inn for three days, one of her companions summoned my wife and myself to her. We went to see what she wanted: on the verge of tears, with the door closed and her maids present, she said, if my memory serves me correctly, these very words:

'"Good sir and madam, heaven will bear witness that I am in my present difficult circumstances, which I am about to disclose to you, through no fault of my own. I am with child and so close to the birth that the pains are already upon me. None of the male servants who accompany me is aware of my need and misfortune: I have neither been able nor wanted to hide the fact from these women. In order to escape the malicious eyes of my own province and so that this critical hour should not come upon me there, I pledged to go to Our Lady of Guadalupe; it must have been her desire that I should enter my confinement at your inn. It now rests with you to help and attend me, with the secrecy you owe to someone who places her honour in your hands. If the reward for the favour you do me, for that is what I wish to call it, does not correspond with the great benefit I expect, it will at least be an indication of my profound gratitude. I wish to begin to show my gratitude by giving you two hundred gold escudos which are contained in this purse." Taking from beneath her pillow an embroidered purse of gold and green, she put it in my wife's hands. My wife took the purse without uttering a single word of thanks or courtesy, as if unconscious of what she was doing and as if she were simple-minded, because she was so awed and mesmerized by the pilgrim. I remember saying to her that it was not at all necessary: for we were not the kind of people who were moved to do someone a good turn when the circumstance offered out of interest rather than charity.

'She continued: "Friends, you must, without delay, find somewhere to take the child I deliver and you must also invent some lies to tell the person to whom you entrust the child. For the time being find someone in the city, but afterwards I want the child taken to a village. As for what will need to be done afterwards, if it is God's will to deliver me safely and take me to fulfil my vow, I will give you instructions on my return from Guadalupe. For by then I will have had time to think about it and choose the most appropriate course of action. I have no need of a midwife, nor do I want one. Other more honourable births I have experienced persuade me that with the assistance of my maids alone I shall overcome the difficulties and will be spared a further witness of my misfortunes."

'At this point she finished her explanation and began to cry copiously, but was partially consoled by the many comforting words which my wife, now almost herself again, addressed to her. To cut a long story short, I went out in search of somewhere to take the child, whatever the time of its birth, and between midnight and one o'clock that night, when everyone at the inn was sound asleep, the good lady gave birth to a daughter, the most beautiful child I had ever laid eyes on, and she is the very one your Honour has just seen. The mother made no complaint during the birth and the child did not come into the world crying. Everyone was affected by a wonderful calm and silence, which befitted the secrecy of such an extraordinary event. She remained in bed for another six days, during which time the doctor visited her every day, but not because she had disclosed the true cause of her suffering to him. The medicines he prescribed were never administered, because she merely wished to deceive her servants with the attendance of the doctor. She told me all this herself once she was out of danger, and on the eighth day she got up with that same swelling, or another resembling the one she had recently been relieved of.

'She went on her pilgrimage and returned twenty days later, by now almost completely recovered, for she was gradually ridding herself of the device she had used after the birth to feign dropsy. On her return the child had, on my orders, already been given to the nurse who would bring her up as my niece in a village two leagues from here. She was christened Costanza, as instructed by her mother who, being satisfied with what I had arranged, gave me a gold chain before departing, from which she removed six fragments, and which I still have in my possession. She explained that whoever returned for the child would bring the missing links with him. She also cut a sheet of white parchment in a zigzag pattern, in the same way and for the same purpose that you put your hands together and write something on your fingers which can be read while the fingers are interlaced, but after the hands are separated the logic is broken because the letters become disconnected. If you put your hands together again the letters join up and correspond with one another so that the whole thing can be read in the normal way. In other words, the one half of the parchment serves as the soul of the other; fitted together they will make sense, but separated it is impossible to make sense of them without guessing the contents of the other half. The larger part of the chain remained in my possession and I have it to this day as I wait for the counter-sign, for she told me that she would send for her daughter within two years, charging me to have her raised, not in accordance with her inherited rank, but as a peasant girl is commonly brought up.

'She also instructed me that if due to some unforeseen event she were unable to send for her daughter so soon, and even if the girl were to mature in years and understanding, I was not to reveal to her the circumstances of her birth. She also asked me to pardon her for not revealing her name or identity, for she was reserving this information for another more important occasion. In conclusion, she gave me another four hundred gold escudos and embraced my wife, all the while shedding tears of affection. She departed, leaving us in awe of her intelligence, courage, beauty, and modesty. Costanza was raised in the village for two years and then I brought her here and I have always dressed her as a peasant girl, just as her mother instructed me. Fifteen years, one month, and four days I have been waiting for the person who is to fetch her and the long wait has destroyed any hopes I had of ever witnessing such an arrival. If no one comes this year I am resolved to adopt her and leave her all of my estate, which is worth more than six thousand ducados, God be praised.

'It only remains for me to tell you, your Honour, if it is possible for me to find words which are adequate, of the goodness and virtue of Costanza. She is, first and foremost, deeply devoted to Our Lady; she goes to confession and takes communion once a month; she can read and write; no woman in Toledo is more skilful at making lace; although she is very modest about it, she sings like an angel and in virtue she has no equal.

'As for her beauty, your Honour has already seen it. Your son, don Pedro, has never spoken to her; it is certainly true that from time to time he serenades her, but she never listens. Many gentlemen, and titled ones at that, have lodged at this inn, and have deliberately delayed their departure for many days in order to feast their eyes on her. However, I know for a fact that not one of them could truthfully boast that she has given him the chance to address a single word to her, let alone two together. This, sir, is the true story of the "illustrious kitchen maid", who is not a maid, and which I have told without departing one iota from the truth.'

The innkeeper fell silent and, amazed by the events the innkeeper had related to him, it was some time before the Chief Magistrate responded. He eventually told him to bring the chain and the parchment, because he wanted to see them. The innkeeper went to fetch them, and when they were shown to him the Chief Magistrate could see that things were as they had been described to him. The chain was in several exquisitely wrought fragments and on the parchment were written the following letters, one on top of the other and separated by the spaces which the other half would fill: T I I T E R E I N. When he saw these letters he realized that they would have to be matched with those on the other half of the parchment in order to be understood. He thought the means of identification clever and deduced that the lady pilgrim who had left such a chain with the innkeeper must be very rich. Since he intended to remove the beautiful young girl from that inn as soon as he had made arrangements for a monastery to take her, he was content for the time being to take only the parchment. He instructed the innkeeper that if by chance someone should come for Costanza, he was to let him know exactly who it was that came for her. That done, he departed as amazed by the story and the circumstances of the illustrious kitchen maid as he was by her incomparable beauty.

All the time that the innkeeper spent with the Chief Magistrate, in addition to the time that Costanza remained with them when they summoned her, Tomás was beside himself with anxiety, his soul besieged by a thousand different thoughts, none of which brought him any comfort. However, when he saw that the Chief Magistrate was leaving and that Costanza remained behind, his spirits recovered and his pulse, which had virtually abandoned him, returned to normal. He dared not ask the innkeeper what the Chief Magistrate had wanted and the innkeeper did not mention it to a soul save his wife, whereupon she breathed more easily and thanked God for delivering them from such a frightful shock.

At about one o'clock the following day two elderly gentlemen of venerable appearance entered the inn accompanied by four men on horseback, having first enquired of one of the lads who was walking in that direction with them whether this was the Sevillano Inn. When they were told that it was, they all went inside. The four men dismounted and went to help the two elderly gentlemen to dismount, a clear indication that the latter were aldermen.* Costanza came out with her customary courtesy to see the newly arrived guests, and scarcely had one of the old gentlemen seen her when he said to the other, 'Don Juan, I believe that we have found all that we came looking for.'

Tomás, who came to feed the horses, immediately recognized two of his father's servants and then his father and Carriazo's, for they were the two elderly gentlemen who were treated with deference by the rest. Although he was astonished at their arrival, he imagined that they must be on their way to look for Carriazo and himself at the tunny fisheries, for more than one person could have informed them that that was where they would find them both, and not in Flanders. However, he dared not allow himself to be recognized dressed as he was: rather, taking a huge risk, he covered his face with his hand and passed right in front of them and went to look for Costanza. As chance would have it he found her alone, and in a rushed and agitated voice, fearing that she would not allow him to speak to her, he said:

'Costanza, one of the two gentlemen who have just arrived is my father, the one that you will hear called Juan de Avendaño. Enquire of his servants whether he has a son called Tomás de Avendaño, for I am he, and this way you will be able to conclude and confirm that I told you the truth about my rank and I shall continue to do so in all matters concerning me. God keep you safe, for until they depart, I do not intend to return to this inn.'

Costanza said nothing in reply, nor did Tomás want her to say anything. Instead he went out again, covering his face as he had done on his way in, and went to inform Carriazo that their fathers were at the inn. The innkeeper called Tomás to come and feed the animals, but since he did not turn up, he performed the task himself. One of the two gentlemen called one of the Galician maids aside and asked her the name of the beautiful young girl he had seen and whether she was the daughter or a relative of the innkeeper and his wife. Gallega gave the following reply:

'The girl's name is Costanza: she's not a relative of the innkeeper, or of his wife either. I don't rightly know who she is; all I can say is the pox on her, because I don't know what it is about her but she won't let any of us other girls here at the inn get a piece of the action. After all, we've got our God-given looks too! No guest comes into the inn without asking who the beauty is, or who doesn't say: "How lovely she is! What a fine-looking one! What a treat for sore eyes! Hard luck on the less well-favoured! May my fortune always be so kind to me!" And as for the rest of us, no one gives us the time of day, not even to insult us.'

'From what you say then,' replied the gentleman, 'this girl must allow herself to be courted and fondled by the guests.'

'Never!' replied Gallega. 'Chance would be a fine thing! You're barking up the wrong tree there! Sir, I swear to God that if she just allowed herself to be seen, she'd make a fortune. She's more prickly than a hedgehog; she's always spouting her Hail Marys; she spends the day embroidering and praying. The day she performs a miracle, I'd like a stake in the profits. My mistress says that she wears her piety like a second skin. It's just too much, honestly!'

The gentleman was delighted by what he learned from Gallega, and without waiting for his spurs to be removed he summoned the innkeeper and, drawing him aside into a room, he said, 'I, sir, have come to relieve you of a possession of mine which has been in your safe-keeping for some years now. To redeem it I bring you a thousand gold escudos, these fragments of chain, and this parchment.'

Saying this, he took out the six fragments of chain which constituted the sign and which he had in his possession. The innkeeper also recognized the parchment and, overjoyed at the gift of the thousand escudos, replied, 'Sir, the possession you wish to redeem is here at the inn, but the chain and the parchment, which will verify the truth to which I believe your honour is referring, are not. I beg you, therefore, to bear with me. I will return shortly.'

He went immediately to inform the Chief Magistrate of events and of the presence at the inn of the two gentlemen who had come for Costanza.

The Chief Magistrate had just eaten, but since he was eager to see how the story ended he straight away mounted his horse and went to the Sevillano Inn, carrying the parchment which was part of the sign. He had scarcely set eyes on the two gentlemen when, with arms open wide, he went to embrace one of them saying, 'Bless my soul! What a pleasant surprise this is, don Juan de Avendaño, my cousin and lord.'

The gentleman returned his embrace, saying, 'My arrival is indeed a pleasant one, since I find you before me, my good cousin, and in the good health I always wish you. Cousin, embrace this gentleman, who is don Diego de Carriazo, a great nobleman and friend of mine.'

'I know don Diego', replied the Chief Magistrate, 'and I am at his service.'

After the two men had embraced and received each other with great affection and courtesy they went into a room, where they remained alone with the innkeeper who already had the chain in his possession, and who said, 'The Chief Magistrate already knows why your Honour has come, don Diego de Carriazo; if you will get out the fragments that are missing from this chain, and the Chief Magistrate will get out the parchment which is in his possession, we will carry out the test which I have waited so long to perform.'

'So,' replied, don Diego, 'it will not be necessary to explain our arrival to the Chief Magistrate again, because he will understand that it concerns what you, innkeeper, have already told him.'

'He told me some of the story, but there is much that I do not know. As for the parchment, here it is.'

Don Diego took out the other one and when they fitted both parts together they formed one whole. The innkeeper's letters which were, as already stated, T I I T E R E I N, corresponded with the letters H S S H T U S G on the other parchment, and once they were combined they read: THIS IS THE TRUE SIGN. They then compared the links of the chain and found that they matched exactly.

'We have the proof!' said the Chief Magistrate. 'Now all we need to find out, if it is possible, is the identity of this beautiful girl's parents.'

'I', replied don Diego, 'am her father; her mother is no longer alive. It is enough for you to know that she was of such prestigious rank that I could be her servant. Since I do not want her reputation to remain a secret in the way that her name must, nor do I want her to bear the responsibility for what must seem a great and blameworthy transgression, let it be known that this girl's mother, the widow of a distinguished nobleman, had retired to live in a village on one of her country estates and there, with her servants and vassals, led a peaceful and quiet existence. Fate ordained that one day, while I was out hunting near the boundaries of her lands, I suddenly desired to visit her, and it was the hour of the siesta when I arrived at her castle, for her grand mansion can justly be called a castle. I left my horse with a servant of mine, and without encountering a soul I reached her room where she was taking her siesta, asleep on a black couch. She was extremely lovely and the silence, the solitude, and the opportunity aroused in me a desire more daring than it was decent, and without stopping to reason with myself, I closed the door behind me and approached her. I woke her and, holding her down firmly, I said: "Dear lady, do not make a noise, for your shouts will merely proclaim your dishonour. No one saw me enter this room, for my good fortune, which is indeed bountiful in permitting me to enjoy you, has sent all your servants to sleep. Even if they were to respond to your shouts, they would have to take my life as I lay in your arms, and not even my death would be able to restore your shattered reputation." In short, I took her by force and against her will and she, exhausted, overpowered, and distressed, either could not or did not want to say a word. Leaving her in that state of delirium and shock, I retraced the same steps I had taken to enter the room and made my way to the village of a friend of mine, which was two leagues distant from hers.

'The lady moved from that place to another, and without my ever seeing her, or even trying to, she lived there for two years, at the end of which time I learned that she was dead. About twenty days ago a steward of this lady summoned me, writing with great insistence that it was a matter pertaining to my happiness and my honour. I went to see what he wanted of me, not for a moment anticipating that he would tell me what he did. I found him on the point of death and, to cut a long story short, he briefly explained that when his mistress was dying she told him what had taken place between us and how as a result of that violation she had become pregnant, and that to hide the swelling she had gone on a pilgrimage to Our Lady of Guadalupe, how she had given birth to a daughter at the inn, and how she was to be called Costanza. He gave me the signs with which to find her, namely, the chain and parchment that you have seen. He also gave me thirty thousand gold escudos which his mistress left as a dowry for her daughter. He also told me that the reason he had not given them to me straight after his mistress died, nor disclosed what she had entrusted to his confidence and secrecy, was pure greed and the desire to enjoy the money himself. However, since he was about to give an account of himself to his Maker, he gave me the money and explained how and where I could find my daughter in order to unburden his conscience. I took the money and the signs, and recounting the details to don Juan de Avendaño, we set off for this city.'

Don Diego had reached this point in his narrative when they heard loud shouts outside the main door: 'Tell Tomás Pedro, the stable lad, that they've arrested his friend, Asturiano; tell him to go to the jail, for he's waiting for him there.' When he heard the words 'jail' and 'arrested', the Chief Magistrate ordered that the prisoner and the constable in charge of him should step into the inn. It was relayed to the constable that the Chief Magistrate, who was inside the inn, was ordering him to enter with the prisoner and he was obliged to do so.

Asturiano came in with his teeth covered in blood and looking a very sorry sight, held in a very firm grip by the constable. As soon as he entered the room he recognized his own father and Tomás's. Taken by surprise and desperate not to be recognized, he covered his face with a handkerchief and pretended to wipe away the blood. The Chief Magistrate enquired what the young lad had done to be carried off in such a sorry state. The constable replied that he was a water-carrier known as Asturiano, to whom all the boys in the street shouted: 'Give us the tail, Asturiano! Give us the tail!' He then briefly recounted why they asked him for the tail, which greatly amused everyone present. He went on to say that the boys were still pestering him with their demand for the tail while he was going out along the Alcántara bridge, and so he had got down from his ass and chased after them. He caught hold of one of them whom he had beaten half to death, and when they tried to arrest him he had resisted and that was why he was now in such a sorry state.

The Chief Magistrate ordered him to uncover his face, but when he defiantly refused to do so the constable went over to him and took the handkerchief away, whereupon his father recognized him and said, his voice faltering with emotion, 'Don Diego, my son, what has happened to you? What clothes are these? Haven't you grown out of your picaresque mischief yet?'

Carriazo fell on his knees at his father's feet and his father, with tears in his eyes, held him in his arms for a long time. Since don Juan de Avendaño knew that don Diego had been travelling with his son, don Tomás, he asked him where he was. Don Diego replied that don Tomás de Avendaño was the boy who gave out the barley and hay at that inn. When Asturiano said this the whole company was astounded, and the Chief Magistrate ordered the innkeeper to fetch the stable boy.

'I don't think he's here,' replied the innkeeper, 'but I'll go and look for him.' With that he went off in search of him. Don Diego asked Carriazo to explain the meaning of these metamorphoses and what had induced him to become a water-carrier and don Tomás a servant boy. Carriazo replied that he could not give a satisfactory answer to these questions in public, but he would answer them in private.

Tomás Pedro was hiding in his room, hoping to observe from there, without being observed himself, what his and Carriazo's father were doing there. The arrival of the Chief Magistrate and the general commotion at the inn mystified him. Someone told the innkeeper that he was hiding upstairs and so he went up to get him, and using force rather than persuasion he made him come down. He would not have gone down when he did if the Chief Magistrate himself had not gone into the courtyard and called him by name, saying, 'Come down, sir, my good kinsman, there are no bears or lions lying in wait for you down here.'

Tomás came down, and with his eyes lowered in shame he very humbly knelt in front of his father, who embraced him with the same overwhelming delight as the father of the Prodigal Son when he recovered his lost child.

Meanwhile a carriage belonging to the Chief Magistrate had arrived to take them back to his house, for the great celebration they planned did not permit returning on horseback. He had Costanza summoned, and taking her by the hand he presented her to her father saying, 'Don Diego, receive this precious gift and value it highly as the most treasured possession you could ever desire. As for you, beautiful maiden, kiss your father's hands and give thanks to God for remedying, elevating, and improving the lowliness of your situation.'

Nervous and trembling, Costanza, who could neither understand nor guess what had happened to her, could only kneel in front of her father. Taking his hands she began to kiss them tenderly and bathe them with the many tears that flowed from her very beautiful eyes.

While this was happening the Chief Magistrate had persuaded his cousin, don Juan, that they should all accompany him to his house, and although don Juan declined the invitation the Chief Magistrate was so persuasive that he was forced to concede and they all entered the carriage. However, when the Chief Magistrate told Costanza to enter the carriage with the others her heart sank and she and the innkeeper's wife fell into each other's arms and began to cry so bitterly that it broke the hearts of all those who heard it. The innkeeper's wife said, 'How can it be, my precious child, that you are going away and leaving me? How can you bear to leave this mother who has raised you so lovingly?'

Costanza wept and replied in terms that were no less tender. Moved by this scene, however, the Chief Magistrate ordered the innkeeper's wife to get into the carriage with her, saying that she need not be parted from her daughter, for such she considered her to be, until she left Toledo. So the innkeeper's wife and all the others got into the carriage and went to the Chief Magistrate's house, where they were received by his wife who was a lady of high rank. They ate an exquisite and sumptuous meal, after which Carriazo explained to his father how Tomás had taken a job as a servant at the inn because of his love for Costanza; for he was so passionately in love with her that even if he had never discovered that her origins were so distinguished, being the daughter of such a father, he would have married her believing her to be a maid. The Chief Magistrate's wife then dressed Costanza in clothes belonging to her daughter who was the same age and size as Costanza. If she had looked beautiful in the attire of a peasant girl, she looked divine dressed as a lady of the court. The borrowed outfit suited her so well that she gave the impression that she had been born a lady and always worn the best and most fashionable clothes.

Among so many happy people, however, there was inevitably one sad individual, namely don Pedro, the Chief Magistrate's son, who immediately realized that Costanza was not destined to be his. He was right; for between them the Chief Magistrate, don Diego de Carriazo, and don Juan de Avendaño arranged that don Tomás should marry Costanza, with her father giving her the thirty thousand escudos which her mother had left her; the water-carrier don Diego de Carriazo should marry the Chief Magistrate's daughter, and don Pedro, the Chief Magistrate's son, would marry a daughter of don Juan de Avendaño. Her father offered to obtain the dispensation necessary because of their blood kinship.

So everyone was happy, contented, and satisfied, and the news of the marriages and the good fortune of the illustrious kitchen maid spread throughout the city and crowds of people came to see Costanza in her new attire, in which, as has already been stated, she looked every inch a lady. They saw the stable boy, Tomás Pedro, transformed back into don Tomás de Avendaño and dressed as a gentleman. They also observed that Lope Asturiano was quite the gentleman too, once he had changed his clothes and abandoned his ass and pitchers. Nevertheless, when he walked down the street in all his finery, some people still asked him for the tail.

They remained in Toledo for a month and then don Diego de Carriazo, his wife and father, Costanza and her husband don Tomás, and the Chief Magistrate's son, who wanted to meet his future bride, all returned to Burgos. The innkeeper of the Sevillano was now a rich man, with his thousand escudos as well as the jewels which Costanza gave her mistress; and she always called the woman who had raised her by this name. The story of the illustrious kitchen maid inspired the poets of the golden Tagus to celebrate and extol the incomparable beauty of Costanza, who still lives with her fine stable boy, and Carriazo likewise with his three sons. The latter do not take after their father, are blissfully unaware of the existence of tunny fisheries, and are all studying in Salamanca. As for their father, he only has to lay eyes on a water-carrier's ass to recall and see vividly before him the one he purchased in Toledo. He fears that when he least expects it that distant voice will echo in some satire: 'Give us the tail, Asturiano! Asturiano, give us the tail!'

THE DECEITFUL MARRIAGE

As the soldier hobbled out of the Hospital of the Resurrection, which is outside the Campo Gate in Valladolid, he supported himself on his sword. From this posture, the shakiness of his legs, and the yellowness of his complexion it was plain to see that, although the weather was not very hot, he must have sweated out in twenty days all the fluid he most probably acquired in a single hour.* He walked with the unsteady, faltering steps of the convalescent, and as he passed through the city gate he saw a friend coming towards him whom he had not seen for six months. Crossing himself as if he had seen an apparition, the friend came up to him and said, 'What is this, Ensign Campuzano? Can you really be here in this part of the world? As God is my judge, I imagined you flourishing your pike up there in Flanders rather than dragging your sword round here. Why are you such an awful colour and why are you so weak?'

Campuzano replied, 'As to whether I am in this part of the world or not, Graduate Peralta, the fact that you see me before you answers your question. As to the other questions, I can only reply that I am leaving that hospital after sweating out fourteen sores which I was saddled with by a woman I was foolish enough to take for my own.'

'So you married?' declared Peralta.

'Indeed, I did,' replied Campuzano.

'It must have been for love and affection,' stated Peralta, 'and that kind of marriage always incurs repentance.'

'I couldn't say whether it was for affection,' replied the ensign, 'although I can confidently state that it was for infection, for from my state of matrimony, or rather acrimony, I have suffered so much pain of body and mind that in order to ease the aches of my body I have had to suffer forty sweats and I have yet to find relief for the torments of my mind. But since I am in no condition to hold long conversations in the street, you must excuse me. Another day and in more comfortable circumstances I will relate my experiences to you, for they are stranger and more marvellous than anything you have heard in all the days of your life.'

'I beg to differ', countered the Graduate, 'for I wish you to come with me to my lodgings and we'll do penance together* there, for a

stew is just the thing for an invalid and although there is sufficient
only for two, my servant will make do with a pie. If your convales-
cence will allow, a few slices of Rute ham will serve as an hors-
d'œuvre, together with the goodwill which I offer as a special
appetizer, not only on this occasion but whenever you wish.'

Campuzano thanked him and accepted the invitation and what he
offered. They went to the Church of St Lawrence, where they heard
Mass, then Peralta took him to his house, gave him what he had
promised, offered his services to him again and, when they were finishing their meal, asked him to relate to him the events which he had
earlier mentioned in such intriguing terms. Campuzano needed no
persuading and began his story as follows:

'You will no doubt remember, Graduate Peralta, how I shared
lodgings in this town with Captain Pedro de Herrera, who is now in
Flanders.'

'Yes, I do,' replied Peralta.

'Well, one day,' continued Campuzano, 'as we were finishing our
lunch in the Solana Inn where we were lodging, two ladies of genteel
appearance came in accompanied by two maids. One of them went
over to talk to the captain by the window while the other sat down
on a chair next to me. Her veil hung low over her face and prevented her features from being seen except where they could be
glimpsed through the fineness of the veil. Although I begged her out
of courtesy to remove her veil, she was not to be persuaded, a determination which further inflamed my desire to see her. To fan the
flame even more, whether by chance or design, she revealed a snow-
white hand adorned with expensive rings. I was on that occasion
looking extremely dashing myself, with that big chain you must have
seen me wearing, and the hat with the band and feathers and my
brightly coloured soldier's uniform, cutting such a gallant figure in
the eyes of my own madness that I was convinced that I could sweep
any woman off her feet. Anyway, I asked her to remove her veil, to
which she replied:

'"Do not press me further; I have a house, arrange for a page to
follow me, for although I am more respectable than this response
implies, nevertheless, in order to see whether you are as discreet as
you are handsome, I shall be happy for you to see me."

'I kissed her hands to thank her for the great favour she did me,
in return for which I promised her pots of gold. The captain ended

his conversation, the ladies departed, and a servant of mine followed them. The captain told me that what the lady wanted him to do was to deliver some letters to another captain in Flanders, whom she claimed was her cousin, although he knew that he was actually her lover. I was still inflamed with passion after seeing those snow-white hands and desperate to see her face, and so the following day my servant led me to her house where I freely gained admittance. Inside I discovered an elegantly furnished home and a woman no older than thirty, whom I recognized by her hands. She was not excessively beautiful but sufficiently so for men to fall in love with her when she spoke, because she did so in such soft tones that on reaching your ears they penetrated your very soul. I had long and amorous conversations with her. I boasted, swaggered, bragged, made offers and promises, and went through all the motions I thought necessary to win her good favour. However, she was accustomed to hearing similar or even greater offers and arguments and seemed to be giving them more attention than credit. In short, in the four days I continued to visit her our conversation achieved nothing of consequence and I failed to pick the fruit I desired.

'During the period of these visits I always found the house empty and caught neither sight nor sound of either false relations or true friends. She was served by a maid who was more crafty than simple. Finally, treating our romance like a soldier who is about to be redeployed, I put pressure on my lady, doña Estefanía de Caicedo (for this is the name of the one who has reduced me to my present state), and she replied:

'"Ensign Campuzano, it would be folly to try and pass myself off as a saint. I have been a sinner and I still am, but not to the extent that my neighbours gossip about me or that I attract the attention of strangers. I have inherited no wealth from either parents or relations and yet my household effects are worth at least two-and-a-half thousand escudos, and if they were auctioned these items would sell as soon as they were put on display. As the owner of this property I am looking for a husband to submit to and obey. In addition to my reformed life-style I will promise to spare no effort in pampering and serving him, for no prince employs a cook with a more appetizing repertoire or who knows how to put the finishing touches to a meal as I do, when I wish to display my housekeeping skills and put my mind to it. I know how to oversee the house like a butler, toil in the

kitchen like a maid, and grace the drawing-room in my capacity as
lady of the house. Indeed, I know how to give orders and demand
obedience. I waste nothing and I conserve a great deal; I know how
to extract the utmost value from a real. My white linen, of which I
possess a great deal of very fine quality, was not purchased from
shops and drapers; it was spun by my own fingers and those of my
maids. And if I could weave at home, I would also have woven them.
I am singing my own praises for there is no dishonour in stating what
necessity demands. Lastly, let me say that I am looking for a husband
who will protect me, instruct me, and honour me, not a lover who
will pay me court and then insult me. If you would like to accept
the prize I am offering you, here I am, with nothing extraordinary
to recommend me, willing to comply with whatever you command,
without advertising my availability which is tantamount to entrusting my reputation to matchmakers. For no one is in a better position
to settle the arrangements than the parties in question."

'At that moment my brains were located, not in my skull, but in
my feet. Since the pleasure I was experiencing was greater than anything I had ever imagined and the extent of her property was on
display before my eyes and I was already converting it into ready
cash, I dispensed with all arguments that were not prompted by my
desire, which had clapped my reason in irons. I told her that I was
the lucky one to receive such a heaven-sent companion, almost as if
by miracle, in order to make her the mistress of my worldly goods.
These were not so inconsiderable as to be worth, when one included the chain I wore round my neck and some other pieces of jew-
ellery I kept at home and the proceeds from the sale of some of my
fine soldier's outfits, less than two thousand ducados. Pooled with her
twenty-five hundred this amount would be enough to allow us to
retire to the village where I was born and where I still had some
property. Adding the cash to the value of the property and selling
our produce in season could provide us with a happy and comfortable life. In short, our betrothal was settled upon there and then and
we set about getting ourselves registered as bachelor and spinster of
the parish, and during the three holy days that came together at
Easter the banns were read and on the fourth day we were married.
The ceremony was attended by two friends of mine and a youth
whom she introduced as her cousin. When I greeted him as a
kinsman in the kind of highly courteous terms I had until then been

addressing to my new wife, my intentions were so corrupt and treacherous that I prefer to say no more on the subject. For although I am telling you the truth, it is not the truth of the confessional, which could not remain unspoken.

'My servant moved my trunk from my lodgings to my wife's house. While she looked on I locked my magnificent chain up in it and I also showed her three or four others which, although less impressive in size, were of superior craftsmanship. I also showed her my fine clothes and feathers and I gave her the four hundred odd reales which I had in my possession to cover household expenses. The honeymoon lasted six days, during which time I wallowed in the comforts of the house like a poor son-in-law in the home of his rich father-in-law. I trod on rich carpets, slept in linen sheets, lighted my way with silver candlesticks, had breakfast in bed, got up at eleven, lunched at two, and slept the siesta in the drawing room, while doña Estefanía and her maid danced attendance on me. My own servant, whom I had only ever known to be lazy and sluggish, was suddenly as swift as a deer. When doña Estefanía was not at my side she was to be found in the kitchen, totally engrossed in the preparation of dishes that would tease my palate and excite my appetite. Sprinkled with orange-blossom water and other perfumes, my shirts, collars, and handkerchiefs were an Aranjuez of scented flowers.*

'The days flew by, as do the years which are similarly subject to the dictates of time. As they sped by and I found myself so pampered and my needs so well attended to, the base intentions with which I had entered into that enterprise began to change for the better. The honeymoon came to an end one morning when, as I lay in bed with doña Estefanía, there were loud knocks at the front door. The maid peered out of the window and withdrew immediately, saying, "Well, she's very welcome, I'm sure! She's here sooner than she said in her letter the other day."

'"Who's here, child?" I asked her.

'"Who?" she repeated. "My mistress doña Clementa Bueso, that's who, and with her is don Lope Meléndez y Almendárez and another two menservants and Hortigosa, the duenna she took with her."

'"Hurry, child, for goodness' sake, and let them in!" exclaimed doña Estefanía at that point. "As for you, sir, if you love me, don't get upset or reply to anything you may hear said against me."

'"Who's going to say anything to offend you, especially in front of me? Tell me, who are these people, for their arrival seems to have distressed you?"

'"I don't have time to explain to you now," replied doña Estefanía, "all you need to know is that everything that happens here is a bluff and has a plan and purpose which you'll understand in due course."

'Although I wanted to say something in reply, I had no opportunity to do so for at that moment doña Clementa Bueso came into the room, resplendent in a dress of green satin richly bordered with gold lace and a cape of the same material and edged with the same trimmings, a hat with green feathers, and a fine veil which concealed half of her face. She was accompanied by don Lope Meléndez y Almendárez, who was no less splendidly dressed in rich travelling clothes. The duenna Hortigosa was the first to speak, when she said, "Heavens! What is the meaning of this? My mistress's bed occupied and what's worse, occupied by a man! I must be seeing things. To be sure, instead of an inch señora Estefanía has taken a mile, presuming upon her friendship with my mistress."

'"I couldn't agree more, Hortigosa," replied doña Clementa, "but I am to blame. I'll never learn not to choose friends who only know how to be friendly when it suits their purpose."

'To which doña Estefanía replied, "Do not distress yourself, doña Clementa Bueso, and believe that what you are witnessing in this your own home is not what it seems; and when you have been enlightened, I know that I shall be blameless and you shall have no cause for complaint."

'During this exchange I had put on my breeches and doublet, and taking me by the hand doña Estefanía led me into another room where she told me that this friend of hers wanted to play a trick on don Lope who had arrived with her and whom she intended to marry. The trick was to let him believe that the house and all its contents belonged to doña Clementa, with the intention of offering them as a dowry, and once the marriage was contracted she was not concerned about the deception being discovered, so confident was she in the strength of don Lope's love for her.

'"And then I will get back what is mine, and it will not be held against her or any other woman for trying to get an honourable husband, even though it may involve some trickery."

'I replied that it was a great gesture of friendship that she intended making and advised her to think about it carefully, for it might afterwards be necessary to resort to law in order to recover her goods. She, however, replied with such persuasive arguments and cited so many obligations which compelled her to aid doña Clementa, even in matters of greater consequence, that against my will and better judgement I had to comply with doña Estefanía's wishes. She assured me that the ruse could only last a week and that in the meantime we would stay with another friend of hers. We finished dressing and then, when she went in to say goodbye to doña Clementa Bueso and don Lope Meléndez de Almendárez, I instructed my servant to pack up the trunk and follow her; I also followed her, without saying goodbye to anyone.

'Doña Estefanía halted at the house of a friend of hers and before we went inside she spent a good while in conversation with her, at the end of which a maid came out and invited my servant and myself inside. She led us to a narrow room in which the two beds stood so close together that they looked like one, because there was no space between them and their sheets were touching. In short, we were there for six days and there was not a single hour in all of that time in which we did not quarrel, because I kept telling her how stupid she had been to lend her house and property, even if it had been to her own mother.

'I ranted and raved so often that one day, when Estefanía said that she was going to see how the business was faring, our landlady asked me the reason why I quarrelled with her so much and what she had done to make me reproach her so much and accuse her of crass stupidity rather than unstinting friendship. I told her the whole story, and when I got to the point of telling her of my marriage to doña Estefanía, the dowry she had brought with her, and how foolish she had been to lend her house to doña Clementa, although it was with the laudable intention of winning such an eligible husband as don Lope, she began to cross herself so rapidly and repeat the words "Good Lord, what a wicked woman" so often that I found it highly disconcerting. Finally she said:

'"Ensign, I don't know whether I'm acting against my conscience in revealing this to you, but I think it would play on my mind even more if I were to remain silent. But let's trust in the Lord and good fortune and long live truth and may falsehood be damned. The fact is that doña Clementa Bueso is the real lady of the house and mistress of the property which was presented to you as dowry; everything doña Estefanía has told you is a pack of lies. She has neither house, nor property, nor clothes other than the ones she stands up in. What gave her the time and opportunity to play this trick was the fact that doña Clementa went to visit some relatives of hers in the city of Plasencia, and from there she went to pray for nine days at Our Lady of Guadalupe, and in the interim left doña Estefanía to look after the house because, when all is said and done, they are great friends. When you think about it, you can hardly blame the poor woman, since she managed to acquire such a fine husband as the good Ensign."

'As she finished speaking I began to despair, and would no doubt have surrendered to the sentiment wholeheartedly if my guardian angel had been a moment later in coming to my rescue and whispering into my heart that I should remember that I was a Christian and that the greatest sin a man could commit was to despair, for it is a diabolical sin. This revelation brought me some comfort but not enough to prevent me from seizing my cloak and sword and rushing out in search of doña Estefanía, intending to inflict exemplary punishment on her.

'However, fate, whether to pervert or aid the course of my affairs I cannot say, ordained that I should not find Estefanía in any of the places I expected to find her. I went to the Church of St Lawrence, commended myself to Our Lady, sat down on a bench, and in my distraught state fell into a deep sleep, from which I would not have stirred so soon had I not been woken up.

'With my mind full of dismal thoughts I went to doña Clementa's house and found her perfectly at ease as mistress of the house; I dared not say a word to her because don Lope was present. I returned to the house of my landlady, who told me that she had related to doña Estefanía how I knew all about her trickery and deception and that Estefanía had asked her how I had reacted to such news. She had told her that I had taken it very badly and that, in her opinion, I had gone out with the express intention of doing her harm. In short, she told me that doña Estefanía had gone off with the whole contents of the trunk, leaving me nothing but a single suit of travelling clothes.

'That was the last straw, but the good Lord took me by the hand again! I went over to look at my trunk and I found it gaping open like a grave waiting to receive its corpse, and that corpse should rightly have been me if I'd had enough wits about me to be able to feel and acknowledge the full extent of my misfortune.'

'It was a great misfortune indeed,' interjected Peralta at that moment, 'that doña Estefanía should have carried off so many fine chains and hat bands for, as the saying goes, everything seems worse on an empty stomach.'

'This loss did not grieve me at all,' replied the Ensign, 'because of the saying: "Don Simueque thought he was deceiving me with his squint-eyed daughter, but by Jove, I'm deformed all down one side."'

'I fail to see what bearing that saying has on your story,' replied Peralta.

'Then let me explain,' replied the Ensign. 'The value of that dazzling display of chains, hat bands, and baubles could not exceed more than ten or twelve escudos.'

'That's impossible,' cried the Graduate, 'for the one you wore round your neck looked as if it was worth more than two hundred ducados.'

'As indeed it would,' replied the Ensign, 'if truth corresponded with appearance; but since all that glisters is not gold, the chains, hat bands, jewels, and baubles were mere imitations, but they were so well-crafted that only close examination or the heat of fire could reveal the deception.'

'In that case,' said the Graduate, 'as far as you and the lady Estefanía are concerned, you're quits.'

'And so much so,' replied the Ensign, 'that we can reshuffle the deck, but the trouble is, Graduate, that she can rid herself of my chains but I cannot so easily shake off her treachery; and, after all, whether I like it or not, she's mine and I'm stuck with her.'

'Thank the Lord, señor Campuzano,' said Peralta, 'that she had feet and could walk away and that you are not obliged to look for her.'

'That's true,' replied the Ensign, 'and yet, even without looking for her, she occupies my thoughts and wherever I am, I'm staring disgrace full in the face.'

'I don't know what to say to you,' said Peralta, 'except to remind you of two lines from Petrarch,* which go:

> Ché, chi prende diletto di far frode,
> Non si de' lamentar s'altri lo 'nganna.

which translates as: "he who takes pleasure in deceiving must not complain when he is himself deceived." '

'I'm not complaining,' replied the Ensign, 'but feeling sorry for myself. For the guilty man does not fail to feel the weight of punishment just because he recognizes his guilt. I fully acknowledge that I wanted to deceive and was myself deceived, when I was given a taste of my own medicine, but I cannot help feeling sorry for myself. And so, to get to the main point of my story (for that is what we can call my account of what happened to me), let me just say that I learned that doña Estefanía had gone off with the cousin whom I mentioned being present at our wedding and who had for many years been her lover through thick and thin. I had no desire to look for her, because it would have been asking for trouble. Within a few days I had changed my address and my hair-style, because my eyebrows and eyelashes began to moult and the hair on my head gradually began to fall out too. I went bald before my time, because I had contracted a complaint known as alopecia, or more commonly, "hair loss". My head was well and truly as bare as my pockets, because I had neither hair to comb nor money to spend. My illness kept pace with my needy condition, and since poverty knocks honour to the ground and leads some people to the scaffold and some to the hospital, while it compels others to stand begging and pleading at their enemies' doors, it is one of the greatest misfortunes that can befall an unhappy man. Rather than sell the clothes which would have to clothe me and sustain my honour when I recovered my health in order to pay for treatment, I entered the Hospital of the Resurrection when they were offering sweat cures and there I have endured forty sweats. They tell me I shall get well, if I look after myself; I have a sword, and as for the rest, may God provide the solution.'

The Graduate, amazed at the story he had been told, once again offered his services.

'Well, it does not take much to astonish you, Peralta,' said the Ensign, 'for I have other incidents to relate which exceed all imagination, for they go beyond the bounds of nature. You must content yourself with the knowledge that they are of such a kind that I consider my misfortunes worthwhile since they brought me to the hospital where I saw what I shall now relate, which neither you nor anyone else will ever believe.'

All these preambles and commendations with which the Ensign

prefaced his account of what he had seen aroused the curiosity of Peralta to such an extent that, with no fewer commendations of his own, he asked him to relate to him immediately the wonders he had to tell.

'You must already have seen', said the Ensign, 'two dogs who walk around the town at night bearing lanterns for the begging brothers as they ask for alms.'

'Yes, I have seen them,' replied Peralta.

'And you must also have seen or heard', said the Ensign, 'what is said about them; that if by chance alms are thrown down from windows and fall on the ground, they immediately go and illuminate the spot where they have fallen, and they stop in front of those windows where they know alms are usually given, and although they walk off so meekly that they are more like lambs than dogs, at the hospital they are lions, guarding the premises with great care and vigilance.'

'I've heard rumours to that effect,' said Peralta, 'but they do not particularly surprise me, nor should they.'

'But what I am about to tell you will, and without crossing yourself or raising objections and harbouring doubts, you must be willing to believe it. The fact is that one night, the night before my final sweat treatment, I heard and as good as saw these two dogs with my own eyes, the one called Scipio and the other Berganza, lying on some old matting behind my bed. In the middle of the night, as I was lying awake in the darkness, thinking about my past affairs and present misfortunes, I heard voices talking close by and I listened very carefully to see whether I could discover who was talking and what they were talking about. I soon realized from the nature of their conversation that it was the two dogs, Scipio and Berganza, who were doing the talking.'

Campuzano had scarcely finished speaking when the Graduate got to his feet and said, 'I've heard quite enough, thank you very much, señor Campuzano, for up until now I was in two minds as to whether or not I should believe what you told me about your marriage, but what you are now telling me about hearing dogs talk convinces me not to believe a word you say. For the love of God, Ensign, don't go repeating this nonsense to anyone other than a good friend like me.'

'Don't take me for such a fool,' retorted Campuzano, 'that I don't realize that only by some miracle could dogs talk. I am well aware that if thrushes, magpies, and parrots talk, they are merely repeating words which they have learned and memorized, because they have tongues capable of pronouncing them. That is not enough, however, to enable them to speak and answer in the measured speech which the dogs used, and so, many times since I heard them, I have been unwilling to believe my own ears. I have preferred instead to interpret as a dream something which I really and truly, being fully awake and in full possession of all five senses which God was pleased to grant me, heard, listened to, took note of, and finally transcribed, with every word in its proper place and not a single one missing. There is sufficient evidence there to convince and persuade you to believe the truth of what I say. The subjects they discussed were lofty and varied and more appropriate to the debates of wise men than the pronouncements of dogs. And so, since I could not have invented them myself, in spite of my reservations and against my better judgement, I have come to the conclusion that I was not dreaming and that the dogs were talking.'

'Whatever next!' exclaimed the Graduate. 'We've returned to the times of Maricastaña,* when pumpkins could talk, or even Aesop, when the cock conversed with the fox and animals talked to one another.'

'I would be one of them, and the most irrational beast of all,' retorted the Ensign, 'if I believed such an age had returned, but I would also be a foolish beast if I refused to believe what I heard and saw and what I shall dare to swear with an oath that obliges and even compels incredulity itself to believe. But let us assume for a moment that I have been deceived and that what I believe to be true is a dream and that to persist in the matter would be folly, would it not amuse you, señor Peralta, to see transcribed in the form of a dialogue the things which these dogs, or whatever they were, had to say for themselves?'

'As long as you waste no more breath trying to persuade me that you heard dogs talk, I will gladly listen to the dialogue,' replied the Graduate, 'for since it has been written and recorded by your own ingenious hand, Ensign, I already judge it to be good.'

'There is another matter,' said the Ensign, 'for since I was listening so attentively and my mind was in such a sensitive state, while my memory was receptive, sharp, and unpreoccupied by other thoughts (thanks to the large quantity of raisins and almonds* I had eaten), I learned it all by heart and the following day I wrote down all that I had heard in virtually the same words, without looking for rhetorical flourishes to embroider it, nor adding or subtracting anything to improve it. The conversation did not take place on a single night, but on two consecutive nights, although I have only one—the life story of Berganza—written down. I intend to write the story of his companion Scipio (which was narrated on the second night) when I can see that this one does not meet with disbelief or, at the very least, derision. I've got the dialogue tucked away in the front of my shirt. I put it in dialogue form to avoid having to insert "Scipio said, Berganza replied" which tends to lengthen the narrative.'

With these words, he drew a notebook from his breast and put it in the Graduate's hands. The latter laughed as he took it, as if he were not taking seriously what he had heard or what he was about to read.

'I shall lie back in this chair,' said the Ensign, 'while you do me the favour of reading these dreams and follies, whose only virtue is the fact that you can lay them aside when they annoy you.'

'Make yourself comfortable,' said Peralta, 'for I shall not be long reading through this.'

The Ensign lay back in his chair, the Graduate opened the notebook, and on the first page he saw the following title—

THE DIALOGUE OF THE DOGS

*Story and dialogue that took place
between Scipio and Berganza,
who are commonly known as Mahudes's dogs
and who belong to the Hospital of the Resurrection,
which is in the city of Valladolid,
outside the Campo Gate.*

Scipio. Berganza, my friend, let us trust the safety of the hospital to luck tonight and withdraw to the peace and quiet of those mats. There we can enjoy this unprecedented gift which heaven has granted us both at the same time without being observed.

Berganza. Brother Scipio, I hear you speak and I know that I am speaking to you and I cannot believe it, for it seems to me that our speaking goes beyond the bounds of nature.

Scipio. That is true enough, Berganza, and the miracle is all the greater because we are speaking coherently, as if we were capable of reason, while we are actually so lacking in it that the main difference between men and animals is that men are rational beings and animals are not.

Berganza. I understand everything you say, Scipio, and the fact that you are saying it and that I understand it reinforces my sense of wonder and astonishment. It is indeed true that during the course of my life I have on many and various occasions heard talk of our great qualities, so much so that it appears that some people have been inclined to suspect that we possess a natural instinct, which is so lively and acute in many things that it strongly suggests, but falls short of actually demonstrating, that we possess some sort of understanding capable of reasoning.

Scipio. What I have heard praised and commended are our good memory, gratitude, and great fidelity, and to such an extent that we are often represented as the symbol of friendship. In fact, you must have noticed (if you have ever looked) that where there are alabaster casts on tombs of the people who lie buried within, when they are man and wife, they place between their feet the effigy of a dog, to signify that in life the friendship and fidelity they observed was inviolable.

Berganza. I am well aware that some dogs have been so overcome by feelings of gratitude that they have even flung themselves into the grave with the dead bodies of their masters. Others have stationed themselves upon the graves where their masters lay buried, neither moving nor eating until their own lives came to an end. I also know that, after elephants, dogs give the strongest impression of possessing understanding; then horses and finally, apes.

Scipio. That is true, but you will also readily admit that you have neither seen nor heard of any elephant, dog, horse, or monkey talking. This leads me to believe that our unexpected ability to speak falls into the category of things known as portents. When such things are seen and witnessed, experience shows that some great calamity is threatening mankind.

Berganza. In that case I'll not be far wrong if I take as a portent something I recently heard a student say when he was passing through Alcalá de Henares.

Scipio. What did you hear him say?

Berganza. That out of five thousand students who were studying at the university that year, two thousand of them were reading medicine.

Scipio. And what do you infer from that?

Berganza. I infer either that these two thousand doctors will have patients to cure (which would be a great calamity and misfortune) or they will die of hunger.

Scipio. Be that as it may, portent or no portent, the fact is that we are speaking; for whatever heaven has ordained should happen, no human effort or wisdom can prevent. So there is no point in our starting to dispute the whys and wherefores of our speech. It would be more sensible to make the most of this happy day, or happy night, and since we are so comfortable on these mats and we do not know how long this good fortune of ours will last, let us take advantage of it and talk the night through, without allowing sleep to deprive us of this pleasure which I have desired for so long.

Berganza. And I too, for since I was strong enough to gnaw a bone I have desired the power of speech, to say the many things which have been stored up in my memory for so long that they were either going mouldy or being forgotten. But now that I find myself so unexpectedly endowed with this divine gift of speech, I intend to enjoy it and take the greatest possible advantage of it, making haste to say everything I can remember, although it may come out jumbled and confused, because I do not know when this blessing, which is on loan to me, will be revoked.

Scipio. Let's do it this way, Berganza, my friend: tonight you will relate the story of your life and the course of events which has brought you to this present moment, and if tomorrow night we can still speak I will relate mine to you. For it will be more profitable to spend the time telling our own stories than trying to delve into other people's lives.

Berganza. Scipio, I have always thought you wise and I have always thought of you as a friend and now more than ever. As a friend you want to relate your adventures to me and hear mine; and in your wisdom you have apportioned time for us to be able to do just that. But first check whether anyone is listening.

Scipio. No one, I think, although there is a soldier close by undergoing a sweat treatment, but at the moment he will be more inclined to sleep than listen to anyone.

Berganza. Well, if I can speak with this assurance, listen: and if what I am saying tires you, caution me or tell me to be quiet.

Scipio. Speak until daybreak, or until someone overhears us; for I will very gladly listen to you, without stopping you unless I think it necessary.

Berganza. I believe that the first time I saw the sun was in Seville and in its slaughterhouse, which is outside the Puerta de la Carne,* from which I would surmise (were it not for what I shall later recount) that my parents must have been the sort of mastiffs reared by the practitioners of that chaotic trade, people known as slaughterers. The first master I knew was a certain Nicholas Snub-Nose, who was a robust, stocky fellow with a bad temper, like everyone else practising the trade. This same Nicholas taught me and some other pups how to go with the mastiffs and attack the bulls by biting their ears. I very easily became an expert at this.

Scipio. I am not surprised, Berganza; for since wrongdoing comes naturally, it is easily learned.

Berganza. The things I could tell you, brother Scipio, about what I saw in that slaughterhouse and of the shocking goings-on there! First of all, you must understand that all those who work there, from the youngest to the oldest, are people with little conscience and no soul, fearing neither the king nor his justice. Most of them are living with their fancy women; they are like vultures, maintaining themselves and their mistresses on what they steal. Every meat day morning a large crowd of young women and youths gathers before dawn, each of them carrying a bag which is empty when they arrive but full of joints of meat when they leave, and the servant girls carry away sweetbreads and half-loins of pork. No beast is killed without these people making off with their tithes and first-fruits of the tastiest and prime cuts. Since there is no one to oversee the meat trade, each can bring what he likes, and the first beast to be killed is either the best or the cheapest and by this arrangement there is always plenty. The owners trust these upstanding citizens I speak of, not to refrain from stealing from them (which would be asking the impossible), but to exercise restraint in the devious cuts which they make into the carcasses, for they trim them and prune them as if they were willows or vines. But nothing shocked me more or struck me as more scandalous than to see that these slaughterhouse workers kill a man as easily as a cow. At the slightest provocation and without a moment's hesitation they plunge their horn-handled knives into the belly of a man as if they were slaying a bull. It's a miracle if a day goes by without quarrels and injuries and sometimes even deaths. They all pride themselves on being tough and they even fancy themselves as ruffians. There's not a man among them who does not have his guardian angel in St Francis's Square,* whose favour has been bought with pork joints and ox tongues. In short, I once heard a wise man say that the king had three things to win in Seville: the Calle de la Caza, la Costanilla, and the slaughterhouse.*

Scipio. If you're going to take this long to describe the condition of the masters you've had and the failings of their professions, it will be necessary to ask heaven to grant us speech for at least a year, and even then I fear, at the rate you're going, you won't get through half your story. I want to point something out to you, and you'll see the truth of it when I relate my life story. Some stories are intrinsically appealing, others are made appealing in the way they are told. What I mean is that there are some stories which give pleasure although they are narrated without preambles or verbal ornamentation. There are others which need to be dressed up with words and gestures of the face and hands and changes in the tone of one's voice, in order to create something out of nothing. Weak and feeble tales are thus transformed into witty and enjoyable ones. Don't forget to put this advice to good use in the rest of your story.

Berganza. I will, if I can and if the overwhelming urge to speak will allow, although I think I'll have great difficulty restraining myself.

Scipio. Watch your tongue, for the greatest evils in human life arise from it.

Berganza. Let me tell you, then, that my master taught me to carry a basket in my mouth and to defend it from anyone who wanted to take it away from me. He also showed me his mistress's house, and by doing so saved her maid the need to come to the slaughterhouse, because I used to deliver to her in the early morning what he had stolen during the night. One day, just as the sun was rising, I was duly delivering her ration when I heard my name being called from a window. I looked up and saw a very beautiful girl; I stopped for a moment and she came down to the front door and called my name again. I went up to her to find out what she wanted, which was none other than to remove what I was carrying from the basket and replace it with an old shoe. Then I said to myself: 'Flesh to flesh.' When she'd taken the meat from me the girl said: 'Go on, Gavilán, or whatever your name is, tell Nicholas Snub-Nose, your master, not to trust animals, and if you're dealing with a skinflint, you've got to take what you can get.' I could easily have retrieved what she'd taken, but I didn't want to touch those pristine white hands with my dirty, slaughterhouse mouth.

Scipio. You did the right thing, for it is the prerogative of beauty always to be respected.

Berganza. Precisely; so I returned to my master without the ration and with the shoe. Not expecting me back so soon, he caught sight of the shoe and guessed the trick that had been played on him. He took out a horn-handled knife and lunged at me so violently, that if I hadn't dodged you would never have heard this tale, nor the many others which I intend to tell you. I was off like a shot, and taking to my heels behind San Bernardo* I headed toward the open fields and wherever God and luck would lead me. That night I slept in the open air and the following day I had the good fortune to come across a flock or herd of sheep and lambs. As soon as I saw it I thought I'd found my haven of rest, considering it the natural and proper occupation of dogs to guard livestock, for it is an activity demanding great virtue and consisting in the defence and protection of the weak and helpless against the powerful and mighty. I'd scarcely been spotted by one of the three shepherds who were looking after the flock when he called me with the words 'Here, boy!', and wanting nothing better than to obey I went up to him with my head hanging and my tail wagging. He ran his hand along my back, opened my mouth, spat in it,* examined my teeth, assessed my age, and told the other shepherds that I showed every sign of being a thoroughbred animal. At that moment the owner of the flock came riding up on a grey mare with short stirrups and carrying a lance and shield, which made him look more like a coastguard than a sheep farmer. He asked the shepherd:

'What dog is this, for he looks a fine beast?'

'You can be confident of that, sir,' replied the shepherd, 'for I've examined him thoroughly and there's not a mark on him to hint or suggest that he won't be a great dog. He's just arrived here and I don't know who he belongs to, but I do know that he's not from a flock round these parts.'

'In that case,' replied their master, 'put Leoncillo's collar on him straight away, the dog that died; give him the same rations as the other dogs and stroke him so that he gets attached to the flock and stays with it.'

With these words he went off and the shepherd immediately put a steel-studded collar round my neck, after first giving me a large helping of bread and milk in a bowl. They also gave me a name, calling me Barcino. My belly was full and I was happy with my second master and new occupation. I showed myself to be careful and diligent in guarding the flock, never leaving it except at siesta time, which I used to go and spend either in the shade of a tree or some bank or rock or bush beside one of the many streams that flowed through those parts. During these hours of rest I was not idle, for I used to exercise my memory in recalling many things, especially concerning the life I had lived in the slaughterhouse and the life led by my master and all those like him, who are obliged to pander to the outrageous whims of their mistresses. Oh, what things I could tell you, things I learned in the school of my butcher-master's lady. However, I must be silent or you'll think me a long-winded gossip.

Scipio. Since I've heard that one of the great poets of antiquity claimed that it was difficult not to write satire,* I will allow you to gossip a little, as long as it is to enlighten rather than draw blood.* What I mean to say is that you can point the finger but not injure or kill anyone in the point you make. For gossip's a bad thing, even if it makes a lot of people laugh, if it kills someone; and if you can be amusing without it, I will think you very discreet.

Berganza. I shall take your advice and eagerly anticipate the time when you'll tell me of your adventures. For from someone who is so well able to recognize and correct the mistakes which I make in relating my affairs, one can confidently expect that he will relate his own in a way that offers instruction and pleasure at the same time. Anyway, to resume the broken thread of my story, I was saying that in the silence and solitude of my siestas I used to ponder, among other things, that what I'd heard about the life of shepherds could not be true, at least about those shepherds my master's lady used to read of in books when I went to her house. For they were all about shepherds and shepherdesses and how they spent their whole lives singing and playing pipes, flutes, rebecks, flageolets, and other unusual instruments. I used to stop and listen to her reading and she'd recount how the shepherd Anfriso sang sublimely and divinely in praise of the peerless Belisarda and how there wasn't a single tree in all the mountains of Arcadia, at whose foot he had not sat down to sing from the first moment the sun emerged in the arms of Aurora until it set in the embrace of Thetis. Not even after black night had spread its dark and raven wings over the face of the earth did he cease his sweetly sung and even more tunefully bewailed laments. She did not forget to mention Elicio, more lovestruck than bold, of whom she recounted that, neglecting both his love and his flock, he concerned himself with the cares of his fellows. She also recounted how the great shepherd of Fílida, the unrivalled painter of portraits, had been more trusting than fortunate. Concerning the swoonings of Sireno and the repentance of Diana, she declared that she thanked God and the wise Felicia, who with her enchanted water unravelled that web of entanglements and shed light into that labyrinth of obstacles. I remembered many other books of that kind that I'd heard her read, but they were not worth recalling.*

Scipio. You are putting my advice to good effect, Berganza; have your gossip, apply your sting, and move on and let your intentions be pure even if your tongue does not seem to be.

Berganza. In matters of this kind the tongue never trips up unless one's intentions stumble first, but if by chance I should gossip, whether by accident or with deliberate malice, I'll give to anyone who reproaches me the same reply that Mauleón, the stupid poet and pseudo-academic from the Academy of Imitators, gave to someone who asked him what *Deum de deo** meant; he replied that it meant 'day by day'.

Scipio. That was the answer of a simpleton; but if you are wise, or wish to be, you must never say anything for which you have to apologize. Carry on.

Berganza. I was saying that all the reflections I've spoken of made me realize how different the manners and habits of my shepherds and the rest of that crowd were from the shepherds I'd heard depicted in books. For if my shepherds sang at all, they did not sing tuneful and well-composed songs but 'Beware of the wolf, Joannie', and other things of that nature. This was not to the accompaniment of flageolets, rebecks, or flutes, but to the sound of one shepherd's crook knocking against another or tiles being clicked between their fingers. Nor did they sing in delicate, rich, and wondrous tones, but with hoarse voices that, whether solo or in unison, gave the impression that they were not singing but shouting or grunting. They would spend most of the day de-lousing themselves or mending their sandals. Nor was there a single Amarilis, Fílida, Galatea, or Diana among them, nor any Lisardo, Jacinto, or Riselo; they were all called Antón, Domingo, Pablo, or Llorente. All this led me to the conclusion that I think everyone must reach, that all those books are well-written fantasies for the entertainment of idle readers and there is no truth in them whatsoever. For if they were true there would be some vestige of that blissful existence among my own shepherds and some trace of those pleasant pastures, spacious forests, sacred mountains, beautiful gardens, clear streams, and crystal fountains. There would similarly be echoes of those amorous declarations which were as modest as they were elegant, and of a shepherd swooning here and a shepherdess swooning there, the sound of pastoral pipes to one side and a flute to the other.

Scipio. Enough, Berganza; stop rambling and get on with your story.

Berganza. Thank you, Scipio, my friend, for if you hadn't warned me, my tongue was getting so accustomed to wagging that I wouldn't have stopped until I'd described to you an entire book of the kind that had me deceived; but the time will come when I'll tell you everything more coherently and eloquently than now.

Scipio. Look at your feet and you'll come back to earth, Berganza. What I mean is you should remember that you're an animal without powers of reason, and if you're currently showing signs of having some, we've already agreed that it's something supernatural and unprecedented.

Berganza. That might be the case if I were still in a state of innocence; but now that I remember what I should have said at the beginning of our conversation, not only am I not amazed at what I'm saying, I'm astonished at what I leave unsaid.

Scipio. So you can't tell me what you remember now?

Berganza. It's a certain incident which took place when I was with a great witch, a disciple of Camacha of Montilla.

Scipio. Then tell me what happened before you carry on with your life story.

Berganza. I'll do no such thing until the proper time; be patient, and listen to my adventures in the order in which they took place, for you'll enjoy them more that way, unless your desire to know the middle before the beginning vexes you.

Scipio. Be brief, and say what you want to in the way that you want to.

Berganza. Let me tell you, then, that I was happy with the job of guarding the flock, since it seemed to me that I was eating the bread earned by my labours and the sweat of my brow and that idleness, the root and source of all vices, had no business with me. If I rested during the day, at night I did not sleep because wolves often attacked us and prompted the call to arms. No sooner had the shepherds said 'After the wolf, Barcino!' than I was off, ahead of the other dogs, in the direction in which they indicated the wolf was to be found. I would cover every inch of the valleys, scour the hills, leave no stone unturned in the forests, leap across ravines, and cross highways. When I returned to the flock the following morning, having failed to find the wolf or even a trace of it, panting, weary, exhausted, with my feet torn to shreds by fallen branches, I'd always find among the flock a dead sheep or a lamb with its throat torn open and half eaten by the wolf. I despaired when I realized what little effect my exertions and diligence were having. The owner of the flock would come and the shepherds would go and meet him with the skin of the dead animal. He would blame them for their negligence and order the dogs to be punished for their laziness. The blows would rain down on us and the reproaches upon them. So, one day, seeing that I was being punished although I was blameless and that my effort, speed, and courage were of no use in catching the wolf, I decided to change tactics, and rather than wander far from the flock in search of it, as I usually did, I stayed close by. For since that's where the wolf came, that's where I'd be more certain to catch it. They sounded the alarm every week, and one very dark night I was able to catch sight of the wolves against whom it was impossible to guard the flock.

I crouched behind a bush while the other dogs, my companions, went on ahead, and from there I observed how two shepherds took hold of one of the best lambs in the fold and slaughtered it so brutally that the following morning it really looked as if the wolf had killed it. I was shocked and amazed to see that the shepherds were the wolves and that the very people who were supposed to be guarding the flock were tearing it to pieces. They immediately informed their master that the wolf had struck, gave him the skin and a portion of the meat and ate the bigger and better part themselves. Once again he reproached them and once again the dogs were punished. There were no wolves and the flock was dwindling. I wanted to denounce their treachery but I was dumb. The whole affair left me feeling bewildered and distressed. 'Good heavens!', I said to myself, 'who will put an end to this evil? Who will have the power to persuade anyone that the defenders are on the offensive, that the sentries are sleeping, that it doesn't pay to trust anyone and that those who guard also kill?'

Scipio. Very well said, Berganza, for there's no greater or more subtle thief than the one living in your own house. That's why people of a trusting nature die in far greater numbers than cautious people. But the trouble is that it's impossible for people to get on in the world without trusting and confiding in others. But enough of that, I don't want us to sound like preachers. Carry on.

Berganza. I'll continue, then, and say that I decided to leave that job, although it seemed so good, and choose another where if I didn't get rewarded for doing it well, at least I wouldn't be punished. I returned to Seville and entered into the service of a very rich merchant.

Scipio. What method did you use to get a master? For the way things are nowadays, it's very difficult for a decent fellow to find a master to serve. The lords of this world are very different from the Lord of heaven. When the former take a servant they firstly scrutinize his lineage, then they test his skill, take a good look at his appearance, and even want to know what clothes he possesses. To enter God's service, on the other hand, the poorest is the richest and the humblest comes from the most distinguished line. As long as he's willing to serve him with a pure heart his name's written in the wage ledger and the rewards are so rich in quantity and proportion that they surpass his wildest dreams.

Berganza. All this is preaching, Scipio, my friend.

Scipio. I agree, and so I'll be silent.

Berganza. With regard to your question as to how I went about securing a master, all I can say is that you already know that humility is the basis and foundation of all virtues, and that without it there's no virtue worthy of the name. It smooths obstacles, overcomes difficulties, and is a means which always leads us to glorious ends. It makes enemies into friends, assuages the anger of the irate, and undermines the arrogance of the proud. It's the mother of modesty and the sister of moderation. In short, with humility vices can achieve no profitable triumph, because with its softness and meekness it blunts and dulls the arrows of sin. So, I took advantage of this same humility when I wanted to enter the service of a particular household, having first examined and looked at the house very carefully to see whether it could maintain and accommodate a big dog. Then I would go up to the door and whenever anyone who looked to me like a stranger went in, I would bark at him and when the master came I would lower my head and with my tail wagging I would go up to him and lick his shoes clean with my tongue. If they sent me away with a beating I endured it and went back to fawn on the very person who was administering the beating, for no one did it a second time after seeing my determination and noble bearing. In this way, after two attempts I was inside the house. I served well, they came to like me and no one sent me away, unless I took my own leave or, more precisely, went off of my own volition, and perhaps I had found such a good master that I might have been in his service to this day, if I had not been dogged by bad luck.

Scipio. I used the same method you mention to enter the service of the masters I had.

Berganza. Since we've had the same experience in these matters, I'll tell you about them in due course, as I've promised. Now listen to what happened to me after I left the flock in the care of those rogues. I returned to Seville, as I said, which is the asylum of the poor and refuge of the dispossessed, for it's so vast that not only is there room for the little people, but even the great can go unnoticed. I approached the door of a large house belonging to a merchant, went through my usual routine, and very soon found myself settled inside it. They took me in and kept me tied up behind the door during the day and left me free to roam around at night. I served them very carefully and diligently; I barked at strangers and growled at people who were not very well known in the house; I stayed awake at night, patrolling around the yards and up on the terraces, the self-appointed watchman of my own and other people's houses. My master was so pleased with my good service that he gave orders that I should be well treated and given a ration of bread and the bones that were cleared away or thrown down from his table, as well as the kitchen left-overs. I showed my gratitude by endlessly jumping up and down whenever I saw my master, especially when he was returning from a trip. I gave so many signs of delight and jumped around so much that my master gave orders that I should be untied and allowed to roam free both day and night. As soon as I found myself free I ran up to him and ran circles around him, but without daring to touch him with my paws. I recalled to mind that Aesop's fable in which the ass was such an ass that it wanted to caress its master in the same way that a pampered lapdog of his did, for which it earned itself a good beating. I interpreted this fable to mean that what is elegant and graceful in some people is out of place in others. Leave it to the jester to tell jokes, leave the clown to his conjuring and his somersaulting, and the *pícaro* to his silly comments; let the low fellow who has devoted himself to such things imitate birdsong and the diverse gestures and actions of man and beast; but let the gentleman of distinction refrain from these activities, for no such skill will bring either credit or honour to his name.

Scipio. That's enough, Berganza, proceed with your story, I get your meaning.

Berganza. If only I were as well understood by those people to whom I'm referring when I say these things as I am by you. For I'm so good-natured that it sorely grieves me to see a gentleman making a fool of himself and boasting that he can do conjuring tricks with cups and pine cones and that no one can dance the chaconne as well as he. I know one gentleman who used to brag that, at the request of a sacristan, he had cut thirty-two paper flowers to place upon the black drapes of a monument, and he made such a song and dance about these cut-out flowers that he used to take his friends to see them as if they were viewing the banners and spoils of enemies upon the tombs of his parents and grandparents. This merchant, then, had two sons, one of twelve and the other about fourteen, both of whom were studying grammar at the school of the Company of Jesus.* They went there in great state, accompanied by their tutor and their pages, who carried their books and what were known as their portfolios. Seeing them travel with such ostentation, in sedan chairs if it were sunny and in coaches if it rained, made me consider and reflect upon the unassuming manner in which their father went to the Exchange to conduct his business, for the only servant he took was a negro, and sometimes he even went as far as riding on a rather unprepossessing mule.

Scipio. You should know, Berganza, that it is the custom and practice of the merchants of Seville, and indeed of other cities, to display their power and wealth, not in themselves, but through their children. For the shadow these merchants cast is greater than the men themselves. Since it is rare for them to attend to anything other than their wheeling and dealing, they conduct themselves modestly, and since ambition and wealth yearn for public display, they are flaunted instead in their children, whom they treat and endow with authority as if they were the sons of some prince. There are others who procure titles for them and seek to attach to their breasts the insignia which so clearly distinguishes people of substance from the plebeians.

Berganza. It is ambition, but a noble ambition, when a man seeks to improve his condition without detriment to another party.

Scipio. Rarely or never is ambition fulfilled without causing harm to someone else.

Berganza. We've already said that we mustn't gossip.

Scipio. I know, and I've not gossiped about anyone.

Berganza. I've just confirmed the truth of what I've heard said many times. A malicious gossip will ruin ten reputable families and slander twenty decent people, and if anyone reproaches him for what he's said, he'll say that he's not said anything amiss, and if he has said something, then he didn't mean it disrespectfully, and if he'd thought that someone would take offence, he wouldn't have said it. To be sure, Scipio, a man has to be very wise and very circumspect if he wants to sustain two hours' conversation without his words bordering on gossip. For I find in myself, although I'm an animal, that I've only to open my mouth a few times before the words come rushing to my tongue like flies to wine, and all of them malicious and slanderous. And so I repeat what I've said before: that we inherit our evil words and deeds from our earliest ancestors and we ingest them with our mothers' milk. This is clearly seen in the way a child has barely got his arm out of his swaddling clothes when he raises his fist as if to avenge himself on the person he thinks has offended him. And almost the first word he articulates is to call his nurse or mother a whore.

Scipio. That's true and I confess my error and beg you to forgive me, since I've forgiven you so many. Let bygones be bygones, as the children say, and from now on let's not gossip. Proceed with your story; you left it when you were referring to the ostentatious way in which the sons of your master the merchant used to go to the school of the Company of Jesus.

Berganza. I commend myself to Him in all things and although I understand that refraining from gossip will be difficult, I intend to use a remedy which I've heard was used by a man who swore a lot. Having repented of his bad habit, each time he swore after repenting he would pinch himself on the arm or kiss the floor, as penance for his sin, but he continued to swear all the same. So each time I go against your precept or my own intention not to gossip, I'll bite the tip of my tongue until it hurts and reminds me of my sin, in an effort not to do it again.

Scipio. Your remedy is such that if you use it I wager that you'll have to bite your tongue so often that you won't have a tongue left to bite, and that way you'll be powerless to gossip.

Berganza. At least I shall make an effort, and may heaven make up for my shortcomings. And so, let me tell you that one day my master's sons left a portfolio in the courtyard, where I happened to be, and since I'd been trained to carry the basket of my master the slaughterer, I picked up the portfolio and went after them, determined not to let go of it until I reached the school. Everything went as planned; when my masters saw me coming with the portfolio in my mouth, gently held by its ribbons, they ordered a page to take it from me, but I wouldn't allow him to do so, nor would I release it until I'd carried it into the classroom, which made all the pupils laugh. I went up to the elder of my masters, placed it in his hands in what seemed to me to be a very polite manner, and then remained squatting on my haunches at the classroom door, giving all my attention to the teacher who was reading from the lectern. I don't know what it is about virtue, since I've had little or no contact with it, but it delighted me to witness the loving care, dedication, and attention with which those blessed fathers and teachers taught those boys, training the tender shoots of their youth to stand erect and not become twisted or stray from the path of virtue, which they were taught along with their letters. I reflected on how they scolded them gently, punished them compassionately, inspired them with examples, encouraged them with rewards and gently and tolerantly bore with them. Finally, they depicted the ugliness and horror of vice and portrayed the beauty of virtue, so that, hating the one and loving the other, they would attain the end for which they were created.

Scipio. Very well said, Berganza, because I've heard it claimed of these blessed individuals that as statesmen there are none so prudent as they are anywhere in the world, and as guides and leaders along the path to heaven they have few rivals. They are mirrors which reflect honesty, Catholic doctrine, peerless wisdom, and finally, profound humility, the foundation on which the whole edifice of human happiness is built.

Berganza. All this is as you say. And so, to continue with my story, I must tell you that my masters were happy for me to carry their portfolios all the time, which I did very gladly. As a result I lived like a king, and even better, because my existence was a carefree one. The students took to playing games with me and I became so tame with them that they used to put their hands in my mouth and the smallest among them used to climb up on my back. They used to throw down their caps or hats and I would put them very carefully back into their hands with signs of great pleasure. They also got into the habit of feeding me whatever they could get their hands on, and enjoyed watching, when they gave me walnuts or hazelnuts, how I cracked them open like a monkey, leaving the shell and eating the soft part. There was one who, to test my skill, brought me a large quantity of salad in a handkerchief, which I ate as if I were a human being. It was winter-time, when you can get buttered muffins in Seville, with which I was so well supplied that more than two *Antonios** were pawned or sold so that I could have my lunch.

In short, I lived the life of a student, free of hunger and the itch, which is about as much as anyone can say to stress how good it was. For if the itch and hunger were not such basic features of student life, none would be more agreeable or entertaining. For virtue and pleasure are equal partners and one spends one's youth learning and having a good time. I was removed from this blissful and peaceful state by a woman, whom I think they call a reason of state* in those parts, a woman with whom one complies only by disregarding many other forms of reason. The fact is that those teachers got the impression that their pupils spent the half-hour between lessons, not revising their studies, but playing with me, and so they ordered my masters not to bring me to school any more. They obeyed and took me back home to my former job of guarding the door. Since my old master did not recall the kindness he had shown me in allowing me to roam free day and night, I once again submitted my neck to the chain and my body to a mat they put down for me behind the door. Oh Scipio, my friend, if you knew how hard it is to suffer the transition from a happy state to a wretched one. Listen: when wretchedness and misfortune continue over a long period of time, they either end suddenly in death or the very continuation of one's suffering becomes a habit or custom, which usually provides relief when it is at its most intense. But when you suddenly emerge from an unhappy and calamitous situation to enjoy a quite different set of prosperous, happy, and joyful circumstances, and shortly afterwards you return to your original sufferings and former troubles and misfortunes, the pain is so overwhelming that if life does not end, then it is an even greater torment to continue living. As I say, then, I went back to my canine rations and the bones which a negress from the house used to throw down for me, but even these were decimated by two tabby cats who, being unfettered and agile, could easily relieve me of what did not fall within the radius of my chain. Brother Scipio, may heaven grant you the blessings you desire, if you will let me philosophize a little, without getting annoyed. For if I failed to tell you the things that have just come to my mind concerning what happened to me at that time, I don't think my story will be complete or have any value at all.

Scipio. Be careful, Berganza, that this urge to philosophize which you say has come over you, is not a temptation of the devil, for gossip has no subtler veil to soften and conceal its dissolute wickedness than for the gossip-monger to claim that every word he utters contains the wisdom of a philosopher, that speaking ill of people is justifiable reproof, and exposing the defects of our fellows is a worthy and conscientious act. There's no gossip-monger in existence whose life, if you look at it and examine it carefully, will not be full of vice and insolence. As long as you bear this in mind, philosophize as much as you like.

Berganza. Rest assured, Scipio, that I shan't gossip any more, because I'm determined not to. The fact is, then, that since I was idle all day and idleness breeds thought, I took to revising in my memory some of the Latin phrases which stuck there from among the many I heard when I accompanied my masters to their studies. As a result, I do believe that I found my mind much improved and I decided that if I were ever able to talk I would take advantage of them whenever the opportunity arose, but not in the way that some ignoramuses tend to use them. There are some Spanish writers who from time to time pepper their conversation with the odd snippet of Latin, giving the impression to those who do not understand that they are great Latinists while in reality they are scarcely able to decline a noun or conjugate a verb.

Scipio. I consider this a lesser evil than the one committed by those who really do know Latin. For among them there are some who are so foolish that even when they are talking to a cobbler or a tailor the Latin flows like water.

Berganza. From that we may infer that the man who spouts Latin in front of another who does not understand it sins as much as the one who speaks it without understanding it himself.

Scipio. Well, there's another observation you can make, that there are some people who know Latin and are still asses.

Berganza. There's no doubt about that. The reason's clear, for when in Roman times everyone spoke Latin as their mother tongue, there must have been some idiot among them and speaking Latin didn't prevent him from being stupid.

Scipio. In order to know how to be silent in one's mother tongue and speak in Latin, discretion is necessary, brother Berganza.

Berganza. So it is, because it's just as easy to say something stupid in Latin as in the vernacular. I've seen educated men who are fools, scholars of the language who are bores, and people whose Spanish is riddled with Latin phrases, which can easily cause annoyance not once, but many times.

Scipio. Let's change the subject; start explaining your philosophies.

Berganza. I already have, it's what I've just been saying.

Scipio. What exactly?

Berganza. What I said about Latin and Spanish, which I began and you concluded.

Scipio. You call slander philosophy? So that's what we're about! Make a virtue, Berganza, of the cursed plague of gossip and give it whatever name you like, for it will earn us the title of cynics, which means slanderous dogs.* For your own sake, shut up and proceed with your story.

Berganza. How am I to proceed if I must shut up?

Scipio. What I mean is get on with it now, for you're making it look like an octopus, the way you're adding tails to it.

Berganza. Speak correctly: for you don't call them octopuses' tails.

Scipio. That was the mistake made by the man who said it was neither clumsy nor wrong to call things by their proper names, as if it were better, if you have to name them, to refer to them by way of circumlocutions and roundabout expressions, which is less offensive than to hear them called by their proper names. Decent words reflect the decency of the person who speaks or writes them.

Berganza. I want to believe you; but my fortune, not content with having removed me from my studies and the delightful and well-ordered existence that they gave me, tying me up behind a door and exchanging the generosity of the students for the meanness of the negress, this fortune also ordained that I should be jolted out of what I considered to be my peace and quiet. Listen, Scipio, take it as a true and proven fact that bad luck seeks out and finds the unlucky man, even though he may hide himself in the remotest corners of the earth. I say this because the negress who worked in the house was in love with a negro who was himself a household slave. He slept in the porch between the main door and the inner one, behind which

I myself used to lie. They could only meet at night, and in order to achieve this they had either stolen or copied the keys. So most nights the negress would come down and, after stopping my mouth with a piece of meat or cheese, she'd open up for the negro, with whom she'd have a good time, aided and abetted by my silence and at the expense of the many things she stole. Some days my conscience would be plagued by the negress's bribes, although I believed that without them my ribs would be showing and I'd shrink from a mastiff to a greyhound. But, in fact, prompted by my natural goodness, I wanted to do my duty by my master, for I took his wages and ate his bread. This is the duty not only of honourable dogs, who are renowned for their gratitude, but of all servants everywhere.

Scipio. I do concede that this, Berganza, may pass for philosophy, for they are arguments composed of sound truth and good sense. Carry on and don't go adding threads, to say nothing of tails to your story.

Berganza. First of all I'd like to ask you to tell me, if you happen to know, what philosophy means, for although I use the word, I don't know what it is; all I can gather is that it's a good thing.

Scipio. I'll tell you briefly. This term is made up of two Greek words, 'philos' and 'sophia'; 'philos' means 'love' and 'sophia' means knowledge; so 'philosophy' means 'love of knowledge' and 'philosopher', 'lover of knowledge'.

Berganza. You know a lot, Scipio. Who the devil taught you Greek words?

Scipio. You really are simple, Berganza, if that impresses you, for these are things that every schoolboy knows, and there are also those who pretend to know Greek when they don't, just as there are those who pretend they know Latin when they are ignorant of it.

Berganza. That's just what I'm saying, and I'd like such people to be put in a press and the juice of what they know squeezed out of them until the pips run dry, so that they don't go round deceiving everyone by flashing their tatty Greek and phoney Latin, as the Portuguese do among the negroes in Guinea.

Scipio. Now, Berganza, you may indeed bite your tongue, and I mine, for everything we say is slanderous.

Berganza. Yes, but I'm not obliged to do what I've heard it said that Charondas* of Tyre did, when he passed a law decreeing that no one should enter his city's council chamber bearing arms, on pain of death. He forgot about this and one day he entered the council meeting wearing a sword. This was pointed out to him and he remembered the penalty he himself had imposed. He immediately drew his sword and ran it through his breast; he was the first to make and break the law and he paid the penalty for it. What I said was not legally binding, but merely a promise to bite my tongue when I gossiped; nowadays things are not so strict and severe as in ancient times; today they pass a law and tomorrow they break it and perhaps it's right that it should be so. One minute a man promises to mend his ways and the next he's fallen into even greater vices. It's one thing to praise discipline and another to impose it on oneself, and indeed, there's many a slip 'twixt cup and lip. Let the devil bite his own tongue for I don't want to bite mine or perform heroic deeds behind a mat, where no one can see me or praise my good intentions.

Scipio. By that argument, Berganza, if you were a human being, you'd be a hypocrite and all the works you performed would be for appearance's sake, insincere and false, covered by the cloak of virtue, and merely to win you praise, just like all hypocrites.

Berganza. I don't know what I'd do then, but I do know what I want to do now and that's not to bite my tongue while I've so many things left to tell you that I don't know how or when I'll be able to get through them all, especially since I'm afraid that when the sun rises we'll be left in the dark and deprived of speech.

Scipio. Heaven will arrange things better than that. Continue your story and don't wander from the beaten track with irrelevant digressions. That way, however long your story may be, you'll soon be finished.

Berganza. I was saying, then, that having seen the insolent, thieving, and indecent behaviour of the negroes, I decided, like a good servant, to put a stop to it by whatever means lay in my power, and I was so successful that I achieved what I set out to do. The negress used to come down, as you've heard, to have a fine time with the negro, confident that the pieces of meat, bread, or cheese which she threw down for me would keep me quiet. Gifts can achieve a lot, Scipio.

Scipio. So they can. Don't get distracted, continue straight on.

Berganza. I remember that when I was a student I heard a master recite a Latin proverb, which they call an adage and which went like this: 'Habet bovem in lingua.'

Scipio. Oh, how inopportunely you've got in your bit of Latin. Have you already forgotten how we recently criticized those who insert Latin phrases into their Spanish conversations?

Berganza. This bit of Latin fits in very well here; for you need to understand that one particular coin used by the Athenians was stamped with the figure of an ox. Whenever a judge failed to say or do what was right or just, the people would say: 'He's got an ox on his tongue.'

Scipio. I don't see the relevance.

Berganza. Isn't it quite clear, if the negress's bribes kept me silent for a long time, so that I neither wanted nor dared to bark at her when she came down to meet her negro lover? That's why I repeat that gifts can achieve a great deal.

Scipio. I've already agreed that they can, and if it weren't for the fact that I don't want to go off on a long digression now, I'd prove with a thousand examples just how much they can achieve. But perhaps I'll tell you some time, if heaven grants me the time, opportunity, and the power of speech to tell you my life story.

Berganza. May God give you what you desire, and now listen. My good intentions finally triumphed over the negress's wicked gifts. One very dark night, as she was coming down to her customary recreation, I attacked her without barking, so as not to throw the whole household into uproar, and in no time I'd torn her nightdress to shreds and bitten a slice out of her thigh. This ruse was enough to keep her safely tucked up in bed for more than a week, feigning I don't know what manner of illness for the benefit of her master and mistress. She recovered and came back another night, and once again I attacked her and, without biting her, I scratched her all over as if I'd been carding wool to make a blanket. Our battles were waged in silence and I always emerged the victor, while the negress came out of them in bad shape and even worse temper. Her anger was clearly manifested in the condition of my coat and the state of my health; they took away my rations and bones and gradually my own bones began to poke through my skin. Nevertheless, although they took away my food they couldn't take away my bark. The negress, however, to finish me off good and proper, served me up a sponge fried in butter, but I recognized her evil intent. I saw that it was worse than swallowing poison, because if you eat it your stomach swells up and you never survive. Since it seemed impossible to guard against the traps laid by such angry enemies, I decided to put some distance between us and get out of their sight.

Finding myself loose one day I went out into the street without saying goodbye to anyone, and within a hundred yards I had the fortune to meet the police officer I mentioned at the beginning of my story,* who was a great friend of my master Nicholas Snub-Nose. No sooner had he seen me than he recognized me and called me by my name. I also recognized him and when he called me I went up to him with my usual ceremonies and caresses. He grabbed hold of my neck and said to his two constables: 'This is a famous guard dog, who used to belong to a great friend of mine; let's take him home.' The constables were delighted and said that if I were a guard dog then I'd be very useful. They wanted to hold on to me while they led me off, but my master told them that it wasn't necessary and that I'd go with them because I knew him. I forgot to mention that the steel-studded collar that I was still wearing when I upped and abandoned the flock was removed by a gipsy at an inn, and that in Seville I went without one. The police officer, however, gave me a collar studded with Moorish brass. Consider for a moment, Scipio, how my wheel of fortune turns: yesterday I was a student, today I'm a constable.

Scipio. That's the way of the world, and there's no reason for you to start exaggerating the ups and downs of fortune, as if there were a great difference between serving a slaughterer and serving a constable. I cannot suffer or endure with patience the way some men complain of ill luck when the best luck they ever had was to cherish the hope and ambition of becoming a squire. How they curse their fate! How outrageously they insult it! And for no other reason than to persuade those who hear them that from exalted, prosperous, and happy circumstances they have fallen upon the hard and unfortunate times they now see them in.

Berganza. You're right; and you need to understand that this police officer was friendly with a notary with whom he went around. They had as mistresses two women who were not simply more bad than good but thoroughly disreputable. It's true that there was something pleasing in their features, but also all the brassiness and slyness you associate with whores in their manner. These two acted as net and bait to catch fish out of water in the following way. They dressed so provocatively that their appearance spoke for itself, and anyone could tell a mile off that they were loose-living ladies. They always went after foreigners, and when the merchant fleet came to Cádiz and Seville for the autumn fair they could smell the profit in the air and no foreigner could escape their clutches. When one of these greasy fellows fell into the hands of one of these fair creatures, they would inform the police officer and notary which inn they were going to, and when the former were together the latter would pounce and arrest them for consorting with prostitutes. But they never took them to prison because foreigners always redeemed the offence with money.

It so happened that Colindres, for that's the name of the police officer's girlfriend, caught herself a greasy, grubby foreigner. She agreed to have supper and spend the night with him in his lodgings. She gave her boyfriend the tip-off, and no sooner had they undressed than the police officer, the notary, two constables, and myself walked in on them. The lovers were startled, the police officer exaggerated the offence and ordered them to get dressed quickly to be taken to jail. The foreigner got upset and the notary, moved by charity, stood up for him and by dint of his pleading alone reduced the fine to a mere one hundred reales. The foreigner asked for his chamois breeches which he'd put on a chair at the foot of the bed, where he had money to buy his freedom. The breeches, however, failed to materialize, nor could they, because as soon as I entered the room the smell of bacon reached my nostrils, which really made my day. I sniffed it out and found it in the pocket of the breeches; more precisely I found a prize joint of ham, and in order to enjoy it and be able to get it out without making a noise I dragged the trousers into the street, where I threw myself upon the ham with all my energy. When I returned to the room I found the foreigner ranting in a strange and God-forsaken tongue, which was nevertheless comprehensible, that he wanted his trousers back because he had fifty gold escudos in them. The notary assumed that either Colindres or the constables had stolen them and the police officer had the same thought; he called them aside, no one confessed, and they all cursed one another. When I saw what was happening I went back out into the street where I'd left the breeches in order to retrieve them, for the money was of no use to me. I didn't find them because some lucky passer-by had already carried them off. When the police officer saw that the foreigner had no money to pay the bribe, he began to grow desperate and it occurred to him to extract from the landlady of the premises what the foreigner did not possess. He called her and she appeared in a state of undress, and when she heard the shouts and complaints of the foreigner and saw Colindres naked and crying, the police officer in a fit of anger, the notary disgruntled, and the constables pilfering objects from around the room, she was not best pleased. The police officer ordered her to cover herself up and accompany him to jail, for permitting men and women to consort together in her establishment. That did it! That's when the shouting really began and added to the confusion, for the landlady announced: 'I'll have none of your tricks, Mr Police Officer and Mr Notary, for I can see what you're up to. You'll not threaten or scare me; shut up and be off with you, otherwise I swear I'll throw a fit and make every detail of this story public knowledge. For I'm well acquainted with the lady Colindres and I know that the police officer's been her pimp for many months; and don't make me speak any clearer than that, and give this gentleman his money back and we'll all be satisfied. For I'm a respectable woman and I've got a husband with his patent of nobility,* his *a perpenan rei de memoria*,* and his lead seals, God be praised. And I do my job efficiently without bothering anyone. I've got my prices listed where everyone can see them, so don't come to me with these tales for, as God is my judge, I know how to look after myself. I'm a fine one to arrange for women to come in with the guests. They've got their own room keys and I've not got the eyes of a Sphinx to see through seven walls.'

My masters were dumbstruck as they listened to the landlady's outburst and saw how their lives were being read like an open book, but since they could also see that she was the only one they were likely to extract any money from, they insisted on taking her to jail. She protested to the heavens at the outrage and injustice they were committing, in her husband's absence and he being such a distinguished citizen. The foreigner was bellowing for his fifty escudos. The constables insisted that they had not seen the breeches, God forbid such a thing. The notary was urging the police officer on the quiet to look through Colindres's clothes, for he suspected that she must have the fifty escudos since she was in the habit of exploring the pockets and other hiding-places of the men who got involved with her. She claimed the foreigner was drunk and must be lying about the money. In short, it was a scene of confusion, shouts, and oaths that showed no sign of abating, nor would it have done if at that very moment the Magistrate's lieutenant had not entered the room. He had been on his way to visit the lodging house and the voices had led him to the scene of the uproar. He demanded to know the reason for the shouting and the landlady told him without sparing any detail. She pointed to the nymph Colindres, who was by now dressed, denounced her public liaison with the police officer and exposed their tricks and manner of stealing. She exonerated herself by claiming that with her consent no woman of ill repute had ever entered her establishment. She made herself out to be a saint and her husband a paragon of virtue and called to a maid to run and bring from a chest her husband's patent of nobility, so that the lieutenant might see them. She explained to him that when he saw them he'd realize that the wife of such an honourable man couldn't do anything wrong, and if it was her occupation to keep a lodging house, it was because she had no choice, and God knew how difficult it was, and whether she wanted to have some kind of income and daily bread to get by on rather than do that work. The lieutenant, annoyed by her endless chatter and presumption of nobility, said to her, 'Dear landlady, I want to believe that your husband has a patent of nobility so that you can claim that he's a gentleman innkeeper.'

'And a very respectable one,' replied the landlady. 'And what line is there anywhere, whatever its pedigree, that does not have some skeleton in its cupboard?'

'What I'm telling you, madam, is to cover yourself up, because you're coming to jail.'

This piece of news knocked her to the floor, where she lay scratching her face and shouting. In spite of this, the excessively severe lieutenant took them all off to jail, namely the foreigner, Colindres, and the landlady. I later learned that the foreigner lost his fifty escudos and another ten which is what they made him pay in costs, the landlady paid the same amount, and Colindres walked through the door scot free. The very day they released her she hooked a sailor, who paid up what the foreigner should have done, by informing her accomplices in the same way. So you see, Scipio, how many people were seriously inconvenienced by my greed.

Scipio. It would be more apt to say by the cunning of your master.

Berganza. Listen, then, for their mischief went much further than that, although it pains me to speak ill of police officers and notaries.

Scipio. True, for to speak ill of one is not to speak ill of them all.

For there are many, very many notaries who are good, loyal, law-abiding men, eager to satisfy without injuring anyone. They don't all delay their cases, nor collude with all parties, nor charge more than their due, nor go prying and inquiring into the lives of other people in order to cast aspersions on them, nor join forces with the judge for a spot of 'you scratch my back and I'll scratch yours'. Neither do all police officers consort with vagabonds and rogues or have mistresses like your master did to aid them in their ruses. Many, very many are gentlemen by birth and conduct themselves in a gentlemanly manner; there are many who are not impetuous, impudent, ill-mannered, or thieving, such as those who wander round the inns measuring foreigners' swords, and when they find them a hair's breadth beyond the legal limit, they reduce their owners to ruin. They don't all release as soon as they arrest and act the judge and lawyer when they feel like it.

Berganza. My master set his sights higher than that and he pursued a different course; he boasted of his valour and of making some famous arrests, and he kept up the illusion of valour without any danger to his own person but at great cost to his purse. One day in the Puerta de Jérez he took on six notorious villains unaided, without my being able to help him in any way, because I had a rope muzzle on my mouth, for that's how he kept me during the day although he removed it at night. I marvelled at his boldness, spirit, and daring; he moved in and out of the villains' swords as if they were made of straw. It was wondrous to behold the agility with which he attacked, his thrusting and parrying and the way he measured the situation, his eye ever alert to the danger of being taken from behind. In short, in my estimation and that of everyone who witnessed or learned of the fight, he became a new Rodamonte,* having driven his enemies from the Puerta de Jérez as far as the marble columns of the College of Master Pedro, a distance of more than one hundred yards. He left them safely locked up and went back to collect the trophies of the battle, namely, three scabbards. He then went to show them to the Magistrate who, if my memory serves me correctly, was then the licentiate Sarmiento de Valladores, renowned for the destruction of Sauceda.* People stared at him as he passed through the streets and pointed their fingers at him as if to say: 'That's the plucky fellow who dared to take on the biggest thugs in Andalusia singlehandedly.'

He spent the rest of the day parading round the city and nightfall found us in Triana, in a street next to the Molino de la Pólvora. After my master had spied out the land (as they say in their slang), to see whether anyone was watching, he slipped into a house. I followed behind and in a courtyard we found all the thugs who had taken part in the fight, without their cloaks and swords and with their tunics unbuttoned. One man, who must have been the host, was holding a large pitcher of wine in one hand and in the other a large glass with which, when he had generously filled it with sparkling wine, he toasted the entire company. No sooner had they noticed my master than they rushed up to him with open arms and toasted him too. He returned the gesture and would have gone on doing so if it had been to his advantage, for he was of an easy-going temperament and keen not to offend anyone in trivial matters. The desire to relate to you right now what went on there would plunge me into a maze from which it would be impossible for me to emerge of my own free will. I refer to such things as the supper they ate, the fights they recounted, the robberies they listed, the ladies whose virtues they commended and those they did not, the compliments that were bandied between them, the absent hoodlums who were remembered, the fencing skills that were demonstrated. Some of them even got to their feet in the middle of the meal to practice the various moves, fencing with their hands and applying elegant terminology to their gestures; and last but not least, there was the figure of the host himself whom they all respected as lord and father. In short, I was able to ascertain that the owner of the house, whom they called Monipodio,* was the accomplice of thieves and abetter of villains and that my master's great fight had been pre-arranged with them, including the detail of withdrawing and leaving their scabbards behind. My master paid for these services there and then, in cash, plus whatever Monipodio claimed had been the cost of the meal, which went on until dawn to the great satisfaction of all concerned. For dessert they passed word to my master of a brand new villain, an outsider, who had just arrived in the city; he must have been braver than the lot of them and they were informing on him out of envy. My master arrested him the following night as he lay naked in bed. If he had been fully clothed I could tell from his physical condition that he would not have allowed himself to have been taken so meekly and with so little risk to his captor. With this arrest, coming so soon after the fight, my coward's reputation grew, for my master was actually as cowardly as a hare, but on the strength of the eating and drinking he financed he preserved his valiant reputation. All the profit he accrued from his official job and his private intelligence leaked away down the drain of his valour.

But be patient, and let me give you the unabridged and unembroidered version of something that happened to him one day. Two thieves stole a very good horse in Antequera and brought it to Seville, and in order to sell it without any risk they used a stratagem which I think was rather inspired and clever. They took up lodgings at different inns and one of them went to the authorities and filed a petition claiming that Pedro Losada owed him four hundred reales which he had lent to him, this being confirmed by a certificate with his signature which he presented as evidence. The Magistrate ordered the said Losada to acknowledge the certificate, and if he did so, they would sequester goods to the value of the debt or put him in prison. It fell to my master and his friend the notary to carry out this task; one of the thieves took them to the inn where the other was lodging, where he immediately recognized his signature, acknowledged the debt, and offered the horse to guarantee it. The said horse immediately caught my master's eye, and he marked it as his, should it be put up for sale. The thief waited for the legal time limit to pass and then put the horse up for sale, selling it for the knockdown price of five hundred reales to a third party my master had employed to acquire it for him. The horse was worth the price it sold for and half as much again. However, since it was in the vendor's interest to make a quick sale, he parted with his merchandise to the first bidder. One thief recovered the debt he was not owed and the other the receipt which he did not need, while my master was left with the horse, which turned out to be a greater bane to him than Sejanus' horse* was to his masters. The thieves immediately moved on to pastures new and two days later, after my master had fixed up the horse's harness and other trappings, he rode him into St Francis's Square, looking more pompous and affected than a peasant in his Sunday best. He was heartily congratulated on his good buy and confirmed in his belief that it was worth one hundred and fifty escudos as sure as an egg was worth a maravedí,* and turning the horse this way and that he acted out his tragedy in the theatre of the aforementioned square. While he was engaged in this prancing and preening, two handsome and richly dressed men arrived on the scene and one of them exclaimed: 'As God is in His heaven, this is Piedehierro, who was stolen from me in Antequera a few days ago!' All four servants accompanying him confirmed the truth of his words, that this was Piedehierro, the horse that had been stolen. My master was stunned, the true owner filed a complaint, documents supporting the claim were produced, and those presented by the true owner were so convincing that the verdict went in his favour and my master was dispossessed of his horse. Word spread of the thieves' ingenious trick and how they had used the arm of the law itself to sell what they had stolen, and almost everyone rejoiced that my master's greed had been his undoing.

His misfortune did not end there; for that very night the Magistrate himself was going out on patrol because he had received information that there were thieves in the San Julián district, and just as they were passing a crossroads they saw a man running away. Seizing me by the collar and spurring me on, the Magistrate exclaimed: 'After the thief, Gavilán! Off you go, my boy. Get him, Gavilán, get him!' Weary of my master's misdeeds and wanting to follow the Magistrate's command to the letter I turned on my own master and, before he could defend himself, I had him on the ground and if they hadn't dragged me off him I'd have avenged more than a score or two. They pulled me off him, leaving both of us much the worse for wear. The constables would have liked to punish me, beat me to death even, and would have done so if the Magistrate hadn't said: 'No one is to touch him, for the dog did as I ordered.'

Everyone understood my meaning and I, without bidding farewell to anyone, escaped through a hole in the wall into the open countryside, and before daybreak I was in Mairena, a village four leagues from Seville. There I had the good fortune to meet up with a company of soldiers who, I heard, were going to embark at Cartagena. Four of my master's ruffian friends were among them and the drummer had been a constable and a great showman, as are all drummers. They all recognized me and they all spoke to me and asked after my master as if I had the power to respond, but the one who showed me most affection was the drummer and so I decided to stay with him, if he were willing, and join their expedition, even if it took me to Italy or Flanders. For it is my belief, and I'm sure you'll share it, that although the proverb claims that 'The fool at home is a fool wher'er he roam', travelling and meeting different people makes men wise.

Scipio. That is so true, and I remember hearing a very clever master I once had say that the famous Greek called Ulysses acquired his reputation for prudence solely on the strength of travelling many lands and meeting many different peoples and races. Therefore, I applaud your intention to go wherever they might take you.

Berganza. The fact was that the drummer, who now had the means to display his showmanship better than before, began to teach me to dance to the sound of the drum and to perform other tricks, which no other dog apart from myself could possibly learn, as you'll hear when I tell you about them. Since we had almost left the district in which they had been recruited progress was slow; there was no administrative officer to keep us in check, the captain was young, but a real gentleman and a very decent fellow; it was not many months since the ensign had left the court and its banqueting hall; the sergeant was experienced and astute and good at mobilizing the company and getting it from its base to the place of embarkation. The company was full of thugs and deserters who behaved badly in the villages we passed through, which resulted in the disparagement of the one person who didn't deserve it. It's the misfortune of the good prince to be blamed by some of his subjects for the faults of his other subjects, because they are each others' tormentors, through no fault of their master. For with the best will in the world he cannot remedy these wrongs, because everything or almost everything to do with war brings with it harshness, hardship, and inconvenience.

In short, through my own talent and the efforts of the man I'd chosen as my master, in less than a fortnight I learned to jump for the King of France* and not for the bad landlady. He taught me how to prance like a Neapolitan horse and walk round in a circle like a miller's mule, and if I hadn't taken care not to be too eager to demonstrate my tricks I'd have made people wonder whether it were some devil in the form of a dog that performed them. He gave me the name of the Wise Dog, and no sooner had we reached our quarters than he would wander around the whole village beating his drum and announcing that anyone wishing to come and see the marvellous tricks and abilities of the Wise Dog could see them performed in such and such a house, or at such and such a hospital, for eight or four maravedís, depending on the size of the village. With this advance publicity, every single person in the village turned up to see me, and no one failed to be astonished and delighted when they did.

My master revelled in the profits he was making and he maintained six friends in the manner of kings. Greed and envy gave the ruffians the idea of stealing me and they looked around for the opportunity to do so, for the business of earning a living doing nothing has many adherents and followers. That is why there are so many puppeteers in Spain, so many who mount sideshows, so many who sell pins and ballads, for all this volume of wares, even if it were sold lock, stock, and barrel, would not sustain anyone even for a day. Yet none of these people set foot outside the eating-houses and taverns all year round. From this I deduce that their current of drinking bouts flows from some other source than the professions they practise. All these people are useless, good-for-nothing vagabonds, sponges which soak up the wine and grubs which devour the bread.

Scipio. No more, Berganza, let's not get back on to that subject again. Carry on, for the night is slipping by and I wouldn't want us to be stuck in the shade of silence when the sun rises.

Berganza. Be silent yourself, then, and listen. Since it's an easy matter to add to what's already been invented, when my master saw how well I could imitate the Neapolitan charger he made me some embossed leather trappings and a small saddle, which he fitted on my back, and on top of that he placed the dummy figure of a man with a small lance for tilting at rings, and he taught me how to run straight at a ring which he placed between two poles. The day I was to do my tilting he would announce that the Wise Dog would tilt at a ring and perform other new and unprecedented feats of skill, which I duly improvised off the top of my head, as the saying goes, rather than make my master out to be a liar.

So we arrived, after several days' march, at Montilla, seat of the great and famous Christian, the Marquess of Priego, lord of the house of Aguilar and Montilla. They gave my master quarters, as he had arranged, in a hospital. He made the usual announcement, and since rumour had already spread the news of the abilities and skills of the Wise Dog, within less than an hour the courtyard was filled with people. My master was delighted to see that the harvest would be a rich one and that day his showmanship knew no bounds. The festivities began with my jumping through the hoop of a sieve, which looked like part of a barrel. He prompted me with the usual questions, and when he lowered a cane stick which he was holding it was the sign for me to jump, and when he held it high it was the sign for me to stay where I was. His first instruction to me that day, the most unforgettable day of my life, was to say: 'Come on, Gavilán, my little friend, jump for that dirty old man you know who dyes his hair black; and if you don't want to, then jump for the pomp and show of doña Pimpinela of Plafagonia, who was a friend of that Galician serving wench who worked in Valdeastillas. Don't you like that order, Gavilán, my son? Then jump for the student Pasillas who signs himself graduate although he's got no degree at all. Oh, what a lazy hound you are! Why don't you jump? Ah, now I get your drift. So jump for the wine of Esquivias, which is as famous as that of Ciudad Real, San Martín, and Rivadavia.' He lowered the cane and I jumped, aware of the malicious and spiteful thrust of his words. Then he turned to the public and declared: 'Don't imagine, worthy senate, that what this dog knows is to be scoffed at. I've taught him twenty-four tricks, the very least of which a hawk would fly to see, what I mean is that it's worth walking thirty leagues to see the least of them. He can dance the saraband and chaconne better than their inventor, he can knock back two litres of wine without spilling a drop. He can sing a 'sol fa mi re' as well as any sacristan. All these things, and many others which I don't mention, you'll see during the time the company remains here. And for the time being let's see the Wise Dog do another jump and then we'll get down to the real business.'

This left the audience he had called senate agog with suspense, and it made them determined not to miss anything I could do. My master turned back to me and said: 'Go back, Gavilán, my son, and with gentle skill and agility undo all the jumps you've just done, but it has to be in the name of the famous witch who's reputed to have once lived here.' No sooner had he said this than the hospitaller, an old woman who looked more than seventy, spoke up and said: 'Rogue, charlatan, cheat, and whoreson, there's no witch round here! If you're referring to La Camacha, she's already paid for her sins and is now God knows where. And if you're referring to me, scoundrel, I'm not and never have been a witch in my life. And if I ever had the reputation of being one, thanks to false witnesses, an arbitrary law, and an impulsive and ill-informed judge, everyone knows the life I lead, not in penance for the witchery I never did, but for the many other sins I committed as a sinner. So, crafty drummer, get out of this hospital, and if you don't, I swear by heaven that I'll make you get out good and proper.'

With that she began to shout such a breathless stream of insults at my master that he was left in a state of confusion and alarm; in short, she simply would not allow the show to go on. My master was not upset by the disturbance because he got to keep the money and postponed for another day and another hospital what had failed to take place in that one. The people went off cursing the old woman, heaping insult upon insult by calling her a sorceress as well as a witch, and a hairy hag as well as an old one.

In spite of this confrontation we remained that night in the hospital, and when the old woman found me alone in the yard, she asked: 'Is it you, Montiel, my son? Is it you, by chance, my son?' I looked up into her face very steadily, and when she saw this she came up to me with tears in her eyes and threw her arms around my neck, and if I'd allowed her she would have kissed me on the mouth; but I found the idea disgusting and would not consent.

Scipio. You were right not to; because there's no pleasure, only torture, in kissing or allowing yourself to be kissed by an old woman.

Berganza. What I want to tell you now I ought to have told you at the beginning of my story and that way we should not have been so astonished to find that we could talk. For let me tell you what the old woman said to me: 'Montiel, my son, follow me and you'll see which room is mine and try to come there tonight so that we might meet alone, for I'll leave the door open. You must understand that I've got many things to tell you about your life which are to your advantage.'

I lowered my head as a gesture of obedience, which was enough to convince her that I was the dog Montiel she was looking for, as she afterwards explained to me. I waited in astonishment and confusion for night to come, in the hope that it would explain the mystery or prodigy of the old woman's words to me, and since I'd heard her called witch I was expecting great things from seeing and listening to her. The moment finally arrived when I found myself in her room with her, which was dark, narrow and low, and lit only by the feeble light of an earthenware lamp. The old woman trimmed it, sat down on a small chest, and pulling me towards her and without uttering a word, she embraced me again and I once again took great pains to ensure that she didn't kiss me. The first thing she said to me was:

'I very much hoped that before these eyes of mine closed to sleep their last sleep, heaven would permit me to see you, my son, and now that I've seen you, let death come and take me away from this weary life. You must know, son, that in this town there once lived the most famous witch the world has ever known, who was called Camacha of Montilla. She was so unique within her profession that the Ericthos, Circes, and Medeas,* of whom I've heard that the history books are full could not rival her. She'd freeze the clouds at will, covering the face of the sun with them, and when she felt like it she would calm the stormiest sky. In an instant she'd bring men from distant lands; she'd wondrously repair young ladies who had been careless in guarding their integrity; she provided a cover of modesty for immodest widows; she annulled and arranged marriages as she pleased. In December she had fresh roses in her garden and in January she harvested wheat. Making watercress grow in a trough was the least of her achievements, as was her ability to make the faces of the living or dead appear, on request, in a mirror or the fingernail of a child. It was claimed that she could change men into animals and that she'd made use of a sacristan in the form of an ass for six years, really and truly, but I've never been able to figure out how it's done. As for the stories that are told about the enchantresses of old, who changed men into beasts, those who know most about it claim that it was merely a case of their beauty and charms attracting men so powerfully that they fell madly in love with them. They then kept them in a state of subjection and made them do whatever they wanted, so that they seemed like beasts. But in you, my son, experience is showing me that the contrary is true; I know you are a rational person and I see you in the form of a dog, unless this is being done by means of the art known as *tropelia* which makes one thing appear as another. Whatever the case may be, what grieves me is that neither your mother nor I, who were both pupils of the good Camacha, ever knew as much as she did; not through any want of intelligence, skill or determination, for if anything we had too much rather than too little of these qualities, but through her own spiteful nature, because she never wanted to teach us the greater skills, because she wanted to keep them to herself.

'Your mother, boy, was called Montiela and she was almost as famous as Camacha; my name is Cañizares, and if I'm not as clever as the two of them I have at least the same good ambitions as either of them. The fact is that your mother's determination to enter a circle and be locked up in it with a legion of demons could not be equalled by Camacha herself. I was always a bit timid and content to conjure up half a legion; but, with due respect to both of them, in the matter of concocting the oils with which we witches anoint ourselves, I put them both in the shade, as I shall do to any who follow and observe our rules today. For you must understand, son, that since I've seen and still see that my life, which speeds along on the swift wings of time, is drawing to a close, I've wanted to give up all the vices of witchcraft in which I was engulfed for many years, and I'm left with the curiosity to be just a sorceress, which is a very difficult vice to abandon. Your mother did the same; she abandoned many vices and she did many good works during her lifetime, but in the end she died a witch. She didn't die of any illness but of grief when she learned that Camacha, her teacher, was envious of her because she considered it a mark of disrespect that she was getting to know as much as she did, or because of some other jealous dispute which I never fully understood. So when your mother was pregnant and nearing the moment of the birth, Camacha acted as her midwife and delivered what your mother gave birth to and showed her that it was two dogs. When she saw them she exclaimed: "There is some evil afoot! There is some mischief in this! But, sister Montiela, I'm your friend, I'll conceal this birth and you must concentrate on getting well and rest assured that your misfortune will be buried in silence. Do not be grieved by what has happened for you know that I'm well aware that for days you've been with no one but Rodríguez, that porter friend of yours, so this canine offspring comes from some other source and there's some mystery in the matter." Your mother and I, for I was present the whole time, were amazed at this strange event. Camacha went off taking the pups with her and I stayed with your mother to look after her, for she couldn't believe what had happened to her. Camacha reached the end of her days and in the final hour of her life she called your mother and told her that she'd changed her children into puppies because of some grievance she felt towards her; but she shouldn't be distressed because they would revert to their proper form when they least expected it; but this could not happen until they had first witnessed the following with their own eyes:

> They will resume their proper guise
> When they observe with their own eyes
> The arrogant laid low,
> The meek raised to the skies,
> By a hand empower'd to do so.

'This is what Camacha said to your mother at the time of her death, as I've already told you. Your mother wrote it down and learned it by heart, and I also fixed it in my memory in case the time would come when I'd be able to tell one of you. In order to identify you, I call all the dogs I see of your colouring by your mother's name, not because I think that the dogs will know the name, but to see whether they respond to being called by names which are so different from other dogs' names. This afternoon, when I saw you do so many things and heard you called the Wise Dog, and saw how you looked up at me when I called you in the yard, I thought you must be the son of Montiela. So it's with the greatest of pleasure that I can tell you what happened to you and how you can recover your original form. I wish it were as easy as the method Apuleius is said to have used in *The Golden Ass*,* which entailed nothing more than eating a rose. Your transformation, however, depends on the actions of others, and not on your own efforts. What you must do, son, is commend yourself to God here in your heart and wait until these divinations, for I don't want to call them prophecies, come to pass, for since the good Camacha pronounced them they will surely come about. You and your brother, if he is still alive, will see yourselves in the form you desire.

'What I regret is that I'm so close to my end that I shan't have the chance to see this happen. Many times I've wanted to ask my goat* how your affair will end, but I've never dared because he never gives a straight answer to the questions we ask him, but replies in riddles with many possible meanings. So there's no point in asking this lord and master of ours anything, for he mixes a single truth with a thousand lies; and from what I can gather from his replies, he knows nothing about the future with any certainty, only by guesswork. All the same, he's got us witches so fooled, that although he plays lots of tricks on us we can't leave him. We travel a long way from here to see him, to a large field where a large number of us, wizards and witches, assemble. There he gives us tasteless food to eat and other things happen which for the sake of truth, God, and my soul I dare not relate, for they are so filthy and disgusting and I don't want to offend your innocent ears. Some people think that we only go to these gatherings in our imaginations, where the devil places the images of all those things that we afterwards claim have happened to us. Others say that this is not true, and that we are present, body and soul. I tend to think that both these beliefs are true, since we do not know when we go one way or the other, for everything that happens in the imagination is so intense that there's no way of distinguishing it from when we really and truly go. The inquisitors have carried out some experiments in this area on some of us they've imprisoned, and I believe that they've found what I say to be true.

'I should like to renounce this sin, my son, and I've worked hard to do so: I've taken refuge in the role of hospitaller; I take care of the poor, and some die who leave me the wherewithal to live on in what they bequeath me or what they leave amongst their rags, which I painstakingly pick clean. I pray rarely and in public, and I gossip a great deal, but in private. It suits me better to be a hypocrite than a self-confessed sinner: the illusion of my present good works is gradually erasing my past misdeeds from the memory of those who know me. Indeed, false sanctity harms no one except those who practise it. Listen Montiel, my son, let me give you this piece of advice: be as good as you possibly can, and if you have to be bad, try to disguise the fact as much as you possibly can. I'm a witch, I don't deny it; your mother was a witch and a sorceress, and I can't deny that either; but the good face that we showed to the world gained us a favourable reputation everywhere. Three days before she died we'd both been on a great spree in a valley in the Pyrenees and yet she died so peacefully and calmly, that if it were not for the grimaces she made a quarter of an hour before she gave up the ghost, she looked at that moment as if she were lying on a bridal bed strewn with flowers. The fate of her two children weighed heavily on her heart, and so firm and resolute was she that not even in the throes of death itself could she bring herself to forgive Camacha. I closed her eyes and went with her to the grave; there I left her, never to lay eyes on her again, although I've not given up hope of seeing her before I die, because it's been rumoured in the village that she's been seen wandering about the cemeteries and crossroads in different forms, so perhaps I'll see her one day and I'll ask her whether she wants me to do anything to ease her conscience.'

Every single thing the old woman told me in praise of the woman she claimed was my mother was a dagger piercing my heart, and I wanted to attack her and tear her to pieces. If I held back it was to prevent death from carrying her off in such a wretched state. In the end she told me that she intended to anoint herself with oils that night to go on one of her customary outings. While she was there she intended to ask her master what was going to happen to me. I wanted to ask her what oils she was talking about and it would seem that she read my thoughts, because she answered me as if I'd actually asked the question, because she said:

'This oil with which we witches anoint ourselves is composed of the juices of herbs, which are very cold, and it's not, as popular opinion would have it, made from the blood of the children we suffocate. On this point you may also ask what pleasure or profit the devil gets from making us kill innocent creatures, because he knows that if they're baptised, and are therefore innocent and without sin, they go straight to heaven, and he receives special punishment for every Christian soul which escapes his clutches. The only other thing I can say on the matter is what the proverb says: "that some people will tear out both eyes if their enemy will tear out one." He also does it for the grief he causes the parents when he kills their children, which is the greatest grief imaginable. What matters most to him is to make us commit such cruel and perverse sins at every turn; and all this is permitted by God because of our sins, for without his permission I've seen from experience that the devil can't harm an ant. This is so true that when I once asked him to destroy the vineyard of an enemy of mine, he replied that he couldn't even touch a leaf of it, because it was not God's will. You'll be able to conclude from this, when you become a man, that all the misfortunes which befall people, kingdoms, cities, and villages; sudden deaths, shipwrecks, falls, in short, all the evils that are called harmful, come from the hand of the Almighty and his permissive will; and the evils and ills that are called culpable proceed from and are caused by ourselves. God is without fault; from which we infer that we are the authors of sin, giving it form in our thoughts, words, and deeds with God's consent because of our sins, as I've said. Now, son, you may well ask, if by chance you can understand me, who made me a theologian, and you may even say to yourself: "Curse the whore! Why doesn't she give up being a witch, since she knows so much about the matter, and turn to God, since she knows that He's readier to forgive sins than permit them?" If you were to ask me, this would be my reply: that the habit of vice becomes second nature and this vice of witchery becomes something of flesh and blood. When you're caught up in its fiery heat, it produces a chill which freezes and numbs your soul even in its faith, which causes it to forget itself, and it does not even remember the terrors with which God threatens it, nor the glory to which He invites it. Indeed, since it's a sin of the flesh and of sensual pleasure, it's a power which deadens all the senses, bewitching and possessing them and preventing them from functioning as they should. And so the soul, rendered useless, weak, and downcast, cannot even rise to the contemplation of a single worthy thought. Allowing itself to be submerged in the deep abyss of its wretchedness, it won't reach out to touch the hand that God is extending to it, out of sheer pity, so that it may raise itself up. I've got the kind of soul I've described to you: I see and understand everything, but since sensual pleasures have my will in chains, I've always been evil and always shall be.

'But let's change the subject and go back to the matter of the oils; let me tell you that they're so cold that they deprive us of all our senses when we anoint ourselves with them. We end up stretched out and naked on the floor, and then, it's claimed, we experience in our minds all those things we think we experience in reality. On other occasions, as soon as we've anointed ourselves it seems to us that we change form and, turned into cocks, owls, or crows, we go to the place where our master is waiting for us, and there we resume our usual shape and enjoy pleasures which I shan't describe to you, because they are so loathsome that the memory is scandalized at the recollection and the tongue similarly shrinks from relating them. In spite of all this, I'm still a witch and conceal my many faults beneath a cloak of hypocrisy. It's true that if I'm esteemed and honoured by some as a good woman, there are many others who insult me to my face or within my hearing, using names fixed in their memory by the fury of an angry judge who in times gone by had dealings with your mother and myself. He passed his anger on to a torturer who, not having been bribed, applied all the force and vigour of his arm to our backs. But that's history, just as everything becomes history; memories fade, no one lives twice, tongues tire of gossip, and new events make us forget past ones. I'm a hospitaller, I put on a show of good conduct, my oils give me my moments of pleasure; I'm not so old that I may not live another year, for I'm seventy-five years old, and now that I can no longer fast because of my age, nor pray because of dizziness, nor go on pilgrimages because of the weakness in my legs, nor give alms because I'm poor, nor think good thoughts because I'm fond of gossip—and in order to do good one must first think good thoughts—my thoughts must always be bad. And yet I know that God is good and merciful and that He knows what will become of me, and that's enough. And let's end this conversation here for it's truly making me sad. Come, son, and watch me anoint myself; for troubles are easier to bear on a full stomach; gather rosebuds while you may; and you can't cry while you're laughing. What I mean is that although the pleasures the devil grants us are unreal and false, they still feel like pleasures, and pleasure is much greater when it is imagined than actually experienced, although where real pleasure is concerned the contrary must be true.'

When she'd finished this long harangue she got up, and taking the lamp she went into another, narrower room. I followed her, tormented by a thousand conflicting thoughts and amazed at what I'd heard and what I expected to see. Cañizares hung the lamp on the wall and quickly stripped down to her chemise. Taking a glass pot from a corner she put her hand in it and, murmuring to herself, she anointed herself from head to foot, for she was not wearing a headdress. Before she completed the operation she told me that she would either remain in the room, unconscious, or she would disappear from it, and that I shouldn't be afraid nor fail to wait there until morning, for I'd learn what still remained in store for me before I became a man. By lowering my head I indicated that I would do so, and with that she finished applying the oil and stretched out on the ground like a corpse. I put my mouth close to hers and saw that her breathing had stopped altogether.

I must confess something to you, Scipio, my friend: that I was very frightened to find myself locked up in that narrow room with that awful figure before me, which I'll describe to you as best I can. She was more than seven feet tall and a veritable sack of bones covered with a dark, hairy, leathery skin. Her belly, which was like a sheepskin, covered her private parts and hung half-way down her thighs. Her breasts were like the udders of a wrinkled, dried-up cow; her lips were black, her teeth were like fallen tombstones, and her nose was hooked and misshapen. With her wild eyes, dishevelled hair, sunken cheeks, scraggy neck, and shrivelled breasts she was, all in all, a bag of diabolical skin and bones. I began to study her carefully and was suddenly overcome by fear as I considered the awful spectacle of her body and the even worse occupation of her soul. I wanted to bite her to see whether she'd come round, but I could find no place on her person where I could do it without revulsion. Nevertheless, I grabbed her by an ankle and dragged her out into the courtyard; but not even this stirred any sign of consciousness in her. There, out in the open and in sight of the sky, the fear went away, or at least it subsided enough to give me the courage to wait and see the outcome of the activities of that awful woman and what she had to say about my affairs. Meanwhile I asked myself: 'Who made that wicked woman so wise and yet so evil? How does she know the difference between harmful and culpable evil? How does she understand and speak so much about God and yet do so much of the devil's work? How does she sin so deliberately without the excuse of ignorance?

The night passed as I thought about these things and the day discovered us both in the middle of the courtyard, she still unconscious and I crouching nearby, alert and watching her ugly and frightful form. People came out of the hospital and surveying the scene some said: 'Old Cañizares is dead, then; look how disfigured and skinny her penance has left her.' Other more practical onlookers took her pulse and, discovering that she still had one and that she was not dead, assumed that she was in ecstasy and that her sheer goodness had caught her up in a rapture. There were others who said: 'There's no doubt this old whore's a witch, and she's anointed; for saints do not go into such indecent raptures, and up until now, amongst those of us who know her, she's considered more of a witch than a saint.' Other curious people went so far as to stick pins deep into her flesh, but not even this was sufficient to arouse the slumberer. She didn't come to her senses until seven o'clock in the morning, and when she found herself riddled with pinpricks, bitten on her ankles, bruised as a result of being dragged outside from her room, and exposed to the view of so many staring eyes, she thought, and thought correctly, that I was the author of her dishonour. So she lunged at me, and putting both hands around my throat she tried to strangle me, saying: 'Oh, you ungrateful, ignorant and malicious scoundrel! This is the thanks I get for the favours I did your mother and those I intended to do for you?'

Seeing that I was in danger of losing my life in the claws of that fierce harpy, I shook myself free, and grabbing hold of the long folds of her belly, I shoved and dragged her all around the courtyard while she cried out for someone to save her from the jaws of that malignant spirit.

When they heard the evil old woman's words most of the onlookers thought I must be the kind of demon that always bears a grudge against good Christians, and some came up and threw holy water over me, others did not dare to pull me off the old woman, while yet others shouted that I should be exorcised. The old woman grunted, I dug my teeth in deeper, the confusion grew, and my master, who had by now arrived, attracted by the noise, despaired when he heard people say that I was a demon. Others, who knew nothing of exorcisms, brought three or four sticks and began to beat my back. Smarting with pain I let go of the old woman and with three bounds I was out in the street, and with a few bounds more I was outside the town and being followed by a crowd of children who shouted at the top of their voices: 'Keep out of the way, the Wise Dog's gone mad!' Others said: 'He's not mad, he's a demon in the shape of a dog!'

After my beating I hastily left the village, with a large crowd in pursuit who undoubtedly believed I was a demon, not only because of the things they had seen me do, but because of the old woman's words when she woke from her accursed sleep. I was in such a hurry to get away and out of their sight, that they believed that I'd been spirited away like a demon; in six hours I covered twelve leagues and arrived at a gipsy camp in a field near Granada. I stopped there for a while because some of the gipsies reco_ﬂized me as the Wise Dog and very readily welcomed me. They hid me in a cave to prevent me being found if anyone came looking for me, and intended, as I later learned, to make some money out of me as my master the drummer had done. I was with them for three weeks, during which time I got to know and observed their manner of life and customs, which are so remarkable that I must tell you about them.

Scipio. Before you go any further, Berganza, it would be a good idea to stop and think about what the witch told you and ascertain whether the great lie you believe can possibly be true. Look, Berganza, it would be utterly absurd to believe that Camacha changed men into beasts and that the sacristan served her in the form of an ass all the years it's claimed that he did. All these things and others like them are deceptions, lies, or manifestations of the devil. If we seem at the moment to possess some understanding and power of reason, since we can talk although we're really dogs, or have the form of dogs, we've already said that this is a wondrous and unprecedented event. Although it's actually happening, we mustn't be persuaded until the final outcome shows us what we ought to believe. Do you want it explained more clearly? Just think of the vain and silly conditions that Camacha stated were necessary for our restoration as men. And what must appear to you like prophecies are nothing but fairy stories and old wives' tales, like the ones about the headless horse or the magic wand, with which people entertain themselves round the fireside on long winter nights. If this were not the case, it would have come to pass, unless the words are meant to be taken in a sense I've heard called allegorical, where the meaning is not what the words literally say, but something which, although different, may be similar. So to say:

> They will resume their proper guise
> When they observe with their own eyes
> The arrogant laid low,
> The meek raised to the skies,
> By a hand empower'd to do so.

and understand it in the sense I've mentioned, it seems to me to mean that we'll recover our form when we see that those who were yesterday at the top of the wheel of fortune are today humbled and laid low at the feet of misfortune and despised by those who held them in highest esteem. Similarly, when we see that those who a couple of hours ago had no other role to play in the world than increase the number of its inhabitants, are now raised so high by good fortune that we've lost sight of them. If at first we couldn't see them because they were so small and timid, now we can't touch them because they are so great and exalted. If recovering the form you mention were dependent on this, we've already seen it happen and it happens all the time; which leads me to deduce that it's not in the allegorical sense, but in the literal that Camacha's words are to be understood.

Yet the solution to our predicament is not to be found there either, for we have many times observed what the verses say and we are as much dogs now as we ever were. So Camacha was a lying trickster, Cañizares a rascal, and Montiela a malicious and wicked fool, begging your pardon, in case she's the mother of both of us, or yours alone, for I don't want her for a mother. I declare, then, that the true meaning's a game of ninepin bowling, where the pins that are stand-ing are promptly knocked down and raised again by a hand with the skill to do it. Think, then, whether over the course of our lives we've ever witnessed a game of ninepins and if as a result of it we've turned into men, if that's what we are.

Berganza. I declare that you're right, brother Scipio, and that you're wiser than I realized; and from what you've said I've reached the conclusion that everything we've experienced until now, and what we're experiencing at the moment, is a dream and that we're dogs. But that should not prevent us from enjoying this blessing of speech and the great honour of human conversation for as long as we can. Therefore, don't get bored with hearing me relate what hap-pened while I was with the gipsies who hid me in the cave.

Scipio. I'll gladly listen to you, in order to oblige you to listen to me when I, God willing, recount my own life story.

Berganza. The life I led with them made me think about their many wicked customs, their cheating, their tricks, and the thieving which the women as well as the men carry out. Have you noticed just how many of them there are scattered around Spain? They all know one another, they maintain constant contact with one another, and they shuffle and swap the stolen goods among themselves. They owe their allegiance not so much to their king as to one they call the Count. He and all his descendants bear the surname Maldonado, not because they are descended from that noble line, but because the page of a gentleman of that name fell in love with a gipsy girl, who would not return his love unless he became a gipsy and took her as his wife. This the page did and found such favour with the rest of the gipsies that they elevated him to the position of lord over them, declared their allegiance to him, and as a sign of their loyalty, bring him a share of the goods they steal, if they are of any consequence. To provide a cover for their idleness they occupy themselves in forging objects out of iron and making instruments to assist them in their thieving; so you'll always see them wandering the streets selling tongs, drills, and hammers while the women carry trivets and spades. All the women are midwives and in this they have the advantage over our own, because without expense or assistance they give birth to their offspring and wash the babies in cold water as soon as they're born. From this moment until they die they are hardened and exposed to the inclemencies and rigours of the elements, and so you'll observe that they're all vigorous acrobats, runners, and dancers. They always marry their own kind, to prevent the outside world from becoming acquainted with their evil customs; the women respect their husbands and there are few who cause them offence through contact with men outside their society. When they beg for alms they employ more trickery and deception than prayers; since no one can trust them they do not enter into service, and so become idlers. I've rarely if ever, if my memory serves me correctly, seen a gipsy taking communion at the altar rail, although I've been inside a church many times. They think of nothing but how they can deceive and where they can steal; they compare notes on thieving and the methods used to commit it.

While I was present one day, a gipsy related to some others a thieving trick he had once played on a peasant. This gipsy had an ass with just a hairless stump of a tail and on the end of this he attached another normal tail which looked like its own. He took it to market where a peasant bought it for ten ducados, and when he'd sold it and received payment he asked him whether he'd like to buy another ass which was the brother of this one, and just as good as it, for he'd sell it to him at a better price. The peasant told him to go and get it, for he'd buy it, and that while he was waiting for him to return he'd take the ass he'd bought to his lodgings. The peasant went off and somehow or other the gipsy managed to steal back from him the ass he'd bought. He immediately removed the false tail and left it with its own bald version; he changed its saddle and halter and then had the nerve to go and look for the peasant so that he'd buy it off him. He found the peasant before he'd missed the first ass and in no time at all he'd bought the second. When he went back to his lodgings to get the money to pay the silly ass found the four-legged one missing; and although he was very silly, he suspected that the gipsy had stolen it from him and did not want to pay up. The gipsy went looking for witnesses and brought back with him the men who had received the tax on the first beast, and they swore that the gipsy had sold the peasant an ass with a very long tail which was very different from the second one he was selling. An officer of the law was present throughout these proceedings who took the gipsy's part so earnestly that the peasant was obliged to pay for the ass twice over. They related many other thefts, all or most of which involved animals, for it's in this discipline that they're graduate students and practise most of their skills. In short, they're an evil breed, and although many wise judges have declared against them this hasn't encouraged them to mend their ways.

After three weeks they wanted to take me to Murcia; I passed through Granada, where the captain whose drummer had been my master was already stationed. As soon as the gipsies found out, they locked me up in a room at the inn where they were staying; I heard them state the reason and I didn't like the journey they were taking, so I decided to get away, which I did, and as I was leaving Granada I came across an orchard belonging to a *morisco*.* He gladly took me in and I stayed even more willingly since I got the impression that he would only expect me to guard the orchard, a job which in my reckoning would be less troublesome than guarding the flock. Since there was no negotiating over salary, it was an easy matter for the *morisco* to find a servant to command and myself a master to serve. I was with him for more than a month, not because the life I led was so satisfying, but because of the satisfaction I gained from becoming acquainted with that of my master and, through his, that of all the *moriscos* who live in Spain. The things I could tell you, Scipio my friend, about this *morisco* rabble, if I weren't afraid of not being able to say it all in a fortnight! And if I had to be specific I wouldn't finish in two months. But, as it is, I'll have to say something, so listen to what I saw in general or made a particular note of concerning these worthy folk.

It would take a miracle to find a single man among so many who truly believes in the Holy Christian laws; their sole intent is to make money and hoard what they make, and to achieve this they work and do not eat. As soon as a coin of any value comes into their possession, they condemn it to life imprisonment and eternal darkness; by virtue of always earning money and never spending it, they are amassing and accumulating the largest cache of money in Spain.

They are money-boxes, moths, magpies, and weasels; they acquire, hide, and swallow it all. Just think how many of them there are and that every day they earn and hide away some quantity of money, and bear in mind that a slow fever can be as fatal as a sudden one; and as they increase in number, so the number of those who hide money away also increases and will surely continue to grow *ad infinitum*, as experience shows. They do not exercise chastity, nor does any man or woman among them take holy orders; they all marry and they all multiply because sober living favours the propagation of their race. War does not weary them, nor do they overtax themselves in the work they do; they steal from us with the greatest of ease and from the fruits of our property, which they sell back to us, they make themselves rich. They do not employ servants, for they perform such tasks for themselves; they do not spend money on their children's education because the only art they practise is that of robbing us. I've heard it said of the twelve sons of Jacob who went into Egypt, that when Moses brought them out of that captivity, six hundred men came out, to say nothing of women and children. From this you may infer how the generations of these *moriscos* will multiply, for they are incomparably greater in number.

Scipio. Solutions have already been sought for all the injuries you've mentioned and roughly outlined: for I'm well aware that those of which you say nothing are graver and more numerous and no proper remedy has yet been found. However, our state is guarded by very wise men who realize that Spain is rearing and nurturing all these *morisco* vipers in its bosom, and with God's help they will find a sure, prompt, and effective solution to such a dangerous situation. Go on.

Berganza. Since my master was stingy, like the rest of his race, he fed me on millet bread and any left-over gruel, which is what he normally lived on himself; but heaven helped me to bear this wretched state of affairs in the strangest way, as you're about to hear. Every morning at daybreak a young man would come and sit at the foot of one of the many pomegranate trees in the garden, dressed like a student in flannel that was no longer black and plush but faded and threadbare. He'd spend his time writing away in a notebook and from time to time he'd slap his brow or bite his nails while gazing heavenwards. Sometimes he became so engrossed in his thoughts that he moved neither hand nor foot, nor did he blink, so deep was his absorption. Once I went up to him without his noticing me; I heard him muttering to himself and after a long while he gave a loud exclamation: 'I swear that it's the best octave I've ever written in my life!' As he quickly scribbled in his notebook, he looked extremely pleased with himself, all of which gave me to understand that the poor fellow was a poet. I made my usual affectionate overtures to assure him of my tameness; I settled at his feet and he, reassured by this gesture, fell back into his reverie. Once again he scratched his head, once again he became caught up in a rapture, and once again he scribbled down what he had invented. While he was still absorbed in this activity another youth came into the garden, a handsome and smartly dressed young man with some papers in his hand, from which he read from time to time. He came up to the other young man and asked, 'Have you finished the first act?'

'I've just put the final touches to it,' replied the poet, 'and it's as elegant as you could wish.'

'How does it go exactly?' asked the new arrival.

'Like this,' said the first young man. 'His Holiness the Pope enters in full regalia, accompanied by twelve cardinals, all dressed in purple, because the action of my play took place at the time of the *mutatio caparum*,* when cardinals did not wear red but purple. It is therefore most appropriate, for the sake of poetic truth, that my cardinals should come on stage in purple. This is a very significant aspect of the play and the audience would certainly cotton on, for such incongruities and errors often occur. I cannot be mistaken on this matter, because I've read up on the whole Roman ceremonial, just to get the vestments right.'

'And where', retorted the other, 'do you expect my theatre manager to get purple vestments for twelve cardinals?'

'Well, if you take even one of them away,' replied the poet, 'pigs will fly before I give you my play. Goodness me! Waste such a grandiose spectacle? Try to imagine right now what it will look like on stage—His Holiness with twelve solemn cardinals and the other attendant ministers they will undoubtedly have with them. By heaven, it will be one of the greatest and most exalted sights ever to be seen in a play, including *Daraja's Bouquet*!*

At this point I realized that one was a poet and the other an actor. The actor advised the poet to thin the cardinals out a bit, if he didn't want to make it impossible for the manager to stage the play. To this the poet replied that they should be grateful to him that he did not include the whole conclave in attendance at the memorable event he planned to recall to the memory of the audience in his masterpiece. The performer laughed and left him to his task in order to apply himself to his own, which was to rehearse his part in a new play. After writing a few verses of his magnificent play the poet very calmly and slowly removed from his pocket some crusts of bread and what seemed to me to be about twenty raisins, for I counted them, although I'm not sure whether there were as many as that, because there were some crumbs of bread mixed in with them which increased the volume. He blew the crumbs away and one by one he ate the raisins together with their stalks, for I didn't see him throw any away. He helped them down with the crusts, which looked mouldy because of the fluff they had collected in his pocket, and they were so hard that although he tried to soften them by moistening them in his mouth more than once, they stubbornly refused to yield. All of this was to my advantage because he threw them to me saying: 'Here, eat them up and much good may they do you.' 'Look,' I said to myself, 'what nectar or ambrosia this poet gives me, such as the gods and his very own Apollo are said to live on up in the heavens!' In short, a poet's lot is, on the whole, a wretched one; but my own need was greater because it forced me to eat what he threw away.

All the time he was writing his play he came to the garden every day and I always had crusts to eat, for he very generously shared them with me, and then we'd go to the water-wheel where we'd satisfy our thirst like kings, I lying down and he drinking from a bucket. When the poet began to stay away, however, and my hunger remained, I decided to leave the *morisco* and go into the city to seek my fortune, for he who moves on finds better luck. As I entered the city I saw my poet coming out of the famous monastery of St Jerome, and as soon as he saw me he rushed towards me with open arms and I went up to him with renewed signs of delight at having found him. He immediately began to produce pieces of bread which were softer than the ones he used to bring to the garden and to feed them to me without first chewing them himself, a kindness which redoubled the pleasure I felt at satisfying my hunger. The soft pieces of bread and the fact that I'd seen my poet leaving the said monastery made me suspect that he'd received charity there like so many others. He made his way toward the city and I followed him, determined to have him as my master if he were willing, assuming that I could live humbly on the left-overs of his bounty. For there's no greater or better purse than charity's own, for her liberal hands are never touched by poverty, and so I don't agree with the proverb that says: 'A heartless man gives more than a penniless one', as if a heartless miser would give anything, while the poor but generous man at least offers his goodwill when he has nothing else to give.

We eventually stopped at the house of a theatrical manager who, as far as I can recall, was called Angulo the Bad, to distinguish him from another Angulo* who was not a manager but an actor and the most amusing the theatre has ever known. The whole company assembled to hear my master's play, for I already considered him as such, but in the middle of the first act they all began to leave, one by one and two by two, except for the manager and myself, who were the only audience remaining. The play was so bad that, although I know nothing at all about poetry, even I thought that Satan himself had written it in order to ruin and humiliate the poet completely and utterly. He tried to swallow his embarrassment as he realized that his audience had deserted him. This was nothing in itself, but his prophetic soul whispered a warning of the misfortune that was threatening him: all the players came back, more than twelve in number, and without saying a word they grabbed hold of my poet and, were it not for the authority of the manager, who intervened with shouts and pleas, they would surely have tossed him in a blanket. The incident left me reeling, the manager out of humour, the players in high spirits, and the poet sulking. Although he was scowling, the latter very patiently retrieved his play, and tucking it into the breast of his tunic muttered: 'It's not worth casting pearls before swine.'

When he'd said this he very calmly walked away. I was so embarrassed that I neither could nor wanted to follow him; and I was right not to do so because the manager made such a fuss of me that I felt obliged to stay with him, and in less than a month I emerged a consummate performer of farce and a great mummer. They put an ornate muzzle on me and taught me how to set upon any member of the audience they chose; and while farces in general ended with beatings, in my master's company they'd end with me being set loose on the crowd. I'd knock them down and trample all over them, which made the ignorant audience laugh and generated a lot of profit for my master. Oh, Scipio, if only I could tell you what I witnessed in this and another two companies of players I had dealings with! But since it's impossible to reduce it to a succinct and brief account I'll have to leave it for another day, if indeed we are to have another day when we can communicate with one another. Do you see how long my discourse has been, and how many and how varied my experiences? Have you considered how many journeys I've made and how many masters I've had? Well, everything you've heard is as nothing compared with what I could tell you concerning what I noted, discovered, and observed in these people: where they come from and how they live, their customs and practices, work and leisure, ignorance and wit, together with countless other things, some of which are for private consumption and others for public proclamation, while all are memorable and enlightening to those who venerate false images and artificially contrived beauty.

Scipio. I fully appreciate, Berganza, the wide range of issues that emerged to prolong your discourse further and it is my opinion that you should save them for a more specific account when we're at leisure and not afraid of being interrupted.

Berganza. So be it, and now listen. With one such company I arrived in this city of Valladolid, where they dealt me such an injury in one farce that it almost finished me off. I couldn't avenge myself because I was wearing a muzzle at the time and afterwards, in cold blood, I had no desire to: for premeditated revenge smacks of cruelty and a mean disposition. This occupation tired me, not because it was demanding, but because I saw in it things simultaneously in need of amendment and punishment; but since it fell to my lot to perceive the wrong rather than be able to remedy it, I decided to turn my back on it and so I sought sanctuary, like those who abandon their vices when they cannot indulge them, although better late than never. Let me tell you, then, that when I saw you one night carrying a lantern for the good Christian Mahudes, I thought you contented and well and virtuously employed. Full of righteous envy I wanted to follow in your footsteps, and with this laudable intention I approached Mahudes who immediately chose me as your companion and brought me to this hospital. What has happened to me in it is not of such little consequence that it doesn't warrant space in my story, especially what I heard from four patients, whom fate and necessity brought to this hospital and to four adjacent beds. Forgive me, for it's a short tale; it won't wait and fits in very well here.

Scipio. Of course, I forgive you, but hurry for I don't think day can be far off.

Berganza. Let me explain that in the four beds at the end of this infirmary there are an alchemist, a poet, a mathematician, and one of those amateurs who come up with crackpot political schemes.

Scipio. I remember having seen these good people.

Berganza. Well, one afternoon last summer, when all the windows were closed and I was getting some air beneath the bed of one of them, the poet began to complain pitifully of his lot, and when the mathematician asked him what precisely he was complaining of, he said it was about his wretched luck.

'Have I not reason enough to complain?' he continued. 'After respecting the law which Horace sets down in his *Ars Poetica* that a work should not be published until ten years after it is completed, I have one that I worked on for twenty and another twelve have gone by since. It is lofty in subject matter, admirable and novel in its plot, elegant in its verse, entertaining in its episodes, marvellous in its construction, for the beginning corresponds with the middle and the end, so that all these things together constitute a poem that is elevated, sonorous, heroic, delightful, and substantial. Yet, in spite of all these qualities, I cannot find a patron to whom to dedicate it, a patron, I might add, who is intelligent, liberal, and magnanimous. What a wretched and depraved century we live in!'

'What's the book about?' asked the alchemist.

The poet replied, 'It concerns what Archbishop Turpin* never got round to writing about King Arthur of England, with a further supplement to the *History of the Quest for the Holy Brail*, all of it in heroic metre, partly in octaves and partly in free verse; but all of it with dactylic stress and when I say that I'm talking dactylic nouns and not a single verb among them.'

'Poetry,' replied the alchemist, 'makes little sense to me; and so I'm unable to appreciate fully the misfortune of which you complain, for although it might be great, it could not equal my own. It is because I lack instruments or a patron to support me and furnish me with the things required by the science of alchemy that I'm not currently rolling in money and in possession of greater riches than all the Midases, Crassuses, and Croesuses* put together.'

'Have you ever, Mr Alchemist,' the mathematician enquired at that point, 'experimented with extracting silver from other metals?'

'I have', replied the alchemist, 'not yet extracted any successfully, but I know that it really can be done, and I'm only two months away from having the philosopher's stone, with which one can get gold and silver from common stones.'

'You have indeed been exaggerating your misfortunes,' said the mathematician at that point, 'for, when all is said and done, one of you has a book to dedicate to someone and the other is very close to extracting the philosopher's stone. But what shall I say of my own misfortunes, for I'm so alone and know not where to turn? I've been pursuing the fixed point for twenty-two years and from time to time it's almost been within my grasp, and when I think that I've found it and that there's no way it can slip away from me, when I least expect it I'm amazed to find myself far away from it again. The same thing happens to me with the squaring of the circle, for I've been so close to discovering the solution that I'm quite baffled as to why I don't have it in my pocket by now. So, my torture is comparable with that of Tantalus,* so close to the fruit yet dying of hunger, near the water yet perishing of thirst. At times I think I've hit upon the truth and at others I find myself so far away from it that I must once again climb the mountain I've just descended, with the stone of my labours upon my back, like some latter-day Sisyphus.'*

The political crank had been silent until now but here he broke his silence to say:

'Poverty has brought together in this hospital four of the most woebegone individuals in creation and I wash my hands of trades and occupations which are neither amusing nor provide their workers with food to eat. I, sirs, am a political theorist, and at different times I've provided his Majesty with many pieces of advice, all of them to the advantage of the kingdom and none of them to its detriment. This time I've written a memorandum in which I beg him to put me in contact with someone to whom I may communicate a new idea of mine, which is so good that it will clear all his debts. But judging by what has happened to my other memoranda, I imagine that this one will end up on the rubbish heap like all the others. But because I don't want you to take me for a fool, although it means making my idea public knowledge, I want to tell you what it is. A petition is to be raised in the Cortes* obliging all his Majesty's vassals between the ages of fourteen and sixty to fast on some chosen and appointed day once a month on bread and water, converting the cost of all food-stuffs on that day, such as fruit, meat and fish, wine, eggs, and vegetables into money and giving it to his Majesty and swearing that not a single penny's been withheld. In this way, in twenty years he'll have no need of clever schemes and be free of debt. If you do the calculations, as I have, there are certainly more than three million people in Spain between the stipulated ages, excluding the infirm and those who are either too young or too old, and none of these can spend less than one and a half reales every day, at the very least. I'm happy for it to be no more than a real, and it cannot be less, even if they eat chaff. It's certainly not something to be scoffed at, having three million reales delivered to you cut and dried every month. This would be to the advantage rather than the detriment of those who fast, because by fasting they would please heaven and serve their king; some might even find that fasting was beneficial to their health. This is my idea, plain and simple, and it could be collected by parishes, without incurring the cost of commissioners who are the ruin of the state.'

They all laughed at the idea and the crank, and he also laughed at his own nonsense. I was amazed to hear the things they said and to realize that, in general, people of like dispositions came to end their days in hospitals.

Scipio. You are right, Berganza. Do you have anything else to say?

Berganza. Just two things, with which I'll put an end to my speech, for I think that day is breaking. When my master went to beg alms one night at the house of the Chief Magistrate of this city, who is a great gentleman and one of very high principles, we found him alone and it occurred to me to take advantage of this private audience to inform him of certain comments I'd heard made by an old patient at the hospital concerning the scandalous situation of the young girls who live on the street. Since they don't enter into service they turn out bad, and so bad that every summer they fill all the hospitals with the wretches who chase after them, an intolerable bane requiring a speedy and effective solution. As I was saying, I wanted to say all this to the Magistrate and I raised my voice, thinking I could speak, but instead of pronouncing reasoned arguments I merely barked quickly and so loudly that the annoyed Chief Magistrate shouted to his servants to drive me out of the room with a beating. A lackey who answered his master's call (it would have been better for me if he had been deaf at that moment) picked up a copper pot which came to hand and whacked me so hard in the ribs that I bear the marks of those blows to this day.

Scipio. And this is what you're complaining of?

Berganza. Don't I have reason to complain, then, if, as I said, I've been in pain until now and if I don't think that my good intention deserved such punishment?

Scipio. Look, Berganza, no one should interfere unless they are called upon to do so, nor meddle in affairs that do not concern them. You must remember that the advice of a poor man, however good it may be, is never admissible, nor should a poor man have the presumption to advise the great and those who think they know everything. Wisdom in a poor man is cast in shadows; want and wretchedness are the shadows and clouds which obscure it, and if by chance it comes to light, it is judged to be folly and treated with scorn.

Berganza. You are right, and learning by my own mistakes, from now on I'll follow your advice. Another night, and with the same motive, I went into the house of a distinguished lady, who was holding in her arms one of those little dogs they call lap-dogs, which was so small she could have hidden it in her bosom. When this same dog saw me, she jumped out of her mistress's arms and set upon me so fiercely, barking all the while, that she didn't stop until she'd bitten my leg. I looked at her again with a mixture of respect and annoyance and said to myself: 'If I came across you in the street, you rotten little beast, I'd either ignore you or tear you to pieces with my teeth.' Looking at her it occurred to me how even cowards and the mean-spirited are bold and daring when they enjoy positions of favour and are only too willing to insult those better than themselves.

Scipio. A good example of this truth you utter is provided by those little people who dare to be insolent in the shadow of their masters. If by chance death or some other accident of fortune fells the tree under which they shelter, they immediately reveal and expose what little courage they actually have. The truth of the matter is that they are worth no more than the value lent them by their masters and protectors. Virtue and understanding are one and immutable, whether naked or adorned, alone and accompanied. It's certainly true that they may suffer in people's estimation but not in the true nature of their merit and worth. And with this let us bring our speech to a close, for the light which is coming in through these cracks shows that the day is well advanced. This coming night, if this great blessing of speech has not abandoned us, will be mine, so that I can tell you my life story.

Berganza. So be it, and be sure to come to this same place.

The graduate finished reading the dialogue and the ensign woke up at one and the same moment and the graduate said, 'Although this dialogue may be invented and never really took place, I consider it so well written that the ensign may proceed with the second.'

'If that's your opinion,' replied the ensign, 'that will encourage me to get down and write it, without entering into further debate with you as to whether the dogs really spoke or not.'

To which the graduate replied, 'Ensign, let's not get into all that again. I appreciate the craftsmanship of the dialogue and its inventiveness, so be satisfied with that. Let's go to the Espolón* to exercise our bodies, since I've already exercised my mind.'

'Let's be off,' said the ensign.

And off they went.

EXPLANATORY NOTES

Prologue

3 *don Juan de Jauregui*: contemporary poet-painter. A portrait of Cervantes once claimed to be by Jaureguí and dated 1600 has proved not to be genuine.

César Caporal Perusino: a minor Italian writer who produced his own *Viaggi di Parnasso* in 1582.

5 *Heliodorus*: Greek writer probably of the second century AD, whose Byzantine work, *The Ethiopian History* or *History of Theagenes and Chariclea*, was a model for Cervantes's *Persiles*. Now known only to scholars, it enjoyed a certain vogue in the sixteenth and seventeenth centuries.

'Weeks in the Garden': a work promised here and in the prologue to the *Persiles* but probably never written, although one critic claims to have discovered a fragment.

Vale: (Latin) Farewell.

The Little Gipsy Girl

7 *the subtle art of thieving*: Cervantes's original words refer to 'the science of Cacus', the thief who stole the cattle of Geryon from Hercules.

sarabandes: the saraband was a popular seventeenth-century dance, considered licentious by some because it involved energetic movement of the whole body.

8 *St Anne*: the mother of the Virgin Mary.

9 *gentleman most just*: a reference to Joachim, the father of the Virgin Mary.

10 *Argus*: a reference to the giant in Greek myth who had a hundred eyes, a symbol of vigilance.

cuarto: a coin worth 4 maravedís. Other coins referred to in this story are: ochavo (2 maravedís); escudo (400 maravedís); real de a ocho (272 maravedís); real de a cuatro (136 maravedís); real (34 maravedís).

Queen Margaret: Margaret of Austria, wife of Philip III, 1598–1621.

11 *Austrian sun*: a reference to Philip III, while the 'tender dawn' refers to his daughter, the princess Anne, born 1601.

that filled heaven and earth with woe: the star in the first line of this verse refers to Philip IV, who was born on 8 April 1605, a Good Friday, hence the later reference to the 'black darkness of that day'.

her private heaven beautify: the following six stanzas refer to the different groups of people in her entourage.

12 *mighty Jupiter*: probably a reference to Phillip's powerful favourite, the Duke of Lerma.

Ganymedes: Ganymede was a beautiful Trojan youth who was kidnapped by Jupiter and made cupbearer of the gods on Olympus. This is a reference to pages and other royal attendants.

13 *Eagles with two heads bestowed*: the double-headed eagle was the symbol of the Habsburgs.

the Phoenix: a reference to St Lawrence, who was martyred by being roasted on a grid.

15 *Calatrava*: one of the three knightly orders in Spain, the others being Santiago and Alcántara.

16 *Great Ballad Anthology*: the *Romancero general*, published in 1600.

17 *the gold-bearing Tagus*: the river which flows through Toledo and through Portugal and into the Atlantic.

23 *... end of your term*: outgoing officials were obliged to stay in office for a time to deal with complaints regarding their conduct and even pay financial compensation.

27 *Flanders*: Spain was at war with its possessions in Flanders from the mid-sixteenth century until the Treaty of Utrecht in 1713.

Salamanca: the University of Salamanca was founded *c.* 1230.

28 *plus ultra*: the motto of Charles V, printed on coins.

Belmonte's henchmen: the Marquis of Belmonte used to pocket the money of French merchants who passed through his territory.

29 *finds his name inscribed on street corners*: it was customary for the fans of actors and dramatists to paint their names on walls.

30 *Poetry has to be handled ... everyone who comes into contact with her*: critics tend to associate Preciosa herself with this personification of poetry.

the Genoese: depicted in the satire of the day as money-grabbing.

32 *don Juanico*: Preciosa proceeds to make fun of the use of the affectionate diminutive.

42 *the Stygian lake*: the River Styx, in the underworld.

45 *pelota*: a game believed to be of Basque origin in which players hit the ball around a walled court, rather like in modern-day squash, with baskets strapped to their hands.

48 *Peña de Francia*: a village to the south-west of Salamanca.

52 *twenty leagues back*: Andrés had previously referred to Peña de Francia as being thirty leagues back. Cervantes is equally careless with the age of the Jealous Old Man.

68 *the licence ... to authorize the nuptials*: these formalities had been introduced to prevent clandestine marriages. The issue is introduced to increase the suspense as the denouement reaches its climax, and it also reflects Cervantes's desire to combine romance and realism.

70 *Pozo*: Cervantes refers to a certain *licenciado* Andrés de Pozo in his survey of Spanish poets in the *Voyage to Parnassus*.

Rinconete and Cortadillo

71 *Walloon collars*: also known as a Vandyke collar, this was a fine white linen collar which hung deeply over back and chest.

73 *quínolas . . . parar . . . andaboba*: these games have no specific English equivalents.

74 *pious place*: probably Mollorido.

the vigilance of an Argus: the hundred-eyed giant; see note to p. 10 above.

80 *my good gentleman of Murcia*: slang for thieves; *murciar* means 'to steal'.

81 *sent to the end of the world . . . on the voyage of a lifetime*: euphemisms for hanging and life imprisonment as a galley-slave respectively.

84 *Perrillo sword*: Perillo was the nickname of a Moriscan swordmaker, and it became the trademark for his famous swords.

85 *stupendous . . . salvage*: stipend and suffrage respectively. These words and later examples are being intentionally misused to emphasize the ignorance of Monipodio.

89 *don Alonso Pérez de Guzmán the Good . . . cut*: (d. 1309); he allowed his captured son to be executed rather than surrender the stronghold at Tarifa into Moorish hands.

90 *the good St Blas*: reputed to protect his devotees from ailments of the throat and, in this ironic context, from death by hanging or garrotting.

95 *that sailor from Tarpeya . . . that tiger from Ocaña, in*: the first reference is the misquoted first line of a ballad, probably well known to contemporary readers: while Cariharta calls Repolido a 'sailor [*marinero*] from Tarpeya', the first line actually reads 'Nero watches [*Mira Nero*] from Tarpeya, while Rome burns . . .' Hircania, in Asia Minor, was famous in ancient literature for its fierce tigers; Ocaña, in Castile, was not.

97 *Judas Mackerel*: i.e. Judas Maccabaeus, the Hebrew leader who reconquered Jerusalem in 164 BC. He was one of the 'Nine Worthies' of medieval legend.

Morphous: Orpheus, the great musician of Greek mythology, who descended into Hades to retrieve his wife, Euridice, but lost her again when he turned round to see her. Other names are similarly distorted by the speaker's ignorance.

Marion: Arion, a Greek poet of the seventh century BC. He was thrown overboard by the crew of his ship but carried safely to Corinth on the back of a dolphin.

the other great musician: probably a reference to Amphion who, with his brother Zethus, fortified the city of Thebes. The music of Amphion's magic lyre caused stones to move into position in the city wall of their own free will.

some musical Hector: Trojan hero, one of the principal figures in the Trojan War.

98 *seguidillas*: a Spanish dance in fast triple rhythm.

102 *juniper oil*: greasy and foul-smelling, it was used to treat mange in cattle.

sanbenitos and horns: sanbenitos were either yellow garments with a red cross or black ones with painted flames worn by penitents or impenitents respectively when undergoing punishment by the Inquisition; horns marked a man as a cuckold.

The Glass Graduate

107 *maccatella, polastri*: small meatballs and chicken respectively.

109 *the 'Hours' . . . 'Garcilaso' without commentary*: a Book of Hours was a collection of short liturgical prayers to be read at different hours of the day in honour of the Virgin Mary. Garcilaso de la Vega (1501–36) was the first great poet of the Spanish Golden Age and his work inspired long commentaries during the reign of Philip II. It is significant that Garcilaso should be singled out in this story for he 'finally broke by his example the old Spanish prejudice that the aristocratic profession of arms was incompatible with a serious dedication to letters': P. E. Russell, *Spain: A Companion to Spanish Studies* (London: Methuen & Co., repr. 1977), 285, the very tension which underpins this strange tale. Garcilaso also spent his formative years in Italy and died young as a result of battle wounds; unlike Rodaja, however, he was a distinguished member of the Court.

Madrigal . . . Descargamaría: famous Spanish wines.

110 *the Vatican*: the Vatican hill does not actually count as one of the seven hills on which ancient Rome was built. The 'other five', as Cervantes's text should read, are: the Aventine, Capitoline, Esquiline, Palatine, and Viminal.

agnus deis: cakes of wax stamped with the image of the Lamb of God, and blessed by the Pope.

111 *Our Lady of Loreto*: a reference to the belief that the basilica at Loreto contained the house of the Virgin Mary, which had been transported from Nazareth by angels.

the most exalted and significant message: presumably a reference to the Annunciation.

Calypso: a nymph who delays Odysseus for seven years during his journey home.

115 *Mount Testaccio*: one of five artificial hills in Rome, a dumping ground for shipments of pottery, bricks, tiles, crockery, etc. that had arrived broken.

Daughters of Jerusalem . . . your children: Luke 23: 28. The Graduate recites this and later quotations in Latin, which was more accessible to Cervantes's contemporary readers than it is to the general reader today.

116 *Old Christian blood*: social acceptability and mobility were dependent on claims of purity of blood. It was the peasant class, however, who probably had the stronger claims because they had not been rich enough to intermarry with wealthy Jews and Arabs. 'Saturday' refers to an individual of Jewish origin and to the fact that New Christians celebrated the sabbath on Saturday, like the Jews.

   wicker basket: of the kind used to transport goods on beasts of burden, hence the need to balance the weight of both sides.

   They arrived in Valladolid: the Court resided at Valladolid between 1601 and 1606.

117 *In former times . . . great wealth*: Ovid, *Ars Amatoria*, iii.

   There is a god . . . hearts: Ovid, *Fasti*, vi. 5.

   But we . . . gods: Ovid, *Amores*, iii.

121 *Honour a physician . . . them*: Ecclesiasticus 38: 1–4.

122 *Tantalus*: a mythical figure best remembered for his punishment in Hades, which was to stand in water up to his chin beneath fruit-bearing trees. Both food and water moved tantalizingly out of his reach whenever he tried to eat or drink.

123 *I don't want you transferring it to Genoa*: it was commonly believed that Genoese merchants were siphoning money out of the Spanish economy.

124 *Against puppeteers*: these travelling puppet shows presented religious as well as secular subjects. On two memorable occasions Cervantes presents puppeteers as tricksters. His most inspired farce, *The Marvellous Puppet Show*, exploits this tradition, while a picaresque character, Ginés de Pasamonte, assumes the role of a puppeteer in *Don Quixote, Part II*, chaps. 25–7.

125 *River Jordan*: it was traditionally believed that bathing in the River Jordan restored youth.

126 *In the hand . . . honour*: Ecclesiasticus 10: 5.

127 *In Madrid . . . the part in between*: Madrid was renowned for its dry climate and clear skies while Valladolid was notorious for its mud and fog.

128 *Touch not mine anointed*: Psalm 105: 15.

   Polla and cientos: card-games, resembling ombre and piquet.

129 *Rueda rather than Rodaja*: both words signify 'wheel', presumably a reference to the wheel of fortune.

The Power of Blood

138 *'Eco . . . salcicie'*: Cervantes's Italian is imperfect. It translates as 'There are fine chickens, pigeons, ham and sausages here'.

139 *Spanish*: the word in the original text is 'romance'.

148 *holy formalities . . . today*: a decree by the Council of Trent in the mid-sixteenth century required preliminaries to a wedding, thus rendering

clandestine marriages invalid. In *The Little Gipsy Girl* the marriage between Preciosa and Juan cannot go ahead until these formalities have been addressed and in *The Deceitful Marriage* the couple register themselves as unmarried and then the banns have to be read out in church prior to the wedding.

149 '*You are . . . my soul*': some editors, including Sieber, incorporate this sentence into the end of Leocadia's speech. It makes more sense, however, if Rodolfo is the speaker since he is the subject of the next sentence.

The Jealous Old Man from Extremadura

150 *Not so long ago . . . somewhere in Extremadura*: the vague geographical reference and the location of the story in a vaguely recent past are devices reminiscent of the opening lines on *Don Quixote, Part I*. Extremadura is a poor and arid province in south-west Spain. There were many Extremadurans among the *conquistadores* of the New World. Although the protagonist of this story does not subdue the land he does make a lot of money out of it.

like a second prodigal son: the parable is recounted in Luke 15: 11–32.

the great city of Seville: due to its monopoly on trade with the New World in the sixteenth century, Seville had become one of the boom towns of that period.

Tierrafirme: in Peru.

esparto mat: this served as a bed for the poor passengers. The Spanish word *mortaja* more commonly translates as 'shroud'.

151 *Cartagena*: then a city port in Peru, it is now part of present-day Colombia.

to avoid any difficulties: Cervantes is probably referring to the confiscation of non-registered imports.

152 *the most jealous man in the world*: the Extremadurans were proverbially known for their jealous nature, so to call Carrizales 'the jealous old man from Extremadura' in the title was to signal how excessively jealous he was. There is also word-play in the original between *extremeño* (Extremaduran) and *extremado* (extreme, extremely).

153 *to confirm their claim to nobility*: it was quite common for families to verify each other's claims to nobility or purity of blood (i.e. the absence of Moorish or, more importantly, Jewish connections).

twenty thousand ducados: a gold ducado or ducat was the most valuable coin in the currency.

He blocked up all the windows . . . street: Carrizales is reverting to the former Arab tradition of having windows which faced inwards, a custom that had begun to be replaced in sixteenth-century Seville.

154 *a turnstile*: the presence of the eunuch lends the house connotations of the harem, while the installation of a turnstile (a sort of hatch with revolving partitions fixed in a door or window, through which objects

could be passed without hand contact) conjures up the image of a convent.

154 *recently imported negro slaves*: having just arrived in Spain, these *bozales* are scarcely able to speak Castilian.

156 *Argus*: mythological watchman; see note to p. 10.

157 *nuns . . . golden apples*: a reference to the mythical tree of golden apples guarded by the Hesperides in a garden on Mt Atlas. It had been a marriage gift from Mother Earth to Hera. It was also protected by an ever-watchful dragon, Ladon. Significantly, it was Hercules' eleventh labour to appropriate some of these apples, which he succeeded in doing partly through trickery.

158 *knew the negro's name*: Loaysa has already addressed the negro by his name on the same page.

159 *Star of Venus . . . bars of a window*: all these ballads were popular at the time.

Abindarráez and . . . his lady Jarifa: these Moorish lovers were featured in numerous ballads.

the great Sufi Tumen Beyo: a captain-in-chief of Alexandria who died in 1517.

sacred sarabands: see note to p. 7.

Prester John of the Indies: a legendary Christian priest and king, said to have ruled a far-eastern kingdom in the Middle Ages.

164 '*How it grieves me*': line from a dance popular at the end of the sixteenth century.

166 *Absalom*: the superlative beauty of this son of King David is recorded in 2 Samuel 14: 25.

167 *who jumps for the King of France*: the idiom means to do whatever one is bidden, from a command given to performing dogs (cf. the English 'Die for the Queen').

168 *Jew's harp*: a small, lyre-shaped instrument played between the teeth.

171 *like a newly appointed professor*: it was a custom of the time to carry the new professor shoulder high in triumph.

172 *the true history of Charlemagne . . . Fierabras*: the 'history' is heavily embroidered with legend. *Fierabras*, the gigantic son of the saracen Emir of Spain, is the subject of an Old French epic poem, where he is defeated and converted to Christianity by Charlemagne's paladin Olivier.

the Cave of Cabra: a deep gorge in the province of Córdoba.

173 *they look like emeralds*: a reference to the green eyes of the stereotypical Renaissance beauty. They are normally a female attribute admired by the male.

177 *Oh duennas . . . good intentions*: duennas are depicted in a negative light in the literature of the time, cf. Doña Rodríguez, *Don Quixote, Part II*, chap. 48. The later reference to their 'long and elaborate headdresses' identifies the type by its costume.

182 *almost eighty*: at the time of his return from the Indies, just over a year earlier, Carrizales was only sixty-eight years old. Cervantes is not renowned for the painstaking revision of his work.

The Illustrious Kitchen Maid

185 *rentoy . . . presa y pinta*: two popular card games.

outside the city walls of Seville: the *barbacanas* comprised the area outside the city where *pícaros* and other low-life types congregated.

186 *Zahara*: Zahara de los Atunes, in the province of Cádiz, Andalusia.

Zocodover: a square in Toledo.

Zahara to Barbary: Moorish pirates often attacked the Spanish coast at that time, sometimes kidnapping Christians, taking them back to North Africa and demanding a ransom for them. Such a raid is described in another of Cervantes's *Exemplary Stories* (not included in this volume), *The Generous Suitor*. Cervantes himself was captured at sea and held captive by the Moors for five years.

Tetuan: a city in the north of present-day Morocco and one of the destinations of Spanish captives.

187 *Elysian fields*: the dwelling-place of the blessed after death in Greek mythology.

'Three ducks, mother . . .': when someone was said to be singing this first line of a well-known ballad, it signified that he was untroubled by his journey. In fact, Carriazo's journey covered more than three-quarters of the length of the Iberian Peninsular.

189 *Cano Dorado . . . Mancha*: the first four fountains are in the city of Madrid while Corpa is in the province of Madrid. The exact location of Pizarra de la Mancha is unknown.

190 *Flanders*: see note to p. 27.

191 *Puñonrostro*: chief officer of justice or *asistente* in Seville from 1579 to 1599.

192 *Sangre de Cristo*: a Moorish archway on the eastern side of Zocodover Square and leading to the street where the Sevillano Inn stood.

194 *Sagrario . . . the great plain*: the Sagrario is a chapel in Toledo Cathedral; Giannello's engine raised water from the River Tagus to the city; St Augustine's is a monastery famous for its views; the Kings' Garden was part of the flood plain and the great plain is situated to the north of Toledo.

Order of Alcántara: see note to p. 15.

194 *the temptations of St Anthony*: Anthony of Egypt (AD 251–356), gave up all his worldly possessions at the age of twenty to live as a hermit. The account of his life and miracles, written by Athanasius, records that the devil several times attacked him in the guise of wild animals.

195 *flageolets*: a high-pitched member of the recorder family.

199 *big-nosed poet*: a reference to the Latin poet Ovid (43 BC–AD 17), author of the *Metamorphoses*, with a play on his full name, Publius Ovidius Naso.

200 *no two canons . . . as pampered*: the lack of chastity among the clergy was often alluded to in the comic literature of the period.

204 *Portia . . . Penelope*: all three women symbolize virtue and constancy. Portia was the wife of Brutus, Minerva the Roman goddess of wisdom, and Penelope the wife of Odysseus.

206 *lethal rays . . . Costanza's eyes*: it was a belief at the time that the eyes emitted rays. The idea is often elaborated in the poetry of the time and recurs in the second of the three poems in this story.

207 *Compás*: an area in front of the brothel in Seville.

chaconas, and folías: Latin-American and Portuguese dances respectively.

208 *give . . . two fresh figs*: ie to make the contemptuous gesture of thrusting the thumb between two fingers.

Pésame and perra mora: along with the *zambapalo* (in the penultimate line of the song), three more popular dances.

210 *sphere*: in this poem Costanza is addressed in terms of the Aristotelian composition of the universe. The uppermost region of the heavens or Empyrean, believed in antiquity to be the home of the gods, is mentioned first, followed in descending order by the *primum mobile* or first cause, the Crystalline, the Firmament, then the spheres which correspond to the sun and planets: Saturn, Jupiter, Mars, the Sun, Venus, Mercury, and the Moon.

the father: Saturn, the father of the gods, who ate his children.

warrior adulterer: Mars, the god of war, caught in adultery with Venus.

fourth heaven and second sun: the sphere of the Sun, and Venus.

grave ambassador: Mercury, the messenger of the gods.

211 *you are this sphere*: the earth was believed by the ancients to be the centre of this system.

212 *Prester John of the Indies*: see note to p. 159.

213 *Danish maids*: an ironic reference to the chivalric romance *Amadís de Gaula*. Princess Oriana's lady-in-waiting was Danish.

214 *the four prayers*: the *Pater Noster*, the *Ave Maria*, the *Credo*, and the *Salve Regina*.

219 *primera*: a popular card game.

220 *dos y pasante*: a special version of *quínola* which enabled the player to double his winnings.

Tamburlaine (or Timur the Lame): (d. 1405), last great Mongol emperor, who in the fourteenth century ruled over vast areas of Asia and present-day Europe.

221 *the Hydra's head*: a monster with nine heads in Greek mythology. A head that was cut off would be replaced by two new ones.

229 *aldermen*: civic dignitaries; members of a town's ruling council.

The Deceitful Marriage

237 *sweated out . . . in a single hour*: the soldier has been receiving a long course of sweat treatments for the syphilis it took him much less time to acquire.

do penance together: Peralta is inviting Campuzano to eat with him.

241 *an Aranjuez of scented flowers*: the royal palace of Aranjuez, with its ornate gardens, is situated to the south of Madrid.

245 *from Petrarch*: *Trionfo d'Amore*, i. 119–20.

248 *the times of Maricastaña*: a distant and mythical past when incredible events occurred.

large quantity of raisins and almonds: part of the medical treatment of syphilis.

The Dialogue of the Dogs

252 *Puerta de la Carne*: Meat Gate, because it led to the slaughterhouse.

253 *St Francis's Square*: the location of both Town Hall and Magistrate's Court. Corrupt officials are the criminals' 'guardian angels'.

Calle de la Caza . . . the slaughterhouse: all three places were the haunts of criminals.

254 *San Bernardo*: according to Sieber (vol. ii, p. 305, n. 20), the slaughter-house was close to the San Bernardo district of Seville, and most of its employees lived there.

255 *opened my mouth, spat in it*: this action was believed to ward off evil spirits.

256 *one of the great poets . . . difficult not to write satire*: a reference to Juvenal, *Satires*, i. 30.

enlighten rather than draw blood: the distinction is between two sorts of penitents in religious processions. Some carried candles (*de luz*) while others (*de sangre*) whipped or punished themselves in some other way.

many other books . . . not worth recalling: a reference to pastoral literature. Some of the names quoted are characters in the better-known works. Diana and Felicia appear in the most famous Spanish pastoral romance, *The Seven Books of Diana*, published by Jorge de Montemayor in 1559; Elicio appears in Cervantes's own pastoral entitled *La Galatea*, an early work published in 1585. Fílida features in *Fílida's Shepherd* by Lius Gálvez de Montalvo (1582).

257 *Deum de deo*: 'God of God', from the Nicene Creed; one of several references to the fact that people recited Latin without understanding it.

262 *Company of Jesus*: the Jesuits had been teaching in Seville since the mid-sixteenth century.

265 *more than two Antonios*: a comically familiar reference to the *Introductiones latinae* (1481) by Antonio de Nebrija, which became the standard text in the study of Latin.

a reason of state: a concept expounded in Giovanni Botero's *Ragione di Stato* (1589), a consideration which overrides all others, and ironic in this context.

267 *cynics . . . slanderous dogs*: the Greek *kynikos* means 'doglike'.

268 *Charondas*: a lawgiver of the sixth century BC, whose legislation is described in Aristotle's *Politics*. Legends about him are found in Diodorus Siculus.

271 *the police officer . . . beginning of my story*: he is not mentioned specifically. He must be one of the 'guardian angels' covering up the goings-on at the slaughterhouse.

273 *patent of nobility*: privileges of nobility or *hidalguía* were offered for sale from 1552 as a means of earning revenue for the crown. Plebeian characters who want to upgrade their status in this way are often the butt of satire in the literature of the period.

a perpenam rei de memoria patents of nobility and other official documents were issued *ad perpetuam rei memoriam*, 'for the perpetual memory of the matter'.

275 *Rodamonte*: Saracen warrior appearing in various epic poems, e.g. Boiardo's *Orlando Innamorato* (1467) and Ariosto's *Orlando Furioso* (1532).

the destruction of Sauceda: a refuge for criminals who were pardoned by Philip II in 1590. It was *not* destroyed.

276 *Monipodio*: the same character who appears in *Rinconete and Cortadillo*.

277 *Sejanus' horse*: ownership of this horse signified death.

maravedí: the smallest-denomination coin.

279 *jump for the King of France*: see note to p. 167.

283 *Ericthos, Circes, and Medeas*: Erictho was a witch in the Roman poet Lucan's *Pharsalia*; Circe was the sorceress who turned Odysseus' men into pigs; Medea was a priestess of Hecate and also a witch.

285 *The Golden Ass*: written in the second century AD by the Roman Lucius Apuleius and often linked with the later picaresque in its comic realism.

my goat: this is the form the devil is supposed to assume on the witches' sabbath.

295 *morisco*: a term used throughout the period of the Reconquest (technically 711–1492) and later to designate any Spanish Moor who converted from the Muslim religion to Christianity. They became a marginalized ethnic group from the early sixteenth century onwards, when a policy of forced conversion from their own Muslim religion was implemented.

297 *mutatio caparum*: the cardinals changed their winter cloaks for lighter ones on Easter Sunday.

Daraja's Bouquet: the *Ramillete de Daraja* was a play on a Morrish theme, now lost, which was mentioned by authors of the period because of its extravagant content.

299 *another Angulo*: Sieber (vol. ii, p. 353, n. 129) refers to a troupe of actors known as Angulo y los Corteses, who performed in Madrid in 1582. Angulo the Bad was a theatrical manager.

301 *Archbishop Turpin*: Archbishop of Reims at the time of Charlemagne, and supposed author of a chronicle of his life and deeds.

Midases, Crassuses, and Croesuses: Midas was the legendary King of Phrygia who was granted his wish that everything he touched be turned into gold; Marcus Licinus Crassus, who lived in the century before Christ, owned silver mines and a large part of Rome; Croesus, the last king of Lydia (560–546 BC), was also famed for his wealth.

302 *Tantalus*: see note to p. 122.

latter-day Sisyphus: his punishment was to roll a large rock up a mountainside only for it to roll back down and his labour to begin again.

Cortes: the Spanish Parliament.

305 *Espolón*: a square bordering on the river in Valladolid.

205 *moriscos*: a term used throughout the period of the Reconquest (technically 711–1492) and later to designate any Spanish Moor who converted from the Muslim religion to Christianity. They became a marginalized ethnic group from the early sixteenth century onwards, when a policy of forced conversion from their own Muslim religion was implemented.

207 *mutatio caparum*: the cardinals changed their winter cloaks for lighter ones on Easter Sunday.

Darvío's Bouquet: the *Ramillete de Darvío* was a play on a Moorish theme, now lost, which was mentioned by authors of the period because of its extravagant content.

209 another *Angulo*: Sieber (vol. ii, p. 353, n. 120) refers to a troupe of actors known as *Angulo y los Corteses*, who performed in Madrid in 1582. *Angulo the Bad* was a theatrical manager.

210 *Archbishop Turpin*: Archbishop of Reims at the time of Charlemagne, and supposed author of a chronicle of his life and deeds.

Midas, Croesus, and Crassus: Midas was the legendary King of Phrygia who was granted his wish that everything he touched be turned into gold; Marcus Licinus Crassus, who lived in the century before Christ, owned silver mines and a large part of Rome; Croesus, the last king of Lydia (560–546 BC), was also famed for his wealth.

211 *Tantalus*: see note to p. 122.

latter-day *Sisyphus*: his punishment was to roll a large rock up a mountainside only for it to roll back down and his labour to begin again.

Cortes: the Spanish Parliament.

212 *Esgueva*: a square bordering on the river in Valladolid

A SELECTION OF **OXFORD WORLD'S CLASSICS**

American Literature

British and Irish Literature

Children's Literature

Classics and Ancient Literature

Colonial Literature

Eastern Literature

European Literature

History

Medieval Literature

Oxford English Drama

Poetry

Philosophy

Politics

Religion

The Oxford Shakespeare

A complete list of Oxford Paperbacks, including Oxford World's Classics, OPUS, Past Masters, Oxford Authors, Oxford Shakespeare, Oxford Drama, and Oxford Paperback Reference, is available in the UK from the Academic Division Publicity Department, Oxford University Press, Great Clarendon Street, Oxford OX2 6DP.

In the USA, complete lists are available from the Paperbacks Marketing Manager, Oxford University Press, 198 Madison Avenue, New York, NY 10016.

Oxford Paperbacks are available from all good bookshops. In case of difficulty, customers in the UK can order direct from Oxford University Press Bookshop, Freepost, 116 High Street, Oxford OX1 4BR, enclosing full payment. Please add 10 per cent of published price for postage and packing.